FIRST KISS

Drake held her close. "Oh, Misty—Misty—we have to see one another. There must be a way."

"I—I don't see how, Drake," she said, turning slightly in his arms. His lips were close to hers.

"I'll think of something," he vowed. "I have to see you, Misty!"

Looking into that lovely face, he wanted nothing more than to lay her back on the ground in the bower of the weeping willow and give vent to all the passion churning deep inside him. But that was not how he wanted it to be when he made love to Misty the first time. He wanted more than that.

His eyes looked deep into hers. "Let me kiss you just once, love," he pleaded. "I promise that's all I'll ask."

Her long lashes fluttered and she stammered, "I've never been kissed before, Drake."

He wanted to be as honest with her as she was being with him. "I know, Misty, and that's why this kiss is so special. I want to be the man who gives you that first kiss—and I intend to be the first man who makes love to you."

He said no more as he bent his head to meet her honeyed lips. She might never have been kissed before, but she knew by natural instinct how to respond . . .

ROMANCES BY BEST-SELLING AUTHOR COLLEEN FAULKNER!

O'BRIAN'S BRIDE (0-8217-4895-5, $4.99)

Elizabeth Lawrence left her pampered English childhood behind to journey to the far-off Colonies . . . and marry a man she'd never met. But her dreams turned to dust when an explosion killed her new husband at his powder mill, leaving her alone to run his business . . . and face a perilous life on the untamed frontier. After a desperate engagement to her husband's brother, yet another man, strong, sensual and secretive Michael Patrick O'Brian, enters her life and it will never be the same.

CAPTIVE (0-8217-4683-1, $4.99)

Tess Morgan had journeyed across the sea to Maryland colony in search of a better life. Instead, the brave British innocent finds a battle-torn land . . . and passion in the arms of Raven, the gentle Lenape warrior who saves her from a savage fate. But Tess is bound by another. And Raven dares not trust this woman whose touch has enslaved him, yet whose blood vow to his people has set him on a path of rage and vengeance. Now, as cruel destiny forces her to become Raven's prisoner, Tess must make a choice: to fight for her freedom . . . or for the tender captor she has come to cherish with a love that will hold her forever.

Available wherever paperbacks are sold, or order direct from the Publisher. Send cover price plus 50¢ per copy for mailing and handling to Penguin USA, P.O. Box 999, c/o Dept. 17109, Bergenfield, NJ 07621. Residents of New York and Tennessee must include sales tax. DO NOT SEND CASH.

SWEET SEDUCTION

WANDA OWEN

**ZEBRA BOOKS
KENSINGTON PUBLISHING CORP.**

ZEBRA BOOKS are published by

Kensington Publishing Corp.
850 Third Avenue
New York, NY 10022

Copyright © 1996 by Wanda Owen

All rights reserved. No part of this book may be reproduced in any form or by any means without the prior written consent of the Publisher, excepting brief quotes used in reviews.

If you purchased this book without a cover you should be aware that this book is stolen property. It was reported as "unsold and destroyed" to the Publisher and neither the Author nor the Publisher has received any payment for this "stripped book."

Zebra and the Z logo Reg. U.S. Pat. & TM Off.

First Printing: September, 1996
10 9 8 7 6 5 4 3 2 1

Printed in the United States of America

*This book is for my dear husband, Bob.
Happy Anniversary, honey!*

Part I

Summer's Splendor

Chapter 1

Melanie Bennett knew she should be getting back to the house. She'd left her little sister taking an afternoon nap and her little brother busily whittling a slingshot when she strolled down the path.

Once she reached the shady riverbank and sat down against the trunk of a tree, she found it so pleasant and serene she hesitated to leave.

She watched the fishing boats moving under the wooden bridge. The catfish would have to be jumping on this kind of afternoon. She could see the men jerking their poles up to take fish off their lines.

She heard a whippoorwill's distinct call. A wagon filled with people rolled across the bridge; two of the passengers were girls about her age, all dressed up in calico dresses with bright bows in their hair.

She found herself envying those two young girls, for surely they had mothers. Her own had died a few years ago and her life had not been the same since then.

It had been her younger brother who first called her Misty

because he couldn't pronounce Melanie. The nickname had stuck; now everyone called her Misty, even her father.

Perhaps the name fit her, for her eyes had often been misting with tears lately. She wasn't at all happy that her father was courting a widow. She couldn't understand how he could have forgotten her sweet mother so soon.

Melanie was glad she'd inherited her mother's golden hair and green eyes. There was no question about it—she was her mother's daughter, with the same traits and gestures.

Truth be told, Melanie had never been fond of her father. The older she got, the more she realized what an overbearing man he was.

By the time she was thirteen, she came to realize that her mother wasn't a happy woman. She'd come upon her sitting by the riverbank one day, her face buried in her lap, crying. Melanie had turned to go back so her mother would never know she'd seen her.

Today she sat in the same spot, thinking about the passengers in the wagon going into Crowley as a lot of people did on Saturday afternoons, shopping or visiting with neighbors and friends.

It had been weeks since her pa had taken her, Jeff, and Lavinia to town with him. He'd been too busy courting his Widow Gordon. Melanie didn't think she was as pretty as her mother but she had a more voluptuous figure. That must have been what caught her pa's eyes. That and the fact that her husband had left her a fine farm which provided her with a good living.

Mike Bennett had a small amount of land by the river and worked at a lumber mill on the outskirts of Crowley, but there never seemed to be enough money.

Since their mother had died, nobody was sewing clothes for the family. Misty tried, but she didn't seem to have a talent for it. The nicest dress she had was a pretty gingham one that a neighbor lady had made for her. She'd also made her six-year-old sister one out of the same material. Then last week, she'd brought two chambray shirts for Jeff. Misty could not have been more pleased, for she'd mended and mended the old ones he could still button. He was growing like a weed.

Jeff was going to be a husky fellow like his pa. He was big for ten. From the time spring came until the weather got cold, he went around in his bare feet. The weather was going to get cold in a few weeks so Misty had to ask her pa to take Jeff to town to buy him a pair of shoes.

Pa got his wages on Saturday after six days of work at the lumber mill so this afternoon would be the time to do it. She rose reluctantly and started back to the house.

Her father was just pulling up to the gate in his wagon. He called out, "Been down by your riverbank daydreaming again, girl?"

"Can't see anything wrong with that, Pa," she said, going through the gate.

"Daydreaming don't put beans on the table, girl. Hard working does that," he barked.

"I figure I've put in a hard day's work. The house is clean and I've got Lavinia's, Jeff's, and my hair washed for the week," she remarked, knowing very well he was just itching to have something to criticize.

"You trying to smart-mouth me, girl?"

"No, pa—I was just telling you what I'd been doing today."

Walking behind her into the house, he was reminded of Beth when she was young and lively with that golden blond hair swaying around her shoulders. In the last years of her life she never wore it that way. She pinned it in a coil at the top of her head.

Mike Bennett was a robust man towering a few inches over six feet. He was thirty-seven years old, and had a zest for living but never enough money to indulge it. After he worked hard all week, when Saturday afternoon rolled around he liked to go to town and drink with his buddies and watch the pretty girls stroll down the street.

In the last few years of Beth's life, she had cramped his style, so he didn't take her with him. She was left at home with the kids. Only his youngest seemed to have an affection for him—she still ran eagerly to have him swing her up in his strong arms. His ten-year-old son was a mama's boy but Mike had no one to blame for that but himself.

Like Misty, he disliked his father. At an early age, he had chanced to see something that made his young heart fill with hate. He'd seen his father slap his pretty mother's face when she'd dared to stand up to him.

He'd rushed back to his room and kicked the wall to give vent to the rage consuming him. That night he couldn't look at his father across the supper table. He even thought about sticking a butcher knife in his father's evil heart that night. Only his mother's deep religious convictions kept Jeff from actually doing such a deed.

Jeff made a vow that he would leave home as soon as he could. He worshipped Misty; without her, he didn't know what he would do.

As young as he was, he knew about his father courting Georgia Gordon. Well, he'd never call *her* "Mother!"

When he and Misty had entered the front room, he was putting the finishing touches to his slingshot. Mike didn't even look his way, for little Lavinia came running to him and he picked her up. "How's my baby girl, eh?"

Misty went into the kitchen to add wood to the cookstove. She'd forgotten to fill up the kettles, so there wouldn't be any hot water for a while.

She prepared herself for a harsh tongue-lashing, but she was hardened to that after the last few years. One thing Mike Bennett did not yet realize was that he didn't intimidate her. She had two very good friends in Ed and Geneva Walters. They lived nearby on acreage four times as large as Bennett's. It was Geneva who had made Jeff's shirts and the gingham dresses. She visited often since Misty's mother died.

Misty was most grateful for her kindness. Geneva had known Beth and liked her very much but they'd never been close because her husband Ed had never cared for Mike Bennett. But this hadn't kept her from coming to the house when she knew that Bennett was working at the lumber mills.

Misty didn't know what to expect from her father and his plans for this evening but she, Jeff, and Lavinia had to have some supper. She began to peel some potatoes and onions and slice some tomatoes.

Mike sauntered into the kitchen and he had only to test the water in the kettles to go into a rage. "Damn, not a drop of hot water, girl! See what your daydreaming did? Your pa has no hot water to wash up with."

She didn't look up but just kept peeling the potatoes. "You won't have to wait long, Pa. Besides, since I'm more or less in charge of Jeff and Lavinia, I must tell you Jeff's going to need shoes. He's gone barefoot all summer but now winter's coming on."

"Can't do it this Saturday, Misty. I'll take him to town next Saturday," he mumbled. He paced back and forth around the kitchen, knowing he was due over at Georgia's within the hour. Three kids at home could pose a problem for a man when he was trying to court a demanding woman like Georgia. She didn't have any children so she wasn't very understanding.

Misty watched him pace. She knew he was going to tell her he wouldn't be here for supper.

"Oh, going over to Georgia's this evening, Pa?"

"Yes—yes I am. It's her birthday," he stammered.

"I see. You know, Pa, since you got paid today if you'd just give me some money I know I could get Ed and Geneva to take me and Jeff to Crowley on Wednesday. They always go on Wednesday and Saturday. I know you've been going over to the Gordon place on your Saturdays," she said in a syrupy-sweet voice. He fell for her little deception.

"That's a good idea, Misty," he responded eagerly. Digging into his pocket, he gave her a generous amount of money. It soothed his guilty feelings.

When he finally left the kitchen with the two kettles of hot water, she took out the roll of bills. A smug smile came to her face. She had enough to buy Jeff some sturdy shoes and a pair of pants, which he needed badly.

As she puttered around the kitchen, putting a plate of sliced onions and tomatoes and setting the table, she planned how she'd start working on her pa to get her and the kids the things they needed.

While her potatoes fried in one big iron skillet, she put a dozen slices of slab bacon in another one. The three of them were enjoying their feast when Mike said goodbye and ambled out the front door in his best shirt and pants.

Two miles up the road, Ed and Geneva Walters encountered him as they were returning home from Crowley.

Geneva remarked to her husband, "Going to see his fancy lady, no doubt. Oh, that poor little Misty! My heart goes out to her, Ed. What a burden on that young girl's shoulders!"

"Well, you know my feelings about Mike Bennett, Geneva! Beth was a fine lady but she picked the wrong husband," Ed remarked. "It was common knowledge that he played around long before Beth died."

"I know, Ed. I'd heard the gossip right after little Lavinia was born, "Geneva replied. She voiced her concern that the three children lacked the clothing they needed since Beth was gone. "That's why I try to make a few things and take them over to Misty."

"Geneva, whatever you want to do for Misty, you have my approval," Ed assured her.

"You're a good man, Ed Walters, and I'm a lucky woman to have you."

"I'm the lucky one, Geneva," he said and smiled at her.

SWEET SEDUCTION

Their wagon rolled on down the dirt road toward the Bennett place. Jeff had gone out in the backyard to try out his new slingshot and Lavinia sat in the front room playing with her doll. Misty had stacked the dishes and gone out to sit on the front step for a while. She was in no hurry to tackle the dirty dishes as she knew her pa would be gone for hours.

She watched the Walters' wagon rolling down the rutted road. Geneva called out to Misty, "**How** are you doing, honey?"

"Oh, just fine, Mrs. Walters. Been to Crowley?" Misty asked as she leaped up from the steps and headed toward the gate.

Ed Walters suddenly realized how much the sixteen-year-old Misty looked like her eighteen-year-old mother had looked. Something about the friendly, eager expression on her face and those sparkling green eyes reminded him of the girl he had once known and lost his heart to, but nothing had ever come of it. Mike Bennett had appeared in Crowley about that time, and Ed had not had a chance against the virile, good-looking twenty-one-year-old who'd drifted into Arkansas from Louisiana.

"Yes, honey, we're on our way home now. Got a lot of pretty new material at the store, so I'm making you and Lavinia more dresses," she told Misty.

"Oh, Mrs. Walters—you're so nice! I don't know what we'd do without you," Misty said.

"You're a sweet girl and a good one too, Misty. I'm—I'm glad to do what little I can. Now, we'd best be on our way. Ed's got some chores to tend to and it'll be dark soon. You take care of yourself. I'll bring your new dresses over as soon as I get them made."

As she and Ed went toward their home, Geneva sighed, "Oh, my heart goes out to that child. She should be having carefree days like any young girl her age. Oh, I detest that Mike Bennett, Ed."

"He's not a man to admire. I figure Beth might not have had much will to live left in her. Thirty-four is damned young to die. She sure changed during the years she was married to Mike. I remember a laughing, happy girl of seventeen," Ed told his wife.

"That's right—I keep forgetting you two knew one another when you were growing up," Geneva remarked, recalling how he'd told her that his father's property adjoined Beth's family's farm.

When they got home, Ed went to the barn and Geneva puttered around the house, putting away the things she'd bought and getting supper warmed up. But she got an idea as she moved busily around her kitchen. She'd suggest to Ed that maybe next Saturday they could take the three Bennett children with them to town for a little outing.

She knew her goodhearted Ed would have no objections. Come Monday, she'd get busy making pretty floral dresses for Misty and Lavinia.

Ed Walters went around the barn, attending to his chores. He had to admit that had he not gone to Tennessee to work for his uncle in Memphis, he would very likely have started to court Beth Boyer. But he'd met his sweet Geneva in Memphis and returned to Crowley with her as his new bride.

Beth had married Mike Bennett, so their courtship never really got started. Still, it sickened him to hear that Beth had married a man he considered to be a scoundrel.

He welcomed anything Geneva wanted to do for Misty. God knows, she needed a friend like Geneva now that her mother was gone!

Misty was glad when Sunday came to an end and it was bedtime. It had been near dawn when Pa finally got home Saturday night so Sunday he was of no company to any of them. Jeff had taken his fishing pole and gone down on the riverbank to spend the entire afternoon; Lavinia managed to get a little attention when he wasn't napping in his chair.

Misty did her usual chores and cooked Sunday dinner for the four of them.

Monday morning, he was back at the lumber mills and at least there was peace in the house. Misty put in a busy day getting the family wash done and Tuesday she spent the afternoon pressing clothes.

Tuesday night, Misty was caught unprepared when her father began to quiz her about going to town the next day with the Walters. Something urged her to lie. She answered, "Yes, I told Mrs. Walters you gave me money to buy Jeff a pair of shoes so they're stopping by here. I'll leave Jeff in charge of Lavinia, Pa."

"Yeah—yeah, that's fine, Misty," he said in a sober tone. "Just thought if you hadn't said anything yet that Jeff's shoes could wait until next week. Seems I'm running short," he mumbled.

"But I have, Pa."

"Yeah—never mind, girl," he said, leaving the kitchen. She knew exactly what was troubling him. He was going over to the widow's Thursday night and wanted to buy her some little trinket.

She knew he would never know whether she went with the Walters or not and she could walk into Crowley. Come heaven or hell, she was going to take that money and get Jeff his shoes and pants.

So that was exactly what she did the next day. She wore the only nice dress she had and her worn sandals. She owned no nice stockings or slippers.

She walked the mile to Crowley and went directly to Marshall's Mercantile and purchased a sturdy pair of shoes that would take Jeff through the winter. As she'd figured, she was able to buy him a pair of dark blue twill pants. She was thrilled to still have enough to buy her and Lavinia pretty satin ribbons for their hair.

She was in the highest of spirits when she finally left the store and began to walk to the outskirts of town. It was exciting to see how she seemed to draw attention from the people she passed on the street. But Misty was a beautiful girl and her simple little gingham dress molded to the soft curves of her young body.

The sun was still high in the sky so she knew she had plenty of time to get back to the house before her father returned from the mills.

Misty was not prepared for two things that would happen to her when she'd walked about a quarter of a mile from town. The strap broke on her left sandal, so she was forced to take it off. A few more steps told her she'd best remove both of them.

As she was removing the other sandal, she became aware of a horse approaching. She turned to see a most magnificent beast coming toward her. Atop the fine stallion was a man dressed in a black shirt and pants, his hair just as dark.

As he suddenly pulled on the reins to look down at her, she looked up at him. He was the man that all young girls dream about. Misty didn't know such a handsome man could exist.

He grinned at her. "You look like a young lady in distress." He leaped down from his horse.

"I'm afraid my sandal broke. But then they're old so it was bound to happen," she said.

"Come—I'll take you home, wherever home is. Those dainty feet should not have to walk on this rough road."

"Oh, no—I couldn't do that," she protested.

"Oh, and why not?" he asked with an amused grin. She was the prettiest thing he'd ever seen and obviously as innocent as an angel, which was what she looked like to Drake Dalton.

"Oh, I just couldn't."

"I'm no monster. If I was, I'd only gobble up ugly girls and not pretty ones like you."

Misty could not help laughing. He knew that he had made her feel a little more relaxed. He said, "If you fear that your parents would object to a stranger bringing you home, then I'll take you nearby so you'll have only a short distance to walk in those pretty bare feet."

Reluctantly, she remained silent. But Drake Dalton could be a very persuasive man, and introduced himself. "I'm Drake Dalton and I've just arrived in Crowley. Now tell me your name."

"Misty. Misty Bennett. Well, actually, my name's Melanie but everyone calls me Misty," she said.

"Well, Misty, come and let me play the gallant by saving your feet."

She allowed herself to be hoisted up on the black horse, then directed him to the bank of the river.

"I can easily walk the rest of the way to the house now. I often walk barefoot to this spot. I—I like it here by the river," she said.

He smiled at her. "It's a nice place. So you come here often, eh?"

"Yes, I love it here."

He leaped down and reached up to help her. "You see, Misty? You're home safe and sound."

She'd never known the touch of a man's hands on hers. She felt her heart start pounding faster.

"I thank you for bringing me home. Now I must go."

"Good afternoon, Misty. It was nice to have met you. I look forward to seeing you again."

She turned around to look at him as she began to walk up the incline. "I would wish that, too, but I doubt that you will," she murmured with a melancholy air.

That was enough to make Drake Dalton curious about this divine little creature he'd chanced upon in this remote little hamlet in Arkansas. She was like a little wood nymph, he thought. She was like something untouched by the world and so refreshing. But what was she so afraid of?

Drake watched her scamper up the hill as she pulled her skirt up above her ankles so she could move faster. Her golden hair flowed back and forth around her shoulders and Drake stood there for a moment just to absorb her beauty before he mounted his horse and rode away.

He knew why he had left England to come to this remote place but now he had found something that whetted his interest just as much as the land he owned.

It was a girl named Misty!

Chapter 2

Misty was glad she had over two hours to get settled before her father arrived. It had been an afternoon like none she'd ever known. But she'd accomplished what she'd set out to do. Her brother had winter shoes and a new pair of pants and little Lavinia was excited about the ribbons for her hair.

Supper that night was leftovers from the night before, but it didn't matter to Mike Bennett. He was in a disgruntled mood because he was going to be calling on Georgia tonight empty-handed.

Nothing could have dampened Misty's spirits that evening. She floated on a cloud. Drake Dalton was everything she'd imagined a man should be. He was a Prince Charming and a knight in shining armor riding to her rescue.

That night she lay in her bed thinking about being close to him with his arms encircling her as he guided the huge black horse.

For the first time in her uneventful life, Misty had a

wonderful secret. She went about her chores the next day in the highest of spirits.

She told her father about the purchase of Jeff's shoes and pants. Mike snapped at her, "Thought what I gave you was to buy shoes."

"Got a good buy so I used the rest for the pants Jeff needed," she told him. Now all she had to do was pray Lavinia wouldn't say anything to him about the ribbons. She'd cautioned her not to.

That Thursday night when Mike Bennett went to court the widow he had to go emptyhanded. As he rolled down the road in his wagon he thought to himself that his daughter was a conniving little miss.

Misty had no qualms about lying about going into town with the Walters. In the weeks that followed, she was to find that lying to her pa made her life easier to endure and far more pleasant.

She was sure things had not gone too well between him and the widow Thursday night. He was like an old soretailed cat the next morning and Friday evening when he came in from the mills.

But his foul mood and tongue couldn't dampen Misty's spirits. Mrs. Walters had come by the house at mid-afternoon with a pretty floral frock. Misty loved all the bright yellow and red flowers on the black background of the cotton material.

It had a square neckline and puffed sleeves and fit her perfectly. Geneva had told her, "Now if your pa will let you, me and Ed want to take you, Jeff, and little Lavinia into town with us Saturday afternoon. You say something to him—we'll be coming about two."

Misty exclaimed, "Oh, Mrs. Walters, I will! I certainly will. I'll just pray he'll let us."

"Can't see any reason why he'd mind. He's known us for years. Give you a chance to wear that pretty new dress, too."

Misty remembered she also had that red satin ribbon to wear in her hair.

Before the day was over, Misty was to have another nice surprise when she went down to her spot on the riverbank before she started supper. Jeff was somewhere fishing, and he'd promised as he left the house that he was going to catch some fish.

She'd laughed and said, "You catch 'em and I'll fry 'em, Jeff." She'd watched him go down the path with his fishing pole and can of worms, his straw hat at a cocky angle on his curly head. He was growing so, she thought to herself. He was going to be tall like his pa. Give him another year and he was going to be as tall as she was.

Lavinia had crawled up on her cot and was sleeping soundly as she usually did in the afternoon. Misty figured she had a good hour to take a rest down on the riverbank.

Like her brother Jeff, she walked down in her bare feet. Just as she approached the large old weeping willow, it dawned on her that she had no sandals to wear tomorrow if she was allowed to go to town with the Walters.

She sank down to the ground and leaned back against the trunk to stare out at the river. Tears began to stream down her cheeks. When would she be able to talk her father into giving her more money to buy herself sandals?

Actually, it had been her intention to get a pair of winter shoes for Lavinia next. She had an old pair of black leather lace-up shoes which would do her for the winter, but Lavinia needed shoes badly.

Something suddenly caught her attention on the green grass a few feet from where she was sitting. She leaned over to take a closer look at the black objects.

Her hand picked up a pair of the prettiest hand-tooled black leather sandals she'd ever seen. A note had been placed inside one of them. It was a short, simple message from Drake Dalton stating that a lady could not be without her sandals. With a smile she excitedly began to put them on, praying they would fit. Amazingly, they fit perfectly!

How could he possibly have known her size? What she could not know was that Drake Dalton was quite a connoisseur when it came to ladies. The twenty-five-year-old Englishman had squired the daughters of many wealthy British families.

His father was Lord Devin Dalton and his mother was a lovely French woman his father had married and brought back to England. It was from his French mother, Adrienne, that he'd inherited his black hair and dark brown eyes.

His father was a tall, lanky gentleman with reddish blond hair, blue eyes, and fair complexion. In fact, he was so fair that he looked pale and frail, but in truth, nothing about him was frail.

Lord Devin Dalton was an overbearing man who dominated his family. Drake had found himself bucking up against him by the time he was fifteen. His three younger sisters were intimidated by their lordly father like his mother was, but never Drake.

His sister Ellen dared to challenge him once in a while, but poor little Suzanne and Valeria trembled with fright when he roared at them.

Most would have assumed that he and his three sisters were blessed to be born to such wealth. They lived in a three-story grey stone house with a stream of rippling water running the length of the property. The children had tutors by the time they were six years old. There were fine thoroughbreds in the Dalton stables—Drake had been presented with his own stallion on his sixteenth birthday.

On the north side of the estate was a forest which provided all kinds of game. Drake was initiated to hunting when he was sixteen.

As a youth, Drake was too young to understand why his mother was so tormented. She had never adjusted to life in England and constantly yearned for France. Devin's ways were not hers and their marriage had never been one of love. It had been arranged by her father.

She had been a ravishingly beautiful French mademoiselle who'd caught the eye of the thirty-five-year-old English lord. She'd been allowed no choice as to whether she wished to marry him back in 1820. Suddenly, she'd found herself married to a stranger and leaving her beloved France.

By the time she'd been married to Devin one year, she had borne him a son who was christened Darren. She never called him that. Instead she called him Drake because he'd reminded her of the renegade black drake that swam in the channel with the other swans. The channel was the one place Adrienne had found serenity in this foreign place.

The second year she was married to Devin she presented him with a daughter, Ellen. Adrienne was a small woman and two births so close together began to drain her strength. But Devin was a selfish man. The only ploy Adrienne had to keep him from her was faking illness. For a year and a half she managed to keep from getting pregnant, but by the fifth year of their marriage her little Suzanne was born. She adored this baby.

After Suzanne's birth, Adrienne became desperate, vowing that Devin Dalton would never have her again. For two years, she turned away from him, even locking her bedroom door.

But one night Devin was drunk and in a rage, so he broke the door down and raped her. She found herself pregnant for the fourth time.

Her last child, Valeria, was born in the spring. After her daughter's birth, Adrienne heard the doctor harshly admonishing Devin. "I told you after Suzanne's birth that she should not have more children. I'll take no further responsibility, Devin. I almost lost her this time."

As soon as Adrienne was able to leave her bed, she went to the kitchen and returned to her bedroom with two fierce-looking knives. One was placed under her pillow every night and one was hidden in her dressing room.

The first night she was to join her husband at the dining table, her intense dark eyes glared at him. "Never come near me again, Devin. I've had all the children for you that I intend to have. I'll kill you or myself before you'll ever have another child from me."

Something about her manner convinced him that she meant exactly what she said. He never came to her bedroom again.

But Adrienne began to wither like a dying flower and her little daughter gave her no pleasure. She tried to fight the feelings consuming her but every time she looked at Valeria she remembered the night of her brutal conception.

By the time Drake was sixteen, Adrienne sensed that he was unhappy. She was pleased to realize that he had not inherited his father's selfish heart. He was the joy of her life. Oh, he was so very handsome! He possessed the romantic heart of the Frenchman. There was nothing about him that reminded her of her English husband's cold reserve.

Drake was only seventeen when he strolled down by the channel and saw his mother sitting and weeping. He rushed to sit beside her, taking her in his arms. "Mother—Mother, why do you weep so? Tell me so I can help."

"Oh, my Drake, my darling Drake! What would I have done without you? Forgive me for giving way to a weak moment," she said, trying to regain control of herself.

"I love you, Mother. I want to help if I can. I—I don't like to see you unhappy."

"Oh, Drake, my unhappiness has nothing to do with you." She told him the story of why she called him Drake instead of Darren, the name his father had insisted upon. Perhaps because Adrienne knew she would not live much longer she told her son about his inheritance from her family—it was in a country far across the ocean. She wanted him to know of it even though he had a few years before he'd be twenty.

She didn't want Devin enjoying the benefits of that. It was to be Drake's land.

Misty kept looking down at the pretty sandals. Now she could go to town with Mrs. Walters.

When she leaped up from the ground to go back to the house she forgot to take them off. She knew she had to get busy in the kitchen if she wanted to get him in a good mood to ask his permission to go to town. How wonderful it would have been to have a father like Ed Walters, she thought as she sliced two large tomatoes and an onion. She grabbed two handfuls of potatoes to fry.

Jeff had done himself proud and brought back twelve nice perch. Fish, fried potatoes, and cornbread cakes ought to make her pa happy.

When Mike Bennett came through the back door, Misty had the cornbread cakes done and stacked in a platter while the potatoes fried. She was busily rolling the fish in cornmeal while the grease was already spitting in the iron skillet.

"Hello, Pa. Jeff caught us a nice mess of fish this afternoon," she said as she greeted him.

"Howdy, girl. Got to say everything smells good," he remarked as he walked over to pour some water in a basin and wash his face and hands.

Misty was encouraged. He was actually civil to her. But she still waited to say anything about tomorrow. Supper went well and they were all sated when they got up from the table. Jeff went out to gather a load of wood as he always did after supper.

Lavinia scampered into the front room to resume playing with her doll. Misty was cleaning off the table when her father's voice called to her, "Where'd you get them new sandals, girl? Get yourself a new pair of shoes yesterday?"

"No, Pa. Mrs. Walters gave them to me today. Aren't they pretty?" Misty smiled up at him.

"Guess you could say they are. That Mrs. Walters is mighty nice to you," he remarked.

"She sure is. You know what she wants to do, Pa? She wants to take me, Jeff, and Lavinia to town with them tomorrow. I told her I'd ask you tonight. Can we, Pa?" She could hardly breathe while she waited for his answer.

"Oh, I suppose so. The Walters are respectable people," he said as he went out of the room. He had plans with Georgia for tomorrow evening anyway. He knew one thing and that was that he had a stop in town before he came home. He was going to buy her one of them bottles of toilet water she splashed all over herself. That ought to put her in a sweet mood tomorrow night.

When Jeff came in with an armful of wood, Misty whispered to him, "We're going to get to go with the Walters, Jeff. Now don't get him riled about anything this evening, honey, or he could change his mind."

Jeff's face brightened with excitement. With an impish grin, he said, "Going to my room, Misty, and do some drawing so I won't say anything wrong."

Misty gave him an approving smile and nod. She was glad to have a quiet, peaceful evening. She put the kitchen in order and took Lavinia to get her to bed. Jeff remained in his room the rest of the evening.

Misty told her father good night and went to the room she shared with Lavinia earlier than usual. In the dim light she hung her new dress on a peg and got out clean undergarments. She finally removed her new sandals and put them on the oak chair. She also got out Lavinia's things for the morning.

As she moved quietly, she thought about the fact that in the last week she'd lied to her pa twice now. But once again tonight, she'd saved herself from his wrath. Oh, what a price she'd pay if he ever found out!

She got into her nightgown and dimmed the lamp. His

mellow mood had to be because he was anticipating being with Georgia Gordon tomorrow night.

By the time she lay back on her pillow, another man occupied her thoughts. She'd never met or even imagined a man like the tall, dark, handsome Drake Dalton.

Chapter 3

A day before Drake Dalton's twentieth birthday he'd left Dalton Manor, intending never to return. He had only one regret—leaving his sisters behind—but soon they'd all be married and living in their own homes.

From that day to this, he was Drake and not Darren Dalton. Adrienne's premonitions had come true and she was not there when he turned twenty. Three months earlier, she'd died quietly in her sleep.

The memory of the private moment they'd spent down by the channel when she'd told him about the majestic black drake among the swans would be etched in Drake's memory forever.

He also recalled an early evening when she'd not been feeling well and had dinner served in her room. After dinner with his father and sisters, Drake had gone to see her. She looked so weak and pale. There was an urgency in her voice when she spoke to him.

"Drake, when something happens to me, go to France and seek out my younger brother, Bayard. He will help you.

You have an inheritance from your Grandmother Benoit. I want you to have it, not Devin. He doesn't deserve it."

"Mother, please don't be so morbid," he protested, taking her hand.

"I couldn't if you were still a little boy, Drake, but you're nineteen now. I've never had anyone to talk with, my son, for it was never my choice to leave France. That decision was made by my father, much to my mother's chagrin. Bayard wrote me of my mother's deep discontent after I left."

"So you didn't love my father when you married him?"

"I hardly knew him, Drake. When I did get to know him I detested him. I am sorry, but I can't lie to you. Not at a time like this."

He realized that this was all she wished to discuss about her marriage to Devin Dalton when she quietly dismissed him, "Just go to Bayard, dear. Promise me, Drake."

"I promise, Mother. I will go to your brother in France." He bent down and kissed her gently on the cheek. His heart was heavy when he left her room that night. He knew there was nothing he could do to help her.

The morning her maid found her dead, it was a cold winter day and a dense fog shrouded the grounds of the manor house. When Drake and his sisters were informed of their mother's death, Drake made a quick exit from his father's library. The rest of them assumed that he wished to be alone in his sorrow.

But Drake had been doing his mourning for weeks. He went directly to her room. She'd told him three months earlier that she'd never had anyone to talk with, so he felt she must have kept a journal. He wanted to find it before it got into his father's hands.

He searched her desk and found a thick leatherbound journal. He wanted one other thing—a dainty little emerald ring and bracelet he used to see her wear so often. He put them in his pocket and quickly exited the room.

Two days after his mother's funeral he'd left Dalton Manor and sailed to France to seek out Bayard Benoit.

Bayard was thirty-nine years old and had never married. He'd become a prosperous lawyer in Paris. He lived in an elegant town house because he had no desire to take over the grand country estate left to him after his parents died.

Drake liked his uncle instantly and understood why he had preferred to remain a bachelor. He'd seen his parents' disastrous relationship and also knew about his older sister's miserable marriage.

Bayard told Drake that he was only fifteen when Adrienne had left France. He recalled the grand wedding in Paris of Lord Dalton to his sister before they sailed back to England.

"It was a vindictive act on the part of my father because Adrienne stubbornly refused to bow to his wishes and give up the young man she truly loved. He did a despicable thing. My mother, Michelle, never forgave him. She died of a broken heart and I grew to hate my father, I'm sorry to say."

Drake could certainly understand for he, too, hated his father. His visit to Paris lasted two years. He lived with his uncle and learned everything about his French heritage. When Bayard took him to the countryside and the seaport cities Drake found himself intrigued.

He worked at various jobs during his two years in Paris and also read every page in his mother's journal. He found it a most pathetic story.

Then it came time for him to announce to Bayard that he wanted to seek out the inheritance left to him by his Grandmother Benoit in a remote spot called Arkansas, which had been settled by the French in the 1800s.

Drake had to admit he was most curious about this place across the ocean. He hired on with a French sea captain whose ship was traveling to the east coast of this strange country. Bayard supplied him with all the legal documents he would need once he arrived to claim his six hundred and forty acres.

Bayard asked him to keep in touch for he was eager to know what he would find when he got there. "That's no small farm, Drake."

Drake had laughed. "Don't worry, I'll keep you informed of all my adventures."

It was late summer when Drake arrived in the States after a taste of what it was like to be a seaman. His skin was bronzed from the sun and sea breezes and his long, black hair hung to his broad shoulders.

Although he was a stranger in this new country, Drake realized that women found him very attractive. One such pretty lady was more than eager to hire him as her driver. He moved into her carriage-house apartment, and for the next six months performed services for her other than just driving. Her elderly husband was fond of the young Englishman, never realizing that his young and vivacious wife was cheating on him. Mr. Aston paid Drake a generous fee, most of which he was able to save during that six months' stay.

His next stop was Virginia, where he worked for a horse-breeding stable. He already had an appreciation for fine horseflesh because his father kept thoroughbreds. He stayed almost a year at the Harrington Stables. When he was ready to leave Virginia, he rode away on his own fine black stallion, Duke. He'd struck a deal with Sam Harrington and purchased the horse. He'd explained to Sam why he was in this country and that his destination was Arkansas.

Sam admired the young man, for he was a hard worker; he had no idea he was the son of an English lord. Drake never let that be known to anyone.

As he and Duke traveled over the Smoky Mountains, Drake found himself more and more intrigued with this country where the countryside changed so vastly. It seemed to have everything. He'd seen the eastern seacoast cities and he'd enjoyed the lush green countrysides of Virginia. Now he was traveling over the heavily forested mountains, admiring the picturesque views.

As he'd promised Bayard, he'd written a letter at least monthly. He suddenly realized he was almost two years older than he was when he'd started on his quest.

When he emerged from the Smoky Mountains he knew he wasn't too far from Arkansas. He and Duke had entered the state of Tennessee, and once again the countryside was changing. The land was flatter and dotted with farms and rows of cotton and corn. He figured that this was what he would find in Arkansas.

He came upon the wide and muddy Mississippi River when he and Duke arrived in Memphis. He'd heard about an awesome earthquake that had struck this area, causing the flow of the river to reverse itself. He lingered in Memphis for a couple of days, wanting to get to know the people.

He found them friendly and outgoing. He roamed around the wharves, where he saw bales of cotton being loaded on boats and the barges going up and down the vast Mississippi.

Drake absorbed everything around him. He rode Duke down broad streets lined with elegant homes and huge magnolia trees with pungent white blossoms. Drake realized that this was a rich, fertile land. Everything seemed to flourish.

He saw beautiful women shading their faces with their parasols. They had flawless complexions, like gardenia blossoms. Ah, the ladies were just as lovely as any he'd seen in England or France!

On his last night in Memphis he strolled down Beale Street and encountered two black men and an attractive mulatto singing a lively tune. He stood and listened for a while.

The next morning he and Duke headed across the Mississippi to Arkansas. He traveled through a few small hamlets, feeling lucky to find one place with a little inn. He had to admit he was curious about what he was going to find when he arrived at his destination.

What he found when he reached his property the next day was a little frame house which consisted of four rooms. Lucky for him, there were lamps, oil, and a few furnishings. It was obvious that no one had lived there for months. Drake swatted at cobwebs as he surveyed the rooms. At least he had oil to light the lamps. Looking at his map, he saw he was between two little hamlets, Crowley and Lepanto. He rode into Lepanto and purchased a pot, skillet, and coffee pot. He bought coffee, a loaf of baked bread, and a shank of ham. He lingered around the little store, trying to remember what else he needed. He was tired and not thinking clearly. By the time he left he had delighted the clerk by buying tins and knives and forks. He also bought eggs. The clerk detected his accent and knew he was a stranger. "Got some fresh milk, mister. You need a quart?"

"Yes, miss," he said.

When he got back to the little shack, he sat down at the kitchen table to drink milk from the tins and put some cheese between the slices of the bread. That was his dinner.

But the next morning, he woke up to the birds singing in the trees and the sun streaming through the windows. Drake got up from the bare bed and built a fire in the old cookstove to brew himself a pot of coffee. The strong black liquid was a meager breakfast, but it woke him up and filled his belly.

His work was cut out for him once he'd spent the morning surveying the inside and outside of the house. A paint job and a couple of window replacements would spruce up the outside, once all the knee-high weeds were cut.

It was the inside of the house that was going to take some doing. He would have to furnish it and clean it from bottom to top. There were a few nice features. The small front room had a little stone fireplace and there was a multitude of shelves in the roomy kitchen. There were two bedrooms.

A porch ran across the front of the house, which had a

back porch off the kitchen. The barn needed a roof and a lot of repairs.

Drake sat at the kitchen table and made an extensive list of priorities. Then he headed for town.

The clerk in the general store was delighted at the size of Drake's bill. He bought sheets for the old bed and more items for the kitchen. He also bought a bucket, mop, and broom so he could start cleaning the place.

It took him a week to clear the inside of cobwebs and clean the walls, ceiling, and floors. But he had sheets on his bed and a clean kitchen to prepare his meals. Now he was ready to purchase a flat-bedded wagon and a team of horses, which he needed desperately to bring supplies. He could carry very little back from town astride Duke.

By the second week, Drake had acquired one comfortable chair and a table for his front room so he could sit in the evenings to make out his list for the following day. His pantry was well stocked, but the bedroom was still bare except for a bed and chest. He hung his clothes on pegs; he'd acquired a couple of outfits of what he called "working clothes."

Duke occupied the one dry stall out in the barn, which was also being fixed up. He'd hired three fellows to reroof it and patch up the broken planks on the walls. The flat-bedded was used to haul grain and feed for the three horses and other bulky supplies. By the end of the third week, he was feeling rather proud of his accomplishments and sat down to write a long letter to Bayard.

The next day he went to town to post the letter and get some information from the clerk at the general store, who seemed to know everyone. He was ready to begin work on his house.

This was the afternoon he chanced to come upon the beautiful little Misty Bennett. It had been a while since he'd had time for pretty girls and it had been a much longer time since he'd met a young maiden as sweet and refreshing.

He'd sensed that she was a little frightened about accepting his offer to take her home. The look in her eyes reminded him of a little doe.

He had the wildest desire to kiss those rosebud lips and run his fingers through all that lovely golden hair, but he restrained himself. He was going to seek her out, he promised himself.

So the next day when he rode Duke into town, he purchased the sandals for her. On his way back home, he went by the spot where he'd seen her. He lingered there for a half hour hoping she might come by, as she'd told him she often did.

He could see why she liked this spot so much. He took the liberty of sitting awhile in the arbor under the weeping willow. It was so pleasant, with the river only a few feet away and birds chirping. Wild ferns grew near the shady riverbank, where purple and red verbena sprang up between the boulders.

He left the sandals there in the hope that she would find them. One day he'd see her there, he knew. For he would be coming this way again!

Chapter 4

On Saturday morning Misty moved at a frantic pace to get Jeff's hair washed and cut. She pressed his best shirt—he looked so fine all dressed up in the shirt with his new pants and shoes. "My, my—if you don't look handsome, Jeff! Now don't go off the porch. Sit in that swing and behave yourself or I'll paddle your behind!"

Then she washed Lavinia's hair. Once she had Lavinia all dressed and a ribbon around her hair, she turned her attention to herself.

When the Walters arrived at two, they were ready. Geneva couldn't have been more pleased when she saw all three of them sitting on the front porch in their best clothes.

They rushed out to the wagon and Geneva exclaimed about how nice they all looked. "We're going to have ourselves a nice afternoon," she declared as they took seats on the bench Ed had placed in the back of the flat-bedded wagon.

Crowley's one main street was a beehive of activity with

all the farmers and their families coming into town to do their shopping and visit with their neighbors.

Ed took charge of Jeff and went to make some purchases and Martha went her way as she always did. Jeff liked Mr. Walters. He was a gentle, kind man who spoke with a soft voice and didn't roar like a lion as his father always did. Ed put his order in at the grain store and then stopped by for some hardware. He wanted to buy the young man something so he pretended to need a new pocket knife. He knew how Jeff like to whittle. Jeff was overwhelmed when he walked out with the finest pocket knife he'd ever seen.

They'd also stopped by the general store and he'd come out of there with a new straw hat. The two of them were laughing when Ed said. "You look downright like a dude, young fellow."

Jeff was thinking how nice it would be to have a pa like Mr. Walters. Jeff wasn't the only one having his own private musings—as he and Jeff walked up the street together, Ed Walters was thinking that he wished he'd been blessed with a fine kid like Jeff. He'd never known the joy of having a son.

There had been times when he'd pondered why he and Geneva had never been blessed with a child. He'd never know the answer to that, but he did know that he'd given the ten-year-old a very exciting time today. That was enough for Ed.

Martha was having just as fine a time with Misty and Lavinia. She'd taken them to the mercantile, where she had to purchase a long list of things. Like Ed, she was generous. She had only to look at little Lavinia's shoes to urge Misty to pick out some slippers. Misty chose a pair that was practical for the winter, but she said to Geneva, "You don't have to do this, Mrs. Walters. You give us so much."

"Honey, I don't have any sweet little girls to buy pretty things for. I wish I did. It's a pleasure for me, dear."

Before they left the mercantile, Martha had called Misty

over to look at the bolts of material. "Pick out a pretty one, Misty, and I'll make you, me, and Lavinia matching frocks," she giggled with girlish enthusiasm.

Misty laughed, "Oh, Mrs. Walters—you're going to have me spoiled." But she would not dampen her happy mood so she roamed along the counter and chose a lovely shade of russet.

She told Misty, "While I settle up my bill, Misty, why don't you take Lavinia to the drug store and buy her one of those fruited ice cones." She took out a handful of coins out of her purse and said she would join them shortly. "I'm going to have a little visit with Matilda, before I join you and Lavinia," she told Misty.

So Misty took Lavinia's hand and the two of them went to the drug store and sat at a small table to enjoy the fruited ice cones. Lavinia had wanted grape and Misty had ordered strawberry.

Misty's back was to the front door so she hadn't seen Drake Dalton enter the store. He had purchased some medical supplies when he spied Misty. He glanced down at her feet and saw the sandals. With a pleased smile he sauntered up to her table.

"Well, Misty—we meet again," he greeted her.

She looked up at him and found herself trembling with excitement. He was so handsome and his eyes seemed to see right through her.

"Hello, Drake," she said in a slow drawl.

"I see you found the sandals. Now who is this pretty little miss?" he asked, knowing she had to be Misty's younger sister.

Lavinia looked up at him with a big smile because he'd called her *pretty*. Misty said, "This is my little sister, Lavinia. I do thank you for the sandals but you didn't have to do that."

"I know that, Misty, but I wanted to. I like your special

little spot, as you call it. May I share a few moments there with you sometime? Maybe some Sunday afternoon?"

She quickly responded, "Oh, no, Drake—I'm never there on Sunday."

"Oh—then on Saturday?"

"Yes, a Saturday would be fine—in the mid-afternoon."

Misty might not have known it but the clever Drake Dalton already knew a few things about her: She was not allowed suitors and her father was very strict. He could understand that—she was so breathtakingly beautiful.

When a matronly lady came over to greet Misty, Drake assumed she was Misty's mother but when he was introduced, he realized she was just an acquaintance.

He thought Mrs. Walters was a very nice lady and told her he was new to the community. "I arrived here from England just a few weeks ago, Mrs. Walters. My grandparents purchased land here years ago and now I'm taking it over. It's the old Benoit property. You know of it?"

"Certainly do, young man. Welcome to our community and our country. Come to see us anytime. Our door is always open," Geneva said warmly.

"I thank you, Mrs. Walters. Now I must go. It was a pleasure to meet you, ma'am, and it was nice to see you again, Misty." He looked down at little Lavinia. "It was very nice to meet you, Lavinia."

"Thank you, sir," she replied. Her older sister was feeling very proud that she'd been so mannerly.

Drake Dalton said his goodbyes and left the store. Misty told Mrs. Walters how she'd happened to meet the Englishman on her way to town to buy Jeff's shoes.

"Well, he seems like a very nice gentleman and he'll make a fine addition to our town, I'd say," Geneva remarked as Misty and Lavinia rose from the table to go with her to meet Ed and Jeff.

While his family had been enjoying themselves with the Walters, Mike Bennett arrived home and was shaving before going over to Georgia's. He'd stopped by the store and bought her a bottle of lilac toilet water. By the time the Walters had loaded up their purchases at the general store and the grain warehouse, it was almost six.

As they were pulling up in front of the Bennetts' front gate, Mike's wagon was rolling away about a hundred feet ahead of them, heading for the Gordon farm. Geneva exchanged glances with her husband. He didn't deserve these three fine children, she thought to herself.

"Misty, got a fine idea. What do you say you three just come on home with us for supper? Ed will bring you home afterwards."

"Oh, Mrs. Walters—you've already done so much for us," Misty said.

"For mercy's sake, honey—it's been a fun afternoon for us. Come on, Misty. I got a big old hen already baked and a couple of cherry pies. Now don't that make you hungry, Jeff?" she asked, glancing back at him.

"Sure does, Mrs. Walters," Jeff said and grinned.

"Makes me hungry, too, Mrs. Walters," Lavinia chimed in.

Misty began to laugh, "Guess I'd better not go against the two of them or they'll make me miserable tonight."

Ed guided the team on up the road. When they arrived at the Walters' house, the girls and Martha went into the house and Jeff helped Mr. Walters with the supplies. When they'd emptied out the back of the wagon, Ed said, "Young man, you just saved me many a step. Sure wish I'd had myself a son."

Jeff looked up at him with a pleased expression. "Wish I'd been your son, Mr. Walters. Sure wished I had."

Ed said nothing but gave him a pat on the shoulder. His heart went out to the young lad. He thought to himself about the very sad life Beth must have had with a man like Bennett.

Jeff went to the barn and helped Ed unharness the horses. When they got back to the house, Geneva had her hen and some potatoes in the oven. Misty had set the table and sliced a loaf of bread. Geneva was setting out some of her jars of relish, pickled beets, and spiced peaches.

By the time darkness gathered around the countryside, the Walters' house was glowing with lamplight as they enjoyed the scrumptious meal.

After dinner, Ed suggested to Jeff that the two of them go out on the front porch so he could have himself a smoke while the ladies cleaned up.

While Misty helped Geneva, Lavinia occupied herself in the front room with a little teddy bear that Geneva had had since she was a child.

"You're spoiled us today, Mrs. Walters. I can't recall when we've had such a day as this," Misty said.

"Truth is, Misty, I can't recall when Ed and I had such a pleasant day. You know, I was always sorry I never gave Ed a son or daughter. I know he's missed that," Geneva confessed.

"Life's not fair, is it, Mrs. Walters? Some people don't appreciate their blessings when they have them. Guess I learned that when Ma died. She was too young to die but she did," Misty declared.

"No, guess you're right, Misty. Life isn't fair or kind at times," Geneva replied.

A short time later, Misty announced it was time to go home. "It's Lavinia's bedtime." Geneva went out to the porch to tell Ed to get his wagon ready. She went back into the house and gave Misty the wool shawl she'd purchased for her at the mercantile store. She wanted to be sure the girl had something warm to wrap around her shoulders when the cold weather came.

Misty couldn't hold back the tears when she saw the lovely cream-colored shawl. She embraced Geneva as she used to embrace her mother. "Oh, Mrs. Walters—I love you."

"Well, I love you, too, Misty, and you just remember that, you hear?"

"Yes, ma'am—I will." Misty called Lavinia and they left for home. Jeff talked like a magpie to Mr. Walters all the way there. Misty realized he was just hungry for a man to talk with, and Ed knew that, too.

While Ed was gone, Geneva sat in the front room in a thoughtful mood. Misty was far older than her years. Life had made her more serious than most girls her age.

When they got home, the first thing Misty did was put one very tired six-year-old sister to bed. She'd had a very eventful day.

Jeff was not about to go to bed. He was too excited about his new straw hat and fine pocket knife. He was a little chatterbox for the next hour. Misty's heart went out to him when he said, "Wish Mr. Walters was my pa, Misty. I told him that tonight. I like him! Me and him can talk. You know what, Misty—he's going to take me huntin' with him. He says we're going in the woods and get ourselves a wild turkey."

"Oh, Jeff—that will be fun. Yes, Mr. Walters is a real fine person and so is Mrs. Walters." She smiled as she began to move around the front room to dim the lamps, announcing it was time they went to bed. She was feeling sleepy and she knew Jeff and Lavinia were, too.

She put on her nightgown and placed the shawl in the drawer of her chest. As she lay there she thought about all the gifts the Walters had given them and the dinner they'd had with them. What a Saturday it had been!

For Misty, the most thrilling part was seeing Drake Dalton again. He was every bit as good looking as she'd recalled.

Now that she was sixteen, Misty's romantic daydreams were influenced by the fairy tales her mother had read to her when she was little. But she also knew that a man's kisses were not always sweet. At least, that was the impression she got when she was thirteen and saw her father force his kisses on her mother. She'd torn herself out of his embrace, saying, "Dear Lord, Mike—the kids are right here in the house. You crazy? It's the middle of the afternoon."

Misty would never forget the look on her father's face as he glared at her. "You're a cold bitch, Beth! Did you know that? I wonder what ever attracted me to you." He'd marched out of the kitchen and her mother had begun to cry. Misty had felt so sorry for her and wanted to run to her, but she didn't. Instead, she'd rushed back to her room.

She lay thinking that Mr. Walters would never speak to his wife that way. Misty knew it was that day that she had begun to hate her father. Calling her dear, sweet mother a bitch was something she could never forgive or forget.

She and Jeff felt the same way. He wished he'd had a father like Ed Walters. And she knew that the man she gave her heart to one day would have to be a good man with a kind and generous heart like Mr. Walters.

Chapter 5

When Drake left Crowley that Saturday afternoon, his wagon was loaded with a few more pieces of furniture. With an amused grin he thought about the reaction his father would have if he could see how his son was living in Arkansas.

But strange as it all seemed, Drake rather liked the intrigue and challenge. During the last few weeks he'd tried to absorb everything around him—the people as well as their culture. He'd listened intensely to everyone he'd talked with and he'd surveyed the lands surrounding his farm. He had to become a planter and knew nothing about crops. It was not a horse breeding area like Virginia or even like Tennessee, where he'd worked for many weeks.

He had to learn about cotton and corn and hire a foreman by the time spring came, which meant building a small cottage on his land. But he had the winter ahead of him and he was not hurting for funds.

Bayard had a very unexpected surprise for him. His mother had not mentioned anything but the land, but there had also been a large sum of money included in that inheritance.

One day he hoped to have Bayard come to visit. He admired his uncle and realized why his mother insisted he go to France to seek her brother out if something happened to her.

Drake was still reading her journal but he had gotten to the part where she'd written that the doctor had told her as well as Devin that she should not have any more children. He'd begun to realize just how callous and selfish his father had been. He never wrote a letter to his father, only to his sisters when time finally permitted him.

After he'd returned from town and unloaded a settee and two tables from his wagon, his front room took on a more pleasant look. It didn't seem so vacant now that three lamps burned brightly on the new tables.

After dinner he'd sat in the lamplight and marked a few more items off his long list of things to accomplish.

He was just about ready to start dimming his lamps when he heard a noise just outside his front door. It was a black night—the moon and stars were blotted out by clouds.

Drake opened the door slowly and saw a large black dog looking up at him.

"Well, hello—big fellow. What brings you to my door, eh?" Drake saw the friendly wag of his tail and bent down to pat the dog's head. "Are you hungry? Is that it?"

Drake opened his door, inviting him to enter, but he noticed immediately he was limping. Laboriously, the dog managed to get through the front door before he sank down on the floor.

"You've got a problem, haven't you, fellow?" Drake knelt beside him to check out his right front paw and he found the culprit—a thorn. Drake gave a quick yank to remove it, then patted the dog's head again. "You're going to be fine now. Feel like something to eat?"

The big dog seemed to know what he was asking and

followed him into the kitchen. Drake cut him a slice of ham and broke up a piece of the bread. The dog ate it greedily. When the dog finished it, Drake put down a bowl of water and then dimmed the lamp. The dog followed him back to the front room and Drake opened the door to give him his freedom. "You ready to go home now?"

But the dog chose not to go. Instead, he curled up by Drake's feet, his tail wagging, and looked up as if to say he wished to stay right where he was.

Drake smiled. "You telling me you don't want to go out? Well, fellow—I'm going to bed." The dog followed him to his bedroom as he undressed and crawled into bed. Then he curled up by the side of Drake's bed and began to lick his paw, seeming perfectly content as Drake dimmed the lamp on the nightstand.

He assumed he had himself a dog whether he liked it or not. He was sure of it by the time Sunday night came around. The big black dog had lingered with him as he'd worked in the front and back yards, cutting weeds and grass.

That night he and the dog ate bacon, eggs, and more of the bread Drake had bought in in Crowley. He didn't know how to bake biscuits.

That night, Drake decided he had to get some carpenters lined up to build a small house for the foreman before winter set in. One old settler had told him that December, January, and February could bring real cold weather to Arkansas.

He also had to get a good supply of wood for his fireplace and cookstove. That was one thing he didn't have to go out to buy—he had plenty of woods right on his own land. He was already anticipating doing some hunting in a few more weeks.

That had been one of his greatest pleasures on his father's country estate—roaming through the woods, looking for game.

On Monday morning, he rode into Crowley and Lepanto to put out the word that he was in need of carpenters. He figured the best places to leave the message were the general store and the grain warehouse. The men who had repaired his barn were back working at the lumber mills.

Before he went back home late that morning, he went by the hardware store to purchase a rifle and a shotgun, along with some ammunition. He also picked up some tools for the fireplace. Almost daily, he noticed things he needed. Never had he realized just how much it took to outfit a place. But he was learning!

Drake had no idea about the flurry of gossip he'd created in the hamlets of Lepanto and Crowley. The young ladies, as well as the female clerks who waited on him, were all fascinated by the tall, handsome Englishman who had moved into their community. The older gents found him a nice, mannerly fellow but the younger men resented him. They found the young ladies they were with always ogled him as he rode down the street on his black stallion.

But Drake had never given any of the young fellows a reason to be jealous—he simply tipped his hat in a friendly way and nodded as he rode by. Most of the time he'd been too preoccupied by the many things he had to accomplish when he was in town.

He had seen many pretty maidens walking down the streets of the two small towns but the fairest of all, as far as Drake was concerned, was little Misty Bennett.

His practical side told him he had to put thoughts of Misty aside for now. But somehow, her face came to haunt him, sometimes in the evening as it had the other night after he'd seen her in the drug store.

He felt the need to find a good hiding place in the little house for the velvet case containing his mother's emerald ring and bracelet. When he'd looked at the jewelry, he thought that Misty's green eyes sparkled like the stones. He'd never seen anything more beautiful!

* * *

Drake had written a letter to Ellen, his oldest sister, and she was elated to receive it. She'd often wondered about him after she'd received the letter from him in Paris. Drake had never written to his father. He had now read all of his mother's journal and placed it back in the drawer of the chest.

Before she'd gone to the dining room that evening, she had let Valeria read the letter. Suzanne no longer lived at Dalton Manor. She'd married the wealthy young Lord Edward Warrington. Ellen was delighted to sit down to write a letter to Drake now that she had his mailing address. She was eager to tell him he was going to be an uncle come springtime.

Valeria was as excited as Ellen had been when she read his letter. "I have missed him, Ellen. Haven't you?"

"Oh, yes, Valeria—I've missed him very much. Who knows, maybe one day you and I might just cross the ocean to see him. I'm going to write him tonight."

"I'll write him too, Ellen, and give you my letter."

"He'll like that, Valeria," Ellen declared as she tucked the letter from Drake in the pocket of her skirt. She planned to take it with her when she went downstairs for dinner. Maybe, after all this time, her father's heart would be more mellow toward his son.

Ellen recalled his harsh words when she'd told him about the letter she'd gotten from Drake when he was in Paris and living with Bayard. He'd roared at her, "I've no son, Ellen. Know that from now on. Darren is no longer my son!"

Being the boldest of the Dalton daughters, Ellen was once again going to approach him. She found herself admiring him for going to a strange country to seek this inheritance. It all sounded very adventuresome and she longed to see him again.

But she knew she could never leave Valeria back here in this gloomy old place—for that was what it had become after her mother's death and Drake's leaving. And then six months earlier, Suzanne had gotten married.

She'd kept hoping some fine young suitor would come to call on Valeria, but their father was so strict that it wasn't easy. Suzanne was the lucky one; the young man enamored of her was the son of Devin's friend, Arnold Warrington, so Devin approved of her marriage to young Edward.

But Valeria was not the beauty Suzanne was. If Ellen was honest, she had only to look in the mirror to know that she was not as attractive as her youngest sister.

Ellen was aware that she might be called a spinster, but she knew better! She had a great capacity to love a man when and if she found the right one. So far, he'd just not appeared, and she was in no hurry to compromise. She liked her job tutoring and she earned wages which gave her a feeling of independence. She had no chance to spend much of it, so she had a nice amount carefully put away.

Ellen knew one day she would leave. She remembered many things about her mother which disturbed her. She knew one thing—she'd never marry a man like her father, regardless of how wealthy he was.

Two months after their mother died, their father called each of them into the library and presented them with one piece of her jewelry. Ellen wondered what he planned to do with the rest of the collection. She had no way of knowing that Drake had helped himself to two pieces before he'd left.

She was the only one who dared to speak up to her father that night when he gave her the pearl necklace her mother often wore. But Ellen remembered that there were pearl earrings to match the necklace, so she asked her father, "May I have the earrings that match these pearls, Father?

Mother always looked so lovely when she wore them. I would cherish them very much."

"Of course, Ellen. Of course you can," he'd said.

So that was her share of her mother's jewelry. Suzanne had been given a sapphire ring and little Valeria was thrilled to receive a ruby and diamond ring.

Suzanne's husband would provide her with her own jewelry collection just as he'd taken her to live in an elegant mansion after they returned from their honeymoon in Paris and Austria.

Ellen had been pondering whether her father was beginning to think about taking a new wife. He left the manor more often and she felt sure it involved a woman.

It was then that she decided that no other woman was going to wear her mother's furs, so she went to the storage room and chose a sable muff and cape along with an ermine cloak. Those and three gowns which Ellen had always admired were put in her armoire. Why shouldn't she have them instead of some strange woman her father might marry? Her mother would have wished her to have them.

Ellen had not one qualm about doing what she did, but she did feel guilty about not choosing something for little Valeria. The next afternoon she went back to the storage room and selected three gowns and a lovely mink cape and muff for her.

She dared her father to question her about the missing items. She'd point out that they were her mother's and she would have wished them to have them. But weeks went by and nothing was said. Devin was not aware of the missing clothing—he hadn't even discovered that Drake had taken his mother's ring and bracelet.

Ellen was right about one thing: he was thinking about taking another wife. Lady Dianne Winters was a widow and he was more than ready for a lady to be warming his bed. The thirty-eight-year-old Dianne had encouraged him to pursue her recently at a soiree he'd attended in London.

She was a voluptuous woman, nothing like the petite Adrienne. Her hair was the color of copper and her blue eyes had a devious glint. Everything about her titillated Devin. He was ready for a spirited lady after Adrienne, who had been like a lifeless rag doll. The French bride he'd picked had been nothing like the promiscuous French ladies he'd heard about. He'd been terribly disappointed in her from the minute he'd brought her back to England. He could not have fathomed that if she had been in love with him, she would have been a completely different woman. He always blamed her for her coolness when he should have been blaming himself. Adrienne was a very warm and passionate woman, but Devin was never a perceptive man. He was so self-absorbed and conceited that he blamed her for everything that went sour in their marriage.

He would never have believed that Adrienne found him a fumbling bore when they indulged in intimacy. She quickly turned into an ice maiden because she found him so dull. She had often wondered how Drake, Ellen, Suzanne, and Valeria had been conceived.

Her secret was that when she was forced to endure Devin's awkward lovemaking, in her mind she was making love to Francois, who the man she loved whom her father had disapproved of. Each time she'd given way to that fantasy she'd found herself pregnant.

That night at dinner when Ellen, Valeria, and their father had gathered in the elegant dining room, Ellen told her father about her letter from Drake. "He's in a place called Arkansas, Father. He sounds very happy living in a little four-room house," she added.

Lord Dalton quickly dismissed her. "I've no interest in anything Darren is doing or attempting to do, Ellen."

Ellen never took the letter out of her pocket but she glanced across the table at Valeria to see her expression. As soon as dinner was over the two of them went upstairs and Devin was left alone downstairs. He knew that the ghost of Adrienne still haunted the house. He was sick of it and ready for a change.

As Valeria and Ellen were mounting the stairs, Valeria remarked, "Father is a cruel man, isn't he? I realized that tonight. He never forgives if you cross him."

"Yes, Valeria—he never forgives," Ellen replied. They said their good nights and Ellen went to her room to write to Drake. Valeria also sat at her desk to write to her brother.

The evening had made an impact on Valeria and it was reflected in her one-page letter. She wrote that she wished she was with him. "It's gloomy around here now, Drake," she murmured aloud.

She finished her letter and took it to Ellen before she went to bed. Before Ellen put it in the envelope with her much longer one, she could not resist reading it. She was sad to know just how unhappy her younger sister was.

Being twenty-three and having certain liberties that Valeria did not have, Ellen decided to do a little exploring to find out what passage would cost her for her and Valeria to go to America. Then there was the cross-country trip to get to Arkansas. A boat traveled southward down the eastern shoreline, veering into the seaport city of New Orleans. From there one boarded a steamboat up the Mississippi River to a place called Memphis, in the state of Tennessee. Then it was an overland trip to Drake's land another sixty miles away. Ellen knew no one had ever considered her to be anything but a clever, serious woman, but right now she was thinking like a frivolous young girl. Drake seemed utterly enchanted with his new country and she was more than ready for a change.

Only one thing stopped her from starting out immediately for Arkansas, and that was money. She would have to work as a tutor for another three weeks to earn the wages she would need to get her and Valeria to America.

She said nothing to Valeria about her trips into London. She'd checked out passage and studied maps, being a meticulous person about anything she did. There was no reason to discuss any of this with Valeria.

One thing she had not considered was that if she didn't book passage in the next eight weeks, her voyage would have to wait until spring. Winter crossings were dangerous.

Chapter 6

Misty had no idea when her father arrived home on Saturday night—she had fallen asleep early. But his bedroom door was shut when she woke up. She prepared breakfast for Lavinia, Jeff, and herself.

Jeff went out to cut some wood for her cookstove, proudly wearing his new straw hat. Lavinia went out in the back yard to play while Misty washed their dirty dishes. Her father still slept. Misty figured he was all tuckered out after his night with Georgia. How she detested that woman!

She worked around the kitchen with all kinds of thoughts rushing through her mind. Dear Lord—what if they should get married? She'd leave, she told herself. But how could she leave Jeff and Lavinia behind? No, she couldn't bring herself to do that.

It was late morning when Mike finally emerged from his bedroom and went into the kitchen to pour himself a cup of coffee. He'd seen Misty out on the front porch sweeping. He wasn't in the mood for his usual hearty breakfast so he just reached in the pan to take one of the cold biscuits and put some jam on it.

It didn't taste too good to him. He blamed it on that damned liquor of Georgia's. It and his stomach didn't get along. He hadn't liked it after the first taste, but he hadn't wanted to offend her.

When Misty came back into the house, she saw her father sitting at the table eating the cold biscuit. "Want me to fry you a slice of ham and some eggs, Pa?"

"Nope, this is fine," he told her. When he finished his coffee, he ambled out on the front porch, figuring a little fresh air might make him feel better.

Jeff was whittling with his new knife as he greeted his father. " 'Morning, Pa."

" 'Morning, Jeff. Where'd you get that fancy straw hat?"

"Mr. Walters bought it for me—he also got me this pocket knife." He held it up to show it to Mike.

"My, my—now ain't he the generous one!" Mike remarked with a tone of sarcasm.

"Mr. Walters is a real fine man. And generous. Mrs. Walters is just as nice. They took us home to have supper with them last night. Boy, it was good!"

"Sounds like the Walters could get a young fellow like you spoiled real easily," Mike remarked as he turned to go back into the house. The fresh air had not helped.

Truth was, Mike didn't begin to feel like a human being again until after suppertime. He began to feel even better when Misty herded Lavinia and Jeff off to their beds. All he'd heard all day and night was praise for the Walters. He was sick of hearing how wonderful they were.

They'd never seemed too friendly to him. They both seemed to like his wife, Beth, but he always felt they looked down their noses at him. He figured it was because he was a stranger who'd come to Crowley only eighteen years ago.

He'd always felt the little community was a bit clannish.

They didn't seem to want an outsider, so Mike didn't try to be overly friendly. It irked him that they were warm to Beth and gave him the cold shoulder.

A good night's sleep Sunday night had him feeling fit to go to work early Monday morning. He was grateful that the awful feeling he'd had was gone. Next time, he would have to refuse that liquor if Georgia offered it to him. He'd stick with a shot of whiskey. He could handle that.

His gift of toilet water had put him back in her good graces and made her more than eager to please him. Please him she surely did, until the wee hours of the morning. He had to say that Georgia was a whole lot of woman for any man!

But he couldn't ask her to marry him. He had nothing to offer her. She had a finer house and a hell of a lot more land. But lately, she'd been hinting around that this didn't matter, that she had enough for both of them.

That was not the only problem. Little Lavinia would not be hard for Georgia to tolerate, but Jeff and Misty could prove to be more than she could endure.

The two of them were so devoted to their mother, he knew they'd never accept Georgia as their stepmother.

For Misty, it was her usual Monday as she went about the house doing the chores. It wasn't until she made a more careful survey of the pantry that she realized that her pa had not stopped to buy any food for the week. He always bought supplies on Saturday afternoon, before he came home.

Mike had made only one stop on Saturday, and that was to buy the bottle of toilet water for Georgia. Misty was at a loss as to what she was going to fix for supper.

Jeff said, "I'll go down and try to catch us a mess of fish, Misty."

"Yes, do that, Jeff." She did have enough meal to make some cornbread cakes. There were only four potatoes left, hardly enough for a meal. Her pa was going to be disgruntled without his morning coffee. But that wasn't her fault.

That wasn't the way Mike Bennett reasoned it when he came into the kitchen shortly after five. There was nothing on the stove, so he asked Misty, "No supper cooking?"

"Pa, you bought no food Saturday afternoon. I'm hoping Jeff's catching some fish. There's no coffee for the morning."

"What you saying, girl?" he roared.

"There's no coffee. You bring supplies in every Saturday after you get paid. I wasn't here when you came in Saturday, so I didn't realize until this afternoon."

Mike knew that what she said was true. He grumbled, "Make me a list quick. I'm going back to town. Got to have coffee in the morning."

Misty did as she was told and handed her father the list. She watched him fumbling in his pocket to count his money before he left. She didn't fool herself that it was his coffee he didn't want to be denied tonight or in the morning. Served him right that he had to go back into town. If he concentrated on his home and family instead of chasing after that fancy widow, this would not have happened.

Jeff had sat out on the riverbank until six before he gave up. There were only six perch on his line but Misty told him to clean them.

"Pa not home yet, Misty?" he asked as he started out the back door with a pan and a knife.

"He's been home but there was no coffee so he's hightailed it back to town to buy food for us."

Jeff broke into a grin as he went out the back door. He cleaned his six fish and Misty fried up a large stack of cornbread cakes and sliced a big white onion. Her table was set and the four potatoes were sliced and frying in the skillet when Mike returned.

Misty didn't put the fish on a platter after she fried them.

A devious streak hit her and she knew what she was going to do.

She put the food away and brewed up a pot of coffee for her father. When the cornmeal-battered perch were fried, everyone was seated at the table. Her father had his coffee, glasses of milk were poured for the rest of them, and the cornbread cakes and potatoes were on the table. But then she took the fried fish and rationed them out. She placed one on Lavinia's plate and one on her plate. She placed two on Jeff's plate, telling him, "You worked hard to get these for our supper tonight, honey."

She placed two on her father's plate. He looked up at her quizzically, but said nothing. Misty knew if she'd put them on a platter he would have taken at least three. Jeff caught her eye and smiled—he knew why she'd done what she did.

Mike left the kitchen table knowing that Misty was a cunning little minx. She wasn't the sweet, docile woman her mother had been. He could not bully her as he had Beth. She irked him like the devil, but he secretly admired her spirit and cleverness.

When Drake returned home Tuesday afternoon, he found that he had himself a fine guard dog—the big black dog was holding a tall, lanky fellow at bay. The man was frantic and yelled at Drake, "Mister, will you call your dog off?"

"Come on, fellow," Drake called to the dog and he came rushing over, his long tail wagging. Drake turned to the man, who was trying to compose himself, heaving a deep sigh of relief that Dalton had arrived home when he had.

Wiping the sweat from his brow, he said to Drake, "Scared me to death, he did. Looks like he could be a mean one if he set his mind to it."

"He just might be," Drake agreed and laughed. "You looking for me or just passing by?"

"If you're Mr. Dalton then you're the one I came to see. Heard you have the need for a hired man. I live just a couple of miles away—staying with my sister. I'm a carpenter but I'll tackle anything you need done around here."

"What's your name?"

"Oscar Wells. Maybe you know my married sister, Rachel Bray?"

"No, I don't. I haven't been here too long so I know very few people." Drake invited him to the front porch so they could talk awhile. He noticed that Oscar kept a lot of space between the dog and himself. A half hour later Drake hired Oscar and said he'd expect him in the morning. Oscar was a happy man when he left to walk the two miles back to his sister's place.

Drake and his dog went on inside before he took the wagon and team to the barn. Patting the dog's head, he grinned. "Guess it's time I gave you a name. Think I'll call you Lucky."

Lucky seemed to approve of his name. He wagged his tail and licked Drake's hand. Together they went back to the flat-bedded wagon—he liked to ride with Drake.

Drake attended to his evening chores before the two of them headed back to the house. He took his packages back to his bedroom before going into the kitchen with the fresh loaves he'd bought at the bakery.

But Drake had to admit he was getting tired of his cooking. He was hoping to hire a man and woman once he had the small cottage built. The man could serve as his foreman and the woman could do some cooking. He had to admit he missed some of the delicious dinners served at Dalton Manor.

The next morning Oscar arrived, riding one of his sister's mules. By the end of the day, Drake was satisfied that he was a hard worker. Lucky seemed to accept him now, but Oscar was still leery of the dog.

The only rest Oscar took during the long day was to sit in the shade to eat the lunch his sister had prepared for him.

Drake rode Duke over to the lumber mills to make a purchase. Duke was ready to kick his heels up because Drake had been using his flat-bedded wagon so often lately.

Mike Bennett got his first look at the tall, good-looking Drake Dalton that early afternoon and asked his buddy, Jeb, who that gent was. "Never saw him around town before."

"He's new to these parts, I've been told. Heard he inherited all that Benoit property. An Englishman, I hear."

"How do you find out so darn much, Jeb?" Mike asked with a chuckle.

"Got a couple of daughters who were raving about the handsome Englishman in our midst the other night. Need I tell you about girls that age? You got a daughter about Mary Sue and Hazel's age. Lord, when a good-looking fellow moves in, girls find out everything they can about him."

"Misty don't have time for fellows yet. She has to take care of her brother and sister," Mike reminded him.

"Well, bless her heart—she does have a lot on her small shoulders, don't she?" Jeb remarked as the two of them got back to stacking the lumber.

"Misty's got plenty of time for courting later," Mike declared in a serious tone. He and Jeb were buddies, but they were hardly the same type. Jeb was a hard worker like Mike, but completely devoted to his wife. Such devotion Beth Bennett had never known. Jeb's daughters never had to work as hard as Misty, who considered them to be pampered and lucky.

Mike thought about his conversation with Jeb as he went home that evening. He'd just realized that Misty was sixteen and at a courting age, as they called it.

That evening he carefully scrutinized her blossoming young figure and saw how her firm breasts pushed against her cotton dress and her hips were rounded below her tiny waist.

Privately, he thought his daughter was very beautiful, far more beautiful than her ma. She had a fine figure already. Fellows would be coming around any day, he told himself. It was strange that he hadn't noticed it until this evening, since he'd always had an eye for a pretty lady.

Misty was just grateful that he was in a pleasant mood. Jeff felt the same way. It seemed to him that his pa had been a little nicer since Sunday. He didn't know what had brought it about, but he welcomed whatever it was.

After supper, Mike and Lavinia went into the front room while Misty started to clean up. Jeff went out to gather in the wood for the morning.

After he filled the wood bin, Jeff dried the dishes. In a low voice he told Misty, "Pa better spend some time getting us some wood cut, Misty. That pile is getting real low. Will you say something to him?"

"I'll say something, Jeff. Don't fret about it."

By the time she dimmed the lamps in the kitchen, she was seething with anger. If her father hadn't been so busy on his day off running over to the Gordon place, he would have already cut their wood for the coming cold weather.

Misty sat down in a chair opposite her father's. Her anger made her bolder than she might normally have been.

"Pa, I have to talk to you," she said in a most serious manner.

"What—what you need to talk to me about, Misty?" he asked. She seemed so solemn that he was caught unprepared.

"Well, it's as simple as this, Pa. Monday night when there was no food in the house, I couldn't cook supper. Well, I can't cook food if I don't have wood for my cookstove. It's running short out there. And there's no wood for heating this winter. Usually, you've started that by now, too," she said, her green eyes piercing him.

"You trying to boss me, little missy?" he asked indignantly as he moved forward in his chair.

Misty replied boldly, "No, not boss you, Pa. Maybe you just haven't noticed the wood pile.

"I—I've noticed. Plan to get to it this week," he mumbled.

She got up from the chair and called to Lavinia to tell her it was bedtime. But her green eyes still glared at her father. What Mike Bennett saw in those lovely eyes was very definitely disapproval!

Chapter 7

Mike Bennett sat in his front room for a couple of hours after all his children had gone to bed. Misty had been right—he'd paid no attention to the woodpile or anything around here for the last four months. Georgia had been a hell of a distraction.

A surge of honesty suddenly went through him. If he hoped to have food on his cookstove and a warm fire when he came in from work this winter, he knew he'd better get his butt busy.

Truth was, he needed to stop by the store for groceries on Saturday afternoon and come home to put in a hour doing chores around the place before suppertime instead of rushing over to Georgia's.

He came up with what he thought might be a solution. He'd pay a call on her on Friday night and hope she'd show a little understanding.

So, Friday night as soon as he'd eaten dinner with his family, Mike cleaned up and announced to Misty that he was going over to Georgia's.

Georgia was pleasantly surprised to see Mike on her doorstep on Friday night. At first she assumed that he just couldn't wait to see her the next night.

But she was disappointed when he explained that he wouldn't be able to come over the next night. She went into a pout. "So, I'm supposed to sit here tomorrow night and twiddle my thumbs, Mike Bennett?" she said, glaring up at him.

"Now, Georgia, honey, don't be that way. I'm not as lucky as you. You got a foreman who takes care of your land and someone who cooks and cleans for you. I've got to cut wood so me and my kids can eat and not freeze to death this winter. Hell, I should have started a month ago."

"Well, you just go and cut your wood, Mike! But I'll make no promises as to what I'll be doing Saturday night." She moved away from him on the settee.

Mike got up to tower over her. "That's your privilege, Georgia. Guess I better be going anyway. I'm a working man with another day to put in."

Georgia made no effort to see him to the door, but remained on her fancy settee, pouting.

Mike leaped up in his wagon and headed for home. He had prepared himself for this reaction. She was a completely selfish woman, but that had been part of her attraction after a woman like Beth. But tonight, he pondered a lot of things as he guided his wagon toward home. As much wild, wonderful pleasure as she gave him in bed, it could have prove to be a living hell to live with her day and night. No woman had ever bossed him around!

Georgia was also doing a lot of private musing. She'd never conquer or rule Mike Bennett completely as she had David Gordon. That was what intrigued her so about this robust, virile man! She didn't want to lose him—no man had ever excited her as much as Mike when they made love. She'd had a dozen lovers during the years she'd been married to David! It hadn't mattered if it was a hired hand on their place or someone she'd met in Crowley or Lepanto.

Georgia had a healthy sexual appetite that David never sated, so she had no qualms about cheating on him. But she wanted to marry Mike Bennett. It didn't matter that he was just a mill worker; he wouldn't have to do that if he married her. The one thorn in her side would be those three kids.

She'd met Lavinia once and figured she would prove to be no problem. But a ten-year-old son and a sixteen-year-old daughter constantly underfoot would certainly cramp her style.

So Georgia decided to do a little investigating on her own during the week while Mike was at the mills. She was going to pay a visit and see for herself how the boy and oldest daughter would react to her.

By the time she went to bed, she'd accepted the fact that she was going to spend Saturday night without Mike warming her bed. She might just get in her fancy gig and go into town. It was something she hadn't done in a long time, but it used to be fun—especially if she ran into her vivacious friend, Lilly.

When Mike went to work on Saturday morning he was no longer fretting about Georgia. The mills closed down an hour earlier on Saturdays, and this time he remembered to buy a good supply of groceries. Since he didn't have to buy a little gift for Georgia, he bought two plump fryers so Misty could fry up a big platter of chicken.

Misty was delighted to see how much food he carried into the house.

"I'm going out back and you'll have a supply of kindling before the sun goes down," Mike said. "We'll just have supper late tonight. Come on, Jeff—you can fill the bin for your sister as I split the kindling," he added as he turned to leave.

Lavinia eagerly went about setting the table as Misty began to wash and cut up the hens. It took two skillets to get the eighteen pieces fried to a crispy brown.

She put on a pot of water to boil the corn. She knew she was going to have two very hungry fellows to feed tonight. Jeff brought in load after load of kindling until the bin was piled high.

She stared out the window, watching the two of them working side by side and thought that this is the way it should be. She also pondered what old Georgia was thinking. She hoped she was madder than a wet cat.

But Misty was wrong. Georgia had gotten all dolled up and took her gig in to Crowley. As luck would have it, she ran into Lilly Johnson when she made her first stop at the drug store.

The two of them gave each other an exuberant embrace, shrieking with delight. They sat at one of the little tables to have a fruit ice. For almost an hour, they caught up on all the gossip. Like Georgia, Lilly was a widow.

Lilly didn't own the vast acres of land that Georgia did, but she had been left a nice fortune and lived in a fine two-story frame house. She had house help and groundskeepers.

For the last year she had been keeping company with Harlan Matthews, a wealthy gentleman about her own age who'd lost his wife three years earlier. Their relationship was not passionate as Georgia's was with Mike Bennett. Truth was, Lilly questioned the relationship Georgia was having with Bennett. What she had heard about it disturbed her greatly.

He could easily be courting her in hopes of marrying her for her wealth. He was only a mill worker and at his age he would probably be just that the rest of his life. His only holding was two acres of property. And he had three children.

She was questioning Georgia's thinking. After all, Georgia was nearly forty years of age. But, Georgia always thought of herself as being eternally young. Despite all her fancy frocks, Georgia no longer looked twenty-five.

Lilly desperately wanted to speak with her about Mike Bennett, but she couldn't seem to find the right moment. She certainly didn't want to offend her dear friend. It wasn't an easy life being a widow—Lilly knew that.

Suddenly there was another distraction to prevent her from speaking to Georgia. Georgia spied the tall, handsome man entering the store. She seemed mesmerized by the sight of him. Her eyes traveled up his long, firm-muscled legs and trim hips to his broad chest.

His dark shirt was unbuttoned and she saw the little ringlets of black hair. Her eyes surveyed his fine-chiseled features and thick black hair. Dear God, she thought, what a magnificent looking man!

She told herself she was going to have to come to Crowley more often! When she could finally find her tongue, she leaned across the table to inquire if Lilly knew who he was. Lilly smiled. She knew Georgia so well.

"He's a newcomer—his name is Drake Dalton. Harlen told me he's taken over the old Benoit property through an inheritance. He's an Englishman and very wealthy from what I hear."

"Well, well, well—the ladies will be swarming all over him like bees after honey," Georgia said with a coy smile.

Certainly Georgia would not be so foolish as to think she could capture his eye, Lilly thought to herself. The young man was in his mid-twenties. In hopes of discouraging her friend, she said, "Can't you imagine how all the little belles around Crowley are going to be throwing themselves at him? Chances are, he already has a lovely lady back in England to bring here as his bride."

"He sounds like the most exciting thing to hit Crowley in years," Georgia declared.

"Well, Georgia, you and I won't be acting silly over him. He's too young for us."

"Speak for yourself, Lilly." Georgia said with a light-hearted laugh.

It was almost five when Georgia headed her gig toward home. She had had a very good time in town.

She was amazed that she didn't miss Mike Bennett's company at all that night. She put away her purchases and refreshed herself before dinner. She went to bed early for a Saturday night—she had plans for the next day and wanted to look her best.

She slept late on Sunday morning and when she did stir the first thing she did was search her armoires, for an appropriate gown. The one she chose had been most flattering on her some ten years earlier.

In her dressing gown, she went to the kitchen to order her cook to send up a breakfast tray and fill a large basket with one of their smoked hams and a large slab of bacon. "I want you to put in four jars of your fine preserves, Samantha. This afternoon I'm welcoming a new neighbor to our countryside."

"Yes, ma'am, I'll prepare it. It'll be ready when you're ready to leave," the black cook said.

Georgia went back to her room to enjoy her breakfast and indulged herself in a perfumed bath. She dressed with special care and styled her hair in a fashion that was not right for her. Georgia still saw herself as a young southern belle, even though those days had passed her by.

Hair hanging down her back did not have the same alluring effect it had when she was in her twenties. The gown she'd chosen was not as appealing as she felt it was. But when Georgia stood in front of her full length mirror she blinded herself to the truth.

At one in the afternoon, she guided her gig toward the Benoit property. When she arrived at the gate of Drake's place she was not prepared to be so suspiciously greeted by Lucky. Drake emerged from the house and admonished the dog gently.

He walked to the gate and greeted her graciously as she introduced herself and told him she'd come to welcome him to the community.

"That's mighty nice of you, Mrs. Gordon. Welcome to my home," he said as he assisted her from her gig.

"I'm sorry I've been so late in coming over, Mr. Dalton, but I just learned of your arrival yesterday," she said as she took his strong hand. She gave him her most attractive smile as she told him she'd brought him a sampling of the fine cured Arkansas hams and bacon. Drake took the basket and held her hand as he led her up the path to his front porch.

Drake was a gracious host. He served her coffee and sat to chat with her but the lady seemed in no hurry. He found himself becoming impatient with her when she continued to linger after an hour.

Drake began to get the impression that the lady had other things on her mind when she made a point of letting him know she was a widow. He'd encountered her type before.

He didn't offer a second cup of coffee and excused himself, leaving the room with her basket.

When he returned to the front room with her empty basket and thanked her graciously, she didn't realize she was being dismissed.

"You're a very generous lady, Mrs. Gordon. I'll enjoy the ham, bacon, and preserves very much, I'm sure. Please come to see me again." He took her hand to assist her up from the chair, then smiled as he said, "Let me see you to your gig, Mrs. Gordon."

Drake had such a winning way about him that Georgia never realized how abruptly she had been dismissed.

Drake went back up the pathway to his house with Lucky trotting behind him. He had better things to do than entertain a silly widow who had more on her mind than just a courtesy call. Drake had only to be around the woman a few minutes to sense that he wanted to be rid of her.

He'd known a lot of women like Georgia Gordon. They

spelled trouble! He had no time for the likes of her. But what he found hard to understand was that they were old enough to be his mother. He found them a disgusting lot.

As Georgia traveled the few miles to her home, it never dawned on her that she'd been charmingly turned away by the handsome Englishman or that he didn't find her attractive or desirable.

What would have really been devastating to her was the fact that Mike Bennett had taken no time to think about her all day Sunday. He had worked from sunup to sundown. Misty had no idea of how many trips his wagon had made to haul wood back for firewood, but she did know he had put in a full day and her heart mellowed toward him.

When he finally came into the kitchen that night, his faded shirt soaked with sweat, she was glad she had fixed him such a good supper.

Her green eyes surveyed his flushed face and Mike saw concern in her eyes. "Oh, Pa—you look so tired." Her hand went up to touch his face and wipe the sweat from his brow. Misty didn't realize what that little affectionate gesture meant to him.

"I am tired but we'll stay warm this winter, I promise you that. Give me another two days and I'll have enough wood cut, Misty."

"I believe you, Pa. I've seen what you've done today." Her kind gesture toward her father helped to change his thinking. His daughter did care for him—she'd shown him that this evening. He'd thought she hated him, but she didn't. He also realized that little Jeff had worked right along with him all weekend. He just hadn't given his kids a chance lately. He was the one at fault.

Mike and Jeff had a ravenous appetite. All eighteen pieces of chicken had been devoured the night before and tonight the same thing happened.

What was really pleasing to Misty as she was cleaning up the kitchen was that she could hear her brother and father laughing and talking in the front room. That sounded so good to her.

When Monday morning came, Misty felt that her father was in a more happy-go-lucky mood than he'd been in weeks. She had hopes that he might be losing interest in Georgia Gordon.

If her pa could always be like he was this weekend, home would be a happier place.

Chapter 8

Oscar Wells had gone home on his sister's mule with his first wages from Drake Dalton. He was feeling real happy about his new job—Dalton was a good man to work for. He paid a fair wage. Now, he'd be able to help Rachel out; she'd known hard times lately. He knew she was going to lose her farm, but there was no way he could come up with that kind of money.

He'd worked hard all week for Drake for he sure wanted him to be pleased and keep him on. This afternoon when Drake paid him he was amazed Oscar had cleared so much underbrush.

Drake saw the huge pile of stacked cuttings. "You've done a grand job, Oscar, and bloody fast, too." When he began to count out his wages, he added some extra.

Gratefully, Oscar thanked him. Drake told him he was ready to send him to the mills Monday morning for the first load of lumber.

"Get some rest over the weekend and I'll see you Monday morning," Drake said as he waved goodbye.

On Sunday afternoon, after Drake had gotten rid of Georgia Gordon, he set fire to the piles of brush and had a mighty bonfire blazing for quite a while.

It was a perfect time because the wind was calm and recent rains had kept the grass green. Lucky didn't like the fire and, for once, he deserted Drake to go back to the house.

Drake was late getting back to fix supper and feed Lucky. He couldn't leave the area until the fires had died down. After he'd eaten and it had grown dark, he went back to satisfy himself that everything was safe for the night.

For Oscar, Monday was slow compared to the days he'd been putting in. He went to the mills for Mr. Dalton and got the lumber unloaded. He said to Drake, "I got all my carpenter's tools. Want me to bring them in the morning and start laying the foundation? All I need to see is the drawings for the cottage and the measurements of the rooms. I've built houses before, like I told you. Later on I'll need another man or two to help me."

"Come on to the house with me, Oscar. We'll have some coffee and I'll show you the plans. It will be a four-room house with a small fireplace for heating. Nothing fancy, just a comfortable place for the foreman I plan to hire before spring gets here."

They sat for an hour at the kitchen table and sipped coffee while Oscar studied the simple drawing. He had helped build much fancier houses, so he had no doubt that he could do this.

"Want me to make a list of things you're going to need, Mr. Drake?"

"Got a better idea, Oscar. Let's go into town—you can do the ordering for me at the mills this afternoon."

"Fine with me, Mr. Dalton."

Oscar and Drake went to town in the flat-bedded wagon and brought back kegs of different size nails and more lumber. Drake made a deal with the manager for the rest of the supplies to be delivered.

SWEET SEDUCTION

When they parted company late in the afternoon, Oscar left about an hour earlier than usual. He was elated that Drake had told him that as of the next day he would be earning a higher wage.

His sister Rachel was so pleased. She had also sold some milk and had gone to town with the money. Mr. Harwood at the bank had given her another month to come up with the money to save her farm.

Truth was, Harwood felt damned sorry for her; she was a hardworking woman and as honest as the day was long. He would not have taken a chance on Rachel Bray except that he knew her dilemma was not of her own making.

Monday morning, after Mike Bennett had gone to the mill, Misty fell into her usual routine. At ten that morning she had an unexpected caller. Geneva Walters was at her door and Misty invited her in.

"Misty—I have your dress made, honey, but I must confess I have another reason for coming," she said as she sunk down in a chair. "You suppose your pa would mind if young Jeff came over to our place for the rest of this week to help with Ed? He turned his ankle out in the barn yesterday evening. The hired hands can handle all the rest, but I could use some help with Ed around the house. He's a big man."

"Oh, I'm sorry to hear that. Well, I know Jeff will be happy to help you out."

Jeff couldn't have been happier as he climbed up in Geneva's buggy. She'd left Ed at the house alone, so she was in a hurry. Unlike Georgia Gordon, the Walters didn't have a cook and a housekeeper.

Martha told Misty that she'd bring Jeff back home on Sunday. She felt sure that in five days Ed would be back to normal.

Misty found her father very understanding when she told him that she'd allowed Jeff to go over the the Walters' until Sunday. Jeff's absence proved to be no problem as far as

Mike could see. Misty provided him with some mighty fine meals all week.

When Friday afternoon rolled around, Mike was not sure what kind of response he was going to get when he went over to Georgia's. He had stopped to pick up a tin of chocolates on his way home.

After supper, Misty realized that her father was going to pay his weekend call on Georgia Gordon.

By Saturday, Misty had to admit she missed Jeff. But he had piled her kindling bin so high that she hadn't had to go out after supper to replenish it.

After she washed her and Lavinia's hair, Misty gave herself a reprieve. She went down to the riverbank to sit in the afternoon sun and let her hair dry.

She had been padding around the house all morning in her bare feet. She wanted to save her good sandals that Drake Dalton had given her. It could be a long time before she'd get another nice pair.

It was a warm, late-August day so she'd chosen one of her sheer batiste tunics with a drawstring neckline and a gathered calico skirt this morning. She figured she should enjoy these sunny days—soon the weather would turn cold. It was a lovely afternoon, with a gentle breeze wafting through the branches of the weeping willow. It was the first moment she'd had to herself for over a week to think about Drake Dalton. Who was he and where did he come from? He had a very distinct accent that was not from this part of the country. Her two very brief encounters with him hadn't told her much.

She wondered when or if they would ever meet again. Even if they didn't, Misty knew she had seen the man she'd dreamed of. He was surely the Prince Charming in all the fairy tales that her mother had read to her when she was a child.

He *was* that tall, handsome hero, and when she'd been

close to him he stirred a sensation in her she'd never known before.

Drake Dalton had done more than daydream about the lovely Misty. He'd ridden into town that Saturday in hopes of seeing her again, but he hadn't spotted her. For once, he'd had nothing to buy.

Before he mounted Duke to ride for home, he stopped to make one purchase—a bottle of toilet water. It was a gardenia fragrance which reminded him of the lovely bushes his mother grew back in England. They couldn't stand England's winters but they bloomed profusely in the summer.

He guided Duke to the outskirts of town and down the dirt road to his place. But, when he should have kept galloping straight ahead, he veered to take the river road and cross the old wooden bridge to the spot where he hoped he might find Misty.

To his delight, he spied her sitting under the willow like a lovely little wood nymph with all that golden hair hanging down her back. As it had dried, soft waves came naturally.

She heard a rider approaching and she was delighted to see that it was Drake Dalton. He gave her a warm smile and dismounted. "How have you been, Misty? I looked all over town for you, then decided to see if I'd find you here."

She smiled up at him. "Guess I'm all right, Drake. It's good to see you again."

"Well, now, that makes my day."

She didn't exactly feel at ease being with Drake, knowing her father was home. She didn't worry about Lavinia running down to the riverbank—she'd sleep for another hour. Jeff wasn't home so she didn't have to worry about him coming upon them.

"I don't go into town every Saturday like most of the other girls. That Saturday you saw me was the first time I'd been there in weeks," she said, trying her best not to show her nervousness.

"Well now, maybe I can change that. What if I came

over here next Saturday afternoon so you and I could go into town? Would you like that?"

"Oh, Drake—I don't know about that," she said, hesitating.

He raised a skeptical brow and asked, "And why not, Misty? Don't you like me?"

"Oh, Drake, I like you very much," she exclaimed quickly. "But my pa would likely not allow me to go with you. He's very strict."

"How old are you, Misty?"

"Seventeen."

"You've never had a beau call on you?"

"No," she confessed.

"I find that hard to believe, Misty. You're so beautiful. The young gents around here must be a bunch of blockheads."

She found herself laughing as she explained that she had no time to meet any people her own age because she was always too busy tending to her brother and sister while her father worked. She explained that her mother had died and she had had to take over the house.

"He has free time off, doesn't he? Can't you have a break from the heavy burden you carry all week?"

"You don't know my pa, Drake. That's not his thinking."

Drake felt sorry for this beautiful girl. He was also forming an instant dislike for that father of hers.

He pulled the bottle of toilet water from his pocket. "Well, maybe this might brighten your Saturday. I know how young ladies like sweet-smelling toilet waters. I should. I have three sisters back in England."

As she fumbled to get the top off, she urged him to tell her about them. He gave her a brief little description, adding, "And I happened to be the older brother."

She could not resist dabbing the sweet fragrance on her wrist as she'd remembered seeing her mother do. Oh, it smelled so divine! She'd have to lie to her Pa again about this gift from Drake, she realized.

"So, your sisters and parents live in England. My, you're a long way from home, aren't you?"

"A very long way, but that's the way I wanted it, Misty." He reached over to take her hand as he told her that his mother had also died. "I had no desire to stay at Dalton Manor after that."

She liked the feel of his strong hand holding hers and found herself feeling comfortable confessing how she'd felt after her mother died.

"I felt so lost and lonely. My mother and I were so close. I, too, wanted to leave and run away but two things stopped me. I had no one to turn to, and there was my sister and brother."

He felt deep compassion for her and understood what desperation she must have felt at her young age, since he was almost nine years older. There was a serious air about Misty that made her different from most silly girls her age. Now he knew why, with the responsibility she'd taken on.

He embraced her, holding her close to him. "Oh, Misty—Misty. We must think of some way to see one another. There must be a way."

Misty had never been embraced by a man—not even her father, although she'd seen him hug Lavinia. But she liked the feel of Drake's strong arms around her.

"I—I don't see how, Drake," she said, turning slightly in his arms with her green eyes looking up at his face. His lips were close to her as he vowed, "I'll think of a way. I've got to see you, Misty!"

Looking into that lovely face, he wanted nothing more than to lay her back on the ground in the bower of the weeping willow and give vent to all the passion churning within him, but that was not how he wanted it to be when he made love to Misty the first time. He wanted more than that.

His eyes looked deep into hers. "Let me kiss you just once, love. I promise that's all I'll ask. I just want to kiss those sweet lips once before I leave."

Her long lashes fluttered and she stammered, "I've never been kissed by a man, Drake."

He sought to be as honest with her as she was being with him. "I know, Misty, and that's why this kiss is so special. I want to be the man who gives you that first kiss and I intend to be the first man who makes love to you."

He said no more as he bent his head to meet with her honeyed lips. She might never have been kissed by a man but she seemed to know naturally how to respond.

After a long, lingering kiss, Drake reluctantly released her. It took all his will power to keep his promise that one kiss was all he'd ask. A liquid fire surged through his firm-muscled body. He said, "I'm going to take my leave, love, and not because I want to but I'll keep my promise. Should I linger any longer I might not prove to be the gentleman I want to be with you."

His hands slipped away from hers as he rose from the ground. "I'm going to see you again, Misty, one way or the other. Nothing will stop that, not even your pa," he swore to her.

She sat still in a dazed state as she watched him mount the huge black horse and ride away. After he had left her, she remained under the willow to think about the warmth of Drake's hands and the feel of his arms encircling her shoulders. The most exciting sensation was when his lips met hers. She'd had no idea that a man's kiss could be so sweet.

Everything changed for Misty after that Saturday afternoon!

Chapter 9

Riding Duke homeward, Drake wore an amused smile. He had to say that it was the first time he'd ever restrained himself from using seduction to have his way with a beautiful young lady. He couldn't even explain it to himself.

He'd learned a lot about Misty Bennett this afternoon. Some things she'd told him made him angry as hell at that father of hers.

The next week it didn't take too much investigation for him to find out a lot about Mike Bennett, which made him feel even more compassion for Misty. He also learned that Bennett was courting the widow Gordon, the flossie who'd come over to his place flaunting her silly self at him.

He found out that in a small community like Crowley, everyone knew everyone else's business, which wasn't exactly to his liking. There was a part of him that wished to remain aloof and private. He figured he was never going to fit into this tight-knit community, so he'd forever remain a mysterious stranger in their midst.

Oscar Wells continued to amaze him. They'd had a lot

of time to talk and Oscar had told him more about himself and his sister. He even told Drake about the crisis Rachel faced. When Drake heard that the bank was going to foreclose on her hundred acres, he generously offered to pay it off.

The amount was astronomical to people like Oscar and Rachel, but Drake found it a small amount to save a hundred acres that Rachel had owned for years.

The day Drake paid off Rachel's loan, she told Oscar, "I must meet this angel of mercy. I—I'm a believer in miracles again, Oscar. I have to admit, my faith had been wavering lately."

She was so grateful that Drake never again had to buy pies and fresh-baked loaves of bread.

Misty had returned to the house Saturday afternoon and slipped the bottle of gardenia toilet water in the drawer of her chest before going into the kitchen to prepare dinner for her pa and Lavinia.

Young Jeff returned home on Sunday feeling very cocky. Ed Walters had insisted that he accept a wage for helping Geneva.

Mike had put in a full day of filling the shed with loads of wood, so another weekend had gone by in a fairly pleasant way.

When Mike returned to work on Monday the first thing he heard from his buddies was that old Georgia had been sashaying around town the last two Saturday afternoons. One of the fellows had chuckled, "That Georgia isn't going to sit around. She's always been a lively one." Mike would probably have gotten into a fight with him had Jeb not restrained him until his temper cooled.

Misty saw a different man when Mike came home on Monday. Tuesday and Wednesday afternoons didn't change his foul mood; Misty had no inkling about what had so suddenly upset him.

She tried to cook good dinners for him and made a point of cautioning Lavinia and Jeff not to rile him in the evenings. But he was constantly barking at all of them.

By the time Friday came around, Misty's nerves were frayed. She felt sure her pa was going to explode with rage. She was glad to see him leave the house to go over to Georgia's that evening.

It was a quiet, peaceful evening, which Misty and Jeff were ready for after such a hard week. Misty had no idea of the hour when her pa returned as she was already in bed. However, the next morning he informed her that he'd be having dinner with Georgia that night.

Obviously, the widow had won out and convinced him that she didn't intend to spend a third Saturday night alone.

Ed Walters had come over early on Saturday morning and asked Misty if he could take Jeff fishing.

"Martha's ailing today so we're not going into town until Monday. I thought it would be a good day to go fishing while she rested. Think maybe I could just bring him home in the morning, Misty? Me and Jeff have good times together."

"That would be just fine, Mr. Walters. Jeff enjoys being with you."

So she began her usual Saturday morning. She put the house in order and washed her and Lavinia's hair. When her father arrived home, he seemed not to notice Jeff's absence so Misty made no mention of it to him.

Mike seemed to have nothing on his mind but getting himself all duded up to go over to Georgia's.

Misty was in no hurry to prepare supper—it was only her and Lavinia, so it would be something simple.

Long before the sun had set, Mike had boarded his flat-bedded wagon to head for Georgia's. To fry up some eggs and ham would take only a little time, so she decided to try on the pretty frock Geneva had given her when she'd brought Jeff home last Sunday.

Things had been so hectic all week that she hadn't taken the time to do it. She knew that the rest of the evening was hers to do as she wished. What was so amazing to her was how Geneva Walters could fit her so perfectly. She loved the new gown so much, she kept it on; Misty realized that there had been a reason for her to keep the new dress on when there was a rap on her door.

Hearing a sudden knock, she went to the front door and saw Drake standing there. With a devious grin he said, "I told you I'd find a way to see you again. I know your father isn't home and not likely to return for the rest of the night."

"Drake—you *are* a cunning devil, aren't you?"

"I am, love, and I don't apologize for it." He strode through the front door. "Now, what do we have left here—a little sister and brother?"

He was so forceful that she had to admire his manner, but she quickly informed him that her brother was with the Walters. "It's just me and Lavinia, Drake."

"Gather up Lavinia. I'm taking you both over to my place for dinner. I want you to see it before the sun goes down."

"Oh, Drake—it sounds wonderful and I'd like nothing better but Lavinia would tell on me. Then I'd be in big trouble with Pa," she protested gently.

"You leave little Lavinia to me. Remember, I've got three younger sisters and there's nothing like a bribe to quiet little sisters' mouths."

"Drake Dalton, you're impossible!" She laughed, for it was obvious he wasn't going to take no for an answer.

"We'll make it work, Misty. Come with me," he urged.

She found it impossible to refuse him.

A few minutes later, the three of them were in the wagon headed for Drake's place. When they got there, Lucky was waiting to greet them and he took to Lavinia at once. She was intrigued with him—they'd never had a dog at their house.

"Well, it seems Lucky has found himself a new friend," Drake remarked.

"Lavinia has, too." Misty smiled, seeing how excited her little sister was.

As they went up the steps to the front door, Lavinia didn't follow them. She sat down on the step and Lucky huddled beside her. When Misty called to her, Lavinia pleaded, "Let me sit here with Lucky, Misty—please!"

"If you'll stay right there on the step—promise?"

"I promise."

Drake led Misty into the house to show her around. It wasn't a large house. In fact, it wasn't much bigger than hers, but the furnishings were much nicer.

"You've obviously done wonders in a short period of time," she remarked as they strolled into the kitchen. On the cupboard counter, three pies were lined up with two fresh loaves of bread. She looked up at him. "And you also cook and bake?"

"No, I can't take credit for that. My hired man's sister sent them this morning," he grinned. He wouldn't have been able to invite them over to eat tonight had it not been for the big basket of food Oscar had brought. There was also a platter of fried chicken and a big pot of beans.

"Come on, let me show you around the grounds before dark. We'll eat dinner later," he said, taking her arm. Lavinia and Lucky accompanied them on their stroll. Drake pointed in the distance to the structure beginning to be built. "That will be my foreman's house. Got to have someone to help me around here. A planter I'm not and I hear this is cotton country."

"It is. This is good delta country—just about anything will grow in this rich soil," she informed him.

"You've lived here all your life, haven't you, Misty?" His hand had taken hers some time during the stroll.

"Yes. I was born in the house where we live."

They turned to go back—it was twilight time. Lavinia picked up a two-foot broken branch to toss it, telling Lucky to fetch it and bring it back to her. Dutifully, he obeyed.

Drake and Misty laughed at their little game all the rest of the way to the house. Drake told Misty, "You see, it was good that you came with me tonight. She's enjoying herself."

She's certainly doing that, Misty admitted to herself.

When they got back to the house, Misty insisted on setting the table while Drake stoked the fire to heat the bean pot.

Lavinia and Lucky sat in the front room on the floor.

When Misty asked her to wash her hands, she leaped up and rushed into the kitchen, declaring in childlike honesty, "I'm starved!"

Drake thought she was cute as she could be as he watched her eat the fried chicken with relish. "She's a little doll, Misty."

Lavinia had no idea he was preparing the bribe he would use to save Misty from getting in trouble. He told her, "I think I ought to just keep you here with me so you and Lucky could play all the time."

"You really mean that, Mr. Dalton?" she excitedly asked and even stopped eating.

"I always mean what I say, Lavinia. But Misty would never allow that. However, I'll make a deal with you: you and Misty can come over here anytime so you can play with Lucky. How would you like that?"

"Oh, I love Lucky and I'd like that more than anything, Mr. Dalton."

"There's just one thing, Lavinia. This must be a secret between the three of us. If you tell anyone about coming here this evening then you might never get to come over to see me and Lucky again," he said with a real serious look on his face.

"Oh, I wouldn't like that at all. I won't tell anyone, not Pa, Jeff, or no one. I promise, Mr. Dalton," she vowed.

Misty sat there with an amused smile. How cleverly he'd worked his little scheme. Later, when they were together in the kitchen, she looked up at him with a teasing glint in her green eyes. "Your poor sisters didn't stand a chance against you, did they, Drake?"

"Oh, I wouldn't say that. They taxed me to the limit at times." He grinned deviously.

When the kitchen lamps were dimmed and they went into the front room, they found one tired dog and little girl sprawled out on the floor, sound asleep.

Drake picked Lavinia up and carried her to the spare bedroom, but he left the lamp burning dimly. He remembered how his sister, Suzanne, was always frightened when she woke up in a dark bedroom.

When he returned to the front room to join Misty, he told her, "I don't think she even knew when I took her off the floor. I left the lamp on dim so she wouldn't be frightened."

Misty realized what a sensitive, understanding man he was. As he sat down beside her, she told him she should be going home. It had been a very big evening for Lavinia.

"She's in bed and sleeping soundly. The night is still young. While we have this time together, I want to know more about you, Misty. I'm not ready to say good night. I haven't had such a wonderful evening in so very long." His hand took hers and he brought it to his lips. "Tell me about Misty Bennett."

She smiled up at him. "Only if you'll tell me about Drake Dalton."

"Ladies first."

For the next half hour she told him about herself and how things had changed so drastically after her mother's death. She told him about Ed and Geneva Walters and how she didn't know what she would have done the last year or two without them.

"Since Georgia Gordon came into his life, Pa's taken leave of his senses, I think. I pray he doesn't marry her. I have to say he has given up the last two weekends to finally get wood cut for the winter, which he'd usually have had done by now. Oh, but that didn't keep him from running over there on Friday nights," she added sadly.

It was apparent that Misty detested this Georgia Gordon and he could understand why after his one encounter with her.

"There you have it, Drake. That's the life of Misty Bennett."

With his eyes warm and adoring, he told her, "And I think I know you a little better. Now, I shall tell you the story of Drake Dalton." As he told her about his life, he realized there was a parallel in their lives. His life had changed so after his own mother's death. He told her how his dying mother had urged him to go to France and seek out her brother.

"So I went to Uncle Bayard and remained there quite a while. He was the one who helped me with all the paperwork on this land. I knew then why Mother had insisted that I go to Bayard. She wanted me to have the inheritance and not my father.

"My parents' marriage was not a happy one, Misty. My mother never adjusted to life in England and yearned to go back to France. It was an arranged marriage, and not for love," he told her with a solemn expression.

"So now you know the story of Drake Dalton and what brought me to this country. I've no desire ever to go back to England, but one day I'll return to France to see my Uncle Bayard."

"Thank you for telling me your story—now I also know more about you," she said.

"It's easy to talk with you, Misty. You're different from most girls your age. But now I know why. You've known hurt and pain in your life."

"I'll admit to that, Drake. It's strange that we should have met, isn't it?"

"But I'm glad we did, Misty, and I honestly think it might just have been meant to be."

Misty searched his face and asked him, "Do you really think that, Drake?"

He never answered her, for he gave way to the sudden impulse to kiss her. This time one kiss was not enough. In the quiet seclusion of his front room, with Lavinia sleeping soundly nearby, Misty was not nervous. After he had kissed her the second time, Misty knew she wanted more and more.

His hands gently caressed the soft fabric of her bodice. He was a man fired with desire. Misty had never known such a wild, wonderful sensation before, but she pressed closer to him. The feel of her soft body against him was enough to tell him he was getting beyond the point of being a gallant gentleman. One kiss was not enough.

"Damn, Misty—I want to make love to you. I have since the first time I saw you," he murmured in her ear.

His heated lips caressed her cheek. His firm, muscled body pressed against her as her arms encircled his neck. Breathlessly she gasped, "Just kiss me again, Drake. I love your kisses."

"Oh, love, I'd kiss you all night long if you wanted me to, but this is going to go beyond kissing and I don't want to do anything you don't want me to do. I'm going to make love to you as a man makes love to a woman."

"Then make love to me, Drake," she said, moaning softly.

Misty found herself gathered up in Drake's strong arms and carried to his bedroom. Swiftly she took off her new frock and undergarments, then Drake left her only long enough to rid himself of his own clothes. Drake had a lot of practice taking his clothing off and ridding ladies of their fancy gowns. Misty's simple little frock proved to be no problem at all.

Just as swiftly she felt his bare body burning against her

and she blazed with a fire traveling the full length of her. As his sensuous lips had caressed hers they were now caressing her breasts and Misty surged against him. Drake had taken other virgins before but this was different. As he began to burrow between her thighs, he whispered in her ear, "Love, have to do something I don't like. I must give you a swift moment of pain—you just keep holding me tight. I promise I'll give you nothing but pleasure when I make love to you after that."

Misty was in such a state of wild passion that she hardly realized when she crossed over from being a virgin to being a woman.

Drake's deep kisses and masterful lovemaking had made it happen that way. His deep voice murmured in her ear, "Now you're my woman, Misty! You will be mine forever."

Breathlessly, she fell into a deep calm after Drake had swept her into a world she never knew existed. He could have stayed in bed with her the rest of the night but there was a little sister in his other bedroom. So he told Misty, "Let me get my clothes on first, then I'll light the lamp for you to get dressed."

Many a time, he'd hastily dressed in a dark room but he knew it was a more complex procedure for a lady.

He walked over to where she still lay, her hair fanned out on the pillow. He cupped her lovely face with his hands and his eyes gazed down at her tenderly. "I adore you, Misty. I've never felt this way about a woman."

Her arms reached up to encircle his neck. "I adore you, Drake Dalton."

"Now, you get dressed and I'm going to the front room so I can waylay little missy before you come and join me." He got up from the side of the bed to leave and closed the door.

Misty got out of bed and gathered up her undergarments. As she was dressing, she had to admit she looked no different now that she was no longer a virgin. When she was dressed

SWEET SEDUCTION

she used Drake's hairbrush to put some order to her tousled hair.

She was ready to join Drake in the front room. He sat puffing on one of his cheroots. "Old Lucky is tired. He's still asleep," he said.

"Drake, I should be getting home. Just in case Pa gets back early. He and Georgia could always have a fuss."

"I understand, love. Let me get Lavinia. I'll lay a blanket in the wagon and we'll let her sleep on the way home."

The clock was chiming ten when Drake carried a sleepy Lavinia out to the wagon. Lucky woke up and went out to the wagon to jump in the back. Drake hoisted Misty up in the seat and leaped up beside her.

As the clock in Misty's kitchen struck eleven, Lavinia was snuggled in her bed and Misty was dimming all the lamps.

Drake and Lucky were headed for home.

Chapter 10

Misty had no idea when her father returned home—once she fell asleep, she slept soundly. However, when she'd first gone to bed, she lay there thinking how it had been in Drake's strong arms, feeling his kisses and caresses. She knew that nothing would ever be the same for her again.

There was no doubt about it; she could no longer claim a girlish innocence—Drake Dalton had brought her into a new world.

Misty was in love for the first time in her life. She was so hungry for affection since her mother had died.

When Mike got up and had breakfast, he hitched up the team to head for the woods. With what he could cut today and next Sunday, he ought to have that shed piled high for the winter.

The pace he'd been going was enough to kill any man, he told himself. Working all day at the mills, keeping Georgia satisfied, and cutting all this wood was making him bone-weary. He went to bed tired and woke up feeling tired.

It would sure be a help when Jeff got to be Misty's age.

He was going to be a husky young man. Misty was small and dainty-looking like her mother, but Jeff was built like him.

Before he left he told Misty, "Tell Jeff to be ready to help me unload wood once he gets back from the Walters'."

"I'll tell him, Pa."

Misty was glad Lavinia slept until after her pa left for the woods. It gave her a chance to remind her not to forget about their secret. "You'll never get to go back over to see Lucky if you let anything slip out, Lavinia."

"I won't forget, Misty. I won't say anything to Jeff, either. But we sure had fun, didn't we?"

"Yes, we certainly did!"

"I really like that Mr. Dalton, don't you?"

"Yes, I do." Misty smiled as she prepared Lavinia's breakfast. For her, it was much more than just liking him.

When Ed Walters brought Jeff back home it seemed that they'd done some good fishing. Jeff had caught six nice bass, so Misty knew what they'd be having for dinner.

Ed told her before he left that Geneva was coming over to see her next week.

"I'll be happy to see her, Mr. Walters," she called out as he put his wagon in motion.

She told Jeff to get into his old clothes—his pa wanted him to help unload the wood.

Misty got busy cleaning the fish. It was a chore she detested but it would sure be good eating when she had them fried.

Seldom had she felt any sympathy for her father but he looked like a weary man by the time he washed up and sat down at the table that night. She had fixed a good meal for them, and she didn't ration out the fish. It was a full, high pile on a big platter. There was also a full dish of fried potatoes, cornbread, and a big plate of sliced onions and tomatoes. Everyone left the table stuffed!

Come Monday morning, everyone in Crowley resumed

their usual routine. Mike was up bright and early. Oscar Wells rode his mule back over to the Dalton place. By now, he and Lucky had become friends so he was out there to welcome Oscar when he came riding up. Drake was getting ready to ride into Crowley and Lepanto to see if he could line up some men to help Oscar do the framework on the house.

By the time he returned, he had hired two fellows who were eager to have some work. They promised to be at his place at seven in the morning. Drake would see if they were men of their word, which meant a lot to him. That was why he liked Oscar so much.

Tom Tulley and Johnny Bigelow arrived on time within a short time of one another. Tom arrived in his wagon—he was older than Bigelow, who rode his roan mare.

At the end of the day, Oscar told Drake, "Think they'll work out fine, Mr. Dalton, if they just keep up the pace they put in today."

Drake was amazed at how quickly the framework was taking shape. Four extra hands made a tremendous difference. He gave Oscar a pat on the shoulder and told him he was doing a fine job. "And tell your sister her food was delicious."

He gave Oscar the pot and platter he'd washed up so he could take it back to Rachel.

Oscar laughed. "She'll have it filled for you again, knowing Rachel. She is a good cook. She's even fattening up this lean body of mine."

Geneva came over to see Misty as Ed had said she would. She brought a huge stack of her fruit turnovers and visited for about an hour. But before she left she asked Misty if the three of them were ready for another trip to town on Saturday afternoon. "My Ed has really taken a shine to Jeff. They have so much fun together."

"We'd love to go with you, Mrs. Walters."

"Well, it's settled then. We'll be by at the same time as before."

Wednesday morning Misty went about her chores in a happy frame of mind, anticipating the trip into Crowley on Saturday. She was thinking she had her new sandals and the sweet-smelling toilet water. Now she even had three pretty frocks to choose from!

But her nice day changed quite suddenly. Just before midday, there was a knock on her door. She saw a buxom woman standing there. Misty's first thought was that she wore her hair in a style too youthful for a woman her age. Her gown had to be expensive, Misty realized, but the neckline should have been higher.

"You have to be Misty. Am I right?" said the woman. "I'm Georgia Gordon."

"I'm Misty," she replied, taking an instant dislike to her. She didn't like her prissy way and her boldness as she walked into the front room without waiting to be invited.

"Well, I took it on myself to come over here to meet the three of you since your father and I have been seeing each other for so long now."

She took a seat in one of the overstuffed chairs. Jeff and Lavinia sat on the floor, while Misty went over to another chair. Out of the corner of her eye, she could see Lavinia and Jeff looking at her.

Forcing herself to be gracious, Misty said, "That's very nice of you, Mrs. Gordon."

"Oh, please, Misty—call me Georgia. After all, Mike tells me you're seventeen. Now, it's different for Jeff and Lavinia— They should call me Mrs. Gordon," she remarked.

It didn't set well with Misty that Georgia should come into their house and be so bossy. A devious streak came out in her as she forced a sweet smile, declaring, "Oh, no, Mrs.

Gordon—my mother taught me better manners than that. I was always to address my elders as Mrs. or Miss."

That was enough to rattle Georgia—she quickly realized that Misty was sharp as a tack. she obviously didn't approve of her at all.

"Well, whatever you wish, dear," Georgia said, trying to gather her composure. She directed her attention to Jeff, as she was usually more successful with men than women. She remarked that he certainly looked like his father.

He sat there stringing his slingshot and finally looked up at her. "But he always tells me I was my mother's boy. Guess he's right about that."

Once again, Georgia found herself tongue-tied. Mike's children were hardly making her feel welcome. His son's eyes registered his disapproval.

So she decided to approach little Lavinia to sweet talk her and tell her how pretty she was.

"Come over here and let me see that pretty hair of yours," Georgia urged.

Reluctantly, Lavinia got up to let Georgia survey her hair. But the little girl was not impressed by the gushing remarks about how pretty she was. There was a fakery about the visitor that Lavinia sensed, young as she was. Now when Drake Dalton had told her that, she was very pleased. She found him to be genuine.

Lavinia didn't linger near Georgia for long.

Misty didn't want to appear to be an ungracious hostess, so she offered Georgia a cup of coffee but it was politely refused. Georgia didn't want to stay long enough to have coffee. Mike's children were an impossible lot!

"No, Misty, I can't stay much longer," she said, purposely letting her lace-edged handkerchief slip from her hand.

Jeff sat on the floor, absorbed in making the final knot on his slingshot.

Georgia trilled at him, "Jeff, dear, would you fetch my handkerchief for me?"

He was already getting up to go outside and test the slingshot. "It's just right there at your feet, Mrs. Gordon." He then announced that he was going to the backyard, and Misty gave him an approving nod. She was utterly disgusted with Georgia Gordon, who was just trying to test Jeff.

"Well, I must be going." She rose from the chair after leaning over to pick up her own handkerchief.

Misty gladly escorted her to the door. Georgia couldn't resist making one snide remark before her departure. "Young Jeff isn't too obliging, is he?"

Misty retorted, "Oh, Jeff is a most obliging person if he needs to be."

Georgia murmured a hasty goodbye and left in a huff. Misty closed the door and went around the house fussing and fuming. Lavinia sensed that her older sister was angry. "You don't like her, do you?"

"I can't stand her!"

Jeff saw her leave and went in the back door. He flopped down in one of the kitchen chairs. "If Pa marries her, Misty, I swear I'll run away from home. Expect I'll be in a heap of trouble when she tells him I wouldn't pick up her handkerchief."

"Not if I can help it, you won't," Misty said. But he was right, for she had no doubt that Georgia would delight in telling her pa that Jeff was rude. But Misty was going to tell him the truth. Whether he chose to believe her was another matter.

Misty was surprised at her pa's reaction that night when she announced that Georgia Gordon had come to see them.

"What'd she want?" he asked as he finished drying his sweaty face. His bushy black brow was arched as he speculated about why she had done it without saying something to him.

"Said she wanted to meet your children," Misty said as she continued to stir her huge pot of stew.

"I see," he mumbled as he went toward his bedroom to get out of his dirty pants and shirt. He didn't like it that Georgia had taken it on her own to meet his kids. He didn't accept for one minute that she had any real interest in them. No, she had another reason for her trip.

Thursday morning Ed Walters came over to the Bennetts to speak with Misty. He always preferred to go through her than speak directly to Bennett.

"I'd like to hire Jeff for Friday and Saturday to do some odds and ends around my place. I'll pay him wages. Thought maybe that might help get him some winter clothes."

"Well, it sure would, Mr. Walters. I'll speak with Pa tonight."

That evening Misty spoke to her father and he was agreeable to Jeff's working for Walters.

She pointed out that Jeff could possibly make enough to buy himself a winter jacket, which he sorely needed.

"Jeff has grown so much the last year, Pa. His old jacket wouldn't meet across his chest and the sleeves are so short."

So the next morning at nine, Ed left with Jeff, who couldn't have been happier about spending two days over at the Walters'. There was such a camaraderie between them that Jeff told Ed about Georgia's visit and he also told him the same thing he'd told Misty. "Swear to you, Mr. Walters, I'd run away before I'd live in the house with that silly woman."

"No, Jeff—don't do that. You could get into more trouble than you could handle. Just come over here to me and Geneva. We'd help you."

Saturday, Mike Bennett put in his full day at the mills and stopped to buy their groceries but he made no effort to pick up a little trinket for Georgia. He was feeling a little out of sorts with her. Damned if she was getting something weekly from him!

Lavinia sat out in the swing and waved to him as he pulled up the drive. She was thinking about what she and Misty had done last Saturday—she was anxious to see Lucky again. It had been a whole week.

Misty was feeling a little crestfallen. This would certainly not be as exciting as last Saturday. Knowing that her pa would be going over to Georgia's, she was already warming up the stew from last night for her and Lavinia. She'd baked a cake so she figured that she and Lavinia could have a piece tonight and there would still be plenty left for tomorrow.

Misty put all the groceries away as Mike stood at the basin table to wash his face and shave.

When everything was put away, she decided to tell Mike about the scene involving Georgia's handkerchief.

"Pa, I want to tell you something before you go over to see Georgia. If she tells you Jeff was rude, then she's a liar."

He whirled around and asked, "What did Jeff do to rile her?"

"That's just it, Pa—nothing. He sat on the floor the entire time she was here, working on his slingshot, speaking when he was spoken to. But just as she was preparing to go, she dropped her handkerchief at her feet. I think she did it on purpose. She asked Jeff to fetch it for her. I thought it very silly when all she had to do was lean over to pick it up. Well, Jeff was getting up to go in the backyard, so he just told her it was right by her feet."

Mike could hardly suppress a smile, knowing Georgia as he did. Truth was, he rather admired Jeff. He shrugged any concerns of Misty's aside.

There was a bold determination in her bright green eyes as she told her pa, "I'll not be Georgia Gordon's slave nor will Jeff. You might let her know that, Pa." With that, she sashayed out of the kitchen to fetch Lavinia for supper. Mike watched her march out of the kitchen, then left to go to his bedroom.

Damn that Georgia—why couldn't she just mind her own business! He could just see her staging such an act. What a demanding bitch!

He had to admit that the last few weeks he had been questioning whether a marriage to her, which would provide him with a more leisurely life, would be worth it.

He had to admit that for a woman her age she had a very hearty sexual appetite. At first, he'd been intrigued, but lately all her demands were wearing thin.

Somehow, he knew that this evening was not going to go well for him and Georgia!

Part II

Golden Autumn

Chapter 11

Lavinia was eager to see Lucky, Misty was yearning to see Drake, and Drake's arms were aching to hold Misty again. But he'd put in a very busy week and Oscar had insisted that he and the two hired men work on Saturday to finish up the framing. By late in the afternoon the four-room house was definitely taking shape.

Oscar reported that the two fellows were fine workers. "Mr. Dalton, give us two more weeks and we're going to have the roof on and the siding done."

Drake paid all three of them a most generous wage because he wanted to keep the men working for him. His generosity had been a godsend to Oscar and his sister.

By the time the three men left and Drake and Lucky were walking back to the house, he realized that the days were getting much shorter.

Yesterday, he had received his first two letters from England and France. One was from Bayard and the other from Ellen, telling him about Suzanne's marriage. It had taken the letter from Ellen so long to reach him that he was probably an uncle by now, he thought ruefully. What really irked him was her news about his father squiring a wealthy widow who lived rear Dalton Manor.

Drake didn't care if he ever saw his father again, especially after he'd finished reading his mother's sad journals. He was glad he'd taken the emerald and diamond ring and bracelet. One day, his bride would wear them and he knew that his mother would have wanted it that way.

He just wished that her body wasn't buried at Dalton Manor. One day he would return to England to visit her graveside, but he never wished to return to Dalton Manor.

He and Lucky had a simple dinner and went out to the front porch to sit by the light of the full moon.

He was in a restless mood. When he finished his cheroot, he told Lucky, "I'm going to leave you for a while, fellow. Taking myself a ride."

He went to the barn and saddled Duke. Lucky seemed to realize he wasn't going along. Drake rode toward Misty's house, then tethered Duke by the willow tree. Through the darkness, he slipped up to the barn to see if Bennett's wagon was gone. Seeing that it was, he knew he was free to knock on the front door.

Misty had just put Lavinia to bed when Drake arrived at the riverbank. She had gone out on the front porch to sit in the glow of the bright moon.

When she saw his tall figure coming up the path, she felt a moment of panic until she recognized him. "Dear God, Drake—you scared me to death!"

"Sorry, love, but I just had to see you tonight. I was hoping I wouldn't find your father's wagon in the barn."

The full moon seemed to glow right on them. The weather was still mild but there were signs of coming autumn.

He took her hand. "I can't stand this slipping around when I want to see you, Misty. It's not my way."

"I know, Drake. It's not mine either. I don't like having to lie. I've been doing quite a bit of that lately. But to tell

Pa the truth—that it was you who gave me the new sandals—would have brought on a furious storm. So I told him it was Mrs. Walters."

She smiled, telling him that Lavinia had been a very good little girl and kept her mouth shut about last Saturday. "But she's dying to see Lucky again. She sure loves that dog."

"Wish I felt free to come over and pick you both up when I wanted to, but I can't," he muttered.

His arms went around her. He was kissing her heatedly when Misty's hands suddenly pushed against his chest. "Oh, God, Drake—it's Pa coming home earlier than he usually does from Georgia's! He can't find you here."

Drake's wagon was some three hundred feet away but he remembered that the Bennett house was the only one on this lane along the riverbank. Drake rose from the step and quieted Misty's fears. "I'll just go around the north side of the house. He'll be going south. Keep sitting here and greet him—that will give me the cue as to when the two of you go into the house."

"All right, Drake," she mumbled. She was shaken by her father's early return. He and Georgia must have had a fuss.

She watched Drake disappear into the darkness as her pa's wagon pulled into the drive. He headed straight for the barn. Drake didn't linger at the corner of the house because he had a team of horses to unharness.

Misty saw him move away from the house. He whispered a hasty good night and dashed through the gate and into the darkness.

He was already riding home before Mike approached Misty. He barely gave her a greeting as he marched on into the house. Misty decided to stay on the porch awhile longer.

She prayed that the three of them would not pay the price of the fuss they must have had. When she did go into the house, she said good night and went directly to her room. She was sure it was a night she'd best not be around him.

Misty had made a wise decision—Bennett was in a very foul mood. Georgia had taxed him to the limit.

But Misty went to bed very apprehensive about how Sunday would go. How would he react to Jeff after what she'd told him earlier tonight?

Mike sat in his front room alone; the clock had not yet struck ten. When he'd arrived at Georgia's, she went through her usual little routine of serving the two of them a drink while her cook prepared dinner. He kept noticing the expectant look on Georgia's face and knew exactly what was going on in that head of hers. She thought he should have been pulling some little gift out of his pocket.

She was in a rather aloof mood by the time they went into her fancy dining room. She picked at the delicious meal the cook had fixed, but Mike ate heartily.

They were just finishing the apple pie when she couldn't resist asking, "Well, I suppose your children didn't mention that I came to your place this week or you would have said something."

"No, Georgia—I was waiting for you to tell me about your visit. Misty told me that night when I got in from the mills."

"Well, I didn't receive a very warm welcome, I can tell you that," she said indignantly.

Mike sighed. "Lord, Georgia—what did you expect? You should have discussed such plans with me first. You've never voiced any interest in meeting my kids."

"I got the idea and I went, Mike."

"I wish you hadn't. I've got good kids, but Misty and Jeff are at an age when memories of their mother are still very vivid in their minds. You ought to know that," he said as the two of them left the table to go into her parlor.

Georgia remained in her pouty mood as they sat down. "Well, your son was very rude to me, Mike."

Mike recalled what Misty had said, so he expected Georgia to say this. He asked her what Jeff had done.

"He wouldn't even pick up my handkerchief for me, as a young gentleman should do. He needs to be taught some manners."

Maybe he wasn't the most devoted father, but this made Mike bristle. "Didn't it fall right by your feet, Georgia? Could you not have reached down to pick it up yourself? You're not that helpless!"

Not in a mood to work her wiles tonight, Georgia leaped up, shouting, "You're just as rude as your son, Mike Bennett!"

Mike rose slowly and gave her a sly grin. "Well, this rude man better take his leave, my lady. I won't be your little lapdog nor would I expect my son to be."

He went to the front door and disappeared into the night, leaving Georgia gasping in disbelief. Nothing had gone as she'd expected.

Mike got into his wagon and headed for home. By the time he finally went to bed, he wondered if things might possibly have worked out for him and Georgia if he'd had no kids. A woman could boss him only so much. Beth had never tried to and he realized that this was probably why they'd stayed together as long as they had.

Truth be told, Beth was too good for him. He always knew that and it was probably the reason why he enjoyed lording over her at times. She was a gentle woman, always gracious and well-mannered. She'd been brought up in nicer family surroundings than he had.

When he woke up on Sunday morning, Misty found him very pleasant when he came into the kitchen. She was delighted to fix him breakfast. She was a little stunned to hear him say, "You're a good girl, Misty. Guess I haven't told you that often enough."

She found herself tongue-tied. "Want another cup of coffee, Pa?"

"One more before I head out for the woods. Today should

do it. If we have a bitter winter, that shed should hold enough to keep us warm. You got a winter coat, Misty?"

"No, Pa—I don't, but Mrs. Walters bought me a pretty wool shawl."

"Don't know why I never thought about it before but I stored all your ma's clothes after she died. I'll get them out and let you go through them. There's bound to be things you might use as big as you are now. Guess that's why I didn't think about it when she died—you were so much younger then."

Misty got very excited. "Oh, yes, Pa—I'd love to have anything that belonged to Mother."

"Well, I'll bring them to your room tonight. She'd want you to have them."

"Oh, Pa, thank you so much!" To Misty, he seemed like a completely different man. She didn't know what had brought it about but whatever it was, she was grateful.

"Got to confess it's only been recently that I'd taken notice of you being a grown-up young lady. Shows you how blind your pa's been."

"Mother was not much older than me when she married you. Yes, Pa—I'm all grown up."

He laughed—and it was so nice for Misty to hear his laughter. After he left, she went about her chores in the highest of spirits. When Jeff arrived home he, too, was happy, for Ed had taken him to town and paid him enough wages to buy a warm winter jacket.

As soon as Ed left, Misty told Jeff to get into his old clothes so he could help his pa unload the wood. She also told her brother about their father's early arrival. "Maybe he's washing his hands of Georgia Gordon, Jeff."

The Bennetts had a very good Sunday. Jeff was there waiting for his pa to come in. Mike was as pleasant with him as he had been with Misty. He told his son, "When I come in the next time, that's it, Jeff."

Almost two hours later, Mike pulled his wagon into the

backyard. When the two of them had the last few logs stacked, Jeff offered, "I'll take the team and wagon to the barn, Pa, if you'll let me."

"Do it, Jeff—I'm tired."

When Mike entered his kitchen, Misty could see he was one weary man. She felt compassion for him, just as Jeff had.

Mike washed his sweaty face and went to his room to change. Wearing clean clothes and sinking down in his comfortable chair by the hearth refreshed him. Mike was a man of tremendous strength. By the time Misty called him into the kitchen, he was more than ready to eat.

It was a very good supper—she felt he and Jeff deserved it. After dinner, it was a sweet sound to hear them in the front room talking and laughing. As she walked in to the front room to join them, it was a welcome sight to see her pa giving Jeff's head an affectionate tousling.

Oh, dear Lord—could she dare to hope there would be real changes? When she went to her room that night, her father had kept his word. There were four boxes of her mother's belongings in her room.

During the next week, Misty began to go through the boxes, sorting everything into various piles. Some gowns and dresses were too worn to keep. The shoes were too big for Misty, so she set them aside. Everything her mother had saved because it had a special meaning to her was put to one side.

Since she and her mother were about the same size, Misty found four wearable gowns. Two of them were very pretty—her mother was a very good seamstress. By the end of the week, Misty had gone through all of the boxes, adding a nice winter coat, a scarf, and gloves to her wardrobe. She had also found a small book in which her mother had written almost daily.

Apparently, her pa didn't know that her mother kept this little journal. Misty put it in her chest under her undergarments. She planned to read each and every page as time permitted.

When Saturday rolled around, Misty was most curious when Mike came in with the groceries to see if he'd start duding himself up to go over to the widow's house. But when he had unloaded the supplies, he began to make preparations which certainly didn't look like he was going to Georgia's.

He brought out his rifle and a tin filled with shells. He told Misty, "Me and Jeb are going hunting overnight. Haven't done that in a damned long time and I've missed it."

Misty knew that something very serious must have happened between him and Georgia last Saturday night—for he hadn't been hunting with Jeb for months.

"Good luck, Pa," she said. Privately, she was praying that Drake would come over tonight. Just she and Lavinia would be home. Jeff had left yesterday to go over to the Walters' because Ed wanted to pay him to stack some wood on the back porch.

Daring to hope that maybe Drake would ride by and see that the wagon wasn't there, Misty asked Lavinia, "You hungry yet? I'm not."

"Not really, Misty. Guess we can eat when we want to, can't we?"

"Sure can, honey," Misty smiled and patted her on the head as Lavinia took her doll and went out to sit in the swing on the front porch. Misty went into her room to brush her hair so she would look pretty just in case Drake did come by. A few minutes later she went out to join Lavinia. The sun was sinking low in the sky so twilight hadn't yet settled over the countryside.

She began to roam around the front yard, plucking some of the flowers. She'd gathered a lovely bouquet by the time she walked back to the steps.

"Oh, how pretty, Misty," Lavinia said as her sister went in to put them in a vase.

Misty figured she might as well get started on supper. It was after six. She set up the table and was preparing to kindle up the cookstove when she heard Lavinia shriek. She almost dropped her pot as she rushed to the porch. "Lavinia?" she asked excitedly. At that moment she looked down on the step to see Drake sitting there grinning up at her.

"Oh, Drake! I heard her scream and it scared me to death."

"Blame me for that, love. I'd just told her I'd come to see if I could take her to see Lucky. I hear your pa's gone hunting overnight, so you two get ready to go in the wagon with me."

Lavinia leapt out of the swing, ready to go. Misty went in to check her cookstove. Luckily, it wasn't too hot because she'd never got around to adding any sticks of wood to the kindling.

She went back to the porch to join Drake and Lavinia. "I'm ready!"

"Then let's be on our way," Drake announced.

The three of them went down the path and through the gate. He swung Lavinia up in the back of the wagon and hoisted Misty into the seat before going around to the other side.

Quickly, they rolled down the dirt road. It was twilight time. All Misty knew was that it was glorious to be sitting in the wagon with Drake, his dark eyes glancing over at her. What she saw in his eyes warmed her. A couple of times he reached over to hold her hand for a moment.

Misty knew she was in love with this handsome Englishman! Now she pondered whether he was in love with her.

Chapter 12

The back of Drake's wagon was filled with boxes, so he had a lot of unloading to do when they arrived back at his place. It had been late in the afternoon when he'd gone into Crowley. The men had worked until mid-afternoon to finish up a job they'd started on the house. He paid all three of them and left immediately for Crowley.

As they rolled into his drive, he'd pointed to the house. "See the house, Misty? It'll be done by winter."

"It's really taking shape, isn't it? Part of the siding is up now, and the roof. Your men have been working hard," she remarked.

Lucky had not forgotten Lavinia, and he was so happy to see her he almost knocked her to the ground.

He escorted the two of them to his house, then excused himself to unload the wagon. It took four trips to get everything out. Before he unharnessed the team, he fired up the cookstove. "I need a hot cup of coffee. How about you, Misty?"

"Sounds good to me, Drake."

There was a fine baked ham in his oven, which Oscar's sister Rachel had sent over along with a huge crock of her baked beans. Rachel tried to send enough food every Saturday morning to keep him fed for the whole weekend.

He hoped Misty and Lavinia liked peach cobbler—Rachel had sent two of them. He'd stopped at the bakery to buy two fresh loaves of bread and the delicious cinnamon rolls he bought by the dozen. He and the woman who owned the bakery were well acquainted. Mrs. Arnold had become very fond of the Englishman.

Other than his groceries, Drake gave no thought to his other purchases of the afternoon, except for two items he took out of the sack.

He excused himself to go to his bedroom—there was something he had bought for Lavinia.

When he came back he was carrying a stuffed teddy bear. "Lavinia, this is for you," he said as he handed it to her.

"Oh, Mr. Dalton—how nice you are," she exclaimed as she snuggled it next to her face and smiled.

He had a simple explanation for the gift. "All my sisters had teddy bears when they were Lavinia's age."

He sat beside a grateful Misty and asked Lavinia, "Now, what are you going to name him? My sisters always gave their teddy bears names."

With an impish smile as she quickly replied, "I'll call him Lucky so when I'm home I'll feel Lucky is with me."

While Lavinia was occupied with the teddy bear, Drake had another gift to present. He reached into his shirt pocket. "This is for you, Misty," he said as he handed her a small box.

When Misty opened the lid she found a lovely little gold locket in the shape of a heart. She'd never owned any jewelry, so Misty was so overcome that her lovely green eyes could not help misting. She looked up at him and Drake saw the tears. "Oh, Drake—I don't know what to say."

"You don't have to say anything, love. Just don't cry. I don't think I could stand to see you cry."

She smiled as he took the locket to fasten it around her throat. Then he turned her around so he could see it on her. "Ah, pretty! Misty, I don't think you know how beautiful you are."

She laughed softly. "I haven't had much time since I was thirteen to ponder whether I was pretty or not. I—I want to believe you—if you think so then that's enough for me."

Lavinia was so occupied with Lucky and her new bear that she was not aware when Drake gave her older sister a kiss. Then he urged her to go into his bedroom to look at the locket in the mirror while he checked the food in the oven.

She came into the kitchen as he was taking the ham and beans out of the oven. He looked up to see her standing there.

"You like it?"

"I love it, Drake.

"As Lavinia said about her teddy bear, it will remind you that I'm with you, Misty, when you wear the locket.

"Yes, Drake—it will. Shall I call her to come to the table?"

"Call her—I know she's starved. So am I!"

She had to admit that she, too, was famished. The thick slices of ham were delicious—she could taste the cloves which Drake had pulled out before he began to slice it. Like Lavinia and Drake, Misty took a generous helping of baked beans.

After dinner, Lavinia went to the front room to play with Lucky and her new teddy bear. Misty and Drake got everything cleaned up and put away.

But this time, Lavinia did not fall asleep. So Drake and Misty had to content themselves by just holding hands and talking. Finally, impatient for a kiss, he suggested they go out to sit in the swing on the dark front porch.

After Drake's first kiss, Misty chanced to notice some distant lightning in the dark skies. She quickly pulled out of his embrace, "Oh, Lord, Drake—you'd better get me and Lavinia home."

"Wha-what's the matter, love?"

"Lightning, Drake. That could mean Pa would be hightailing it home. He and Jeb won't stay out in the woods if storms move in."

Drake wasted no time getting the wagon ready—he saw the flashing light off in the distance. In a few minutes he had the team moving at a fast pace.

They beat Mike Bennett home, but for Misty's sake he didn't press his luck by lingering at the front door. "I'll see you as soon as I can, love." He told Lavinia good night, turning hastily toward his wagon so he and Lucky could get back home before the rains came. The lightning continued to get closer, and now there was the low rumble of thunder.

Misty watched his wagon roll down the drive and then closed the front door and lit a lamp. She told Lavinia to take her new teddy bear to her room. "Pa could be getting here anytime. I have to think up something to explain that teddy bear, Lavinia, and you have to tell him the same thing or you and me will be in trouble."

Lavinia came up with the solution. "Tell him Mrs. Walters got it for me." Misty agreed that that was the best idea, but she knew that this little web of lies was going to catch up with her.

She got Lavinia undressed and into her nightgown. "It's past your bedtime, honey, so crawl into your bed with your new teddy bear and get some sleep."

With a glowing smile she told her older sister, "I got Lucky to sleep with every night, haven't I, Misty?"

"You sure do, honey. You and Lucky can snuggle together every night," Misty said as she dimmed the lamp. By the time she walked back into the front room, the rain was coming down and lightning was flashing brightly. Sharp, resounding explosions of thunder were overhead and she was hoping that Drake and Lucky were safe inside by now.

But they hadn't been quite that lucky. They made it to the barn but by the time Drake got the team unharnessed, heavy rain was falling.

The two of them made a mad dash for the house—when they reached the back door, dog and man were both dripping wet.

Lucky gave himself a mighty shake, sending drips of water spraying over the kitchen floor, but Drake couldn't have cared less. He was heading for his bedroom to get some dry clothing.

All the time he was cussing the storm for moving in when it did. It had robbed him of precious moments with Misty.

He was no more disappointed than Misty, who kept expecting her pa to rush through the door. She looked out the window to see how hard the rain was coming down.

But when Mike hadn't appeared by ten o'clock, she went to her room to change into her nightgown. She waited one more hour before she locked the front and back doors as she always did when it was just her and Lavinia.

When she got up the next morning, it was apparent that her pa and Jeb had braved out the storm. By the time she had made coffee and fixed Lavinia her breakfast, a very weary looking Mike Bennett came dragging through the back door.

He was more than ready to drink a fast cup of black coffee and lie down on his bed, which was exactly what he did. He slept for over six hours. He woke up at two, hungry as a wolf, and Misty fixed him some ham and eggs.

"Catch yourself any coons, Pa?" she asked.

"Yeah, but I let Jeb have them," he told her. His dark eyes fastened on the gold locket she was still wearing. "Well, now—where did that come from, Misty?"

"What, Pa?"

"That fancy little locket around your neck."

"Mrs. Walters, Pa," she quickly responded. But she wondered to herself how she could have been so careless not to take it off last night as she'd intended to do. She cautioned herself to remember to take it off before Jeff returned home from the Walters'.

When her pa left the kitchen, she went to her room and removed the locket and put it into the drawer of her chest.

Then she went into Lavinia's room and put the teddy bear into the little wooden chest at the foot of her bed.

She walked out on the front porch where Lavinia was sitting in the swing playing with her doll, then leaned over to whisper in her ear, telling her where she'd put Lucky.

She lingered in the swing with her little sister for a while before she went back into the house. She'd had something on her mind for a few months now. Tomorrow she was going to get Jeff to help her change the bedrooms.

She saw no reason to consult her pa about it. Jeff was a young man going on eleven and should have his own room. Her little sister could share her bedroom. When Jeff was seven and Lavinia three, the arrangement was fine, but all of that had changed.

Her pa seemed perfectly content to sit in the front room and read the paper he'd picked up in Crowley. But Mike was also having a lot of private musings that afternoon. It had been good to have some time with old Jeb. They got four squirrels their first hour in the woods. By eight, the woods were dark and Jeb suggested they take a break and have some corn liquor. They'd found a cozy spot on an incline and Jeb had gotten out his jug of liquor.

For the next hour and a half they drank and talked. Mike told Jeb how the last four months of his life had been wasted courting Georgia Gordon.

Jeb was a married man with three kids. He did like to go out with a buddy to hunt and get a little drunk, but he'd never cheated on Liza. She knew that, so she never nagged him when he went out occasionally to "kick up his heels," as she called it.

He had never understood why Mike had been attracted to Georgia Gordon; he thought he was courting her because she was wealthy.

He and Mike had been pals for a long time, but that was not to say Jeb always approved of his friend's ways. Beth Bennett was a fine lady and a pretty one. At least she was when she was young, but Jeb saw the changes in her after she'd been married to Mike for ten years.

After they'd been drinking for an hour, Jeb asked, "You think you'd be content with an overbearing woman like Georgia? All her money wouldn't be worth being her lapdog."

Mike had bristled at that. "You saying I'd be that?"

"I'm saying that that might be what she'd expect. There's your kids, Mike. You and Beth had three fine youngsters. How would Georgia be with them?"

"Not worth a damn!" He told Jeb about the the scene she'd had with young Jeff. "Actually, it was over Jeff that we had our big argument. Misty had told me what had happened but Georgia's version was different."

"Then believe Misty," Jeb told him. "From what I've heard, your Jeff is a very good kid. At least, that's what they say around Crowley and Lepanto. Hey, Mike—if that woman is so lazy she can't bend over to pick up her own hankie, imagine how she'd be married to you."

By now the two of them were well into their cups. Lightning flashed and thunder rumbled all around them, but they seemed oblivious.

They talked for another hour, drinking from that jug. Then they sank into a drunken sleep which lasted until long after the storm had passed. When they woke up, the sun was shining high in the sky, so they started for their homes. Mike had told Jeb to take the squirrels—he had a bigger family to feed. Mike had bought a good supply of groceries

Saturday. Two weeks of not buying gifts for Georgia left him with a lot more money.

On his way home early that Sunday morning after he and Jeb had parted company, he thought to himself that all he would have had to do the last four months was travel some ten miles over to Lepanto to a place called Floating Palace Flo's to get the same pleasure he'd gotten from Georgia.

Flo's place was a houseboat, a very fancy houseboat. Flo and Jewel, her partner, had a very prosperous business. The lumber mill workers came into town on Saturdays, their pockets filled with their week's wages. They went to the barber shop for a bath and shave for twenty-five cents. A thick steak could be enjoyed at the River's End, the only inn. By then they were ready to go to Flo's.

Flo's place was very busy on Saturday nights and no one ever left the houseboat disappointed. Flo was a buxom blonde who knew exactly how to please a man. Jewel was an attractive brunette who took on the shyer gents, who felt very bold and daring when they left Jewel. She had a real way about her.

By the time he arrived at his place that Sunday morning, Mike had decided he didn't need the likes of Georgia Gordon. The truth was, he wasn't ready to marry again.

He was very content to spend the afternoon around the house and enjoy Misty's fine supper. Two hours later he went to bed and realized he hadn't missed seeing Georgia at all.

Chapter 13

Mike Bennett went to work the next morning feeling more carefree and happy than he'd felt in a long time. But Georgia Gordon met the new week devastated that she'd had no visit from Mike over the weekend. When he'd left her parlor a week earlier, he'd meant exactly what he'd said. Georgia had to face the stark reality that her wealth was not going to hold this man.

Realizing this, she wanted him more. It had been a lonely weekend. She also knew now that Mike was more devoted to his family than she'd realized. Her foolish little game had yielded her nothing. Now that she had had the long weekend to think about it, it had been a very silly gesture on her part.

She knew the next time she approached his children, she would have to act more intelligently than she did on her first visit. Mike's children were smart, especially Misty. She must have seen Georgia for what she really was—a foolish, silly woman.

For the next three days Mike was constantly in her

thoughts and she racked her brain trying to figure out how to get back into his good graces. She had her pride and she would not crawl.

She could think of nothing. By Thursday she was so depressed that she got into her buggy and paid a visit to her friend, Lilly.

Lilly knew something was wrong with Georgia the minute she walked in the door. "Come on in. This is a nice surprise. I was just sitting here with nothing to do all afternoon," Lilly remarked as she motioned for Georgia to have a seat. "I'm going to get us a cup of coffee, Georgia."

Before Georgia could say anything the feisty little Lilly was making a dash to her kitchen. Every movement Lilly made was fast and furious. She was a tiny lady compared to Georgia—Lilly had prettier and more delicate features and a lovely mane of soft blond curly hair piled atop her head.

She sank down in the overstuffed chair and sighed, "Oh, Georgia—hope your life's been more exciting than mine. I made my usual little trek down the main street Saturday afternoon, but Saturday night I sat here all alone—and all day Sunday. I'm just about ready to accept Henry's offer to come take me to church Sunday morning and go out to his house for Sunday dinner."

"Don't feel too sorry for yourself, honey. I was doing the same thing Saturday night and Sunday," Georgia confessed.

"You telling me that Mike Bennett didn't sashay over to see you all weekend?"

"That's exactly what I mean, Lilly." She ended up telling Lilly everything that had happened between her and Bennett.

"Guess it would have been best to have had Mike take you over to meet his kids for the first time, Georgia. From what I've heard those kids adored their mother. You were walking right into a hornet's nest."

"I know. I didn't know how to cope with any of them, not even that little Lavinia," Georgia admitted.

"How would you, Georgia? You never had any children so you'd have no idea how children think." Lilly wasn't a woman to mince words. It wasn't her nature to do otherwise. "Georgia, let's face it. We're too old to have to put up with kids six, ten, and seventeen. Lord God, what a damnation that would be to me!"

Dejectedly, Georgia sighed, "Well, that leaves me with no option but to forget about Mike Bennett."

"That's a decision only you can make, dear," Lilly said. Secretly, she was thinking it would probably be the best thing Georgia could do. From all she'd heard about Mike Bennett, Georgia would rue the day she married him. He'd go through all her money and leave her brokenhearted, and a lot poorer than when he'd married her.

"I know, Lilly. I know. It's just hard 'cause you know I have strong feelings for Mike. We've been seeing one another almost five months now."

"I've got a great idea. You get in your buggy and come to town Saturday afternoon. You and me will just make a little sashay up the main street and then come back here. I'll fix dinner and we'll have a leisurely bottle of sherry. Let's keep each other company Saturday night, sleep in as late as we want to Sunday morning, and then you can get in your buggy to get back home."

"I'll do it, Lilly."

"Then come next Sunday I'm going to church with old Henry. You might think about doing the same thing with Cyrus. You and I both know he's had an itch to court you ever since he found out you were a widow."

A sly smile came to Georgia's face. "Yes, I might just take a little jaunt over to Lepanto tomorrow, Lilly."

An hour later, as she was guiding her buggy homeward, Georgia's spirits were much higher. At least, Cyrus had no kids! He was wealthier than she was—she'd been concerned about that in her relationship with Bennett. Many times she'd asked herself if he was courting her so he could feather his nest. She'd tried to convince herself that he wasn't, but there was still that little shadow of a doubt.

At least this weekend she had something to look forward to and for Georgia that was enough.

The Bennett house was a pleasant place as Mike went to work daily and came home in the late afternoon in a more mellow mood. Misty, Jeff, and Lavinia welcomed this new Mike. Misty knew she had to take Jeff into her confidence about Drake Dalton. She could easily conceal her locket, but Lavinia forgot and brought out her new teddy bear. Jeff looked over at Misty and asked, "Where did she get that?"

She confessed the secret she and Lavinia had been sharing for almost three weeks. She even told him how she'd first met Drake Dalton when she'd been walking home from Crowley after buying Jeff's shoes. "My sandal broke and I was hobbling down the road. He brought me home—well, not home but to the riverbank. Oh, Jeff, you'd like him just like Lavinia does. He has this big black stallion, Duke, and a big dog named Lucky. That's why Lavinia called her teddy bear Lucky."

"Gosh, he sounds real nice. Maybe I could go over to his house sometimes like you and Lavinia have been doing," Jeff exclaimed.

"I'm sure that could be worked out, Jeff." He listened with fascination as she told him about Drake coming here from England to claim an inheritance from his French grandmother. "You know where the old Benoit property is? Well, you would not believe what he's already done to restore the house and barn as well as all the outbuildings. Now he's building a house for the foreman he hopes to hire before spring. He's not a planter and he knows it. He knows nothing about raising cattle."

Young Jeff found himself intrigued by this man who'd entered Misty's life while he'd been spending so much time over at the Walters the last several weeks. He'd absorbed a lot during those weekends with Ed Walters. Jeff's young mind was spinning. He'd heard Mr. Walters mention a man he'd consider for his own foreman if he didn't already have one.

The foreman told Walters, "You ever have need of another good man, I've got one. He's foreman for Sellars over near Lepanto. He's not getting his wages on time and Jake's a damned hard worker. Know him for years and I can vouch for him. Jake's wife is also discontent 'cause Sellars isn't keeping up repairs on their house."

Walters asked him, "Now what's the man's name? Who knows when I might need another name."

"Jake Meadows."

For whatever reason, Jeff had remembered the man's name so he told all this to Misty.

Misty told her brother he could be just the type of man that Drake Dalton would be looking for.

As the end of the week approached, Misty wondered if her pa would be going over to Georgia's. If he didn't go over there this weekend, it probably meant that they had had such a bad fight that he was no longer going to be seeing her.

Ed Walters didn't want to press his demands on Jeff too far, so he made no effort to seek the boy's services for the coming weekend. He didn't want Bennett to get riled with him.

But he knew he was going to miss the young man's company. Geneva had cautioned him, "We don't want to overdo it. Mike could think we're getting too possessive."

When Saturday came around, Mike returned from the mill as usual with the weekly groceries. He unloaded the wagon and began to shave. Misty assumed he was going to see Georgia. But he turned to ask her what they were having for dinner. "It sure smells good, Misty."

"Chicken and dressing, Pa. You going to be eating here tonight?"

"Sure am, honey. Nothing better than chicken and dressing—you don't think I'm going to miss that, now do you?"

"I didn't know, Pa. I—I figured you were probably going over to Georgia's."

"Nope! I'm going to eat your good dinner and then I'm heading for Bert Horn's. Going to play some poker. Bert's wife and kids have gone to Mississippi to visit her folks for a couple of weeks. So don't keep the lamps burning for me, Misty. It could be morning when I come home." He seemed in a very gay mood.

He reached in his work pants and pulled out some bills. "Misty, this is for you for whatever you wish to buy."

It was another Saturday night that he hadn't had to buy a little gift. He'd had money left from last week's salary after he'd bought the groceries.

"Thank you, Pa," Misty had stammered, thunderstruck.

By six-thirty, the four of them sat down at the table to enjoy Misty's baked chicken and dressing. She was unaware that Drake had driven down the road and saw Bennett's wagon, so he had gone on home and unloaded his supplies. He and Lucky had had dinner—Rachel had sent over a pot roast with an array of fresh vegetables. He had hoped he could share it with Misty and Lavinia, but he had to accept that it was not to be.

After dinner, Drake was restless and went out on the front porch and lit up one of his cheroots. He found himself pacing like the panther which some of the old-timers had told him still roamed these unsettled woods. There were still some bears and wildcats, but as the land was cleared there were fewer sightings.

He gave way to a sudden impulse. He went to the barn and put a saddle on Duke and rode down the river road. The little house was glowing with lamplight. He was pleased to see that Bennett's wagon was gone now, but he still took the precaution of tethering Duke some two hundred feet away.

Misty had just put Lavinia to bed. She went back to the front room where Jeff sat whittling with the knife Ed had given to him. She saw how intensely he was concentrating. "What are you making now, Jeff?" she asked as she took a chair beside him.

"Oh, probably never going to be able to do it. Never tried anything like this—I'm trying to copy a wood carving of a horse like the one I saw over at Mr. Walters'. He has it sitting on his desk," he mumbled.

"Won't know until you try, Jeff." She smiled and gave him an affectionate pat on his head.

"I'll work on it all winter if I have to," he vowed.

"Good for you!"

They were startled by the sudden knock on the door. Misty leaped from her chair to answer it, and a pleased smile lit her face when she saw Drake standing there. "Come in, Drake. This is a wonderful surprise," she exclaimed as he came striding through the door.

He immediately saw the young boy sitting on the floor, the knife and block of wood in his hands. His dark eyes looked up at Drake quizzically.

"Jeff, this is Mr. Dalton." She smiled up at Drake. "This is my brother, Jeff."

Georgia Gordon was completely wrong about young Jeff, who could be very well mannered when he chose to be. He rose from the floor and extended his hand. "Nice to meet you, Mr. Dalton. Misty told me how nice you've been to her and Lavinia."

"Well, it's nice to meet you, Jeff," Drake replied, smiling. He glanced around the room. "Now wait a minute—where's that cute little Lavinia?"

"Just put her to bed a few minutes ago," Misty told him.

"Well, that's just as well because I left Lucky at home." Drake laughed as he followed Misty over to the old settee.

He didn't have to say a word—just the look in his eyes warmed her. His hand took hers and gave it an affectionate caress that had to substitute for the kiss he yearned to give her.

"What are you making there, Jeff?" Drake asked.

"A horse which probably won't end up looking at all like I want it to."

"No, Jeff—tell yourself quite the opposite— It will look exactly the way you've envisioned it."

Jeff looked up and grinned. "You sound like Mr. Walters, Mr. Dalton. He's always telling me I'm too hard on myself."

"Well, your Mr. Walters sounds like a smart man. You must feel highly about yourself if you want others to feel that way. Never say you can't, always say you can!"

Jeff took an instant liking to Drake Dalton. His warm, friendly nature reminded him of Ed Walters. Drake was also quietly observing the young man. He was far more mature than most ten-year-old lads he'd known. He was going to be quite a handsome young fellow by the time he was eighteen. He already had a firm young body, huskily built. From the look of his legs, he was going to be tall.

Drake liked the way his dark eyes were so direct.

He turned to Misty. "Where's your pa tonight?"

"Gone to a poker game at his friend's house."

"I came this way earlier and saw the wagon so I didn't stop, naturally. After I ate I decided to ride over this way and saw the wagon gone."

"I'm glad you did. Think you might enjoy some peach cobbler?"

"Why, of course," he replied eagerly. When she got up, he followed her into the kitchen where he rewarded himself with one long kiss. While he was holding her, he whispered, "Couldn't stand the thought of not seeing you after a long week, Misty. I—I get lonely for you."

"Oh, Drake—it's a long week for me, too. I'm just glad

you and Jeff have finally met. He won't give us away, I can assure you."

"Seeing him tonight, I've got an idea, Misty. Suppose your pa would let me hire him for some odd jobs around my place? From what you've told me, he's a hard little worker and you must know I'd never push him beyond his limit or age."

Her green eyes sparkled brightly. "What a wonderful idea, Drake!"

"It would open the door for me to come over here and see you."

She gave him an impish grin, "Drake, you're a conniving man!"

"Never would I deny that!"

Before they left the kitchen she called out to Jeff to ask him if he'd like some of her peach cobbler, but he turned her down.

Drake ate his cobbler in the front room and Misty took the empty plate back into the kitchen. as she came back, she heard Drake speaking with Jeff.

"Think you might be interested in working for me for, say, three days a week? My carpenters could use a young man to do a lot of errands for them. It would mean my house could be ready quicker." Drake mentioned the wages he'd pay.

That was enough to make Jeff quit whittling and look up at Drake in disbelief. "You'd pay me *that* much, Mr. Drake?"

"Certainly, I would. You'd be worth it to me, young man."

"Lordy, I'm saying yes right now but I'd have to speak with my pa. But I've already helped him get all his wood stored for the winter, so I can't see how he'd object. Can you, Misty?"

"Can't see why he would, Jeff," she said and smiled down at him.

"You ask him, Jeff, and I'll come over here next Wednesday afternoon. If you can, then I'll come over bright and early on Thursday morning to pick you up and bring you home at the end of the day."

"Sounds great to me, Mr. Dalton," Jeff said with a broad smile. His head was swimming at the amount of money he could make working for Mr. Dalton. His pa just had to let him take this job.

Drake rose from the settee to announce that he had to be heading home. At least, he had something to look forward to, for he could see Misty when he picked Jeff up if he got to take the job.

Misty accompanied him out the front door. On the dark front porch, he could take her in his arms and kiss her one more time before he left.

When his lips finally released hers, she told him, "Drake, that's a most generous wage you offered Jeff."

"Worth every penny if it means I'm able to see you, love. Besides, Jeff will give me a full day's work for his pay. I know that! It's a fine young brother you have, Misty. I like him!"

"Well, I could tell Jeff was very impressed with you tonight," she said, still standing in his embrace.

With a devious grin he told her he was far more interested in how he was impressing his sister. Her hand went up to caress his cheek. "You know the answer to that, Drake Dalton, so don't you play coy with me."

His expression grew solemn. "Never change, Misty. Always stay as you are right now. You're like no other girl I've ever known. You're so genuine and honest."

"I can't imagine being any way but the way I am. I'm just a simple girl from Arkansas. How are your young ladies in England?"

"Never met one like you, love," he declared as he finally persuaded himself to take his leave.

Chapter 14

Amazingly, Georgia Gordon found herself having a most enjoyable Saturday afternoon and evening with her good friend, Lilly. But more important, it proved that she wasn't dependent on Mike Bennett.

She'd boarded her little buggy with a valise containing her nightgown, robe, and toiletries. She'd arrived at Lilly's around two that Saturday afternoon; by three, they were going up the main street in Crowley. They'd made stops at the mercantile and emporium, then visited with old friends. Georgia realized how isolated she'd been for months because of her crazy infatuation with Mike Bennett.

Their last stop was at the drug store for fruit ices. Both of them bought bottles of sweet-smelling toilet water and Georgia bought some face powder. Lilly also bought some little satin sacks of sachet to put in her bureau drawers. By the time they left to return to Lilly's house, they were as gay and carefree as two schoolgirls.

Yesterday, she had made an applesauce cake she knew Georgia loved. She also had the butcher carve two fine beefsteaks, she had a fine dinner planned for the two of them.

When they arrived, they sat in Lilly's parlor resting their tired feet and sipping sherry for the next hour. Then they went into Lilly's small but elegant dining room for tender beefsteak, roasted potatoes, and steamed corn. Georgia felt so stuffed she didn't know whether she could eat a piece of the applesauce cake, but somehow she managed it.

As the two of them worked in the kitchen afterwards, Lilly said, "You see, Georgia—you don't need Mike Bennett like you thought you did."

"You know what, Lilly, I know that now and I have you to thank for it! Truth is, I don't think I want him back in my life. I don't want to put up with those kids," Georgia confessed.

They went back into the parlor to have another couple of glasses of wine before getting ready for bed.

They shared a late breakfast the next morning and Georgia prepared to head home. But as she was saying her farewells, she embraced Lilly and said, "Thanks for more than you realize. You go to church with Henry next Sunday and I think I'll make a call on Cyrus over in Lepanto. A man like him is all I can handle."

Lilly suppressed a giggle. "Honey, neither one of us needs a man we can't handle—not at our age."

Georgia went home that early Sunday afternoon with a clearer head than she'd had in months She'd had a good look at her own foolish fancy.

Mike Bennett's head was certainly not clear when he arrived back at his place. He was bleary-eyed and his pockets were empty. He realized as he was guiding his team of horses home that it was a good thing he'd already bought groceries for the next week or he'd probably have bet all that money, too. Playing poker could be like a fever in the blood. A man keeps thinking he's going to win.

Well, he hadn't tonight! He'd drunk too much liquor, which was poison in a poker game. He was angry with himself. Everyone back at his buddy's house were laughing about how they'd cleaned him out.

Dawn was breaking in the eastern sky when he got to his barn and unharnessed his horses. None of his children knew when he arrived back home.

Misty would have slept another hour, had Jeff not awakened her to tell her he was hungry. So reluctantly, she crawled out of her bed and slipped into her robe to go to the kitchen and fire up the old cookstove.

Selfishly, she prepared the coffeepot first. She needed that hot steaming cup of coffee. Then she began to put some slices of bacon into the cast iron skillet. She had a dozen biscuits left over from yesterday, so she put them in a baking pan.

Lavinia and Jeff had their breakfast before Mike finally emerged from his bedroom. For the first time since Beth had died, he faced the fact that he'd been a miserable excuse of a father to his three children. He'd been completely selfish and his three kids had had to fend for themselves for the most part. Misty had taken charge the last few years to make this place run while he'd frittered his time away.

He decided he had no more time to waste on shallow women like Georgia who expected far more from a man than he was able to give.

There was no need to make a trip to the woods today—he was glad of that. Jeff helped him do some chores around the barn, and Mike realized he had some grain to lay in for the winter months. His pa seemed in such a pleasant mood that Jeff felt *that* it was the perfect time to approach him about the job Drake Dalton had offered him.

"How did all that come about, Jeff?"

"You know how word gets around a small place like

Crowley. Guess he heard about me and that Mr. Walters liked the work I've done for him. Anyway, he wants me to work for him for about three days a week and I'd like to do it, Pa. I could buy all my winter clothes with some to spare. Can I do it?''

"Sure, Jeff. You have my permission. But how are you going to get there?"

"Said he'd pick me up and deliver me home in the evening. Seems like a real nice man, Pa. He's trying to fix up the old Benoit property."

Jeff could not recall how long it had been since he'd received an affectionate pat from his pa. Mike tousled his hair and said, "If you want to work for this Mr. Dalton then go ahead and do it." Mike suddenly realized how his son had shot up in height. He was only going on eleven but he was already tall. Mike also noticed how huskily he was built.

"Thanks, Pa. I'll tell Mr. Dalton when he comes over on Wednesday."

He told Misty later that evening that Pa had given permission for him to work for Drake.

"Oh, Jeff—I'm so glad. Drake will be fair with you. Pa seems to have changed lately. Haven't you noticed it, too?"

"Sure have. Started when he quit going over to see that old Georgia Gordon," Jeff said.

On Wednesday Drake rode over to the Bennett place to see about Jeff working for him. Anticipating that he would be coming over, Misty took a brush to her hair at least a dozen times.

Lavinia noticed her sister's constant brushing and gave way to her curiosity by asking why.

Misty tried to shrug her inquiry aside by telling her it kept getting in her eyes. Lavinia had a simple solution. "Tie it back with a ribbon like you usually do."

"Don't worry about it, honey," Misty said when Lavinia left the room, Misty took advantage of her departure by slipping out the bottle of toilet water and dabbing some behind each ear.

Misty realized how much her mind was on Drake's arrival instead of her baking—she'd placed three loaves of bread in the oven and almost forgotten them. She'd pulled them out just in the nick of time. She planned to give one of the loaves to Drake.

It was almost three when he came riding up on his black stallion. Young Jeff was very impressed by the fine horse. His first remark to Drake was praise for Duke.

"You must like horses. I agree with you—Duke is very special. How's your wooden horse coming along?" Drake asked.

"Kinda slow, Mr. Dalton. But I have good news. Pa says I can work for you."

"Great, Jeff. I'll be over at eight in the morning," Drake said, giving him a pat on the shoulder.

He looked up at Misty, who was standing behind the two of them. "Wish I could stay longer, Misty, but I must get back to my place. Some things need attention before the men leave."

Lavinia was still taking her afternoon nap so she didn't know of his visit until later. Misty and Jeff stood on the porch waving as he rode away. Secretly, she thought he was a handsome devil atop that black horse.

She suddenly remembered that she hadn't given him the loaf of bread. The sight of him made her forget everything else. She gasped, "Oh, no!"

Jeff turned to ask what was the matter. She told him about the bread. "Give it to him in the morning when he comes to pick me up, Misty."

The sight of Drake Dalton surely did addle her. At least by the time her pa arrived home a couple of hours later she was more in control. Supper was simmering on the stove. She got her table set up and saw that there were two kettles of steaming water ready for her pa.

Coming home in his wagon that afternoon, Mike Bennett realized that Georgia Gordon had meant absolutely nothing to him. It came to him that day when one of the fellows at the mill poked good-natured fun at him telling him how he'd seen Georgia riding around in old Cyrus Heller's fancy buggy yesterday. "Heller beating your time with that gal, Mike?"

"She's not my gal, Ted. Cyrus can have her," Mike replied cheerfully. "But God pity him."

Cyrus owned a nice place over in Lepanto, but he was about fifteen years older than Georgia. Georgia would certainly have to have a slower pace with old Cyrus than she'd had with him. Old Cyrus could never stand up to that woman!

Georgia just had to have a man! She was a different breed from her good friend, Lilly. Now he'd always considered Lilly to be a feisty little filly and she was actually much prettier than Georgia.

Lilly had been a widow much longer than Georgia, but she'd never remarried after her husband died. He'd never heard any gossip about Lilly and any of the gents around Crowley and Lepanto.

Truth be told he was glad to have Georgia out of his life. It had been good to be free to play poker with his buddies and go hunting with Jeb the last two weekends.

The next morning, Mike left the house at seven and Jeff left with Drake at eight, so Misty and Lavinia were there by themselves. She was delighted to have Geneva Walters pay a visit.

Martha had made new dresses for her and Lavinia out of the same material. That was enough to brighten their day.

Misty had so much to tell her. She told her about Jeff being hired by Drake Dalton, but the news which delighted Geneva most was about the changes her pa had made recently.

"He's worked like a dog to get all our wood up for the winter, Mrs. Walters. Guess taking two full weekends to get that done must have ruffled Georgia Gordon's feathers. Anyway, he's not been going over there and everything has been so much nicer here."

"Oh, honey—I couldn't be happier to hear all this," she said. "Can't tell you what it is about Georgia Gordon, but I could never get close to her even though we've known each other a long time. Guess I never was a very good neighbor."

"Well, I'm just glad she's out of my father's life," Misty declared.

"Well, me and Ed have got to get over to pay a visit to this Mr. Dalton. You know how it is in Crowley—we've heard all the gossip. But he's been out there at the Benoit place for over three months now and we should have welcomed him to our community. I feel real bad about that," Geneva confessed.

"I think you'll like him, Mrs. Walters. He seems like a very nice man." She could have said much more about Drake's kind and generous heart. She could have told her of his gifts to her and Lavinia but she didn't.

It was almost noon when Geneva left, promising she'd try not to go so long without seeing her again. Misty thanked her for the dresses.

Lavinia wanted to put her new dress on as soon as Geneva left, but Misty said, "Oh, no—save it for a special occasion, Lavinia, like when we go to town with the Walters or over to Drake's."

Lavinia was agreeable, so Misty went to the kitchen to check the huge pot of beef stew she'd been cooking for hours. She added a generous amount of potatoes and quartered onions, along with a jar of Geneva's tomatoes.

She intended to send a big crock of the stew home with Drake—she knew he didn't know how to cook. To her, it was a small way to compensate for the lovely sandals and toilet water he had given her.

Drake was not going to put Jeff through a long day, but

he'd found out that the young man was a hard worker. He'd been a big help gathering up the pieces of lumber the carpenters had sawed off and didn't need as they were now sectioning the rooms off in the house. He also carried water out to them during the morning hours. Oscar and the other two men instantly liked Jeff. Lucky liked the way he took his two hands to pet him so on every trip Jeff made from the house to the work site, Lucky began to trail along beside him.

When the clock struck four in Drake's kitchen, he called out to Jeff to come on in. He paid Jeff his first day's wages. "You've put in a good day, Jeff, and been a big help to me and Oscar."

"Thank you, Mr. Dalton. This job means everything to me."

"Well, I'm glad you're happy, because I'm pleased with you, young man."

With a big grin, Jeff said, "Golly, now I can buy Misty and Lavinia something pretty. I've always wanted to do that. I—I don't know what we'd have done without Misty."

The young man's words affected Drake very much. His open, honest expression was enough to tell Drake what a mature young man he was for his age.

But Drake also knew a boy should be able to think of more lighthearted things. As they walked out the door, Drake put his arm around Jeff's shoulder and said, "Jeff, how about you and me taking a ride around the countryside?"

Jeff's dark eyes looked up at him as he confessed, "I'd like that, Mr. Dalton, but I've never been on a horse."

"Well, that's no problem. I'll teach you to ride."

With a big grin Jeff declared, "Oh, I'd like that very much, Mr. Dalton." Jeff decided right there and then that when he got that horse whittled out of that block of wood he was going to give it to Mr. Dalton. But it had to be good!

Drake got him home by four-thirty and Jeff rushed into

the house to get washed up. Misty lingered on the front porch with Drake for a few minutes. He didn't care if Jeff or Lavinia saw him kiss their sister. Before he departed with the crock of beef stew, he told her, "He's a fine lad, Misty. He certainly adores his older sister, as I do."

The rest of the week gave Misty something to look forward to. Every day she had a brief encounter with Drake.

Like Jeff, Misty was amazed by the wages Drake paid him. Saturday had been a very short day, so Drake brought him home at one. He made a very tempting offer to Misty. "Jeff is a young man with money burning a hole in his pocket. What would you think about me coming back over here around three and all of us going into town for a couple of hours?"

Impulsively, Misty accepted his invitation. Her pa had already told her he was not going to be home for supper. He was going to a square dance over at the Harris barn. He hadn't been to a good old square dance in ages. When he and Beth were courting and first married she had been a great dancer and she always looked so cute as he swung her around the floor.

Misty wrote her pa a simple note before the three of them boarded Drake's wagon. If she paid a price for her frivolous act tomorrow, she didn't care. This afternoon they were going to enjoy themselves with Drake.

Enjoy themselves they did! Jeff took his little sister in tow, asking Drake, "Mr. Dalton, may me and Lavinia meet you and Misty somewhere in an hour?"

"Of course, Jeff. We'll meet in the drug store and have one of those good fruit ices."

Jeff took his sister's hand and led her down the main street. Drake took Misty's hand and led her in a different direction. He told her how pretty her dress was, which he did not know was new, and he'd noticed immediately that she was wearing his locket.

They ambled slowly up the street. When they passed by a jewelry store, he asked her to linger a moment.

At a small display window at the front, Misty admired all the pretty pieces. "My goodness, there are so many beautiful things," she sighed.

Nothing Drake saw could begin to compare with his mother's exquisite jewelry.

His slender finger lifted her long hair and he told her, "I think those dainty ears of yours need a pair of pretty earrings, Misty."

"Oh, Drake." She felt him urging her through the door of the shop and knew exactly what he was up to.

When a clerk asked if he could help them, Drake said they wished to see some earrings. As the clerk brought out one tray after another, one pair caught Drake's eyes. They were small with emerald stones encircled with gold filigree.

"Try these on, Misty." He waited for her to get them on and she lifted both sides of her hair.

"How—how do they look, Drake?"

"As I thought they would." He turned to the clerk to ask for a hand mirror so Misty could have a look.

The look on Misty's face told him she loved the way they looked. She had never had a pair of earrings. "You like them, love?"

"Of course I do, Drake."

"Then just keep them on," he said. He turned to the clerk to tell him he'd take them.

The clerk, Roy Greene, noticed Drake's very definite English accent and asked if he was Mr. Dalton. "Don't mean to be bold, but I heard we had an English gentleman. Figured you had to be him."

"You figured right. Yes, my name's Drake Dalton."

"I'm Roy Greene and I'm happy to have been of service to you, sir."

Roy didn't recognize the pretty young miss, but he was

sure she had to be a local girl. Mr. Dalton had obviously not wasted any time getting acquainted.

He might not have recognized Misty Bennett but two women had as they entered the jewelry shop right after Drake and Misty left.

Both of them knew who the man was, but they were curious as a cat about what Misty Bennett was doing with him.

Chapter 15

Samantha Clay and Ethel Barton marched into the shop to a warm, friendly greeting from Roy Greene. He was in great spirits after the nice sale he'd just made. "Well, what can I do for you two ladies?"

"Came in to pick up my brooch, Roy. Is it ready?" Samantha asked.

"Sure is, Samantha," he said turning to go to the back of the shop.

When he came back to hand the brooch to Samantha for her inspection, Ethel asked, "Wasn't that the new Englishman I saw leaving your place?"

"Sure was. Seems like a real fine fellow, too. He made the pretty miss very happy. Without blinking an eyelash, he bought her a pair of emerald earrings," Roy remarked.

Samantha looked up from the brooch to ask, "You say *emeralds,* Roy? They don't come cheap!" She glanced over at Ethel with a skeptical look.

She paid Roy and slipped the brooch in her reticule as they left the shop. As soon as they got out the door, Ethel turned to say, "Well, did you ever! I'd told you Geneva had sorta taken that girl under her wing the last couple of years. Now I just wonder what she'd think about what we found out this afternoon."

"Well, a man don't buy a girl expensive earrings unless there's something going on," Samantha added as they went toward their next stop.

Jeff and Lavinia had explored every corner of the emporium. He was a very practical young man, so he decided on a soft wool sweater to purchase for his little sister. When the cold winter came she'd be good and warm in that. He bought himself another pair of pants so Misty wouldn't have to constantly be washing for him. The only frivolous gift he bought was for Misty. He'd gotten the idea while he and Lavinia were roaming around the emporium and he'd noticed all the ladies with their reticules dangling from their wrists.

So he'd purchased one in a rich shade of green for Misty. He didn't know what to ask for so he just described what he was seeking and the lady clerk knew instantly what he wanted.

After that purchase was made, he told Lavinia they'd better head for the drug store. "My pockets are empty," he said and laughed.

"Yeah, but it sure was fun," Lavinia giggled as they emerged back out on the main street and turned toward the drug store.

After treating all of them to some refreshments in the drug store, Drake helped them into the wagon and leaped up in the seat to head for home.

As the wagon was beginning to roll down the main street, Ethel and Samantha were ambling along one side. Ethel nudged Samantha, exclaiming, "Well, will you look at that, Samantha! He's got the whole Bennett brood with him."

"I—I don't get it!"

Both couldn't wait to get to Geneva Walters to tell their tale.

Drake and Misty had no idea they'd been such a topic of gossip that afternoon. It had not even dawned on Drake that calling Misty "love" in the jewelry shop would lead Roy Greene to jump to conclusions. But then he just didn't know how people in small towns think.

Drake had insisted they stop off at his house for dinner. "Lavinia hasn't had a chance to see Lucky in a while and I've a pork roast big enough for all of us. That sister of Oscar's takes pity on me and sends over a feast every Friday."

Misty knew she would have been fighting a losing battle if she'd dared say no. But she saw no reason not to accept Drake's invitation. Her pa was going to the square dance, so he'd be coming in very late.

They all piled out of the wagon when they arrived at Drake's. Lavinia made a mad dash toward Lucky, who was just as eager to see her. Jeff remained with Drake and Misty, saying, "I better not horn in on her and Lucky right now—Lavinia wouldn't like that."

Drake knew what he was talking about, for Jeff and Lucky had become very close companions. He explained this to Misty.

But Lucky spotted Jeff and rushed to him, leaving Lavinia alone by the front step. Jeff tousled his head and the two of them walked back to Lavinia.

Drake and Misty laughed. "Jeff's a clever little fellow, isn't he?" he remarked.

"I've always thought so," she said.

As she had before when she and Lavinia ate with Drake, she helped him in the kitchen. He confessed, "I could use your advice, Misty. I need so many things for my kitchen, but damned if I know what they are."

"I'd be glad to do that for you, Drake."

He began to pull out all the food Oscar had brought over. Misty had never seen such a huge pork roast. He stuck it in the oven immediately as it was going to take a while to heat up. There were two huge crocks: one held sweet potatoes and the other turnips.

"Drake, there's enough food here for a dozen people."

"Got to do something real nice for Rachel. She's kept me from starving," he said and laughed. "I was getting awfully tired of bacon and eggs."

When everything was in the oven and the table was set, the two of them went into the front room to sit on the settee. Drake just couldn't resist playfully lifting up her hair to gaze at the earrings.

"Look perfect on your pretty ears, love, but this best be our little secret for a while, Misty. Your pa might get the wrong impression."

"I had already thought of that, Drake," she said. She'd already been reminding herself secretly that she must not forget to take them off tonight as she had forgotten about the locket, for her pa would know that the Walters would never buy her something this expensive. Her little white lies had been successful so far but it wouldn't work on these earrings.

Jeff told them he thought he'd better come into the house because Lavinia was getting into a pout because Lucky was paying more attention to him.

"That's very considerate of you, Jeff. Tell me, did you and Lavinia have fun spending your money?" Drake asked.

"Sure did, Mr. Drake. I got Lavinia a pretty blue sweater and got myself another pair of pants. Misty's always washing my pants." Suddenly, like a bolt of lightning had struck him, he leaped up to mumble, "Gosh, I almost forgot."

He rushed out the door and just as quickly dashed back with the gift he'd bought for Misty. He walked over to her and proudly handed her the small package. "That's for you, Misty."

"Oh, Jeff!" She smiled up at him. When she took out the lovely little reticule, she rose from the settee and gave him a big kiss on the cheek. "It's beautiful, Jeff. I've never had one."

"Didn't think you had, Misty, so it's time."

"Thank you, honey. Thank you very much," Misty said as she sat back down beside Drake. She showed it to Drake, who told him he had good taste.

The scene made an impression on Drake. He saw the great depth of love between this young man and his sister. He saw the ease with which they expressed their love.

Seeing how much pleasure it had provided for these two, Drake got the idea to approach Jeff about working an extra day. Another two weeks and the little house would be done so he wouldn't need Jeff's help.

"Suppose you might be able to work on Wednesdays for me, Jeff? The house will be finished in another two weeks, I think."

"I'd like to and I think I could get Pa to let me."

"Then I'll come over on Wednesday morning at the usual time and, if you can, then I'll take you back with me."

It was a late dinner, but the wait was worth it. They were all famished by the time they sat down at the table, and there was enough left for Drake's dinner the next night.

When Misty and Drake finally left the kitchen and dimmed the lamps, they found Lavinia and Lucky curled up on the rug in front of the hearth, asleep. Jeff sat in one of the overstuffed chairs, his head leaning against the back of the chair as he drowsed off.

"Guess I'd best get this sleepy family of mine home, Drake," Misty said with a smile.

"Let them sleep awhile—I have something to speak with you about. Perhaps you might think it foolish for a man in his twenties to seek the advice of a young lady of seventeen. But you are so much wiser than any seventeen-year-old I've ever known. I've got three sisters, as I told you, but none of them have had the responsibility you've had."

Misty had no inkling what he might want her advice about but she was flattered. "I'll do the best I can, Drake."

He told her after he'd gotten this place going he'd finally written a letter to his oldest sister, Ellen. He'd told her of all his grand plans and that he was happier than he'd ever been before.

"Well, I got a letter from her yesterday and it seems like she's ready to gather up my youngest sister, Valeria, and come here. God, I don't want that! This house isn't big enough to accommodate the three of us." He described the vast mansion they'd lived in at Dalton Manor. "For them, these living conditions would be primitive. Hell, they've had servants waiting on them hand and foot all their lives. So you see what a monster I've created."

She sensed the desperation in his voice. She took his hand in hers and gave him a real simple answer. "Drake, this hand better write a letter tomorrow telling your sister the truth. It's as simple as that. You don't have many bedrooms and certainly no servants. Pampered young ladies would find Crowley life not to their liking."

"And Ellen wouldn't find tutoring assignments here."

Misty laughed, "Hardly. The closest city she'd find for that would be Memphis."

"Well, I know what gave Ellen this idea. It seems my father is about to take a new wife and Ellen can't stand her."

"So write your letter and get it posted quickly, Drake."

"Thanks, love." He embraced her for one long kiss, which he knew was all that was possible tonight. But his feelings for Misty went beyond just pleasuring himself. He liked the good feeling he had when she was with him, even when they were just puttering in the kitchen together as they had this evening.

There were so many things about Misty that set her apart from any other girl he'd ever known. They could talk together as they had just now. He liked that straightforward way of hers. He saw that same trait in young Jeff.

He found her far more beautiful of face and soul than the demanding young women in London. Just because they were wealthy and dressed in fancy gowns, a man was supposed to attend every little whim. He'd never seen Misty in a fancy gown but in her simple little cotton frocks she outshone them all. To Drake, she was the most beautiful woman in the world.

Misty had remembered about the earrings and slipped them in the reticule as they were traveling home.

She realized just how late they'd returned home when shortly after she'd got Lavinia to bed and Jeff had gone to his room, she heard her pa's wagon rolling up to the barn. She just prayed that he hadn't seen the lamplight from her window.

She quickly got into her bed and waited apprehensively until she heard him come into the house. She heaved a deep sigh of relief when she realized he went directly to his room.

It would have eased her concern to know that Mike Bennett had met a cute little black-haired lady by the name of Colleen. The two of them instantly warmed to one another.

Colleen was ripe for a man like Mike. Her husband had had a boating accident about eight months ago. She was a feisty little lady in her mid-thirties.

Mike had had a grand time this evening. She had a seventeen-year-old daughter and they lived in Lepanto. She came to the square dance with some friends who felt she needed to get out of the house.

Misty was greeted by a most happy fellow in the kitchen the next morning—he was up much earlier than usual for a Sunday morning. He ate a hearty breakfast. Since he seemed in such a pleasant mood, she decided to approach him about Jeff's working an extra day for Drake.

"He's so pleased with Jeff that he'd like him for an extra day, Pa."

"Well, of course he can. He's a hard worker—and I suppose he wants to?"

"Oh, yes, he wants to. He likes Mr. Dalton."

"That's fine, Misty."

Misty went about her chores feeling happy as a lark. When Mike left the kitchen he told her he wouldn't be home for supper. He had an invitation for dinner.

"Oh, having dinner with Mrs. Gordon?"

"Hell, no! Thought you knew I haven't been seeing Georgia for weeks now. Met myself a real sweet little lady last night. Colleen Carver's her name—she lives over in Lepanto. She's got a daughter about your age and lost her husband in a boating accident."

Misty was stunned that he was so openly discussing his new lady friend.

"Tiny little thing like you, Misty."

Misty smiled. "Well, I hope you have a nice time this evening, Pa."

Around three, Mike shaved and got into his best shirt and pants to go over to Lepanto. Misty had to admit when he left the house, his thick hair all slicked and his best clothes on, he was a very good-looking man, even though he was almost forty.

Jeff was delighted to hear Misty tell him he could work the extra day for Drake.

Drake Dalton spent a lazy Sunday afternoon at his place. As Misty had suggested, he wrote to Ellen. In a very frank, honest manner he let her know that he was not prepared to have her and Valeria live with him. He also stressed that she would find it impossible to find a tutoring position in this remote community. It took him quite a while to write the long letter. He told her of the primitive way he lived compared to life at the their father's fine manor.

Come Monday morning, he would take the letter and post it. He could only pray that it reached England before she started out for America.

Chapter 16

A day didn't go by that Misty didn't take out the velvet reticule and pull out the lovely earrings inside to look at them for several seconds before she put them back.

It seemed that Wednesday morning would never come—Drake was due to come over to see if Jeff could work for him.

It was obvious to Misty that her pa must have enjoyed himself Sunday evening with Mrs. Carver. He was in the best of spirits as he began his new week. Mike Bennett could not recall how long it had been since he'd been this happy.

Colleen was as different from Georgia as day is to night. And she had to be the best darn cook in all of Arkansas.

The interesting thing about Colleen was she was just as independent in nature as Georgia but she wasn't demanding.

Mike liked her attitude toward herself. She frankly admitted that although she was a widow, she wasn't eager to marry again. "My life's well organized, Mike. Hank's death didn't change that. I've had my bakery shop here in Lepanto for five years. I had my interests and Hank had his," she'd said.

Mike found her a contented woman, which he'd always known Georgia wasn't. She was eager to have a man in her life. He didn't find himself reluctant to speak of his children since Colleen often talked about her daughter, Maureen.

"You'll see what I mean about Maureen when you meet her, Mike. She's having dinner this evening with her young man's family."

"And how old is she?" Mike had quizzed her.

"Seventeen."

"And you allow her to be courted by a young man?"

She laughed. "But of course I do, Mike. Hank was courting me when I was seventeen. Think back, Mike—how old was your wife when you were courting her?"

He could only grin and nod his head.

They'd had a lovely visit for almost two hours after dinner but Mike knew he should take his leave. Colleen had to get up at five in the morning to get to her shop. The clock was striking nine, so she was probably ready to go to bed.

At the door, he'd thanked her for a delightful evening and asked if he could escort her to the square dance next Saturday night. But he didn't even try to kiss her. He was just happy to have her accept his invitation.

When Wednesday morning arrived, Drake was there at the appointed hour. Misty's meeting with him was brief but just those few moments were enough for her to go about her day feeling very happy.

Her heart had gone out to little Lavinia since their visit on Saturday night. She had told Misty more than once that she didn't think Lucky liked her as much as he had. "He likes Jeff better than me now, Misty," she'd lamented.

"Honey, Jeff's been over there more than you have," Misty had said, trying to soothe her.

She wouldn't have dared to tell her what Drake confided to her when they'd had a moment of privacy after he'd brought Jeff home Wednesday afternoon. "I let Lucky out just before bedtime as I always do last night and that devil didn't come back. He hasn't been home all day today, Misty."

"Did you caution Jeff not to say anything to Lavinia?"

"Oh, God, yes. I rode around the countryside today but there was no sign of him. I don't know where else to search."

"Maybe he'll find his way home, Drake. I hope so."

Thursday morning when Drake came to pick Jeff up she asked if Lucky had shown up but Drake shook his head. "No sign of him yet."

He had the same answer when he brought Jeff home that afternoon at four-thirty. Misty could see that Drake was upset about his dog's disappearance. She wanted to do something to lift his spirits, so she'd baked an extra blackberry cobbler and an extra pan of cornbread. She'd also prepared a crock from the huge pot of beans and hamhocks for him to take home.

That evening Drake sat in the kitchen eating Misty's beans and cornbread when he heard a scratching on his back door. He leaped up from the table with wild anticipation. Had that old rascal decided to come home?

There was Lucky looking a little worse from wear and a bit gaunt as though he hadn't eaten for a while. "Well, Lucky—what kind of mischief have you been up to? You look like bloody hell."

Misty had left big chunks of ham on the hocks so he gave Lucky that while he finished his dinner. But Lucky was still famished so he cut some slices off of one of his cured hams and put it down.

As he cleared away his table and washed his dirty dishes he knew one thing: he wasn't going through this again. He would have a fence installed around his front and back yards. Lucky was going to have his wings clipped.

At least he was going to have some good news to tell

Misty in the morning. The next day Lucky seemed to have no desire to roam.

Drake was pleased with the house he was having built. It was painted white on the outside and Bigelow was a fine mason so there was a nice woodburning fireplace in the small front room. Drake rather doubted that the three men would need another week to complete the place. All the rooms had been divided off, the walls were now being painted, and the floors were being varnished. As fast as the three of them worked, he could see the little house completed in another four or five days.

Misty was delighted to hear that Lucky had returned home. Drake suspected that Lucky had found himself a lady friend nearby and that was where he'd been for a couple of nights.

A few days later his suspicions were confirmed by a neighbor. Ben Murphy rode over to introduce himself and tell Drake that he'd seen his big black dog around his place for a couple of days.

"My female is a collie. Do you want me to let you know when the pups come along? They might prove to be an interesting lot," he told Drake.

Without any hesitation, Drake said, "I'd like to have one. I was worried crazy about that rascal."

"You've got one, Dalton. I'll let you know. I apologize for not coming over sooner to welcome you to our community. Got to tell you you're doing a hell of a job over here," Murphy told him.

"Well, thank you, Ben. I appreciate that. I've got a long way to go but I'll get there sooner or later. Glad we got to meet today."

"Crazy that it had to be through our dogs," Ben said and laughed. "Guess it don't matter how it happened as long as it happened, Drake."

"Stranger things have happened to get people acquainted with one another."

"You just let me know if I can be of any help. I've lived

here in Arkansas all my life. I'll be glad to tell you anything I can about this new land of yours.''

Drake thanked him. He was the first neighbor he'd met and was about Drake's age, give or take a few years.

Ben Murphy rode away from the old Benoit place impressed by the Englishman, whom he had expected to find reserved and cool. That was what he'd always heard about the English, but it wasn't true about Drake Dalton. He was a warm, outgoing fellow—Ben felt they could become close as they got better acquainted.

That afternoon when he'd ridden his mare back to his place, he'd told his pretty wife Celine that he liked the Englishman very much. "We'll have to have him over here for dinner one night. There's nothing snobbish about him, Celine."

Ben told her Drake wanted one of Princess's pups. He continued to talk about all the things he had already done over there at the old Benoit land.

For people who measured the seasons by the number of daylight hours, there was no question that autumn had arrived in Arkansas. The days were shorter and the nights were longer. Darkness descended almost an hour earlier than it had a month and a half ago. Misty was very aware of it when her pa arrived home and the sun was sinking so much lower in the sky.

The week had gone by swiftly for Misty and she knew why. She'd seen Drake twice a day for the last three days. It was a pleasant week and everything had run smoothly. She found it hard to believe that tomorrow was Saturday once again.

Her pa told her during Friday night supper that he'd be with Colleen at the square dance the next night. Misty was glad to know of his plans.

She also knew that Jeff was going to be a happy young

man this Saturday. He'd worked an extra day for Drake, so he'd have money in his pockets.

When Drake brought Jeff home Friday afternoon, he asked Misty, "Suppose we might do the same thing again this Saturday afternoon?"

She gave him a sly little smile, "I think it can be arranged. Pa's going to the square dance again tomorrow night."

"Perfect! I'll bring Jeff home early tomorrow then."

"Pa will probably leave by four-thirty because he's going to have dinner before the dance," Misty told him.

"Well then, I'll return about five then."

The Walters went into Crowley Saturday morning instead of Saturday afternoon. Geneva wanted to get some canning done that afternoon. "Don't know what it is, Ed, but I can't seem to get it all done like I used to," Geneva declared.

Ed laughed and patted her hand. "Neither do I, Geneva. This old foot of mine is not back to normal. Guess we don't heal as fast as we get older."

"Maybe we should have kept Jeff on longer to help you, Ed."

"Well, it's a little late for that now 'cause he's working for that Mr. Dalton. I've been missing the little fellow."

"Got to get over there and see Misty this next week and see how everything's going with them," Geneva said as they neared the outskirts of Crowley.

As was their usual routine, Ed let Geneva off at the mercantile while he went on to the grain store. After she'd bought the things she needed she went next door to get Ed's favorite tobacco, then met her husband at the meat market and grocery store.

They were going out the door when they ran into Samantha Clay. "Well, how are you two? Don't tell me you're heading for home already. I'd like to have a visit with you, Geneva. Haven't done that for weeks, it seems."

"I know, Samantha, but I fear I can't visit today. We have to get home with these groceries—I've got canning to do."

Samantha was disappointed as she was so anxious to tell Geneva about Misty Bennett.

Drake brought Jeff home around midday after he'd been paid his wages. Drake asked him what he wanted to shop for today when they went to town. Jeff quickly responded by telling him that he was going to save all this money.

"I see. So then we really don't have anything to go into town for this afternoon, eh?" Drake asked.

"Not for me, sir. I—I don't want to spend any of my money."

"Well, then, let's surprise Misty and Lavinia. I'll come over at five as I told Misty and we'll go over to my house and have a backyard picnic. What do you think?"

"Gosh, sir—that sounds like a lot of fun!"

"All right—we'll do it! Don't say anything—we'll just surprise them," Drake said and grinned down at him.

"Won't say a word, Mr. Dalton. I promise."

Misty had to admit she was surprised by their early arrival—Drake didn't stay long after he'd delivered Jeff, but he'd told her he'd be back at five.

From the Bennetts' place he guided his wagon into Crowley. Any picnic had to have lemonade, so he went directly to the drug store. He sent the clerk into a frenzy when he walked in and ordered two gallons.

The young lady looked at him in disbelief. "Are you serious, mister?"

"Very serious, miss. Can you supply that much?"

"I can but it's going to take some time to make all that up," she stammered.

"Very good. I have some other shopping to do, but I'll be back."

With an amused smile he sauntered down the street. He knew that the rumor would probably circulate around the town that the Englishman had to be a little crazy to want so much lemonade.

He went to the grocery store to purchase eggs, a dozen ears of corn, and a large crock of churned butter before he returned to the drug store.

When he left Crowley, Drake had all the fixings for a fine picnic. He knew how to boil a kettle of eggs and corn. Oscar had brought over a huge platter of fried chicken this morning along with a big chocolate cake.

He already knew the perfect picnic spot out in the back yard. There was a tall mimosa as well as an old table he'd moved out of the house when he'd first arrived.

It was a little past two when he returned home. Once he'd unloaded the wagon, he realized he was hungry, so he took one piece of chicken from the platter to munch on as he fired up the cookstove to heat the coffee.

He went out to put the tablecloth on the wooden table. He had to use a firm hand with Lucky, who playfully tugged at it and tried to pull it off.

Lucky had not been too happy the last few days since the picket fence had been installed to enclose the front and back yards. Drake felt no guilt at all since Lucky had plenty of room to stretch his legs, and the fence would keep him out of trouble. The sad look on Lucky's face when he closed the gate didn't impress Drake at all.

He boiled two dozen eggs, then shucked the corn so it was ready to be put into boiling water after he'd picked up Misty.

He took a bath, shaved, and put on his blue shirt, leaving it unbuttoned in a casual way. Then he put on his dark blue pants and the fine black leather boots he'd brought from England.

He thought about all the clothes he'd left behind, but they would not have been suitable for life here. Yet, he'd always liked the fine tailored pants and linen shirts he'd purchased in London. There was nowhere in Crowley to find such clothing.

He figured he'd have to go as far as Memphis to find a decent haberdashery.

A few moments before five, he guided his wagon down the drive toward the Bennetts' place. He just hoped Misty would not be disappointed that they were not going into Crowley.

Mike Bennett was already on his way to Colleen's house. Misty had brushed Lavinia's hair and got her dressed and Jeff had his bath and was dressed a short time after their pa had left. The two of them sat out on the front porch swing. Misty put on the paisley dress Geneva had made for her, then brushed her hair, allowing it to flow loose around her shoulders. When she put on the earrings Drake had bought her, she dabbed some toilet water behind her ears.

She wore his locket around her neck and also wore the sandals. She was convinced that Drake was the most generous man in the world when she thought about all he had done for her and her brother and sister.

As he had promised, Drake's wagon came rolling into the drive promptly at five. He picked up his three passengers and as he leaped up on the wagon seat beside Misty, his right hand reached out for hers and they exchanged smiles.

Jeff and Lavinia were in the back of the wagon laughing and chattering, so Drake took advantage of the moment to tell Misty how pretty she looked.

"Drake, you always make me feel so good," she said and smiled at him.

"That's my intention, love. We're not going to town. Jeff and I made other plans this morning. We're going to have an old-fashioned picnic in my backyard. I hope you're not disappointed."

"It sounds wonderful. Such a perfect evening. The summer heat is gone, so it'll be so pleasant in your backyard."

Drake leaned over to whisper in her ear, "Jeff told me

he wanted to save the salary I paid him today so he had no reason to go to town. Now, I can't say what the young man has on his mind, but he obviously doesn't want to spend it. Just wanted you to know, Misty.''

Misty didn't know what was churning in Jeff's mind but something was and she was glad Drake had told her about it.

Chapter 17

Misty realized as she sat on one of Drake's wooden benches that this was another first for her. She, Jeff, and Lavinia had never been on a picnic before. What a wonderful idea it was!

Lavinia and Jeff were sitting on the blanket Drake had laid on the ground, Lucky between them.

They were already enjoying a glass of lemonade as they waited for Drake to bring out the steaming corn and the crock of butter.

"Come on, kids—that's what a picnic is all about. Everyone just helps themselves to anything they want," he called to Jeff and Lavinia. But he suggested that they sit on the bench while they were eating or Lucky might just help himself to their chicken.

Misty wondered what had caused her to be lucky enough to meet a man like Drake Dalton. He was so kind and generous. This picnic he'd arranged had taken so much effort on his part.

Drake said, "Thank Rachel for all this good fried

chicken—but I can take a bow for the boiled eggs and corn."

Misty giggled, "You see—you can cook more than just bacon, ham, and eggs."

They sat in the yard as twilight gathered and a light breeze wafted through the tall trees. Sounds of the night began to echo in the nearby woods. A turtle dove's cooing and the calls of a couple of whippoorwills reached them from the distance.

Darkness finally drove them inside. Drake lit the lamps in the front room and kitchen as Jeff and Lavinia pitched in to help gather up all the dishes.

"They're damn good kids, Misty. I give you a lot of the credit for that since you've been the one raising them since your mother died."

"My mother really deserves the credit for that, Drake. She was a very loving mother. Her entire life was devoted to her family. She was a very unselfish woman."

All too quickly, the evening came to an end, and once again, Drake had to be satisfied with a few stolen kisses. But he was a patient man—at least, where Misty was concerned.

As they rolled down the rutted dirt road, he leaned over and whispered in Misty's ear. "Somehow—someway I'm going to get you all to myself."

"It will happen, Drake. It must," she said and smiled sweetly at him.

When Jeff and Lavinia rushed into the house, Drake managed to steal another couple of kisses before he finally started back home.

It was midnight when Mike returned. He'd had another wonderful night with Colleen. Each time he was around her, he was more impressed. They had a great time together, constantly laughing and talking, but there was something about her that demanded he behave like a gentleman.

He guessed what it was—Colleen was a lady and she expected him to treat her like one. She was also spunky enough to demand it.

But she was also a very thoughtful, generous woman. When he'd taken her home, before they'd said their goodbyes she presented him with a tray of delectable pastries—cupcakes, cookies, and a fruit tart. She'd smiled and said as she'd handed him the tray, "I know how children love sweets. I thought they might enjoy these."

"That's—that's mighty nice of you, Colleen. We'll all enjoy them. Dare I hope that you'll spend next Saturday night with me? I've enjoyed being with you so much," he said and honestly meant it.

"I'd love to, Mike," she replied. "Since we both have children, perhaps it might be nice to get together for a Sunday night dinner. I'd like to meet your three. If I can keep Maureen home some Sunday night, you could meet her."

"That sounds good to me. I've got three good kids. I come to know that more and more all the time, Colleen."

"I'm sure they are, Mike."

She walked with him to the front door. Mike would have loved to kiss her good night but something restrained him. He didn't want to chance anything with this relationship.

She very graciously thanked him for the evening. "I'll look forward to Saturday night. I've a wonderful idea, Mike. Perhaps you could bring your children over here for Sunday dinner. I could let you know Saturday night."

"That's fine, Colleen."

Mike put the tray in the wagon by him and urged his team into motion. Never during all the time he'd been with Georgia had she made a nice gesture toward his kids as Colleen had tonight.

He was just sorry it had taken him so long to see what a cold-hearted bitch she was.

Come next Saturday night, he intended to bring Colleen a nice gift. All the way home he thought about what would be right. All women liked toilet water, he guessed, but there were so many different fragrances. What would he choose for her?

Colleen reminded him of the sweet scent of lilacs in full bloom. She'd looked so fetching tonight in her lavender frock with ruffled neckline and sleeves.

She looked fragile, but he knew she wasn't after all the talks they'd had. She was sharp and had a very practical head on her shoulders. Her bakery shop would not have been thriving this long if she hadn't been.

She was as light as a feather when they'd danced. The top of her head barely came to the top of his shoulder.

He might not have been ready to admit it to himself yet, but Mike Bennett was definitely smitten by the petite, black-haired lady.

Gossip flowed freely between the two small hamlets of Crowley and Lepanto. Georgia Gordon soon heard about her old lover's new lady.

She'd settled for Cyrus Heller after Mike had quit coming around, but times with Cyrus were rather boring. So the news made Georgia seethe with jealousy. As the week went on, her curiosity got the best of her. She got in her fancy gig one Thursday afternoon to travel over to Lepanto. Her destination was Colleen's Sweet Shop. She wanted the see this lady who'd caught Mike Bennett's eye.

Colleen had already put in a very long day. She'd arrived at her shop at five that morning to start baking all the pastries for a wedding in Lepanto on Friday evening. She was thinking how glad she would be to get home.

It appeared she was due to have one more customer. She looked up to see a fancy-dressed lady coming into her shop. Colleen thought she knew every lady in Lepanto, but she didn't recognize this one.

Colleen greeted her warmly and said, "Good afternoon, ma'am. May I help you?"

"I'm not quite sure what I'd like," Georgia replied.

SWEET SEDUCTION

Colleen got the impression she was scrutinizing *her* more than she was the pastries. She suggested various items, but Georgia finally said she'd take a dozen fruit tarts. As she was paying, Georgia announced, "I'm Georgia Gordon. I live over in Crowley."

"Well, I didn't think I'd seen you in my shop before." Colleen introduced herself and packaged the tarts. Georgia left, concluding that her name had made no impact on the woman at all.

Georgia felt insulted that the woman had not recognized her name, so she went home feeling more frustrated than ever.

Colleen was very pretty—there was no denying that. In her simple little cotton frock and white apron, Georgia could see she had a very nice figure.

But what would have really boggled Georgia's mind was what a perfect gentlemen Mike Bennett had been with Colleen Carver the last two weeks. She would have found it very hard to believe that he hadn't even tried to kiss her.

It never dawned on Georgia that she'd never demanded that Mike respect her. She'd flaunted herself brazenly and Mike had responded as any red-blooded man would have.

Misty certainly had no baking to do for a couple of days. This Mrs. Carver surely had to be a very nice lady to have sent such a tray of pastries. She certainly knew one thing: her father was much kinder now than when he was courting Georgia Gordon.

When Drake brought Jeff home on Thursday afternoon, he told Misty, "I'll have nothing more for Jeff to do after this week. The house is done. Right now, I'm just having him clean up the grounds. Actually, I have nothing for him do on Saturday."

"So tell him, Drake. Jeff will understand."

"But I'm selfish. I'll miss seeing you now that I won't be picking Jeff up," he confessed.

"I know, Drake. I've been doing a lot of thinking about us. I'm tired of living a lie as I've been doing with pa. He might be more reasonable now than he was six months ago," she said, looking up at him.

"Shall we dare to confront him? I leave it up to you—I'm ready anytime," he assured her. "My only hesitation has been my concern for you."

She sighed. "Oh, Drake—I don't think you know how much you've done to change my whole life. I'm ready to face Pa in order to be with you. I hate playing silly games."

"Then let's do it, Misty," he declared, bending down to kiss her, not caring if Jeff or Lavinia saw them. Like Misty, he was tired of silly games!

As he prepared to take his leave, he grinned down at her. "I'd like to take you to that square dance your pa's been going to. I don't even know how to do a bloody square dance but I could sure learn."

Misty laughed. "Drake, we'd make a most awkward pair then—I've never square danced."

"But love, I'll bet we'd do fine. I dare you to try it with me once," he challenged.

She smiled impishly and her green eyes sparkled teasingly. "Drake Dalton, I've already done so many things with you for the first time that I suppose I could try dancing."

His broad chest swelled with a pride—he was glad he had been the first man in her life and he never wanted her to regret it.

With a certain determination in her voice, she said, "I'm going to tell Pa tonight that you've invited me to the square dance, Drake."

"You just do that, love!" he said as he prepared to leave.

Once she had made up her mind, she was amazingly calm about facing her pa. Misty knew many things now that she had not known six months earlier. She was not a child—

she'd left that stage of her life. And now she was no sweet, innocent virgin. Drake had changed all that. She had become bolder. She was a young woman ready to have a beau if she chose to do so.

During the next hour, she puttered around the kitchen putting the finishing touches on their dinner. She'd decided not to ask his permission; she was just going to tell him she was going to the dance with Drake Dalton.

That was exactly how she did it, right at the table while the four of them were finishing supper. Mike was unprepared for her startling announcement. Lavinia and Jeff reacted with excitement, which helped her cause.

When Mike finally found his voice after almost choking on a morsel of food, he glared across the table. "Obviously, there's things been going on I didn't know about."

"Yes, Pa—that's true! But I've no intention of going on this way. I've accepted Drake's invitation to go to the dance. He's an honorable man—Jeff can tell you, if you don't believe me."

Mike could find no argument to give her. He also remembered Colleen's daughter had a beau. Colleen even allowed her to accompany him out in his buggy alone.

To her delighted amazement, he gave her no argument. If his daughter was to be courted, then why not this wealthy Englishman? He was the most sought-after bachelor in Crowley or Lepanto. Misty had caught his eye, so a certain fatherly pride swelled within him.

"Well, Misty, you'll have a chance to meet Colleen Saturday night," he remarked as he prepared to leave the table.

"I'll look forward to that, too, Pa," she said and smiled as she watched him depart.

Mike left for the mills Friday morning and Drake picked Jeff up about an hour later. Cockily, she announced to Drake that she had told her pa. "I didn't ask. I just told him I was going to the dance with you tomorrow night. He gave me no fuss. I couldn't believe it!"

Drake threw his head back and laughed heartily. "What bloody luck!" He picked her up in his arms and whirled her around, not caring that Jeff was observing them.

He lowered her back to the floor and told her he'd see her later as he and Jeff jumped up in the wagon. As they were rolling down the dirt road, Jeff was wearing a big grin. "Mr. Dalton, are you sweet on my sister?"

Drake looked over and smiled. "I'm very sweet on your sister, Jeff. I trust you don't object."

"No, sir—I don't object at all. I think it's great."

He gave Jeff a comradely pat on the shoulder and told him he was glad to hear that. When they arrived at the house Lucky rushed out to meet them, but now that Bigelow had built a fence around the place, Lucky could no longer roam over the countryside.

He gave Jeff instructions about his chores for the day and then got back in the wagon to head for town.

He felt he was soaring to the heavens. He was finally going to be able to court Misty, and he wanted to make tomorrow night special for her.

Chapter 18

Misty was in the gayest of spirits. She breezed about, getting her household chores done and putting a huge pot of beans on her cookstove so she'd have something for their supper tonight and tomorrow night.

She'd already decided which dress she'd wear to the dance. It was not one of the newer dresses that Mrs. Walters had made—it was the emerald green one Geneva had made for her about this time last year for the holiday season. It was her fanciest frock, and Misty felt it would be so perfect with the pretty earrings Drake had bought for her. And the sweetheart neckline would display the locket—she wanted to look especially pretty for Drake tomorrow night.

As she usually did on Saturday morning, she would wash her and Lavinia's hair. Lately, Jeff had seen to the washing of his own hair. That had started about the time he'd begun working for Drake.

Drake spent a lot of time in Crowley that morning. He went to the only furniture store in Crowley to purchase furnishings for the foreman's house, but he couldn't find all the things he needed, so he decided to ride over to Lepanto. He was sorry he hadn't gone there first. The furniture store was nicer and he was able to buy a cookstove and the other pieces to furnish the place. They agreed to deliver them the next morning. Joe Harrington, who owned the store, was delighted; he hadn't made that large a sale in weeks.

Drake took time to saunter down the one main street. It was similar to the one in Crowley, but he found the shops were nicer. The jewelry store had a much finer selection. He couldn't resist buying a lovely gold bangle bracelet that he thought would look perfect on Misty's dainty wrist. He also purchased a small locket for Lavinia.

He took time to walk through the mercantile and bought Jeff a shirt, which would be the first store-bought shirt he had ever owned. The three shirts he had were all made by Geneva over the last two years. His mother had always made his shirts, but he'd grown out of them.

It was almost noon by the time Drake left Lepanto. He decided he would take Jeff home early and give him his wages. He really had no more chores for him, but that didn't mean he wasn't going to spend some time with the young man. He still planned to teach him to ride a horse and take him hunting in the nearby woods. He might just buy Jeff a rifle in a few weeks.

When he arrived home, he called out to Jeff to come in the house and take a break. While they sat at the table having their midday snack, Drake said, "I'm paying you your wages today, Jeff, 'cause I can't come over to get you in the morning. I've got furniture being delivered so I've got to stick around."

"That's fine, Mr. Dalton. Truth is, I've got all the chores almost done."

"You're a hard worker, Jeff, and you move fast. Just because I've no more work for you doesn't mean we're not going to see one another."

With a big smile Jeff said, "I'll miss not coming over here. I'd miss seeing old Lucky."

"You'll still get to see Lucky," he assured the boy as they got up from the table. He told Jeff that when he finished whatever chore he was doing he could call it a day.

An hour later, Jeff came back through the kitchen door to announce he had finished his job. Drake handed him his wages and also gave him the shirt he'd purchased for him.

He thanked Drake, saying, "This is sure a fancy shirt, Mr. Dalton. Never had a store-bought shirt before. Mrs. Walters has been making one for me every now and then."

"You've spoken of the Walters so much. I must meet them. They sound like real fine people," Drake remarked as they boarded the wagon.

"Finest people I've ever known," Jeff declared. Jeff went home feeling rich with the salary in his pocket and the wages he had left from last week's pay.

A half-hour later, Jeff was home and Drake had left with a crock of beans for his supper. Misty had also sliced up some of the pork roast she'd baked that afternoon.

Drake told her he would pick her up the next evening at seven. Misty said, "I'll be ready, Drake."

Misty found herself still amazed that this was all actually happening. She did not know that she had Colleen Carver to thank for her father's mellow manner. When Mike learned that Colleen allowed her seventeen-year-old daughter to have a beau it influenced his thinking. He thought of Colleen as a very wise woman.

Saturday was a busy day around the Bennett house. Mike went to the mills in a happy mood—he was going to see Colleen tonight. Misty got busy washing their hair and Jeff took advantage of not having to work for Drake to go down to the riverbank to do a little fishing.

He didn't even make it back to the house for a midday meal. It was a lazy autumn day, with a bright sun shining and a soft breeze blowing. He leaned against a tree trunk and fell asleep.

It was well past two when he finally woke from his nap and fished for another two hours. Misty had already told him she wouldn't fry up any of his catch for supper. He put his fish in a big zinc tub of water in the backyard when he got back to the house. He'd caught four catfish and a couple of perch.

Mike had come home from the mills and unloaded the things he'd bought at the grocery store. He'd also made another stop by the mercantile to purchase a bottle of lilac toilet water for Colleen and a new shirt to wear to the dance.

He left the house two hours earlier than Misty as he was having supper with Colleen. His wagon was pulled out to the road at five.

Misty called out that Jeff's and Lavinia's supper was ready. "I've got to start getting dressed," she said. She was too excited to sit down to eat with them. She'd nibbled on a slice of the pork roast and gulped three spoonfuls of the beans.

She'd already had her bath and seen that Lavinia took hers. She tried to style her hair so Drake's earrings would show. She finally decided to pull the sides up and let the rest fall down her back.

It was a very attractive hairstyle for Misty—it enhanced the loveliness of her face and she was pleased with the effect.

When Drake's earrings were in place, she dabbed his toilet water on her ears and throat. She realized as she sat at her dressing table that all the luxuries she'd enjoyed the last few months had been provided by Drake, with the exception of the dresses Geneva Walters had made for her.

By the time she had her green frock on, she had to admit she was very pleased with how she looked. With her little green reticule, she was ready for Drake's arrival.

She was happy it was Drake she was going to her first

dance with. She could not have imagined going with anyone else.

She'd seen the new shirt Drake had bought for Jeff, so it didn't surprise her when he came bearing a gift for Lavinia, who was thrilled by the little locket.

Misty was not given the gold bangle bracelet until they were in his buggy, ready to pull out of the Bennetts' drive. He slipped it on her wrist—it looked perfect.

Misty admired the beauty of it. Her green eyes gazed up at him as she stammered, "Oh, Drake—you're always doing so much for me, Lavinia, and Jeff. I can do so little for you."

He leaned over and gave her a gentle kiss. "Ah, love—you've done so much more than you can ever know! You've been the best thing ever to come into my life. I needed someone exactly like you, Misty. I was a very disillusioned man when I arrived in Arkansas, but I'll tell you about that later. Tonight, we're going to have a grand time! Even though you've never been to a dance before and I have no bloody idea how one square dances," he said and laughed.

"Well, that makes me feel better."

"We'll be fine, love!"

"I know," she said and smiled.

That was what made Misty so rare. Drake knew she did trust him and he also knew he would never do anything to betray that trust. He'd never felt that way about any woman. Misty had a way of pulling a very protective feeling out of him. Drake liked the feeling.

When they arrived at the huge building where the square dance was being held, the fiddles and guitars were already resounding in the vacant lot where buggies and wagons gathered. It seemed the people inside were already enjoying themselves—laughter could be heard as Drake came around to Misty's side of the buggy.

Mike Bennett and Colleen arrived only a short time ahead of them. Both were in a very lighthearted mood. Mike had just enjoyed another one of Colleen's dinners—this pretty lady was a superb cook.

Colleen had not had a man bring her a gift in a long time; she felt it was awfully sweet and thoughtful. What was so surprising was that it happened to be her favorite fragrance although he had no way of knowing it.

Mike felt proud to lead Colleen into the gathering. She was a most attractive lady and she acted like one, which impressed him.

There was a large crowd gathered—the dancers were already whirling about the floor, so Mike and Colleen didn't hesitate to join them.

Misty was a little awestruck as they entered and she saw all the couples moving so swiftly. The ladies' full skirts whirled out as the gentlemen swung them around.

When Drake looked down to see the wide-eyed look on her face, he could read her thoughts. She was afraid she'd never be able to do the dances. While he'd never done this kind of dancing, he had been considered a fine dancer in London. He had no doubt he could learn this dance, too.

"Come, let's go over and have a seat. You see, there are several couples just sitting at the tables observing the other dancers. So that's what we'll do for a while."

Misty was more than agreeable to that suggestion. As they made their way to one of the small tables, her green eyes scanned the crowd for her father. He was easy to spot because he was so tall.

Drake left her at the table for a few moments to get the two of them some fruit punch being served by two ladies at a small refreshment table.

There was a pause in the music and Mike and Colleen left the floor to sit and catch their breath. Mike spotted his lovely golden-haired daughter immediately and also recognized the tall, handsome Englishman, Dalton, who'd come to the mills where he worked some weeks ago.

Mike realized just how grown up his daughter was. No

wonder Dalton was attracted to her. She was the prettiest girl in Poinsett County!

He guided Colleen over to a chair so she could relax a moment before he took her over to meet his daughter. She'd laughed, unashamed to confess, "There was a time I wouldn't have been so winded."

"That makes two of us, Colleen."

That was another quality about Colleen that Mike found appealing—he could be relaxed around her. He sure couldn't say the same about Georgia Gordon.

"Colleen, my daughter's here. I'd like you to meet her," he said after they'd rested a few minutes.

"Oh, I'd love to. I've looked forward to that ever since you told me she was going to be here tonight," she said, her eyes sparkling.

He led her over to the table where Misty was seated with Dalton. Her back was turned to them so she had no inkling that her father was approaching.

Suddenly they were beside the table and her father was greeting her. Misty looked up to exclaim, "Pa—I've been looking for you."

Dalton rose from his chair. This was his first face-to-face encounter with Mike Bennett and he wasn't sure what his response would be.

"Pa, this is Drake Dalton," Misty said.

"Nice to meet you, Mr. Bennett. Please join us," Drake suggested.

Mike introduced the two of them to Colleen and they took the two empty chairs at the table.

Misty instantly warmed to Colleen. Maybe it was because she was small like her mother or maybe it was because of the genuine tone of her voice when she said how anxious she'd been to meet her.

"I've a daughter about your age, Misty. My, how nice it would have been if she and her young man had come to the dance tonight," she said before she turned to Drake. "I hear you arrived here just a few months ago, Mr. Dalton?"

"Yes, ma'am. I came here from England to take over the old Benoit estate."

Mike looked over at Misty and asked, "Well, what do you think about square dancing?"

"I—I think I'll probably stumble all over myself out there is what I think, Pa," she admitted. All of them began to laugh.

"Oh, no—Misty, you'll be dancing with ease before the night is over," Colleen assured her. She looked in Drake's direction to ask him if he'd ever square danced.

"I've done a lot of dancing, but never square dancing, Mrs. Carver," he replied.

"Well, we'll take care of that, won't we, Mike? We'll just get over here in a corner and do a little practicing," she declared. "Think I'd like a cup of that punch, Mike."

When Mike rose to get Colleen and himself some punch, Drake accompanied him, leaving Misty and Colleen at the table together.

Colleen was so outgoing she never found it a problem to talk to anyone. She didn't hesitate to tell Misty how beautiful she was. "You must have inherited your mother's fair hair and lovely green eyes."

"Yes, I did."

"Then she had to be a beautiful lady," Colleen said and smiled warmly.

"She was, Mrs. Carver. May I say that I think *you're* very beautiful," Misty declared earnestly.

For another few minutes after Drake and Mike returned to the table, the four of them sat sipping on the punch and had a lighthearted chat.

Drake found that he liked this vivacious woman who had put Misty so at ease. He was very perceptive to her moods, so he knew Misty warmed to her. He also got the impression that Misty was more relaxed around her father than she had been in the past. Somehow, he was sure Misty had Colleen Carver to thank for his change in attitude. In fact, he had to believe that she might have been the influence that had allowed him and Misty to be together.

Colleen's twinkling eyes darted over in his direction as she asked, "Well, Mr. Dalton—are you ready for me to step on your toes?"

With a teasing glint in his eyes, he told her, "Only if you'll call me Drake."

She giggled softly. "Then come on, Drake. I suspect it'll be a short practice session."

Mike took charge of his pretty daughter. With a lot of apprehension, Misty followed her father.

Misty discovered that her father was a very good teacher and she found herself having fun as her father put her through the motions of the dance.

Mike found her as light and agile as her mother had been—Misty had a natural grace so she quickly responded as he guided her.

A half hour later the four of them were out on the floor having a grand time!

Chapter 19

Saturday afternoon when Cyrus came to call on Georgia, she pretended to feel ill rather than go on their usual perfunctory outing and then to his home for dinner. She was glad he didn't wait around when he found her still in her dressing gown.

Georgia had planned it that way and made no effort to be dressed when he arrived at two in the afternoon. It worked and Cyrus got back into his gig and drove away.

As soon as he was gone, Georgia rushed out of her parlor and went to her bedroom to get dressed. She was going into town to see Lilly. She wondered if Lilly was as bored with old Henry as she was with Cyrus Heller.

By three, she was in her own gig going toward Crowley. Lilly greeted her eagerly at the door. "Well, Georgia—this is a real nice surprise. Figured you were with Cyrus," she remarked as she guided Georgia into her parlor.

"Oh, God, Lilly—just couldn't go through it again today. I wondered if you might be in the same mood as I am."

"I am, Georgia. I won't lie to you. Henry is a nice little

fellow, but bless his heart, he's not very lively either. But maybe I have a solution for both of us. I also had to excuse myself from being with Henry this weekend because my nephew arrived yesterday to spend the weekend with me before he travels on to Memphis tomorrow.''

Georgia was feeling a little crestfallen hearing that Lilly's nephew was there, but Lilly quickly told her about their plans for that evening. "Come with us, Georgia. We'll pick you up at seven. It could be fun. I thought Harvey would enjoy going out instead of just sitting around the house. We're going to the square dance.''

"Oh, Lord Lilly—I haven't danced for years," Georgia said.

"So? We can always sit and watch. We'd have a few laughs and see people we both know. Beats sitting at home, Georgia. Who knows? You might find yourself out on the floor before the evening is over.''

At first, Georgia wouldn't commit herself, but she finally relented. She stayed and visited with Lilly until her nephew, Harvey Walker, returned from the barber shop.

He was what Georgia would call a very eligible young bachelor—a good-looking young man with sandy-colored hair and busy blue eyes.

Georgia knew that if he stayed too long in Crowley he'd have a lot of the local girls flaunting themselves at him. But a Crowley miss was not what Harvey was looking for. He was merely traveling through on his way to Memphis. He lived in Natchez, where Lilly's brother owned racing horses.

Georgia understood why Lilly was trying to plot something to add a little spice to the last evening he'd be here.

She bade the two of them goodbye and got into her gig. It was almost five when she arrived back home. She immediately went to her armoire to see what she wanted to wear that evening.

She wanted something bright and gay so she chose a rich blue gown which was actually a little too fancy for a square dance. Her dangling sapphire earrings were hardly in order for this kind of gathering.

As soon as she'd halfheartedly nibbled at the dinner her cook had served her, she went to her bedroom to get dressed. By six she was powdered and perfumed.

She went to her parlor to wait for Lilly and her nephew to arrive. While she waited, she poured herself two very generous drinks of her favorite whiskey.

She recalled how she and Mike would sit in the parlor to enjoy this whiskey for an hour or so after dinner before they'd go into her bedroom to make passionate love. She missed those times—there was no denying it!

She didn't have much hope of this evening proving very lively so she filled Frank's old silver flask with her good bourbon and put it inside her blue velvet reticule.

Lilly and Harvey appeared promptly and the dance was going strong when the three of them arrived. It was a lively crowd and, as Lilly had told her, it was better than sitting home all alone.

She had been at the table with Lilly and her nephew long when she spied Mike's daughter out on the dance floor with that dashing Englishman.

She had to admit she could see why he had no time to spend for her—he obviously had his eyes on the breathtakingly beautiful Misty. She had that look of freshness and youth that Georgia had lost twenty years ago. She also had to admit that a passionate woman had only to look at Dalton to become tittilated.

Her eyes stayed on them until they finished the dance and then followed them over to a table.

What she saw there was enough to make her get out her flask to doctor up the fruit punch. Mike Bennett with that woman he was courting!

Apparently, there had been some changes in his life. He'd given her the impression that he was a very strict father, but Misty was here with him tonight in the company of Drake Dalton.

That rather boggled Georgia's mind. The longer she sat there, the more she seethed. By the time they'd been there about an hour, she'd pulled out the flask twice.

Lilly had been too busy scanning the room and talking with both Georgia and Harvey to notice, but Harvey had seen how Georgia was lacing her punch.

He leaned over to ask her, "Mrs. Gordon, want to try one with me?"

Georgia smiled, "That's mighty sweet of you, Harvey, but it's been too long since I've whirled around the floor like that."

He then turned to Lilly. "What about you, Aunt Lilly?"

"Sugar, I fear I'm in the same fix. You go get yourself some pretty little thing to dance with. See those three young girls standing over there by the refreshment table? Bet any of them would be thrilled to dance with you," Lilly assured him.

Harvey wasn't the bashful sort, so he excused himself to do as his aunt had suggested and quickly secured a dancing partner.

It was not until Mike and Drake went over to the refreshment stand that Mike spied Georgia sitting with Lilly. He moaned, "Oh, God!"

"Something the matter, Mr. Bennett?"

"Fear so, if she spots me. Just saw Georgia Gordon sitting over there. Hell, never expected her to come here. I—I courted her for a few months before I started seeing Colleen. She can be an overbearing witch," Mike mumbled.

Drake could agree with him. He considered her a brazen, pushy woman.

"I just don't want her making a scene in front of Colleen," Mike said as they started back to the table.

"Mrs. Carver is certainly a nice lady. Misty seems to like her," Drake remarked.

"Well, she sure didn't like Georgia!"

"Well, sir—you might think about making an exit sooner than you'd planned," Drake suggested.

"I may just do that. You can explain to Misty."

Being the shrewd gent he was, Drake asked Misty to dance again after she'd taken two sips of her punch. He figured that would give Bennett an opportunity to say something to Colleen and suggest the two of them leave a little early.

Mike took advantage of their time alone. He leaned closer to Colleen. "I've had no time alone with you since we arrived. Would you mind if we left now?"

She smiled up at him. "That's just fine with me and it might just please Misty and Drake. They could have some time alone, too."

When Misty and Drake came back from the floor they said their good nights and Mike took Colleen's arm to escort her toward the door.

When Drake escorted Misty back to the table, she chanced to see Georgia across the room so she was delighted to hear her pa say that he and Colleen were leaving. But as they were making their departure and had almost reached the door, Misty saw Georgia suddenly leap up from her chair. She'd taken two or three steps when Misty noticed she seemed to be swaying. Misty knew she was trying to get to her pa before he went out the door.

Misty had no intention of allowing that to happen so she rose quickly and excused herself for a moment. She knew she could stop Georgia before she could reach them and delay her long enough for her pa and Colleen to get in his wagon.

She did exactly that. Misty took her arm and addressed her, "Well, Mrs. Gordon—it's nice to see you here."

Her slightly glazed eyes looked at Misty and she mumbled, "Oh, hello, Misty. I was trying to get to your pa before he got out of here."

"Oh, I think it best if you don't, Mrs. Gordon."

A scowl creased Georgia's face as she snapped, "How dare you tell me what I should or shouldn't do, Misty Bennett!"

"How dare you be so presumptuous, Mrs. Gordon, to assume he'd have anything to say to you now?"

Drake sat there watching the little scene unfold, an amused smile etched on his face.

She had accomplished exactly what she'd set out to do—her father and Colleen were already rolling down the dirt road to Lepanto.

When Lilly heard Misty's last remarks to Georgia, she came up to take her friend's arm to urge her back to the table. She gave Misty a weak smile and a nod as she led Georgia away.

Misty went back to the table with a smug look of satisfaction. Drake rose to assist her into her chair. He reached down to plant a kiss on her cheek and murmur in her ear, "You're a divine little vixen, Misty Bennett, and I adore you!" They both broke into laughter.

Drake was a selfish man, too, so while they had this golden moment together alone he wanted to enjoy it. He suggested that they leave, too.

But he was certainly not ready to take her home and call it an evening, now that they finally had some time all to themselves. So he headed to his house instead of taking the river road.

They had a lot to laugh and talk about as they traveled. "Hey, we were bloody good out there on that floor, love! You're as light as a feather and a natural dancer," Drake said cheerily.

"Drake—you're sweet. You gave me the courage to try. I was scared to death! My legs felt like jelly."

His strong arm reached over to draw her closer as he sighed, "Ah, Misty! Misty!" That was all he said but he was thinking so much more. He had never known a girl who was so unashamed to be so utterly honest with a man as Misty was. When they arrived, Lucky was at the gate to greet them.

He followed them into the house. Once Drake got the lamps lit, he excused himself to take his buggy to the barn. The first thing Misty did was rid herself of her tight-fitting slippers.

When he returned to the house he spotted Misty's stocking feet. He grinned over at her as he sank down in the overstuffed chair. "Well, if you can do that, so can I." He yanked off his fine leather boots.

They indulged themselves with a piece of Rachel's carrot cake and a steaming cup of coffee.

Misty had never had such a special night—this had been exactly what Drake wanted for her. But both of them knew that this night would not be complete until they sated the passion that had mounted as the night had gone on.

Misty found herself in Drake's strong arms, his hungry lips on hers. Then they were suddenly in Drake's bed and rid of their clothing, their searing flesh pressed against each other.

Misty loved the way his hands caressed her and Drake knew this from the way she moved against him. Nothing could have pleased him more or fired his passion higher.

Their lovemaking could never last as long as Drake would have liked. Misty was such a passionate little minx and gave herself to him so completely that he could not deny himself or her for long.

As they lay there drifting down from the peak of passion, Drake whispered in her ear, "I'm just an evil seducer of a sweet, innocent girl like you, love."

Misty turned slightly to face him with a pleased smile. "Ah, Drake—what a sweet seduction it was, though!"

He pulled her closer and declared, "I love you, Misty. I think I've loved you since the first time I set eyes on you!"

"And I dreamed of such a man as you, Drake, long before

we met that afternoon. I didn't have much to go on but my dreams when we met. But you changed all that for me. You made it come true."

He held her close. "Oh, love. My little love!" He could say no more for he was filled with too much emotion.

Chapter 20

Misty arrived home only a short time ahead of her father, but everything changed for the two of them after that night. They had much to talk about on Sunday. She told him how she'd stopped Georgia from rushing after him and Colleen. "I think she'd been drinking, Pa. I smelled liquor when I got close to her."

"Well, I thank you, Misty. I've no doubt you did smell liquor," he said.

"I like Mrs. Carver, Pa. She's a very sweet lady."

"Well, she liked you, too, Misty. Thought you were about the prettiest thing she'd ever seen."

"But what impressed me, Pa, was she has a warm heart."

Mike confessed that he had been a foolish man ever to get himself mixed up with the likes of Georgia. "I only regret that I neglected you kids during those four months, Misty," he admitted humbly.

Jeff was privy to this part of their conversation and he found himself feeling more kindly toward his father than he'd felt for most of his life.

They had a pleasant Sunday and Mike went back to the mills on Monday morning. Jeff found himself without a job to go to the next week so he spent a lot of time down on the riverbank fishing.

Things were moving at an even slower pace at Drake's place. The house was built and furnished. All he had left to do was find himself a foreman.

He kept Oscar working at little odd jobs. Oscar knew Drake was just being generous to keep him on. He was beholden to Drake Dalton for that.

When Drake told him what he intended to call his place, Oscar worked on a wooden sign to place at the gate of the drive. Drake was so impressed by his handiwork with letters scrolled in the wood—"Dalton's Lair." He smiled and told Oscar, "Put it up at the entrance gate, Oscar."

The money he'd been spending so freely had slowed down this last week.

However, Drake was not getting through the entire week without making one purchase. He could not turn down the fine roan mare. He thought it would be a perfect little filly for Jeff to ride.

He remembered his promise to Jeff that they would go riding together and that he would take him hunting. He meant to keep those promises.

Lilly was sorry she'd been generous enough to invite Georgia to accompany them on Saturday night—and grateful that nothing terrible had happened at the square dance.

She was glad Misty had stopped Georgia before she got to the door. She had to admire the young lady's spirited spunk. She hadn't realized how beautiful Misty Bennett had become in the last year.

She was glad when they'd seen Georgia safely home and had started toward Crowley.

Harvey left the next day for Memphis and Lilly was glad

to have her house back to herself. She thoroughly enjoyed her quiet, peaceful Sunday evening alone.

She felt sorry for Georgia—she was obviously fearful of growing old. That was what was so sad about Georgia. She was a woman in her mid-forties, but she still saw herself as someone in her twenties or thirties.

At least her nephew had had a great time and that was all that really mattered. She doubted that she would be going to another square dance for a long time.

For Georgia, Sunday morning was not a happy time. She had a miserable headache. It had been a long time since she'd awakened feeling like this.

It certainly wasn't worth it since she'd had such a miserable evening. Dear Lilly had had the best of intentions, she realized. Truth was, she left there feeling more depressed than if she had stayed home alone.

It was almost dinner time by the time Georgia began to feel like a human being again and her head had quit throbbing.

She didn't have a glass of wine with her dinner, as she usually did, but just sat in her parlor to do a lot of thinking.

Georgia had not done this since her husband had died. She'd still envisioned herself as a young widow and the feisty young filly she'd been when she'd married. Well, she had to face the fact that she wasn't!

Being married to an older man had made her feel younger than she was, but in fact, she was well into middle age when she'd become a widow.

Late in the afternoon she'd taken a good look at herself in the mirror. She stood there studying how she looked compared to the woman with Mike Bennett. Colleen Carver looked much younger, so it was no wonder he was drawn to her. She couldn't deny that seeing him again had excited her.

She realized now that it would never have worked out for them. Her wealth probably gnawed at his ego. She'd never had any intention of playing the mother role to his three children. It would have driven her insane to have three children roaming around here.

She had to start being more level-headed and settle for a man like Cyrus Heller. This was not to say she wished to marry Cyrus, should he ask her, but they could have an uncomplicated relationship.

She also promised herself to go into Crowley to see Lilly on Monday and apologize for her terrible behavior. When she thought about it, Lilly was the only really close friend she had.

Mike Bennett went back to the mills on Monday a most happy man. He'd finally gotten to hold Colleen and kiss her on Saturday night after they'd arrived at her house. His fierce, hot-blooded nature yearned for much more than that, but Colleen had placed her hands on his broad chest and urged him to release her after a couple of kisses.

She had looked up at him warmly, declaring, "I don't want to do anything tonight that I'd wake up and regret in the morning. I like you too much for that."

"God knows, Colleen, I'd—I'd never want you to do that," he stammered. He released her as he tried to gain his composure.

"I thank you, Mike, for understanding. But you see, I think something worthwhile is worth waiting for. We've both known the impulsive ecstasy of first love. If these wonderful times we're sharing together prove to be love, then I'll be blissfully happy. But I don't wish to be hurt or hurt you. I guess I want to savor every moment."

Colleen always seemed to know the right thing to say. There was so much about her that impressed him. He took her hands in his and brought them to his lips. "Colleen, I've never known a woman like you. I care for you so much that I can be a very patient man."

Before he said good night, he and his family had a dinner invitation for the following Sunday evening.

For Misty, the week started out in grand form. She went about her Monday morning chores singing a happy tune. It was a nice surprise to see Geneva Walters at her door in the late morning.

"Well, Mrs. Walters, how nice to see you! It seems like ages." she said as she ushered her into the front room.

"It has been a while, hasn't it? I trust everything is going well with you?" Geneva asked.

"Oh, just fine, Mrs. Walters. May I get us a cup of coffee?"

Geneva said she'd like one, so Misty went to the kitchen and poured two steaming coffees. She then went over to take a chair across from the old settee. Geneva asked, "Where's Lavinia?"

"She was out in the backyard playing hopscotch the last time I checked on her," Misty said and smiled.

"And Jeff—is he still working for this Drake Dalton?"

"No, ma'am—Drake has no more work for him. But he paid Jeff handsomely for the time he put in. Jeff liked him very much. I think he misses going over there."

"Ed has certainly missed Jeff. Maybe he could spend some time with us now that he's not working for Mr. Dalton."

"Oh, I'm sure Jeff would like that."

"And your pa, how is he?"

"Things have changed a lot around here, Mrs. Walters, since he quit seeing Georgia Gordon. He and Jeff are getting along much better and the same is true for me."

"Well, I'm happy to hear that," Geneva said. She was finding it difficult to approach the subject that had motivated this trip over to see Misty this morning.

She'd run into her two friends, Ethel and Samantha, Saturday afternoon and they'd been anxious to tell her about Misty being in the jewelry store with Drake Dalton and accepting his purchase of a pair of expensive earrings.

Misty couldn't quite figure just what it was, but Mrs. Walters was not her usual self today. Her first thoughts were that she wasn't feeling well, so she asked her.

"Oh, no, Misty—I'm all right, really. I guess I'm just a little concerned about some tales I heard Saturday when I was in town. Now I don't have to tell you that I know you're a good girl, Misty, but I heard that this Mr. Dalton purchased some expensive earrings for you in the jewelry store," Geneva declared with concern.

A slow smile came to Misty's face. Now she understood why Mrs. Walters had acted so strangely. She just wondered what busybodies had told her this, as there were no other customers in the store. But she did recall two older ladies approaching as she and Drake left. She hadn't taken the time to really notice them but obviously they'd surely noticed her.

"Sorry that's caused you concern, Mrs. Walters, because two old busybodies had nothing better to do with their time than spread rumors. Yes, Drake did buy me the earrings but he also bought Lavinia a gold locket and Jeff a nice store-bought shirt. Drake Dalton is a kind, generous man who likes to do nice things for people, expecting no favors in return," Misty declared defensively.

Geneva was taken back by her quick, honest retort. She regretted pressing Misty so hard—it was apparent that she felt a deep loyalty to this Drake Dalton.

"Misty, you don't have to tell me more. I believe you. But please understand my concern for you," Geneva said, hoping she hadn't offended her.

"I'm glad to hear you say that, Mrs. Walters, and when you've had a chance to meet him you'll see for yourself what kind of man he is. He has not only been overgenerous with me but with my brother and sister as well. I love him for that!'' she confessed frankly.

"Then he must be a very fine man and me and Ed should go over to welcome him to our community," Geneva declared.

"That would be very nice of you, Mrs. Walters. I'm sure Drake would appreciate a visit."

Geneva Walters got into her buggy feeling very foolish that she'd questioned Misty just because of some gossip. She was glad she hadn't said anything to Ed about the rumors and now she certainly wouldn't.

When she arrived back home and Ed asked her how things were over at the Bennetts', she said everything was just fine!

Ed immediately made plans to invite Jeff over to spend some time with them when Geneva told him that he was no longer working for Dalton.

At Dalton's place, the pace had definitely slowed down now that it was autumn. Drake's sheds were filled with wood cut for winter and the planters' crops were harvested, so everyone moved at a slower pace.

At least everyone with the exception of Drake Dalton. He was looking for a foreman with a wife who would be his cook for the long winter months ahead when he would be without the generous pots of good food constantly furnished by Oscar's sister, Rachel.

The day he'd planned to tell Oscar he had nothing left for him to do, he never got around to it. Oscar made a suggestion that changed all that.

"Mr. Dalton, give me this next year as your foreman. You know I'm a carpenter—I'm also a farmer and have been all my life. I've plowed field and hoed cotton. And I know how to raise cotton and corn."

"But what about Rachel?"

"She's tired, Mr. Dalton, of running that farm since her husband died. She's willing to come over here and be your cook and housekeeper. Rachel ain't got no hankering to ever marry again at her age. She's just a simple woman. Wish you'd think about it, Mr. Dalton, before you find someone else. Me and Rachel would work hard for you."

Drake was taken back by his proposal. He'd never given any thought to hiring Oscar as his foreman, but the idea of Rachel being his cook and housekeeper certainly appealed to him.

"But what about her farm, Oscar?"

"Well, as it would happen, Mr. Dalton, the man who owns the adjoining property wants to buy Rachel's place for his son since he just took himself a wife. Made her an offer just last week. Rachel could pay you back for the loan you took care of and have some to spare."

A slow smile spread across Drake's face as he said, "Well, you and Rachel get all the loose ends tied up. It's settled then. You'll be my foreman and Rachel will be my cook."

"Oh, thank you, Mr. Dalton! Come springtime, I'll prove I know how to take care of your land," Oscar vowed.

After Oscar left, Drake wondered if he might have had this in mind while he was building the little house. Maybe Oscar had dreamed about living in that cozy place this winter. Drake never faulted anyone for having dreams. He had a few himself.

He had already realized one of them, and that was to get this place where it was today. Everything was going according to his plans, and he had the next three months to think about his next goals. He wanted to make even more progress by the time spring arrived.

So since he didn't have to find a foreman, he would go over to the Bennetts' tomorrow and bring Jeff over to introduce him to the new little mare he'd bought.

It was time he taught that young man how to ride a horse!

Chapter 21

Misty declared it the most golden, glorious autumn of her young life. No longer did she have to tell her pa lies to be with Drake Dalton. He could court her openly and honestly.

As unlikely as it had seemed at one time, Drake and her pa got along just fine since the night they'd met at the square dance. About once a week, Drake came over to get Jeff to take him over to his place to ride the little roan mare. He'd also allowed Jeff to name the mare.

"If she was mine, Mr. Dalton, she'd be called Beauty."

"So Beauty it shall be, Jeff! Yes, I like that, too."

As he'd expected, Jeff took to Beauty and she to him. He and Jeff rode over the countryside at least once a week. It was a wonderful time in Jeff's young life. He told Drake one afternoon that he thought old Lucky was a bit jealous that he had to stay behind that fence and couldn't trail along with them.

"Well, I came to the conclusion that Lucky keeps out of trouble, if he's behind that fence. He's got plenty of yard to roam around in."

Drake and Misty were not the only lovers enjoying the golden autumn months. Mike and his ladylove, Colleen, grew fonder and fonder of one another.

Colleen certainly met with all of Mike's children's approval. On Sundays, the four of them often went over to Lepanto to Colleen's house for Sunday dinner.

Misty had persuaded her pa to let her go into Crowley to purchase a few things to spruce up their little house so they could invite Colleen and her daughter Maureen for dinner one evening.

Mike was very agreeable and took her into town the next two Saturday afternoons to do her shopping. She bought a nice set of dishes and a matched set of glasses. Mike saw that his daughter had good taste when she picked out a pretty tablecloth and matching linen napkins.

He confessed as they went home in the wagon, "A man just don't think about such things, Misty."

"That's only natural, Pa. One more shopping day and I'll have everything I need. Mrs. Carver has had everything so perfect for us when we've gone over there that I wanted it the same way."

"You like Colleen, don't you, Misty?"

"I like her very much, Pa. She's a caring person. That's the difference between her and Georgia Gordon."

"You're right, Misty," he said, giving her an affectionate pat on the shoulder. This was another thing that had changed about her pa in recent weeks that Misty had definitely noticed. After all these years, it seemed Mike Bennett could finally show affection toward his son and daughters. Misty credited Colleen Carver with bringing this out in him.

That next Saturday when they made their trek into town, Misty bought a meat platter and the serving dishes she felt she needed. Mike let her indulge herself by buying candle holders and some tall white tapers.

They were in a lighthearted mood as they boarded his wagon to go home. Mike told her that Colleen would feel very flattered to know she had put so much effort into the dinner.

"Now don't you dare tell on me, Pa," she playfully chided.

"I'd never do that, honey."

That evening Mike went over to Colleen's and Misty and Lavinia spent the evening alone. Jeff was spending the weekend with the Walters. Drake had been unable to come over this evening, as it was moving day for Oscar and Rachel. He'd promised Misty he'd be over on Sunday afternoon.

Actually, she was grateful for a relaxed evening at home after the busy afternoon she and her pa had put in making her purchases.

The square dancing at Harper's Barn was no longer being held now that it was October. Tonight Mike was escorting Colleen to the Farrells' house. The Farrells were the parents of the young man who'd been Maureen's beau for the last year. Young Stephen Farrell had proposed to Maureen and she'd accepted, so the family was having a gala celebration at their home on the outskirts of Lepanto.

Daniel Farrell was one of the wealthiest planters in the community. He owned hundreds of acres of rich delta land and had built a fine two-story stone house. He fashioned the grounds like those he and his wife, Jeanine, had seen in England. They had only one son and he was their pride and joy.

Colleen's station in life was so much more humble than theirs that she had first expected them to object when Stephen courted her daughter, but they hadn't. In fact, Jeanine Farrell had given Colleen all her orders for cakes and pastries for the various functions at their country home, Cottonwood.

Colleen had come to the conclusion that the Farrells approved of her daughter for several reasons. She was a very beautiful girl, with her deep auburn hair and brilliant blue eyes, and she was very well-mannered and gracious.

Maureen had many talents—she could sing like a lark and she also played the piano.

Since Maureen was an only child, Colleen devoted all her energy and time to her. She had her reciting poetry by the time she was five, and taking piano lessons at nine. Her husband had thought her insane when she'd bought a piano from the first profits from her bakery shop, but Colleen had never regretted that purchase. She loved sitting in the parlor listening to Maureen play.

So this evening was very special to Colleen. She'd worked every evening making a dress for the affair. She was a fine seamstress as well as a baker.

Since it was late autumn, Colleen had chosen a lovely purple silk for her gown. Its simplicity made it elegant—she planned to wear her only good jewelry with it. Her husband had bought her a string of pearls and years later Colleen had bought a pair of earrings to match.

She had only two other pieces of jewelry. Her wedding ring, which she still wore, and a pair of gold earrings she wore daily because her daughter had bought them for her.

Georgia made the trip into Crowley to make her apologies to Lilly, who found herself with a very humble Georgia Gordon. As vexed as she'd been with her that Saturday night, she found herself feeling sorry for her this afternoon as Georgia confessed, "I've been a fool, Lilly. You're a much wiser widow than me."

"Well, Georgia—I haven't had the same problems you've had. Dear God, I'm glad Thomas wasn't a planter! I was lucky to be left with this comfortable home and enough money to take care of my needs," Lilly declared.

"Oh, Lord, Lilly I have money but I need someone to organize my affairs and take care of me."

"Well, think about something then, Georgia. Sell that

place and buy a little house here in Crowley. It would be much simpler."

"You've given me something to think about, Lilly."

They had a nice visit and when Georgia left she was in much better spirits. She had decided to accept Cyrus's invitation for the following Saturday.

Lilly laughed infectiously. "Georgia, I'd rather be an old man's darling than the other way left for women like me and you. I've no complaints about my life."

"Guess that's been the difference between us. I've had a lot of complaints about my life, Lilly, but I think I know I can't make up for all those years now. Guess I've finally come to terms with some things," she'd said as she prepared to leave.

But as she traveled down the dirt road in her gig, Georgia thought about something else Lilly said. It made good sense. Maybe she should start thinking about selling her land and getting a nice home in Crowley.

The more she thought about it later that evening the more the idea appealed. That next Saturday when Cyrus came to pick her up she told him her thoughts about selling her land and moving to town.

"You might as well forget trying to sell the land now, Georgia. You won't get any nibbles until spring. Winter's coming on now."

"I know, Cyrus, and, of course, you're right. But I'm becoming tired of running the place," she sighed.

They'd had their usual little jaunt around the local countryside and he was pulling up his gig in front of the large two-story house where he lived. A young man who worked for Heller rushed up to take charge of the gig as Cyrus got out to assist Georgia down.

As they usually did on Saturday, they had returned to Cyrus's house to have dinner together. They'd go into his fancy parlor and have a couple of glasses of sherry. Promptly at six, Heller's cook, Dessie, would announce that dinner was ready and they would go into the dining room.

After they'd had dessert, they would return to the parlor and Dessie would serve them a cup of coffee. It was never later than nine when Georgia got back home.

But somehow, Georgia enjoyed their quiet conversation tonight more than usual, especially after the miserable time she'd had the previous Saturday.

Cyrus lit up one of his cheroots, which he'd been pleased to find out didn't offend her as they had his first wife.

"Georgia, look around here. All this could be yours if you'd marry me. Hell, Georgia, I'm not a demanding man. You know that! I know you're an independent woman and I damn well admire you for that. I wouldn't cramp your style that much—with one exception." He got a twinkle in his eye and showed Georgia a side of himself that she hadn't seen before. "I wouldn't stand for you to take a lover."

Georgia threw back her head and laughed. "Oh, Cyrus! I'd never expect you to."

"Well, you think about it, Georgia, and I'll say no more. Whether you accept my proposal or not, I'll help you sell your land when the right time comes. I do wish you'd come here to share Thanksgiving dinner with me. You've no family here nor have I so let's enjoy the day together."

"I'll be here, Cyrus. I'll also give you my answer on Thanksgiving," she said and smiled.

Heller was very encouraged. She seemed more receptive than she'd been in the past when he'd first proposed.

As he sat on the fancy brocade settee beside her he became bold enough to take her hand in his and draw it up to his lips. "If the answer is yes, Georgia, then there'll be a wedding here at Heller's Haven at Christmas time. I see no reason to waste any time at our age."

"I guess not, Cyrus." She had to admit it was a more outgoing, talkative Cyrus she was enjoying tonight.

He really surprised her as he was taking her home by

asking, "Georgia, if this should all work out and we did have a wedding at Christmas time, come spring, what would you think about taking a delayed honeymoon to France and England?"

"France and England, Cyrus?" she stammered.

"Yes, Georgia. I've always wanted to see the part of England where my mother was born. I figure you'd love to see Paris if we were that close. What would you think about that?"

"Dear God, Cyrus—I'd think that was the most wonderful thing in the world! Truth is, I've never even been out of Poinsett County my whole life!"

"Well, we're only going through this life one time. You and I can't take our money with us when we go," he declared.

"You're right, Cyrus. Absolutely right."

Cyrus didn't try to kiss her when he said good night. He merely told her, "I'll see you next Saturday, Georgia, if that's all right with you."

She didn't hesitate to tell him she'd be ready at the appointed hour. When she went into her house, Georgia was a much happier woman than she'd been when Lilly and her nephew had brought her home last Saturday night.

Before she went to sleep that night, Georgia had already decided to accept Cyrus's proposal on Thanksgiving Day.

Part III

Winter's Chilling Winds

Chapter 22

Drake took Misty on the last picnic they'd share until springtime. He was glad that she had brought her light woolen shawl when they'd traveled to Otter Creek. It had been his idea that they go there after he'd discovered the spot the previous week.

It was an ideal autumn afternoon when they arrived but as they sat on the blanket and had their picnic and talked endlessly as they always did when they were together, the sun sank lower and the air grew cooler.

He'd given her a report on Jeff and what a fine horseman he'd become. "I'm getting ready to take him hunting in the woods behind my place. Told him that last week."

"Oh, he'll love that."

"Now, I must ask you something else, Misty, because I wouldn't want to do anything without your father's permission. I have a very special Christmas gift to give Lavinia if your father would approve. My neighbor is giving me one of Lucky's pups and what I'd like to do is give the pup to

Lavinia when it's ready to leave its mom. What do you think?"

"I'll ask Pa, Drake. Need I tell you that she would be thrilled to have one of Lucky's pups?"

By five the air seemed so cool to Misty that Drake suggested they pack up and head for his house.

By the time they arrived, twilight had fallen over the countryside and the temperature was so cool that the wool shawl felt especially good.

Drake laughed as they went into the house. "I'm going to start up that fireplace immediately."

He kindled up the cookstove to heat up some coffee while Misty made herself cozy in the front room.

What did surprise her was that the Walters had yet to pay a call on Drake. She'd asked him twice if he'd met the Walters yet, but he hadn't. She didn't understand it. She wondered if it had to do with a bit of jealousy. Drake had innocently taken attention away from the two of them, and perhaps they resented that.

Misty had said nothing to her father yet, but she planned to have a big Thanksgiving dinner. She didn't want Drake to be alone, and she thought it would be the perfect time to invite Colleen and her family.

She told Drake about her plans for the holiday. He immediately responded, "I'll look forward to it, Misty. In fact, Jeff and I will go hunting for a wild turkey."

Speaking of family and holidays, Misty asked, "Have you had word from your sister in England, Drake?"

"No, damn it! I wish I would—I'd breathe much easier. I couldn't stand having her under my roof. Ellen tends to be too bossy."

What he didn't tell Misty was that Ellen was so headstrong she might have ignored his letter, which he knew she had to have received by now. For the last three weeks he had hoped to hear from her but he hadn't.

Having her here would have cramped his style in many

ways. It was where he and Misty shared those special stolen moments and he wanted no sister spoiling that for him. And he wanted no sister with her bossy ways trying to tell him how his house should be run. Everything was running so smoothly for him right now.

Each time he made love to Misty it seemed to grow sweeter. He'd never felt about any woman as he felt about her. She asked nothing of him but that he love her. Yet, he felt very protective of her and should she find herself with his child he would have married her in a minute.

He didn't say this to Misty, but he constantly told her how much he adored her and that seemed to satisfy her. He already had decided if any woman would ever wear the jewelry he'd taken from his mother's case, it would be Misty. He knew he'd never feel about another woman as he felt about her.

When her pa mentioned something about the four of them going over to Colleen's for Thanksgiving dinner, Misty quickly protested, "Oh, no, Pa. I've invited Drake to come here. Could we invite Mrs. Carver and her daughter? Drake's going to take Jeff hunting for a wild turkey. He has no family here. He can't have Thanksgiving alone."

"All right, Misty, I'll say something to Colleen when I see her," Mike agreed.

When he said something at the end of the week, Colleen eagerly accepted. Maureen had been asked to have Thanksgiving dinner with her fiancé's family.

Mike returned home to tell Misty that Colleen was delighted to accept her invitation. "But she insists that you let her bring pumpkin pies and maybe a couple of her pecan pies as well. Swears she makes a good one."

Misty laughed, "I've no doubt about that."

It was a thrilling occasion for young Jeff the first time Drake took him hunting. That afternoon, Drake spent time instructing him on how to use the rifle and the two of them did a little target practice. He told Jeff, "Now next week we're going hunting for a turkey, Jeff. Just thought you needed to get a feel for the rifle."

"All right, Mr. Dalton!" he declared excitedly.

As he promised, the next week the two of them did go into the woods and two hours later they came out with not one, but two turkeys.

When they'd spotted the second turkey, Drake had urged Jeff to take aim as he was preparing to do. The turkey fell limp to the ground and Jeff thought his shot had hit the turkey. Drake let him think it. Jeff strutted like a peacock as they walked back to his house. Each of them was carrying a big turkey that weighed at least twenty pounds.

He told Jeff, "You can take home the one you shot and I'll give this one to Oscar so they can have a nice turkey, too."

Rachel was pleased by the big turkey. "Thank you, Mr. Dalton. My, what a lot of good eating this will be."

"Rachel, don't worry about anything for me. I'm having Thanksgiving dinner over at the Bennetts'," Drake informed her.

"Bake you a couple of pies then, Mr. Dalton?"

"No, you just bake pies for you and Oscar."

"Well, have yourself a nice holiday then, and me and Oscar will do the same," she said as he and Jeff prepared to leave.

Later when Drake arrived at the Bennetts' with Jeff and the turkey, Jeff was quick to tell his sister he had shot it. Misty threw her hands up. "Lord, he is a big one, isn't he! I just hope I've got a pan big enough."

Drake laughed. "If you don't, I'll go to town and buy one for you, love!" He suggested she go check as he was going into Crowley first thing in the morning.

She came out of her kitchen a few minutes later and announced that she didn't have one big enough. Drake assured her she'd have a pan to accommodate that turkey when he returned from town.

The next day when he returned from Crowley, he had not only purchased a massive baking pan but he'd also bought a set of wine glasses. "I'll bring a couple of bottles of white wine to have with our dinner," he told her.

"You didn't have to do that, Drake."

"Know I didn't, but I wanted to. I'm looking forward to the holiday. I've a lot to give thanks for, Misty. Life's been good to me this last year. Most of all, I give thanks for meeting you last summer," he said in all seriousness, bending down to kiss her.

"It *was* only this summer that we first met, wasn't it, Drake? I sometimes feel like I've known you forever. I know that sounds silly," she confessed.

"No, Misty—it doesn't sound silly at all. Until I met you, no woman ever meant much to me. I never stayed long with any of them. I think I must have been waiting for you to come along."

"Oh, Drake—I hope that was how it was meant to be. I know it was that way for me."

He kissed her once more before taking his leave. With a devious grin, he admitted, "I'm a very possessive man, Misty, and I'd be bloody jealous if I ever saw another man around you. I consider you my lady!"

She couldn't restrain an impish smile as she playfully tried to mimic his English accent. "And I'd be bloody jealous if I saw you with another woman!"

He roared with laughter and lifted her in his arms, swinging her around. "And I'd want you to be!" Setting her back on the floor, he declared, "Now, you tempting little minx, I've got to go before I get both you and me in trouble."

She stood on the porch watching him drive away in his wagon and she thought she had never been so happy and it was all because of Drake Dalton.

The day before Thanksgiving, she'd labored all day in

the kitchen. She was glad that Colleen was bringing the pies. But there was cornbread to bake for her dressing as well as several loaves of bread.

Because she wanted everything to be so perfect she had carefully charted out everything she had to do. On Thanksgiving morning she was in a frenzy. Their little kitchen table only had four chairs and there were six people eating dinner!

Jeff instantly had a solution. "I'll take the drawers out of the nightstands—you can put a tablecloth over them and Lavinia and I can sit there."

He gave his older sister a smug smile. "You see, Misty? That will take care of the problem."

She smiled and gave his head a playful tousle. "Ah, Jeff—what would I do without you? What a marvelous idea."

Her new tablecloth went on the kitchen table where she and Drake, her father, and Colleen would be eating. She took out another tablecloth to drape over the two nightstand drawers. It worked perfectly.

Misty had gotten up very early that morning to get the turkey in the oven and prepare the dressing. The house was in perfect order.

Mike left in the late afternoon to go pick up Colleen. Drake was due to arrive at six. By four Misty had helped Lavinia get dressed and combed her hair, tying a colorful velvet ribbon at the crown of her curls. "Now, you keep yourself clean, Lavinia," she told her little sister.

She no longer had to boss Jeff about getting dressed— he took full charge of himself. Drake had bought him a hairbrush and Misty had watched him stand in front of the mirror trying to style it in the same fashion that Drake wore his.

It was almost five when she was finally ready to go to her bedroom to get dressed. She had decided to wear the paisley dress Geneva had made for her. She also wore Drake's locket and bangle bracelet. She dabbed her wrists and throat with the toilet water he'd given her, which she only used on special occasions.

The most special gift he had given her, which she prized above all else, were the little emerald earrings.

She pulled the sides of her hair up as she sat at her dressing table, thinking about Mrs. Walters and how she'd quizzed her about the earrings. Somehow, Misty had gotten the impression that she hadn't approved of Drake's gift of the earrings. Ever since that day she had come over to quiz her about the gossip she'd heard from Samantha and Ethel, Geneva Walters had not visited again.

Misty had been so occupied with other things that she hadn't thought about it until now.

She also wondered why they still hadn't paid a courtesy call to Drake. She knew if they'd called on him, he would have mentioned it, but he hadn't.

There was a very simple explanation for what had transpired with Ed and Geneva Walters. They'd never had any children and Geneva had taken it upon herself to be motherly with the three children when she and Ed felt that Mike was sadly neglecting them. Neither of them had ever liked him.

They'd both enjoyed the affection they'd received from the Bennett children for their generosity. But suddenly, everything had changed when Drake Dalton came to the community.

When Drake had hired Jeff to work for him, it meant that Jeff couldn't spend time with Ed, who secretly resented the Englishman. When Geneva heard the gossip from Ethel and Samantha, she had bristled.

Geneva knew she should have been happy when Misty told her how much better things were going for them since her pa was no longer seeing Georgia, but somehow everything she learned from her visit with Misty left her depressed.

The same thing happened with Ed when Jeff had finally come over to spend a weekend after he'd quit working for Drake. All Ed heard from Jeff during that weekend was

Jeff's praise about the Englishman. Jealousy gnawed at Ed. He realized he could not compete with the young and vigorous Dalton. It was apparent that young Jeff saw him as a kind of hero!

So he and Geneva had kept to themselves the last few weeks. They planned a very quiet Thanksgiving day alone.

Georgia had told Lilly about her plans for Thanksgiving. Lilly could not have been happier.

"Georgia, now you're using your head. Ruby and I will be toasting you while we have our dinner here." Lilly laughed and embraced her.

Georgia asked her, "Won't you be spending Thanksgiving with Henry?"

"No, I told him to spend it with his children. I wanted no part of that big bunch of relatives. We'll have Christmas together if he doesn't have to be around all those people. A little family goes a long way with me, Georgia. I like it in very small doses. I don't need bawling babies and a lot of chatter. It drives me crazy. The truth is, that's why I've never allowed myself to get too serious about Henry. He's got too many kids and I don't choose to put up with them," Lilly declared.

Georgia said, "Well, I don't have to worry about that with Cyrus and thank God for that!"

They both wished one another a happy holiday and Georgia left Lilly's to go back home.

It was a very happy Thanksgiving Day around Crowley and Lepanto. Mike Bennett was the first to notice that the air was colder than it normally was at this time of the year so he'd banked up his fireplace and lit the logs just before he'd gone to pick up Colleen.

Cyrus had picked up Georgia at mid-afternoon for their Thanksgiving dinner at six. Lilly and Ruby had shared a turkey dinner and indulged themselves with too many glasses of port, so Ruby had stayed overnight with Lilly.

Cyrus was a most happy fellow that evening when Georgia told him she would marry him. They spent the entire day together so they could make their plans for a Christmas wedding.

Cyrus was as excited as a schoolboy when he took her home around the usual time, but he jested, "You're going to save me a lot of trotting back and forth between Lepanto and Crowley, dear."

She laughed lightheartedly. After Cyrus had taken her home and gone back to his house, she felt a great deal of excitement churning within her.

Chapter 23

It was a very happy Thanksgiving holiday around the two hamlets of Crowley and Lepanto. The countryside slowed as all the leaves on the trees turned various shades of rust and gold. It was a bright, sunny day with just enough of a nip in the air.

Maureen had left with her fiancé about two hours earlier and Colleen was enjoying the time off from her shop. The day before had been hectic and her poor feet were swollen by the time she'd closed her bakery.

It had been glorious to sleep late and have a light breakfast of one of her cinnamon rolls and coffee.

She had the four pies lined up on her kitchen table, ready to take to the Bennetts. There was plenty of time for a warm scented bath. When she had finished bathing, and styling her hair, she dressed in a long-sleeved, white crepe blouse and grey wool skirt with a matching jacket. Her only jewelry was her string of pearls around the high-necked blouse.

Mike arrived promptly at the appointed hour, as he always did. He carried all her pies to his wagon, thinking to himself how nice it would be if he had a buggy to take such an elegant lady to his house. But Colleen did not seem to mind.

Drake was there when Mike returned with Colleen—he could tell Misty was a little nervous.

He gave her a reassuring kiss. "You've got everything looking so fine, Misty. Just calm yourself. Your dinner will be perfect! I can attest to what a good cook you are—remember?"

"Oh, I know, Drake, but I just want everything to be as nice as it's been when we've gone over to Mrs. Carver's. She's such a grand cook!"

The candles were all lit and there was a delicious aroma coming from the kitchen when Mike and Colleen walked through the front door.

Misty had no reason to be concerned—her dinner was scrumptious. It was apparent from the way all her guests devoured everything that they were enjoying it.

Like all her pastries, Colleen's pies were divine—Drake couldn't resist having a second piece of the pecan.

"Mrs. Carver—may I come to your bakery and buy some of these?" he asked.

"Of course, Drake. For you, I'd bake one," she assured him.

Colleen insisted that Misty allow her to help clear up the kitchen and do the dishes. Misty realized that Colleen Carver was a headstrong woman—she would not allow Misty to do it all.

"Mike and Drake can entertain themselves while we get this cleared away, Misty," Colleen said as she tied an apron around her waist.

It was late at night by the time Drake left and Mike guided his wagon toward Lepanto to take Colleen home.

Misty had had only a few brief moments with Drake as she told him good night on the darkened porch. He only got one hasty kiss, but Misty had a chance to tell him she'd spoken to her pa about the pup and Lavinia could have it.

"Wonderful! I was hoping he'd let her have it. I think they're going to be real cute little fellows. I asked for a little female pup," he said as he turned to go down the front steps. Misty watched him fade into the blackness of the night but his words kept echoing in her ears.

When she returned to the front room, Jeff was still there. Misty sank down on the settee, feeling a bit weary after the long day. Jeff had a very serious look on his face as he said, "A lot different from this time last year, isn't it, Misty?"

"Sure is, honey."

"Tell you something, Misty, 'cause I don't feel that way now, but I was thinking about running away this time last year. But Pa changing and meeting Mr. Dalton changed everything for me," he confessed.

"Oh, Jeff, honey—I'm so glad about that," she sighed.

"So am I, Misty, 'cause I didn't like the thought of leaving you and Lavinia. You don't have to worry about me doing that now," he assured her.

"That's good to know, Jeff. I wouldn't want you to do that."

"Well, I don't want to leave home now. Kinda like it around here," he said and grinned. He rose and came over to give her a kiss on the cheek and tell her he was going to bed. "All that good food has made me sleepy."

Misty confessed that she wasn't going to be too far behind him—she was definitely ready for bed.

For Mike, it was a late night because he had to get up to go to work the next morning. Colleen also had to open her bakery on Friday, so she was not going to get the amount of sleep she needed.

But neither of them minded the lack of sleep after the wonderful evening they'd shared. However, Mike did not stay long. He said goodbye at the door, since her daughter was already home and sitting in the parlor. He didn't even get a goodnight kiss.

They exchanged smiles as Mike promised her he'd see her Saturday night.

The next day, Lavinia was already talking about the Christmas holiday coming up next but Misty laughed and shrugged. "Lord, Lavinia—I won't be making any plans for that for a while."

For the next week, she slowed down. She needed to after the frenzied pace she'd kept the last two weeks.

For Drake it was also a lazier week. The day he planned to ride over to the Bennetts' to get Jeff so they could go for their weekly ride, there was a chilling rain that lasted all day.

But it was also a week when Drake began to appreciate Oscar even more. He pointed out to Drake that if they had a few hens and a rooster they would have all the fresh eggs they'd need.

"Another thing, Mr. Dalton, if you had a pair of good milk cows, then we'd have milk daily and Rachel could churn up our butter. Every place needs cows and chickens," Oscar added.

"You see, Oscar—I need you! You got any other suggestions?"

"Well, yes sir, I do but all this is going to cost you some money. Hogs, Mr. Dalton—then you could have shanks of ham and slabs of bacon. Some sows and a good boar would provide a lot of good eating. I can cure a good ham if I do say so, Mr. Dalton."

"Well, I put you in charge of getting us some chickens, cows, and hogs, Oscar."

"I know several farmers who'd be able to furnish you with the things you need. You see, Mr. Dalton, landowners like you don't go to the stores in town to buy milk, eggs, butter, bacon, and hams. They produce it right on their farms."

Drake shook his head as though he was a little out of

Here's a special offer for Zebra Historical Romance Readers!

GET 4 FREE HISTORICAL ROMANCE NOVELS

A $19.96 Value!

Passion, adventure and hours of pleasure delivered right to your doorstep!

HERE'S A SPECIAL INVITATION TO ENJOY TODAY'S FINEST HISTORICAL ROMANCES— ABSOLUTELY FREE! *(a $19.96 value)*

Now you can enjoy the latest Zebra Lovegram Historical Romances without even leaving your home with our convenient Zebra Home Subscription Service. Zebra Home Subscription Service offers you the following benefits that you don't want to miss:

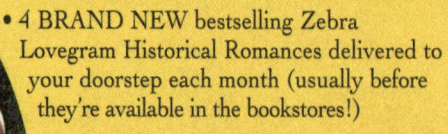

- 4 BRAND NEW bestselling Zebra Lovegram Historical Romances delivered to your doorstep each month (usually before they're available in the bookstores!)
- 20% off each title or a savings of almost $4.00 each month
- FREE home delivery
- A FREE monthly newsletter, *Zebra/Pinnacle Romance News* that features author profiles, contests, special member benefits, book previews and more
- No risks or obligations...in other words you can cancel whenever you wish with no questions asked

So join hundreds of thousands of readers who already belong to Zebra Home Subscription Service and enjoy the very best Historical Romances That Burn With The Fire of History!

And remember....there is no minimum purchase required. After you've enjoyed your initial FREE package of 4 books, you'll begin to receive monthly shipments of new Zebra titles. Each shipment will be yours to examine for 10 days and then if you decide to keep the books, you'll pay the preferred subscriber's price of just $4.00 per title. That's $16 for all 4 books with FREE home delivery! And if you want us to stop sending books, just say the word....it's that simple.

It's a no-lose proposition, so send for your 4 FREE books today!

4 FREE BOOKS

These books worth almost $20, are yours without cost or obligation when you fill out and mail this certificate.

(If the certificate is missing below, write to: Zebra Home Subscription Service, Inc., 120 Brighton Road, P.O. Box 5214, Clifton, New Jersey 07015-5214)

Complete and mail this card to receive 4 Free books!

YES! Please send me 4 Zebra Lovegram Historical Romances without cost or obligation. I understand that each month thereafter I will be able to preview 4 new Zebra Lovegram Historical Romances FREE for 10 days. Then if I decide to keep them, I will pay the money-saving preferred publisher's price of just $4.00 each...a total of $16. That's almost $4 less than the regular publisher's price, and there is never any additional charge for shipping and handling. I may return any shipment within 10 days and owe nothing, and I may cancel this subscription at any time. The 4 FREE books will be mine to keep in any case.

Name _____

Address _____ Apt. _____

City _____ State _____ Zip _____

Telephone ( ) _____

Signature _____

(If under 18, parent or guardian must sign.)

LF0996

Terms, offer and prices subject to change without notice. Subscription subject to acceptance by Zebra Home Subscription Service, Inc.. Zebra Home Subscription Service, Inc. reserves the right to reject any order or cancel any subscription.

4 BOOKS FREE!

A $19.96 value... absolutely FREE with no obligation to buy anything, ever!

ZEBRA HOME SUBSCRIPTION SERVICE, INC.

120 BRIGHTON ROAD

P.O. BOX 5214

CLIFTON, NEW JERSEY 07015-5214

AFFIX STAMP HERE

sorts with himself. "I bloody well should have thought about that, Oscar."

"Come springtime, we'll plant a big garden and then you'll have fresh vegetables any time you want them. Mighty nice to have."

Drake sat there listening to him and realized he was getting an education from this lanky fellow.

Oscar smiled at the expression on Drake's face. "Mr. Dalton, I don't know of anything that gives a man more than his land if he loves and cherishes it. I ain't through yet. There are fruit trees we can plant, too."

The next morning Drake was awakened by a rooster's crowing at the crack of dawn. It was a very impressive sound, but one the Englishman was not used to. Drake sat up in bed, wondering what all the strange noise was about. Then he remembered what Oscar had done, so he turned over and slept for another hour.

The next day Oscar came back to Dalton's Lair with two fine-looking Jersey cows tied to the back of the wagon. In one of the sheds he made nests for the hens to lay their eggs. The barn now housed Duke, the new roan mare, and the team of horses that pulled the wagon. Now there were also two cows occupying stalls. Each evening Oscar went out to milk them.

By Friday he was ready to call on Rachel's former neighbor to see about buying some hogs. He made the deal with Harley but he had no way to get them back to Dalton's place, so Harley obliged by getting the four sows and the boar over to Dalton's. With winter coming on, he was delighted to have the money.

When Saturday evening came around, Drake rode Duke over to see Misty. With a boyish enthusiasm he told her about his new acquisitions.

She realized how little Drake knew about people who lived on farm land. They'd always had chickens and one milk cow, but they had never raised hogs. Mike's friend,

Jeb, raised them so he always brought them bacon, smoked hams, and sausage.

"Well, Drake—sounds like you've had a busy week," she remarked.

"Not me. Poor old Oscar. He's been the one making all the deals and running around."

Saturday evening Drake and Misty spent time quietly at her house. She had fixed turkey pies with a flaky golden crust and made up some little crocks of custard, which Lavinia loved.

After dinner, Drake and Misty sat on the settee having lighthearted conversation.

Misty asked, "Have you had any word from your sister, Drake?"

"No and damn it, it bothers me! I wish to hell I would."

"Has there been time for her to get a letter to you by now?"

"Oh, yes. I should have received a reply around four weeks ago."

"Maybe she wasn't pleased by what you wrote," Misty pointed out.

Drake laughed. "That would be fine with me, Misty, but another thing bothers me. She might have left England before my letter arrived and is en route here. I remember the time it took me to come across the country many months ago."

"So it took that long for you to get to Arkansas?"

"God, it took so many weeks."

To Misty and Drake, it seemed like forever before they were finally alone. Misty was convinced that Drake was the most understanding man in the world.

He rewarded himself with a few kisses but there was no way he would allow his passion to go out of control at Misty's home. So with an ache in his groin, he told her good night and went home. He'd kissed her goodbye with a devious grin. "I'll pick you up next Saturday night, love. We'll have dinner at my house."

"I'll be ready, Drake," she said and smiled slyly. She knew well how he'd had to restrain himself tonight. Since she now knew the passion a man and a woman could feel for one another, she was very aware of Drake's body as it pressed close to her. She could tell by the look in his eyes and the pulsing of his firm muscled body.

She had to admit she was just as hungry for lovemaking as he was when he left. Since Drake had introduced her to the art of making love, she realized that a woman's needs were just as fierce as a man's.

Misty knew that no man could make her feel as he did. She could not imagine ever lying in any other man's arms or giving herself to such sweet, sensuous seduction the way she did with him.

Drake Dalton was the only man who could make her feel that way!

Chapter 24

Life at Dalton's Lair became more fascinating and intriguing to Drake as each week went by. When Rachel brought the first wicker basket of eggs in, a big grin spread across his face as he remarked, "And my own hens did that for me."

Rachel laughed at the twenty-five-year-old. She realized he had lived in such completely different circumstances back in England.

The first time she sat at the churn to make some butter, Drake stayed in the kitchen to watch. Like an anxious young boy, he was constantly asking, "Is it butter yet, Rachel?"

"Not yet, Mr. Dalton," she chuckled. She genuinely liked this young man who had been so kind and generous to her and her brother.

Finally, he had been forced to leave the kitchen and he remarked as he sauntered out the back door, "Takes a bloody long time to make butter, doesn't it, Rachel?"

"Yes, Mr. Dalton—it takes a while," she said and smiled.

After he'd gone out, she was going to have an amusing tale to tell Oscar when she got home.

That afternoon, Drake found himself with a new guest in his house. His neighbor, whose bitch had bred with Lucky, came over with the little black female he'd promised Drake.

"Thought I'd bring her on over this afternoon, Drake. My man, Moses, predicts that we're in for some bad weather and I never question him. He's usually exactly right. Besides, the little girl is very fat so she's only leaving her ma about a week early. Look at the little critter!"

Drake saw a fat little ball of black fur that was absolutely adorable. He was only concerned as to how Lucky would respond. It was still almost two weeks before he'd be giving the pup to Lavinia as a Christmas present.

Drake had no reason to be concerned. The big, awkward Lucky seemed to know he had to be gentle with this small replica of himself.

Cautiously, Drake watched Lucky with the small pup after he took her into the house and made her a comfortable bed with an old blanket.

But the little pup had no desire to get into the cozy bed and stay there. She followed Lucky around the house. In a very firm voice, Drake told Lucky, "This is your daughter, Lucky, so you protect her."

Lucky seemed to understand. He didn't put up a fuss when the pup ate ravenously from the bowl of food Drake put down.

Drake had a fire glowing in his fireplace. By the time he'd cleaned up his kitchen and gone into his front room he saw a scene he'd remember for a long, long time.

There in front of the hearth on the rug where Lucky lay all curled up, the little pup also lay sleeping soundly. Father and daughter seemed to take to one another instantly. Drake sat down to relax and felt very pleased.

What Drake found even more interesting the next morning when he woke up was the little pup was not in the nice blanket bed he'd fixed but had slept in Lucky's bed with him all night.

After Drake had gotten up and dressed, he let Lucky out the kitchen door to roam in the yard as he always did. He made his morning coffee and fixed breakfast.

The fuzzy little black pup was like a lost soul when Drake allowed Lucky to go out. She sat by the closed door and yelped.

Drake reached down to pat her head and assure her that her father would be back shortly and scratch at the door to be let in. He knew Drake would have something to give him from the table as he sat eating breakfast.

Drake had only to open his back door to know that December mornings in Arkansas were just as chilling as they were back in England.

There might not be dense fogs and constant misting rains, but the wind was just as cold. He was more than ready for a steaming cup of coffee. Drake put a couple of slices of ham into the cast iron skillet, for he figured he had to share with Lucky and his daughter. Instead of two eggs, he broke four. He'd already put the baking pan in the oven to warm up the biscuits Rachel had made.

By the time he was ready to sit down, Lucky was scratching at the door. Drake let him in and the little pup was delighted to see him. Drake fixed a plate of two eggs, a biscuit crumbled up, and one slice of ham cut in pieces.

Needless to say, Lucky and his pup devoured all the food long before Drake had finished.

Drake couldn't wait for Misty to see the little pup. He'd already made arrangements that they were to spend this Saturday evening at his house.

Drake figured if Mike could go over to Lepanto to visit Colleen, then Misty should also have free time away from her younger brother and sister.

Drake didn't consider that to be selfish. From all the talks he and Misty had had together, Drake knew that Mike

Bennett had certainly changed. However, Drake also knew the heavy responsibility Misty carried on her shoulders.

She had the right to enjoy herself at least one night a week. Drake had nothing negative to say about Colleen Carver. He thought she was a very nice lady, but it should be Mike staying home with his young children, not Misty.

He'd ridden over to see her at mid-week and invited her to come over to Dalton's Lair on Saturday night. The invitation did not include Jeff and Lavinia.

"Jeff's a big guy now so he can tend to his sister if your father has an engagement," he said.

"I'll be ready, Drake. But I wonder if you'll be able to come here during the next three months. There are going to be Saturdays, Drake, when you won't be able to make it. I don't know about winters in England, but when there's snow or freezing rain, everyone around here stays close to home."

"It would have to be bloody bad for me not to come over to see you, Misty," he responded hastily.

On Saturday evening, Mike Bennett left the house to go over to Lepanto to see Colleen. Shortly after he left, Drake arrived to pick Misty up. She wore a coat she'd salvaged from her mother's belongings. It was much warmer than her shawl.

As she sat beside him on the buggy seat, she told him "Winter has arrived in Arkansas, Drake."

"So, I'm about to spend my first winter in Arkansas, Misty. But don't think I'm not going to be able to see you," he assured her.

When they arrived at Drake's house, he escorted her into the house. He'd already prepared her about the new guest.

Misty was enchanted by the little pup. She was already cuddling her when Drake returned from putting the buggy in the barn. She knew that Lavinia would be thrilled to have this pup.

"Oh, Drake, she's divine!" she exclaimed as she put her back down on the floor.

Drake and Misty had a most romantic Saturday night. They enjoyed a nice dinner and worked together to put Drake's kitchen in order. Misty found Lucky's devotion toward the pup amazing.

In the sweet seclusion of Drake's house they once again made passionate love. Drake had to admit he wished he didn't have to take her home. More and more, he wished she could just remain with him.

Perhaps that was the reason he snuggled up close to her soft body and fell asleep. Usually, he didn't allow himself to drift off, knowing he had to get Misty home before Mike arrived at midnight.

He woke up with a start to see that he'd drifted off to sleep for over two hours. He leaped out of bed and began to get dressed, cussing himself for allowing the luxury of that long nap.

When he was dressed, he gently nudged Misty, "Love, wake up—I must get you home. Your father's going to beat us there tonight. I went off to sleep. Get dressed and I'll get the buggy."

She quickly got out of bed and began to get into her clothes.

The blackness of the night concealed the thick coat of ice on the front steps. The porch was dry, so he wasn't prepared as he started down them. The heels of his boots slid and his long legs went flying up in the air and his back slammed with a mighty force against the steps.

Misty heard his moans and the thud of his body as he hit the steps. She rushed to the front door.

"Oh, God, Drake!" she gasped as she rushed to him.

"No, love—don't get off that porch. There's a glaze of ice on the steps.

"But I must get you in the house, Drake. You're injured."

She could tell he was in a world of pain from the cracking of his voice.

"Give me a minute, love, and let me see if I can push myself up the steps." It took all his strength to push himself up the first step, but the pain was excruciating. As chilly as the air was, he broke out in a cold sweat.

"Here, Drake, take my hand and let me try to help you get up the top step. At least the porch is dry. Now come on or I'm going to go get Oscar to help us," she declared.

"Misty, you'd never make it. You'd fall out there and I couldn't come to help you. Give me a minute and I'll take your hand."

She strained to give him all the strength she had, but it was precious little.

Once he'd reached the top step it took a long time for him to slither through the front door.

He lay back on the floor to rest and catch his breath. Misty closed the door so they could begin to feel the warmth of the smoldering coals in the fireplace.

"Lie there, Drake, and rest while I put another log on the fire. You need to thaw out," she said.

Drake tried to muzzle his moans but it wasn't all that easy. He knew he had to get nearer to the fireplace because it was cold on the floor. He was going to be sleeping there tonight, for Misty couldn't possibly get him up on his bed. He had to just pray Oscar would arrive early in the morning.

As soon as Misty put another log on the fire, she rushed to the bedroom to get a pillow for Drake's head.

"Oh, Drake! I feel so helpless! You need a doctor and I can't get one for you."

His hand went up to caress her cheek as he tried to reassure her. "You're here with me, Misty. I'll be all right, I promise you."

He told her to take the pillow and blanket over by the fireplace. However, he had grave doubts that he'd get any sleep.

SWEET SEDUCTION 235

He gritted his teeth as he forced his body to move across to the hearth. Once he reached the spot where he planned to lie, Misty placed the pillow under his head and covered him with a blanket.

She then went to the kitchen to brew up some hot coffee. There wasn't going to be any sleep in this house tonight. It never occurred to her to worry about what her pa might think when she didn't come home. Right now, that did not concern her.

As soon as she had kindled the fire in the cookstove and had the coffeepot filled with water, she went back in the front room to check on Drake.

"You warm enough, Drake?"

"I'm just fine, love."

"I'm fixing us some coffee. I'll help you sit up to sip some of it."

"Sounds good to me," he said. His faltering voice told her the discomfort he was experiencing, even though he was trying to give her a weak smile.

At two in the morning, Misty sat on the floor with Drake, her small arm was cradling him while he tried to sip the hot coffee.

His dark eyes looked at her. "Ah, Misty—Misty, the luckiest day of my life was when I met you."

"I'm going to remind you to tell me that when you're not out of your head with pain, Drake Dalton," she said and smiled at him, trying to sound far more lighthearted than she was.

When she took their cups back to the kitchen and dimmed the lamps, she went to the bedroom to get another pillow and blanket. She intended to sleep by Drake's side.

When Drake tried a feeble protest, she quickly let him know what a determined, stubborn girl she could be. "I don't want to sleep in a comfortable bed, Drake. I want to be here, beside you, tonight."

She had never seen his dark eyes as warm as they were

in that moment, even when he was in the heat of passion. "Misty Bennett, marry me and then I'll never have to take you home again."

She gave him an impish grin as she snuggled down beside him and lowered her head to the pillow. "I'll remind you of that, too, Drake Dalton, when you're not out of your head with pain."

"I know exactly what I'm saying, love. Give me your hand. At least, I can hold it," he said.

With Drake holding her hand, she could tell each time he was feeling a surge of pain because he held her hand tighter.

Chapter 25

Mike Bennett arrived at his drive about the time the first sleet began to fall. A sudden drop in temperature had changed the misting rains into sleet, which usually did not occur this early in Arkansas.

By the time he'd gotten to the barn, put the horses into their stalls, and made his way to the house, he knew that another hour could have caused him problems getting the ten miles from Lepanto to his place.

His early arrival was due to the fact that Colleen was catering a large wedding the next day and had to get to her bakery to make several trays of finger sandwiches.

She'd spent hours that afternoon baking a three-tier wedding cake and Mike could tell she was exhausted. He realized that she probably wanted just to rest instead of fixing dinner for him.

Mike told her her this but she'd quickly dismissed the idea. "Oh, no, Mike—I'm glad to have you here with me tonight. I need a quiet evening."

The more he was around Colleen, the more he admired

her. She made the most delicious casseroles, and with her fresh-baked bread they were most filling. At Colleen's house, there was always an exciting dessert served at the end of the meal.

"God, Colleen, this chocolate mousse is so good!" Mike declared.

"Glad you enjoyed it, Mike."

He had insisted on helping her clear away the table and do the dishes. He'd stayed only a half hour in her parlor before leaning over to give her a kiss and say he was going to do her a favor by going on home.

"I think you need to get to bed, Colleen."

He was aware that the temperature had fallen several degrees since he'd arrived at Colleen's. If this misting rain kept up during the night and the temperature fell a few more degrees, he wondered if it would turn to ice pellets.

He found Jeff and Lavinia cozy in their beds but Misty was still over at Drake's. But he didn't worry about Misty—he had realized in recent weeks that Drake Dalton was definitely in love with her. Being a man, he recognized the look in Dalton's eyes when he looked at Misty.

Now that he'd gotten to know Dalton, he had to admit he liked him. How could he possibly fault a man who'd been so generous with his family? Colleen had voiced her approval of young Dalton after the night at the square dance.

He had to admit that Misty was probably envied by a lot of the young ladies in Crowley who would have loved to be squired by the handsome Englishman, but his daughter had been the one to catch his eye.

He felt a little smug about that since he'd always known that a lot of the people had never accepted him into their clannish little community.

He didn't stay too long in his front room after he arrived home—he wasn't concerned about Misty as long as she was with Drake. He had that much faith in him by now. But he did spend some quiet moments in private musings before he dimmed the lamps. What he could never tell Misty, Jeff, or Lavinia was that their mother was not exactly what they'd thought her to be and that he was not the overbearing bastard they'd thought him to be.

He would be content to let them have their dream of his Beth. He had realized, though, after they'd been married two months, what he'd known on their wedding night: Beth was not the virgin she'd pretended to be.

He'd said nothing then or in the months to follow, but he saw how quickly her body began to swell and he was convinced that the baby was not sired by him.

To this day, he still did not know who had fathered Misty but he knew he hadn't. There was no doubt in his mind that he had sired Jeff and Lavinia. Misty was so much like her mother that he'd never been able to figure out who her father was. But he knew he had to be a local man.

He would only have had to read Beth's private journals to find out. But he'd never taken the time to do that. Misty had yet to get around to reading them—her life had been too busy and exciting of late.

The next morning when the sun rose, the ice began to melt.

From sheer exhaustion, Drake and Misty had gotten a few hours of sleep. At seven in the morning there was a rap on the front door. Misty leaped from her pallet—it was Oscar, who stood there with a pitchfork to help him make it from his house to Drake's.

"Miss Misty—you didn't get home?"

"I sure didn't, Oscar. Drake fell and hurt his back. It was so bad last night I couldn't walk over to your house to get you. So I tried to make him as comfortable as I could. There was no way I could possibly get him up on his bed so we slept on pallets by the hearth," she said as she ushered Oscar through the front door.

He immediately spied Drake lying on the floor. He wasn't even sure if he could get Drake into bed, but he knew he had to try.

Drake roused from his light sleep to see Oscar towering over him. " 'Morning, Oscar—got myself in a bit of a mess last night."

"Appears you did, Mr. Dalton. We're going to have to see if we can get you into your bed—that's where you need to be."

"Oscar, you sure can't carry me so I'll have to do what I did last night."

"Then that's how we'll do it—I'm going to get those pants off of you and have a look at your back," Oscar said.

Drake suggested to Misty that she get a pot of coffee. "I'll need one by the time Oscar and I make that long trip back to my bed."

After lying on the floor for hours, moving caused Drake very intense pain. Oscar thought he might be able to make it a little easier, so he took hold of Drake's hands. He was certainly not as husky as Drake, but he had great strength.

He literally dragged Drake out of the front room to his bedroom. Once they reached the side of Drake's bed, they took a moment to rest and figure out the best way to get him up on the bed.

"If Misty could lift your feet and legs, I could get a tight hold under your arms and your hands would be free to help, Mr. Dalton," Oscar suggested.

"Well, let's try it—I can't think of an easier way," Drake said.

Oscar called Misty and instructed her as she cradled Drake's lower legs. Oscar was already in position and starting to hoist Drake's body upward. Drake's hand clawed at the mattress to help get him over the edge of the bed.

He couldn't help moaning as he collapsed on the bed. Both Misty and Oscar sank down on the edge of the bed and breathed a deep sigh of relief.

"Thank God, Drake—you're finally in the bed!" Misty declared. "I'm going to go check the coffee."

As soon as Misty left, Oscar told Drake he was going to get his pants off. "You just lie still and let me do the work—you won't have to do a thing."

Drake just allowed Oscar to take charge. Oscar unfastened the belt and waistband before he went to the foot of the bed to start gently pulling on the pants. Very quickly they slipped underneath Drake's buttocks and on down his legs.

"They're off—we'll let you rest awhile before I try to check out your bruises. Sun's out this morning, Mr. Dalton, and the ice is melting fast. I can hitch up the horses and get Miss Misty home. I'm sure her pa's walking the floor about her. Then I'll head on to Crowley to get Doc Smothers to come out here and take a look at you. Rachel will come to stay with you."

"Thank you, Oscar," Drake said.

A short time later Oscar took a look at Drake's back; he found some angry redness but no bruises. His injury had to be internal, Oscar assumed.

He went into the kitchen to tell Misty he was going over to fetch Rachel so she could take care of Drake and the house. "I'll take you home, Miss Misty. I know you've got family worried stiff about you. Then I'm going into Crowley to get the doctor."

"I'll be ready, Oscar. I've got coffee ready for you when you want it. I'll take Drake a cup," she said.

When Rachel and Oscar returned to the house, Misty was sitting by Drake's bedside, helping him drink some of the coffee. She told him she was leaving and bent down to kiss him.

"Afraid I won't be coming over next Saturday, love," he said dejectedly.

"But one way or the other I'll get over here to see you, Drake. It might not be until Saturday but I'll have Pa bring me," she promised.

"One more kiss, Misty," he insisted. She was more than willing to oblige.

A short time later she was in the flat-bedded wagon with Oscar heading for home. He assured her that he and Rachel would take good care of Drake.

She smiled. "Drake isn't going to like lying in bed for a week or so."

"Like it or not, he may just have to. Same thing happened to a man my age he'd be laid up twice as long."

When they arrived at Misty's, Oscar insisted he see her to her porch. He was glad he'd remembered to throw that pitchfork into the back of the wagon—the Bennett house faced the north and the pathway was still coated with ice.

Oscar held her arm as they slowly walked up the pathway. Mike saw his daughter with a strange man and rushed out to the porch. "My God Misty! I've been so worried about you," he said as he came down the steps and took her hand.

"It's been a long night, Pa," she said, quickly introducing Mike to Oscar.

He hastily informed Mike that Dalton had fallen and injured his back. "Miss Misty couldn't even get to my house to get me and my sister, so she just had to stay with Mr. Dalton. I'm on my way to get Doc Smothers now."

"I thank you, Oscar, and I trust Drake isn't too badly injured," Mike said as he held Misty's hand tightly to help her up the steps.

With his pitchfork, Oscar headed back to his wagon as Mike took Misty into the house. She looked weary. Misty found her father very understanding as he led her into the front room and helped her remove her coat.

"Lavinia and Jeff are still sleeping. Do you want to just go to your room and get some sleep, Misty? We can talk later," he said.

"Think I will, Pa. I got almost no sleep all night," she replied.

She went to her room and closed the door. Then she

undressed and crawled into the bed with her undergarments still on, pulling the heavy coverlet up to her chin. She slept for the next five hours.

Mike gave firm orders to both Jeff and Lavinia that they were not to make any noise so Misty could rest.

It was a strange afternoon around the Bennett house. Mike was in the kitchen at mid-afternoon, puttering around the cookstove as he prepared a big pot of beef stew. Lavinia gave him a quizzical look. "Pa, are you sure you know how to do it?"

He laughed and tousled her hair. "I think I can put a pot of beef stew together. Guess you don't remember, honey, but after your ma died I put a lot of meals on the table before Misty took over."

"Guess I don't remember, Pa," she admitted.

"Well, I did, so you just go play and I'll attend to our supper. Misty will have a break from cooking tonight," he said and smiled down at her.

It was almost three when Misty finally woke and got dressed. Her room seemed cold.

The first thing she had to do once she emerged from her bedroom was to answer a great many questions about Drake.

"Well, we had no idea how much sleet had fallen when Drake went to the barn to get his buggy to bring me home. The porch was fine because the roof covered it, but when he started down the steps, they were covered with ice and he went flying. He couldn't get up and I couldn't lift him so he had to drag himself up the steps and across the porch to get inside."

"Lordy, he must have really hurt himself, Misty," Jeff gasped.

"He certainly did, Jeff. So he crawled over to the hearth and that's where the two of us slept last night. He wouldn't hear of me trying to walk over to Oscar's. Of course, he was right. I probably wouldn't have reached the gate before I'd have fallen, too."

"Sounds like he's got himself a good back injury, Misty," Mike said.

"I fear so, Pa. What about you? How did you make it home from Lepanto?"

"I was lucky. Colleen and I had an early night because she had to cater a wedding this afternoon, so I left a couple hours earlier than usual. Sleet began to fall about the time I arrived home, then it was coming down real heavy."

"It must have been from the amount I saw on Drake's steps."

Misty found it very thoughtful of her pa to prepare the stew for supper and took charge of cleaning up after they ate.

While Mike's thoughts were about Colleen, hoping she hadn't found the roads too treacherous to get to the reception, Misty was wondering if Oscar had gotten a doctor to check Drake.

So both of them began the new week wondering about the people they loved.

Chapter 26

Colleen had had no problems getting to the reception as Lepanto did not get the sleet storm Crowley had experienced.

Misty would have been delighted to know that Dr. Smothers had examined the entire length of Drake's back and found that he had some badly bruised muscles around his tailbone, but it didn't mean he had to be confined to bed.

"It's going to hurt like hell every time you move, but you don't have to stay in bed," he said to Drake.

"I can handle that, Dr. Smothers."

Drake had insisted that Rachel return to her house after she'd served him dinner. She'd been prepared to stay in the spare bedroom overnight.

"But Mr. Dalton—I just don't feel right leaving you here alone," she'd protested.

Drake had told her to go on home, but she fussed and fumed all the time after she got there. After she and Oscar had their dinner and she'd put her kitchen in order, she was still upset.

Oscar asked her, "Will you settle down and get yourself

a good night's rest if I go over there and stay through the night with him, Rachel? You're as nervous as a cat."

"Yes, I'd feel a lot better," she declared.

So Oscar went over to Drake's that evening around nine and told him, "Rachel is going to worry all night if one of us isn't over here tonight. Mind if I use that spare bedroom so I can get some sleep, Mr. Dalton?"

Drake laughed. "Be my guest! That Rachel is a little mother hen, isn't she?"

"Yes sir, she is when she cares for someone."

Every time Drake got up he experienced terrible pain, but at least he hadn't broken anything. Once he went to bed, he slept deeply but he wasn't even able to lift a log to bank up his fire to keep the house warm through the night.

Rachel was wiser than he was. He did need someone with him. He slept so soundly that he didn't hear Oscar when he got up quietly and left the house in the morning.

By the time Oscar left, Rachel was back. When Drake woke up, a pan of biscuits baked to perfection was waiting for him, and Rachel was ready to fry up some ham and eggs.

Drake had a hearty breakfast and felt very invigorated. He pushed himself to walk around the house that morning while Rachel went about her chores.

Being a gentle-hearted woman, Rachel saw that Lucky and the newly arrived pup were fed. She also allowed Lucky to have his freedom in the yard but she restrained the pup from following him.

She planned to cook a fat hen for Drake's dinner. He loved her chicken and dumplings so she knew he'd be pleased.

Working for Mr. Dalton had never been a problem for Rachel—he was not demanding and he was very neat. She found it a pleasure to keep his house in order and cook his meals.

She also made him a fruit cobbler, which she knew he

loved. She noticed he had to give way to his discomfort by late afternoon and go to his bedroom.

She sat in the kitchen enjoying a cup of coffee once her chores were done. She was even satisfied that Mr. Dalton could take care of himself during the night. She had already given him orders to let her clean up after his evening meal in the morning.

She placed a plate and silverware on the table for Drake, so that when he wished to eat all he had to do was ladle some of the chicken and dumplings out of the pot.

Rachel was very encouraged when Drake slowly moved into the front room and picked up the silver case holding his cheroots to light one up. Then he went over to the liquor chest to pour himself a drink. With an impish grin, he asked Rachel what he had to look forward for dinner. When she told him he had peach cobbler and chicken and dumplings, he responded quickly, "Lord, Rachel, how you spoil me!"

"Got to get you well, Mr. Dalton. Christmas is just around the corner."

"You're right, Rachel. I have got to get over this. I have gifts to buy." He already had one little girl her gift, but there were several more he wished to buy. He and Oscar had already talked about going to the woods to get their Christmas trees.

By the time the end of the week rolled around, Drake had made great strides. He'd even taken a brief stroll in the front yard just to get out of the house after being inside all week.

Rachel started her preparations for the holiday season by baking two fruit cakes. She told Drake why she liked to bake them in advance. "I moisten them with brandy and wrap them with a cloth. Makes them mighty fine by the time Christmas comes."

"Bet that's mighty tasty," he remarked. Drake was already anticipating Misty's visit on Saturday. He realized she had to depend on her father to bring her over as it was too far to walk.

Drake had been back in his bedroom resting for almost an hour when, for the first time all day, Rachel poured herself a cup of coffee. She was almost ready to go home as she'd prepared everything for the night. Oscar came over about seven to bank up the fire.

When she heard a rapping on the front door, she wondered who it might be. Miss Misty wouldn't be coming at this hour.

A tall, willowy young woman stood there looking down at her. With an aristocratic air, she announced herself she was Ellen Dalton. "I'm Drake's sister from England."

"Come in, miss. I'm Rachel, Mr. Dalton's housekeeper," Rachel said, inviting her to have a seat.

"My valises will have to be brought in. Is Drake here?"

"Yes, miss—he's here. He's resting. Mr. Dalton took a bad fall and injured his back a few nights ago so those valises will have to wait until my brother can fetch them."

Ellen took a seat and began to remove her gloves. "I trust he wasn't injured too badly."

"He's improving but he still takes a rest every afternoon. May I bring you a cup of coffee? I was having one myself when you arrived," Rachel remarked in a friendly manner.

But Ellen found Rachel far too familiar for a servant. "No, but I'll have a pot of tea, though," she replied.

"Fear I can't oblige you, miss. We have no tea in the cupboard."

Ellen looked at her in disbelief. "Drake doesn't drink tea anymore?"

"Far as I know he doesn't. Never brewed any for him since I've been here."

"Wonder when he acquired a taste for coffee." Ellen mumbled. She suddenly recalled that her mother and Drake often did drink coffee.

Ellen rose to remove her fur-collared coat. She'd expected

Rachel to come and fetch it, but that didn't happen. So she laid it across the back of the chair and, in a rather vexed tone, told Rachel, "Well, then I guess I'll have to settle for a cup of the miserable stuff then."

Rachel went to pour her a cup, just yelling from the kitchen to ask if she wanted sugar and cream.

Thus, within the first fifteen minutes of her arrival, did Ellen experience her brother's "primitive" lifestyle in Arkansas.

After Ellen was served her coffee, Rachel excused herself to feed the dogs. One sip caused Ellen to grimace. When Rachel opened the back door to allow Lucky in, the little pup heard him and came scampering to greet him.

Lucky was ready for the food Rachel had placed on the kitchen floor. It was then he noticed the strange lady sitting in the front room so he rushed in to inspect her. He didn't get a friendly pat on his head—Ellen pushed him away. "Get away! Dear God, Rachel—come here and get this mutt!" she cried as the pup's wet tongue licked at her ankle.

Rachel could hardly control her laughter. Lucky didn't like being pushed away. He was accustomed to everyone liking him, so he began to bark at Drake's sister.

Rachel called to him and he went to her side as she bent to pat his head. "He's a real friendly dog, miss. At least, he's friendly as long as you don't strike him. Then I'm not sure what he'd do."

"Don't tell me Drake keeps that monster in the house!" Ellen said and bristled.

"Yes, miss, he does. So you'll be having to get used to Lucky if you stay around here."

Rachel grew nervous—this young lady was already proving to be a headache. She pitied poor Mr. Dalton.

Drake roused from his nap when he heard voices coming from the front room. He prayed it was just a bad dream as he sat on the side of the bed for a second before attempting to get up.

There was no doubt it was his sister, Ellen, in his front room. "Oh, God!" he moaned. Either she'd gotten his letter and, being her usual headstrong self, had decided to come anyway or she hadn't received it in time.

As soon as he arrived in the front room he realized it had already begun to happen. Rachel had a strained look on her face and Ellen sat stiffly, obviously annoyed.

"Well, Ellen—this *is* a surprise!" he greeted her, slowly walking over to plant a kiss on her cheek.

"I'm sorry you're injured, Drake. Rachel was telling me about your fall. I wrote you about my plans," Ellen said after they broke their embrace.

"And I also wrote you. Did you get my letter?"

"I did."

"I see," Drake replied, figuring they'd discuss that later.

Rachel quietly exited the room and gladly turned his sister over to Mr. Dalton. Lucky immediately went to Drake's side and the little pup followed. Rachel went back to her kitchen to put away her fruitcakes and pack up a crock of chicken and dumplings and a cobbler for her and Oscar to have for supper.

When she was ready to leave, she went back into the front room to put more logs in the fireplace. As she'd been doing, she gently admonished Drake. "Now Mr. Dalton—Oscar will come over later to bring in your sister's heavy valises. Your supper is on the stove warming and I've set another place for your sister. Lucky and little one have had their supper so I'll be leaving now. Nice to meet you, miss," Rachel said as she made a quick exit.

Drake observed the strange look on Ellen's face and couldn't suppress a smile. His sister was in for some very rude awakenings.

Drake reached over to light up one of his cheroots. When Ellen finally found her tongue, she stammered, "She doesn't serve your dinner?"

"I'm up to doing that for myself now, Ellen. As I told

you, there are no servants here. Until Oscar and Rachel came I did my own cooking and cleaning."

"Oh, Drake, how could you possibly live like this?"

"So why did you come here after I wrote you about how life was here?"

"Because I couldn't stand the woman Father married. And Valeria got married a couple of months ago."

"You could always have gotten yourself a town house in London and pursued your tutoring," Drake pointed out.

"I think I just wanted to get away from England," she confessed.

"Be prepared, Ellen. You'll have to take a simple job here, like working in a mercantile or bakery. There will be no tutoring. Let me tell you right now so you'll understand about Rachel and Oscar. Rachel is not the kind of servant you're used to. She doesn't run and fetch for you. Her brother is my foreman and she is my housekeeper and cook but we all do for ourselves," Drake informed her.

"I understand, Drake—really I do."

But Drake rather doubted that. He ushered her back to the spare bedroom. "This is the only other bedroom I have."

Ellen's eyes had scrutinized the front room when she'd first arrived, concluding it was not even as luxurious as the servants' quarters on her father's estate. This second bedroom was not half as nice as her maid's room back at Dalton Manor. There was not even a dressing table. There were three pieces of furniture: a bed, a chest, and a chair. Simple little floral ruffled curtains hung at the one window and an ugly coverlet draped the bed.

She grumbled, "Well, I can hardly refresh myself until this man of yours brings my valises in. Is it possible to have a warm bath in the meanwhile?"

"If you wish to heat the three teakettles on the cookstove. That's the way we bathe here, Ellen. I do have a nice big tub."

"Oh, Lord, Drake—I can't believe you live like this!" she moaned.

"Then, love, you should have taken my letter more seriously." He grinned as he left her fussing and fuming—he felt in need of a drink.

He went to the front room after he'd poured himself a generous drink and lit a cheroot. As he sat in the quiet of his front room with a roaring fire, he thought he might buy her a little house and furnish it if she wished to stay, just to get her out of his hair.

Ellen would drive him crazy and she would certainly cramp his style with Misty. The two of them would never get along. Misty would never understand Ellen's high-handed ways and Ellen would never understand Misty's simple, frank manner.

Rachel alerted Oscar to the arrival of Drake's sister as soon as he arrived home at six. Then he rushed over to the house to get the valises carried in, because he didn't want Mr. Dalton doing it.

Having her valises soothed Ellen's ruffled feathers somewhat. She was finally able to get out of her traveling ensemble and into a dressing gown. Since things were so informal, she decided she could spend the rest of the evening in that.

She forgot about taking a bath. She'd go through that ritual tomorrow, she promised herself.

Oscar banked up Drake's fire and said good night. "I'll check on things in the morning, Mr. Dalton," he said before he left to go home, where Rachel had their supper waiting. But Rachel had already told him enough for him to know that this sister was not what Dalton needed.

When Ellen finally emerged from her bedroom in her mauve dressing gown, Drake asked if she was ready to have dinner. "I'll have to get some tea for you, Ellen."

Drake rose from his chair and escorted his sister to the kitchen, where he poured them some coffee. "I'll let you slice Rachel's bread, Ellen." He noticed how awkward she was, so he decided to serve the chicken and dumplings himself. She wanted to find fault with them, but she found them delicious.

The peach cobbler was just as excellent—Ellen had to admit that Rachel was a great cook. She'd never eaten a flakier crust. Drake told her after they'd finished just to stack the dishes on the counter and Rachel would clean them in the morning.

If Ellen thought she'd had some rude awakenings late Friday afternoon, she was to have more the next day.

When she met Misty Bennett, Ellen knew that her older brother had met a young lady who had captured his heart, and she could understand why. She was breathtakingly beautiful!

It was obvious to Ellen that Drake adored her when she saw his face as he rushed out the door to greet her.

Chapter 27

Mike Bennett had put his time in at the mills and had stopped by the store to buy groceries. He'd also bought a gift to take to Colleen and one for Misty. It was interesting to Misty that he'd chosen the same toilet water that Drake had purchased many weeks ago. He told her that he always remembered how she'd pluck the wild jasmine growing in the woods by their house.

"Now you go and get ready, Misty. I'll take you over to Drake's when I go to see Colleen and pick you up on my way home."

"Oh, thank you, Pa. I've been worried about him all week, I have to admit."

"I know you're anxious to see him."

She smiled sheepishly as she turned to leave. An hour later she was dressed and wearing Drake's locket and earrings. She gathered up her coat and reticule and headed for the front room.

"Well, now aren't you pretty!" Mike remarked. Lavinia said, "Yeah, and she smells good, too."

"Well, thank both of you," Misty told them before turning to Jeff to give him some instructions about supper, telling him all he had to do was heat it up. Once again Lavinia spoke up. "You're not going to take both of those cakes to Mr. Dalton, are you, Misty?

Misty sighed, "Oh, Lavinia, bless you! I was about to walk out of here without the cake. No, honey, I'm only taking one."

"Oh, good!" Lavinia declared happily. Chocolate cake was her favorite.

It was five-thirty as Misty and her father rolled down the drive in his wagon. Mike told her he didn't think they'd have to worry about sleet tonight. "But I won't be late, Misty. Colleen has another catering assignment tomorrow. She told me that this is the season her business picks up."

"All right, Pa."

"It will be a little after ten at the latest when I get back here," he said as he pulled up in front of Drake's gate. Lucky spotted her getting out of the wagon and immediately ran to greet her. Mike put his wagon into motion and Misty slipped through the gate—she didn't dare to let Lucky out. She gave him a pat on the head. "Trust your master is better than he was the last time I saw him, Lucky. Bet you've been keeping him company," she said as they walked to the steps.

Drake had looked out the front windows numerous times since early afternoon—he wasn't sure if Mike would bring her by after he got off work.

He was finally rewarded by the sight of her and old Lucky strolling up to the porch, so he knew he was going to have the pleasure of her company all evening. He just wished it was time they could spend alone.

Up to now, his day had been a taxing one. As soon as Rachel had finished cooking his dinner, he told her to go on home early. He sensed that she welcomed his suggestion—Ellen had given her a case of frayed nerves. Ellen's constant invasion of the kitchen or asking for this or that was throwing Rachel into a frenzy.

But going to the door to greet Misty, putting his arms around her, and kissing her made him forget all his problems.

They had a few brief moments together, so he alerted her about his sister's arrival.

"Oh, no—didn't she get your letter, Drake?" Misty stiffened, suddenly feeling very uneasy.

"Yes, but Ellen's a headstrong girl. She's already given Rachel a good case of nerves so I sent her packing. She fixed a roast hen for our dinner tonight. Will you take charge, Misty? Ellen would burn everything," he said and grinned deviously.

"I'll take charge, Drake, but she can help, too. Surely she can set a table or slice bread," Misty giggled.

"Good girl! She's bloody well going to have to learn to do some things around here. I've already told her Rachel is my housekeeper, not my maid."

"Oh, Drake—you didn't need this right now," Misty declared, giving his cheek an affectionate caress.

"No, but it looks like I'm stuck for a while," he replied.

Ellen could not figure out what had intrigued Drake about Arkansas. What really upset her was that she was stuck here until spring came whether she liked it or not.

A winter crossing of the Atlantic was treacherous. It had taken her weeks to get to this horrible place from the east coast, which was where she would have to travel to get passage back to England. But there was no question about it—she was going back. Dalton Manor was paradise compared to this, she told herself as she leisurely soaked in the tub on this gray December afternoon.

Since she'd closed her bedroom door, Ellen began to feel a chill. She was used to a woodburning fireplace in her bedroom.

At least, it did feel refreshing to put on clean undergarments and slip into her robe. There was no dressing table to sit at while she styled her hair, so she used her silver hand mirror. She chose a light wool gown—Drake's house seemed so drafty. One small fireplace supplied little heat.

She'd found that she could only unpack two of her valises, as there was no armoire to hang her gowns in. The one small chest didn't even have enough drawer space for her undergarments and nightgowns.

Ellen knew she had been the worst kind of fool!

By the time she left the house at four-thirty, Rachel was relieved not to be tormented any more by the young miss from England.

But she'd been aware that Drake and his sister had been sitting in the front room together for the last half-hour. The clock chimed four as Ellen had made her entrance into the front room and Drake greeted her warmly. "Well, you look refreshed and attractive, Ellen."

"Ah, if I only had a nice cup of tea right now," she sighed.

"We'll get you some tea, dear."

"You hated father, didn't you, Drake?" she asked.

"Yes, I hate him yet, Ellen, for what he did to a very sweet, gentle lady—our mother."

"So that was why you left to go to Mother's brother in Paris?"

"Yes, Mother knew she was dying—she had no desire to live longer, Ellen. She was weary of life. He drained her dry, this father of ours. She urged me to go to Bayard if something happened to her."

"I wondered, because you left so quickly after she died," Ellen remarked.

"I left because after she was gone, I couldn't stand to sit across the table from him anymore. I took nothing from that place but my mother's journals, which I went to her room to get before he got his hands on them. I knew he would have destroyed them. I also took two of her favorite pieces of jewelry—I considered myself more deserving of them than some strange woman he'd marry. One day my bride will wear them and that would have made Mother happy. From what you've told me, he hasn't waited too long to find himself a wife.'' Drake's smirk revealed the disgust he felt for Lord Devin Dalton.

"May I read Mother's journals, Drake?" Ellen asked.

"Of course you may, Ellen."

"I would like to. I know now that I should not have come here, Drake. I understand what you were trying to tell me in your letter. But I was the only one left there after Valeria married and I detested this woman Father married."

"Ellen, it wasn't that I wasn't glad to see you, but I knew this place wasn't for you. It would take you a long time to adjust to living here. No, it would have been wiser of you to stay in England and just move out to your own private quarters if you wished. Your sisters live there and the lifestyle you've always enjoyed could have continued. You'll never have it here, my dear sister," he told her, giving her hand a gentle pat.

She smiled. "I know that, Drake. I find this place horrible."

"And I find it a paradise, Ellen."

All the time they had been talking, Ellen realized that Drake was preoccupied by other things—he kept pacing over to the window. "It's a couple of hours before dinner so I'd enjoy reading them while you rest."

"Of course, Ellen." He rose from the settee slowly and went to his room to get them.

When he returned, Ellen took them and announced she would see him at dinnertime. Since the moment she'd arrived, she'd noticed that her older brother was different. He was nothing like the man she'd known back in England. That year he'd spent in Paris and the time he'd spent in this remote place had changed him.

He was no longer the happy-go-lucky bachelor he used to be, squiring all the beauties and living in luxurious surroundings. She had instantly noticed how differently he dressed—no more of the fine tailored outfits he used to wear.

But she had to admit he was more handsome than she remembered. His skin was bronzed and there was a sparkle in his dark eyes as he talked about his place. Drake was obviously a very happy man!

Chapter 28

Ellen had not been aware of Misty's arrival until she heard the soft, lilting laughter and Drake's deep, husky voice. She walked out of her bedroom to go to the front room and saw the two of them together. She knew her older brother was entranced by this beautiful girl.

Ellen had to admit she was gorgeous. Her long, golden hair fell over her shoulders and when she turned to look at Ellen her eyes twinkled like emeralds, so brilliant and green.

She was obviously very familar with her brother. Her hand held his as they rose for Drake to make the introductions. Misty quickly responded by saying, "It's so nice to meet Drake's sister." Her eyes were scrutinizing Ellen as Ellen scrutinized her.

The other thing Ellen noticed was that the big dog was curled up by their feet and Misty had the pup on her lap.

Drake rose from the settee to serve some sherry before Misty went into the kitchen. Drake heard his sister remark, "I find your name quaint, Misty."

"My name is actually Melanie but my little brother

couldn't pronounce it so he called me Misty. Somehow, the rest of my family began to call me that, too."

Drake handed Misty one of the glasses. "You'd never told me that."

She smiled. "I guess I hadn't, Drake. Anyway that's the story about how I became Misty instead of Melanie."

Ellen sensed they were more than casual friends. The warmth in their eyes when they looked at one another told her that.

Drake found himself amused by his sister and the various questions she asked Misty. Ellen was curious as a cat about the two of them.

When Misty finished the glass of sherry and saw that Ellen had also finished hers, she got up from the settee and said to Drake, "You just sit here and enjoy one of those cheroots while your sister and I get dinner ready."

Ellen's eyes darted from Misty to Drake. This pretty young lady seemed awfully bossy, but Misty urged her in a friendly manner to come to the kitchen so Ellen could hardly refuse.

When they got to the kitchen, Ellen asked her, "What—what shall I do?"

Misty pointed to the cupboard where she'd find dishes and serving bowls and the drawer where the silverware was. "If you set the table, Ellen, then I can see if I need to add a little kindling to the stove to heat up this food Rachel left."

"What in the world is *kindling?*" Ellen asked.

"It's thin pieces of wood that fire up faster than regular logs in a cookstove," Misty said as she busily moved around the kitchen. It was apparent that she felt perfectly at home.

Misty seemed to be in constant motion, stirring the pots and then getting the bread placed on the cutting board with a large knife. She was so outgoing and talkative that Ellen found it impossible not to respond in the same way.

"Ah, Ellen, we'll have this dinner on the table before

you know it. Now, if you'll slice us some bread I'm about ready to take the roast hen and pan of dressing out of the oven.

Misty had the two pans out of the oven as Ellen struggled to cut that first slice of bread. Misty noticed she was trying to slice it without holding the top of the loaf, so the bread kept sliding around. Misty showed her how to hold the loaf as her knife did the work.

"You see how easy it is?" Misty said and smiled.

"Well, this is a first for me. I never did anything around a kitchen, as you can see. Servants did everything for us as we were growing up," Ellen confessed.

"Well, my life's not been so luxurious, Ellen. I've cooked and cleaned and tended to a younger brother and sister ever since my mother died."

"Oh, Lord—I can't imagine doing all that!" Ellen declared.

"Guess a person does what needs to be done." Misty spooned the vegetables onto a plate. She suggested to Ellen that she announce to Drake that dinner was served.

To Drake's surprise and delight, Ellen was not in a sulking mood because Misty had insisted on having her help with dinner. In fact, the three of them enjoyed Rachel's delicious meal and ate heartily.

For the first time since she'd arrived, Ellen laughed—Misty was telling them about Lavinia thinking she was going to bring both of her chocolate cakes over here this evening. "I made her very happy when she found out I was leaving one there," Misty said and laughed.

"How old is she, Misty?" Ellen asked.

"She's six and Jeff's ten but lately he thinks he's going on twenty. He's trying to mimic Drake—his hero." Her green eyes glanced over at Drake. "Have you noticed lately how he's trying to brush his hair like yours?"

Drake smiled, "I'd noticed."

Misty directed her conversation to Ellen, telling her how

Drake had taught Jeff to ride a horse and had taken him hunting. She told Ellen how the two of them had provided the turkey for their Thanksgiving dinner.

Misty added, "Jeff swore he shot that turkey but I knew it was probably Drake."

It was a far more relaxed evening than Drake had anticipated—his little Misty was doing a grand job of keeping his sister entertained with various tales about her family.

It seemed that Misty, with her simple, unpretentious manner, had performed a miracle because when the meal was over Ellen offered to help her clean up.

By the time Misty was dimming the lamps in the kitchen, Ellen was lightheartedly jesting that she'd had two firsts this evening. "I've sliced bread and dried dishes."

"You'll have a lot of firsts, Ellen, living here with Drake," Misty told her as they went back into the front room.

"Well, I fear I got myself on the bad side with his housekeeper, Rachel. I cut into her fruitcake. She was furious with me this morning," Ellen confided.

"Oh, no," Misty sighed. With an impish grin, she explained to Ellen the reason for Rachel's fury. "She'll get over it, but the fruitcakes are baked in advance and wrapped in a cloth and given a dose of brandy a couple of times before Christmas. Ah, Ellen, they're delicious!"

"I see. Guess I'll have to rely on you to educate me to the ways and customs in this place." She grinned sheepishly because now she understood why Rachel was so angry.

Drake heard their gay laughter as he came back up on the front porch. It was nice to see his sister so agreeable and he was also pleased that Misty wasn't having a miserable evening.

He was also pleased about himself—this had been the best day he'd had since he'd fallen last Saturday night. He told Misty when he went over to sit beside her, "There's a full moon out tonight. There'll be no sleet like there was last Saturday."

"Thank goodness for that," Misty declared.

"So that was when you fell, Drake?" Ellen asked.

"Yes, I was going out to get the buggy to take Misty home. It was dark and I didn't know sleet had been falling, coating the steps. My feet went out from under me and I fell on my rear with a mighty crash."

"So how did you get home, Misty?" Ellen asked.

"I didn't until the next morning. Poor Drake had to slither like a snake just to get inside the front door and we slept on pallets by the hearth. I couldn't get him to his bed and I couldn't walk over to get Oscar to help me," Misty informed his sister candidly.

"My goodness!" Ellen now knew why they seemed so relaxed around one another. Drake sat watching his sister's face. He had never known anyone as frank and honest as Misty Bennett. It would not have occurred to Misty to tell Ellen anything but the truth.

When the clock chimed nine, Drake had given up all hope that he and Misty would have a private moment. But then Ellen seemed to sense that the two of them wanted a few moments together.

So she told them good night. "I've some things to still get unpacked," she said as she rose from her chair. She turned to Misty. "Thanks for teaching me how to slice bread and dry dishes. If I slip in late tonight to get myself a piece of cake it will be the chocolate one. I won't touch Rachel's fruitcake," she said and laughed.

"Good night, Ellen. It was nice to spend the evening with you," Misty said.

As soon as Ellen left, Drake grinned and asked Misty, "So she told you about the set-to between her and Rachel around here this morning? God, I'm just going to send for you, Misty, when they go at it the next time! You seem to be able to do wonders with Ellen."

"I don't think she and Rachel will have that kind of

problem again, Drake. I explained why Rachel was in such a furor and Ellen understood."

Drake's arm went around her waist. "I can't love you the way I'd like to but I can kiss those sweet lips. You're the tonic I've needed all week, Misty."

His strong arms held her close as he kissed her for the longest time. When he finally released her, he sighed, "Oh, love—the day I met you on that country road hobbling along with that broken sandal was the luckiest day of my life, I swear it!

"I'd like to think that, Drake. It was the day everything changed for me."

"It delights me to know that for that's what I wanted to do, my little Misty. I want to be the only man in your life now and forever."

"You are, Drake. Don't you know that? I'd never given myself to any man until you. I can't imagine ever giving myself to any man but you," she declared.

"And you just keep feeling that way."

She never got a chance to respond for there was a rap on the door. Drake left her to answer it. Misty knew it would be her pa coming to pick her up. Drake opened the door and invited him to enter.

Mike came in carrying two pies. "Colleen sent these over, Drake. Said to hope you were feeling much better and it looks like you are."

"Yes, sir—I sure am. That Colleen is an angel. That was the best pie I'd ever eaten. You tell her I thank her very much. But give me another week and I'll probably be able to get over to Lepanto to thank her myself."

While the two of them were talking, Misty went to get her coat and reticule. The two of them said good night to Drake and Mike urged his daughter to button up her coat. "It's getting chilly out there. I think I can say winter's arrived in Arkansas, Drake. Hope you got plenty of wood up, 'cause the next three months you're going to be burning a lot of it.''

"Think I have, Mr. Bennett. Oscar had prepared me very well," Drake assured him.

Drake was very encouraged by the time he went to bed that night. He was sure that one more week was going to find him in very good shape.

When Ellen had gone to her bedroom at nine she was certainly not sleepy, so she began to pursue her mother's journals which dated from her earliest days at Dalton Manor. There was no doubt in Ellen's mind that she left this world an unhappy woman, but she'd obviously also arrived as a young bride at the manor house an unhappy woman. She was not in love with her husband. It was a marriage arranged between her father and the wealthy young English lord. Neither of them had seemed to care about her feelings at all.

Ellen sat on the bed, tears flowing down her cheeks, as she read what her mother had written about how cruelly he'd used his young, virgin bride once he'd brought her back to England where she was a prisoner at his manor house with no one to turn to for help or solace.

The lamp in her bedroom burned much later than Drake's. She had to quit reading when her eyes grew heavy after learning of the agonizing hours her mother spent giving birth to Drake. What was more startling was to discover what the doctor had told her father: she was never to have another child.

She, Susanne, and Valeria should never have been born but they were. So now she understood why Drake hated their father so much. He cared nothing for their beautiful mother except to satisfy his own selfish lust.

She closed the journal, unable to read more of the horror her mother's life had apparently been after Drake was born. She'd never been allowed to visit her beloved France to see the mother she loved so much. She detested Devin and swore she would to the day she died. Ellen had no doubt that she did.

Two things had made an impact on Ellen that she'd never expected or anticipated. Reading this journal had convinced her and that when spring came, she wouldn't return to England as she'd planned. She didn't care if she ever laid eyes on her father again as long as he lived.

Misty Bennett had changed her opinion of this place. She realized how spoiled and pampered she'd been. Ellen had only to listen to Misty to know what a frivolous life she'd lived.

Maybe that was why Drake was so intrigued by this place. He had found something here that had been sadly lacking back at Dalton Manor.

Ellen decided she wanted to know the contentment that Drake had found. Never had she seen him happier than he was tonight, even with the discomfort of his injury.

She was sure that the little green-eyed Misty had added something to Drake's life that he'd never known back in England. She could see that he was completely smitten by this little Arkansas miss.

She could certainly understand her brother's feelings— Misty had cast her bewitching spell on *her* tonight!

Chapter 29

Georgia Gordon realized that time was growing short before her wedding to Cyrus Heller. She had already been to her seamstress, Lizzy McClure, who was busily stitching the lovely ecru lace gown she was to be married in on Christmas Eve.

Lilly had found a lovely gown in the emporium instead of going to a seamstress. It was a deep red taffeta—her garnet jewelry would be perfect with it. Lily was satisfied that she'd look very attractive for the wedding.

Georgia guided her buggy to Lepanto to order her wedding cake from Colleen Carver. Her bakery was far better than the one in Crowley. But she had another reason for going to Colleen's. She wanted to gloat a bit in hopes that her news would get back to Mike Bennett.

By the time she'd left the shop, Colleen had an order for a three-tiered wedding cake and dozens of fancy little pastries. Georgia inquired, "I assume such a large order will be delivered to Mr. Heller's home?"

"Oh, yes, Mrs. Gordon—I personally deliver my orders.

You just let me know the day and the time and it will be there," Colleen said.

Georgia gave her the date and the time. Then with an arrogant air, she remarked, "Well, as you probably know, Mr. Heller is the wealthiest planter around, so he'll expect everything to be perfect."

Colleen smiled—she knew exactly what Georgia Gordon was feebly attempting to do. She was so obvious that Colleen could almost have pitied her. "Oh, yes, I know Mr. Heller. It's been my pleasure to serve him on various occasions," Colleen replied tactfully.

When she and Mike were together that next Saturday evening, she teased him playfully, "Well, Mike, I'm baking your former ladyfriend's wedding cake. Want to help me cater the affair?" There was a twinkling challenge in her eyes.

He laughed. "I think I'll let you handle that one, Colleen. I'd already heard the news about her marrying old Cyrus. I don't expect to get an invitation."

"I found myself feeling rather sorry for her, Mike."

"Sorry for Georgia? Good Lord, Colleen, you must have a heart of pure gold."

"Well, it seemed so important to her to let me know that Heller was the wealthiest planter around here."

"Colleen, being the type of woman you are, you wouldn't be able to understand how a woman like Georgia thinks and feels."

He took her in his arms and gave her a long, lingering kiss. He was more than pleased to find that Colleen was letting down more and more of the barriers she'd put up when they'd first started seeing one another.

Over the last few months Mike had been more devoted to his family and not frittering away his money. He was happy to see how much he'd accumulated in the tin box where he'd been putting all his extra wages.

His boss at the mills bought his wife a new little gig for

Christmas, so he'd put her old one up for sale. Mike made him an offer, and Bert Hollister accepted it, saying, "I just want to be rid of it. Needs a few little things done to it but it's basically in good shape."

That Saturday, Mike paid him in full and found himself the proud owner of his first gig. At last he had something nice instead of that old flat-bedded wagon to take his lady for a drive in on Sunday afternoons. He'd been embarrassed when she'd had to get up in that old wagon.

Mike believed that Colleen was caring more and more for him—he knew he was finding himself more and more in love with her.

But he also faced some stark realities. He had his home and his three children and she had her home in Lepanto and her unmarried grown daughter. Her home was nicer and larger, so how could he ask her to marry him and come to live with him and his family? Also, she had her bakery, which surely earned more money than he did at the mills. So he hesitated to ask her to marry him.

Colleen had pondered these same questions—she had a practical head on her shoulders. She cared for Mike very much and she adored his children but she'd never settle for being a housewife. So she had been praying that he wouldn't ask her to marry him. She would have been pained to tell him no, but she could not have accepted.

Sunday at Dalton's Lair, Rachel arrived at the house. She wondered what new problems she'd face with Drake's sister. It had been so good to get back to her house on Saturday afternoon and have her evening so quiet and peaceful.

The house was ghostly quiet when she let herself in the back door. She tied an apron around her waist and fired up the cook-stove. In a few moments, she had a blazing fire going and the coffeepot was filled.

She spied the chocolate cake over on the cupboard and

knew that Misty must have brought it over yesterday. Nevertheless, she made a check on her fruitcakes, pleased to find them wrapped as she'd left them.

She put the jam on the table and set up the table to serve breakfast. She mixed up a pan of biscuits and sliced some thick slices of ham.

It surprised her to hear someone coming just as she'd placed the biscuits in the oven. It was Ellen, clad in her robe. She greeted Rachel with a different air than she'd had the last two days. Rachel said, "Morning, Miss Ellen."

"How are you, Rachel?" Ellen responded. She didn't ask Rachel to serve her coffee, but went to the stove and helped herself.

She smiled and said to Rachel, "I guess I'm acquiring a taste for this coffee, Rachel."

"I'm glad, Miss Ellen, but we'll have some tea this week. Oscar will be going to town."

As Rachel kept moving constantly around the kitchen, Ellen took a couple of sips. Ellen wanted to let Rachel know that she understood why she was so vexed with her for cutting into her fruitcakes. "I—I now understand why I made you so angry, Rachel, about your fruitcake. Misty explained everything. I just didn't realize about the brandy. We don't do that back in England."

Rachel gave her a warm, understanding smile. "Well, I should not have been so upset. We'll both have to be a little more patient with one another, Miss Ellen."

"Yes. I've never seen Drake happier, so this world of yours must be something. I'm eager to learn more about it—I was so unhappy in England."

Being the kindhearted soul she was, Rachel stopped and asked her, "You weren't content living in that fine mansion Mr. Dalton has told me and Oscar about? He told us about you and his other sisters. Never spoke much about his father, but always used the most glowing terms about you and his mother."

"Drake adored Mother and detested Father," Ellen admitted.

Rachel was utterly amazed by Ellen's changed manner. She thought she might not be so impossible to get along with after all.

"You two look nothing alike. One of you must take after your father and the other after the mother," Rachel commented.

Ellen laughed. "Yes, Drake takes after our beautiful mother. That's why he's so darn good-looking. I have fair hair and blue eyes like my father."

That day and the next, things ran very smoothly around Dalton's Lair. Drake was delighted with the change in Ellen. He had confessed to Rachel that he felt they had Misty to thank for it.

"Didn't know what the hell to expect Saturday evening when Misty arrived, but she had Ellen spellbound with her easygoing way and warm, friendly nature. Ellen could not have disliked her if she'd tried."

"That's Misty! No pretenses about that little miss. She's just what she is—like her or not! Got to admit I wondered about your sister and Misty," Rachel remarked as she was kneading dough.

She asked Drake about himself. "You're getting yourself back to normal, aren't you, Mr. Dalton?"

"I'm about ready to get Duke and give him a good run. I figure he's ready to kick his heels up. I'm thinking about riding into Crowley tomorrow," Drake said as he rose to leave the kitchen to take Lucky and the pup out for a romp.

Oscar was just returning from Crowley. He wanted to have plenty of supplies in the barn for animals with the winter months coming on.

He waved to Drake as he pulled the wagon up to the barn. It was good to see Drake returning to his old self.

Drake realized he could have looked the entire county over and not found a better man than Oscar. And he couldn't have found a better housekeeper than Oscar's sister. More and more he looked upon the two of them as his family, and he was sure they felt the same way.

The next morning he announced to Ellen that they were going into Crowley. Ellen asked, "Are you sure you're up to that, Drake?"

"Well, if I'm not I'll let you bring me home. After all, you had your own buggy and took yourself to all your tutoring classes. I'll be fine, Ellen."

It was an ideal December day, just cool enough that Ellen felt comfortable in her bottle green cape and light woolen gown.

They visited the mercantile and the only emporium in Crowley. Ellen found her brother to be a most generous shopper. She stood by his side as he purchased various items in both stores.

"My goodness, Drake, you're being most extravagant today."

"Christmas gifts, Ellen. For all the people I know."

Ellen made a few purchases but all them were things for herself like stockings and scented soaps.

Drake was feeling lighthearted and glad to be away from home. "Now we're going over to Lepanto. There's a charming little lady I want you to meet—she has a bakery shop there. Makes the most delicious pecan pies you'll ever eat."

"Pecan pie, Drake?"

"I know. I'd never eaten one until recently, but everything Colleen Carver makes is delicious."

The sweet smells of the bakery shop were enough to intrigue Ellen as Drake led her through the door. They were greeted by a petite lady with a lovely face and warm smile. "Drake, how nice to see you up and around. Mike told me about your injury."

"Good to see you, Mrs. Carver. I decided to come over to get one of your pecan pies. I want you to meet my sister, Ellen, who just arrived from England."

"Well, how nice to meet you, Ellen, and welcome to our country. You've arrived at a wonderful time of the year." She looked over at Drake and corrected herself, "Well, except when the sleet comes in."

They all had a laugh. Ellen told her it was a pleasure to meet her and declared her pastries the best she'd ever eaten. "I'm anticipating that pecan pie he's raved about."

Colleen smiled. "I hope you won't be disappointed, Ellen."

"From the delicious aroma as I walked in, I don't think I shall be," Ellen said and smiled at her.

Drake ordered a pecan pie, two loaves of bread, and a dozen fruit turnovers. Colleen packed an extra pecan pie in the sack. After they had chatted awhile and were preparing to leave, she told Ellen, "I put a pecan pie in there for you, Ellen, just in case you like it. I hope to see you again while you're here."

Ellen's departing words set Colleen's shrewd mind to thinking. During the course of their conversation, Ellen had remarked that she'd hoped to find tutoring work, but that Drake had told her that was very unlikely in Crowley or Lepanto.

Colleen had a very wealthy lady who'd been her customer since the time she'd opened her shop. Agatha Fortis gave her a large order to deliver weekly.

She remembered Mrs. Fortis was going to be in need of a companion after the holidays. Agatha had voiced her concerns during one of Colleen's weekly visits. "God, Colleen, I have a housekeeper and a cook but I like getting out of this house to take my little jaunts around this countryside. Lord, it's terrible to get old and helpless. I used to saddle up my horse and ride whenever I pleased."

"You're not helpless yet, Mrs. Fortis. You never will be unless you give up, and you're not the type to do that. You're still a spirited woman but your body won't go along with that."

Colleen had left the estate that afternoon wishing she knew someone to help Mrs. Fortis, but she didn't have anyone in mind.

But this afternoon when she closed her shop, she knew she might just have an answer for Mrs. Fortis as well as Ellen Dalton. What Drake had told her was true—there was no tutoring around Crowley and Lepanto. The closest place she'd find such an assignment would be some fifty miles away in Memphis.

Ellen Dalton might just be the type of young lady Agatha Fortis was looking for as a companion. Agatha would find her interesting, with her distinct English accent.

Chapter 30

Drake and his sister had enjoyed their shopping spree. Drake placed all the packages in a chair but took the pastry he'd bought at Colleen's into the kitchen. When he entered, he wore an expression of boyish delight. "I got a lot of my Christmas shopping done this afternoon, Rachel. Here, I got two of those good pecan pies of Mrs. Carver's. You take one home for you and Oscar. Also got a couple of loaves of bread so you won't have to bake for me and Ellen for a couple of days."

"I don't mind that, Mr. Dalton, and I thank you for the pie." She'd never known a young man as generous and thoughtful as Drake Dalton.

He opened the last box from Colleen's shop and urged her to take half the fruit turnovers. Rachel said, "Mercy, Mr. Dalton—you did have yourself a buying good time, didn't you?"

"Sure did, Rachel." He smiled as he turned to leave the kitchen.

Ellen had gone to her room with her small packages and

Drake gathered up all his purchases to take them to his bedroom. There was one Christmas gift he didn't purchase today—his gift to Misty.

Tomorrow, he was going to take a ride on Duke. He believed that his badly bruised back was completely healed. This Saturday night there should be nothing to prevent him from calling on Misty, unless the weather turned bad. He had to admit, he had a new respect for sleet and ice.

Then it suddenly dawned on him that he could hardly leave his visiting sister alone Saturday evening. He couldn't help feeling a little resentment. It was going to be this way as long as she was here.

That evening as they ate dinner and spent the evening together, he questioned her about her plans for the future. "Now that you've been here almost a week, have you changed your opinion about my new home?"

With an impish smile, she said, "Let's just say I've adjusted to some things, but it is not a life I would wish to live too long. I'd miss London and going to the theatre. I find myself missing Valeria and Susanne. Guess I didn't think this wild venture out as thoroughly as I should have. But there's nothing I can do about it now."

"Of course you can, Ellen. I'll buy your passage back to England."

"I'd take you up on that offer, Drake, if only it was spring, summer, or early autumn. But I won't make an Atlantic crossing in the middle of winter, so I'm stuck until spring arrives."

Drake realized that he, too, was stuck. He mumbled, "God, that's right!"

Nothing more was said on the subject. But he had to give Ellen credit—she had learned a few things. She took charge of clearing away the table and washing the dishes while Drake fed the pup and Lucky. Afterwards, he took the two of them out in the yard for a little roaming around before bedtime.

SWEET SEDUCTION

By the time he returned to the kitchen, Ellen had dimmed the lamps and was relaxing in one of the overstuffed chairs in the front room.

When Drake came in to join her, she told him, "I think I'm going to my room and get into my nightgown, Drake. Then I'll get all propped up in bed and read some more of Mother's journals. I'm finding them so interesting and yet so very sad, Drake."

"I know, Ellen. I felt the same way when I read them," he declared soberly.

"Guess I never realized what a disillusioned, unhappy person she was. She hid that from me most of the time."

Drake admitted it had been the same way with him, except that he chanced to come upon her one day down by the little channel as she sat on the bench.

"It had been one of those days when she needed to talk to someone and I happened to be the one there. I'll never forget that afternoon. I was seventeen but I knew instinctively that mother's and father's marriage was not a happy one."

"What did she tell you, Drake?"

"She pointed to the black swan out in the water and told me how when I was born I reminded her of that fine, majestic swan with my little mane of black hair. She wanted to name me Drake, but Father would not even allow her that pleasure after the difficult time she'd had bringing his son into the world. You'll read it all in her journal. I just happened to hear it from her lips before I read it later after her death," Drake said.

"God," Ellen gasped. "What an unfeeling bastard he is!"

"Yes, that he is," Drake commented.

Ellen said good night and went to her room. Once she was in her nightgown and cozy in bed, she picked up the journal and began to read. She had read about the first months of her mother's marriage to Devin Dalton and how stolen moments, but yet, those moments had been blissfully happy. Drake had never known such happiness moments with any other woman.

As he prepared to leave the house at five-thirty, Ellen told him he looked mighty handsome in his black twill pants and matching jacket. His white shirt was unbuttoned at the neck. She found the garb so different from what he used to wear in England, but she had to admit that he looked just as striking.

"Well, I thank you, little sister, and I'll see you later, unless sleet moves in. If that happens I'll spend the night at Misty's." He laughed as he went out the door.

It wasn't a boring evening for Ellen. After she'd eaten her dinner and cleaned up the kitchen, she fed the little pup and Lucky. She and Lucky had finally warmed to one another and the little pup was so adorable, she'd got to where she picked it up to cuddle it on her lap.

Since she was alone, she changed into her nightgown and robe, but came back to the front room to sit by the hearth to read. Lucky curled up in front of the fire and the pup began to whine the minute she sat down.

Ellen laughed. "You *are* getting spoiled, little one." But she could not resist those pleading black eyes. She picked her up and placed her in the chair beside her so she could lay the journal on her lap.

Lying against her warm body, she hastily went off to sleep. Ellen began to read. She did not move out of the chair for the next two hours.

Ellen drowsed off to sleep until the chiming of the clock roused her. It was already ten. So she gathered up the little pup and dimmed the lamps except for one before she went to her room, stopping by Drake's room to put the little pup in her bed.

It was late when Drake arrived, but Mike had lingered longer at Colleen's than he had the last two Saturday nights. He had left the house sitting proud on the new buggy seat.

SWEET SEDUCTION

After he and Colleen had had their dinner, he took her for a moonlight ride. She told him how nice the buggy was. "I have to say it's much smoother riding than the wagon was, Mike," she said and laughed.

"Damn if I didn't hate coming to get you in that old thing," he confessed.

"It probably bothered you more than it did me."

It was a night for lovers, with a big, full moon shining down on the countryside. Mike couldn't resist the urge to pull up by the riverbank so he could take her in his arms.

But embraces and kisses were all Colleen would allow. Dear God, she wanted him to make love to her! The more she was with him the harder it became to resist him. She found Mike Bennett a most sensuous man with a certain rugged charm. He stirred a wild desire in her.

Mike had sensed lately that Colleen was feeling more intense about him and he knew that if he'd been more forceful she might have succumbed. But it was very important to him that she come willingly and eagerly into his arms when he finally made love to her. So once again, he had released her when her hands began to press against his chest.

He put the buggy back in motion and headed toward Lepanto. It was ten when they arrived at her house. He had planned to tell her good night at the door but Colleen invited him in for a cup of coffee.

"That sounds good to me, Colleen," he said as he followed her into the house.

"Make yourself at home while I go prepare the coffee," she said as she flung her cape aside. A short time later she returned and sat down beside Mike. "Remember, I've no catering to do tomorrow so we can have a little more time together tonight."

"You know, honey, I'll take all the time I can have with you. If I could have my way, I'd be with you much more than I am, but with both of us working like we do, it don't leave much time for pleasure."

"I know, Mike, and I understand that it has to be either Saturdays or Sundays," she said and smiled up at him.

His dark eyes looked deep into hers. "One day, Colleen, maybe we won't have to settle for that. I—I've got hopes that someday we'll have much more than this."

She patted his hand affectionately as she prepared to go to the kitchen to get the coffee. "Let's just enjoy this wonderful time we're having. I have no desire to be with anyone else, Mike."

That was sweet music to his ears. "You're the only lady I wish to be with, Colleen, and it's been that way since the night I met you."

After exchanging those words, it was inevitable that they would embrace and kiss again.

This time when he finally released her, she told him with a twinkle in her eyes that she'd better send him home.

Good-naturedly, Mike rose from the settee, still holding her hand as he moved toward the front door. He grinned. "I know you want me to go before we do something you'd regret. You noticed I didn't say *we'd regret,* for I wouldn't."

She laughed. "Mike Bennett, you are a devil!"

Privately he was thinking to himself that she just didn't know how much she'd tamed him.

Chapter 31

Drake rode up to the Bennetts' place about five-thirty. Jeff was the first to spot him and shrieked with delight.

Lavinia had been sitting in the living room playing with her doll. Hearing Jeff's yell, she leapt off the chair and dashed out the door.

Misty was back in her bedroom putting on one of her nicer frocks, just in case Drake came over as he'd said he would. When she heard his deep voice in her front room, she fumbled with the last button of her bodice before she dashed out to greet him. But she forgot to slip her feet into her little leather slippers before she left.

The sight of her coming toward him with that lovely smile was his reward. He was sure Misty was the most beautiful creature in the world!

"Oh, Drake—you did come! I was so hoping you would."

Drake ran to meet her and his hands took both of hers and he gave way to the impulse to kiss her, even though Jeff and Lavinia were standing right there. He heard the two little imps snickering.

When he released Misty, Drake gave her a wink and told the two of them, "Misty's my girl so I can give her a kiss."

Lavinia quickly responded. "I'm glad Misty's your girl, Mr. Dalton. If I was all grown up, I'd want to be your girl."

Drake laughed. "Well, you can be my girl, too—my little girl."

Since Jeff had not been able to see Drake for the last few weeks, he bombarded him with questions, admitting how much he'd missed their rides together. "Think Beauty has forgotten me, Mr. Dalton?"

"Of course she hasn't—you'll be riding her next week."

"Will I, Mr. Dalton? That'll be great!" Jeff exclaimed, his bright eyes shining.

Looking at the young man's face, Drake made an impulsive decision, as he often did. With Mike Bennett's approval, he was going to give Jeff the little roan mare for Christmas. He'd even furnish enough feed and grain for the winter months.

Young Jeff had provided their supper. He had gone fishing, so Drake was treated to thick fillets battered with cornmeal and fried golden crisp. She also fixed a huge iron skillet of fried potatoes and chopped onions, which Drake loved, and some hushpuppies.

He laughed. "How did they get the name of hushpuppies? I love them and you must give Rachel your recipe. She's never made anything like this."

Misty told him the old folktale she'd heard years ago.

"After the war, food was scarce so the women would make them and toss some to the hungry dogs and admonish them to hush yowling for something to eat. There's another tradition you'll learn about New Year's Day, Drake."

"And what is that?"

"Well, the families of the South were ravaged by the Yankees so all their food was taken but they did have a lot of black-eyed peas left and some were lucky enough to have a shank of ham. So they served a pot of black-eyed peas, ham, and cornbread to be sure the next year would bring good luck."

"And do you have that on New Year's Day, Misty?" he asked.

Her green eyes met his with a most serious expression as she assured him she certainly did. "I wouldn't tempt fate. I always cook a pot of black-eyed peas."

Lavinia grimaced. "They're terrible! I hate them!"

Misty laughed. "I have to admit they're not my favorite. I haven't found a way to make them taste better."

"Yeah, Misty—fix a different pea or bean this year. I hate them, too," Jeff chimed in.

"Just for you and Lavinia, I promise to cook an extra pot of beans but you must eat one spoonful of the black-eyed peas," Misty said.

It was apparent that Misty truly believed in that old Southern tradition so Drake spoke up. "Misty, I'll eat your black-eyed peas."

Lavinia said, "You're going to be sorry, Mr. Dalton."

"I'll remember what you told me, Lavinia," he told her and looked over at Misty.

Jeff went into the front room and sat in front of the hearth to whittle on the wooden horse which was finally taking shape.

Lavinia stayed in the kitchen to finish her cake as Drake and Misty began to clean up. As Misty washed the dishes, Drake dried them. When they were finished he whirled her around and untied her apron, declaring, "I want to take a moonlight stroll with my girl tonight, if you're not too tired, Misty."

"I'm not tired at all, Drake."

They lingered long enough in the front room for Misty to tell Jeff they were going for a walk. Without saying a word to one another, they strolled leisurely toward the riverbank and the giant weeping willow.

The moon beamed through the branches of the willow

tree as they sank to the ground. "Guess this is our special place, love. It's where I kissed you the first time," he reminded her.

"I remember, Drake. It seems so much longer than early summer that you came into my life."

"It's the same with me, Misty. Maybe you were just the beautiful girl I envisioned in my dreams all those years before I met you," Drake said as his arm encircled her back.

Suddenly, she found herself drawn into the full circle of his arms as his head bent so his lips could capture hers.

As it always was when Drake kissed her, passion stirred deeply within her. They both gasped when he released her, for he sensed she was as hungry for lovemaking as he was.

"God, Misty, this is hell, isn't it?" We have nowhere to call our own. It's driving me crazy. Now that Ellen's at my house we've lost the sweet seclusion we had there. God, I wish she'd never come."

"I know, Drake. I know," she said, caressing his face with her hand. "Oh, if only it was summertime, we could have our own private little bower right here under this old willow."

He grinned sheepishly. "I know—I'd already thought of that. I was just thinking as I held you in my arms that I wished this was a warm summer night."

"And we've a long winter ahead of us," she giggled.

He was most serious as he declared, "Well, I'll be a raving idiot by springtime. By the way, Ellen is going back to England. She realized the life she wants is not to be found here—there are no tutoring jobs for her. She and I went into Crowley and Lepanto the first of the week, but she confessed to me that it wasn't like going into London.

"Will she be leaving after the holidays?"

"She can't, Misty. One doesn't cross the Atlantic Ocean in the dead of winter, so we're talking about March at the earliest."

Misty nodded her head. March was a long time away.

"Come on, love—I won't be selfish and keep you out here any longer."

"My shawl and your arms have kept me warm."

"You're sweet, my little Misty, but I insist on taking you to the house. We'll work something out. Damn, I've bloody got to!"

"Oh, Drake!" she said, laughing merrily as he helped her up.

When they got back to the house, Misty left Drake to see about getting Lavinia to bed. The clock chimed nine as she returned to the front room.

Jeff sat there for another hour. Misty told Drake later that Jeff was becoming quite the night owl.

So all they could do was sit and talk about the holidays. Misty told Drake that her pa was going to the woods next Sunday to cut their Christmas tree.

"Lavinia's anxious for us to get it up so Pa promised he'd get the tree next week. But I have no intentions of decorating it that soon," Misty said.

This would be a first for Drake—cutting his Christmas tree in his own woods.

Finally at ten, Jeff wearily got up to bid them good night. Drake admired his carving.

"You really like it, Mr. Dalton?"

"I certainly do!"

Jeff was delighted as this was the Christmas gift he was making for Drake.

After Jeff left and it was only Misty and him in the room, Drake told her, "I've got to have a talk with your father soon, Misty. I wouldn't do anything without his approval, but I'd like to give Jeff the little roan mare. He loves Beauty so much. I think I must have had him in mind when I bought her. I really don't need her. I've got more than enough feed and grain to take care of her all winter. Oscar bought an ample supply."

Misty was astounded and found herself speechless for a

few moments. She finally stammered, "Drake Dalton, I've never known anyone with a heart as generous as yours! You're always giving us so much and we give you so little in return."

"It's simple, love. I love all of you—Lavinia, Jeff, and, of course, you most of all."

"And we all love you, too, Drake, and I think you know that."

"I came here a stranger, troubled and disillusioned about so many things, Misty. Meeting you and your little brother and sister began to make me realize there was such a thing as love. I came to know warmth, to care for who cares for you."

Misty's thick lashes fluttered. "I had no idea you were feeling that way when we first met. You seemed so cocky and sure of yourself."

"To be cocky and arrogant was the way I had been brought up to be, but sure of myself, I wasn't. Coming here to take over the Benoit estate was scaring me to death but it was my salvation. One day, I'll tell you about Drake Dalton and his life before we met. I'm not ready to do that yet," he confessed.

"I'll be here when you're ready to tell me about that other Drake Dalton."

"I know this, Misty, my love, and that's what makes you so dear to me," he told her as he leaned over to kiss her. The chiming of the clock told him how long they'd talked after Jeff had gone to bed. Mike Bennett could be home any time, so Drake prepared to leave.

"I'll see you next Saturday, if not sooner if I can get over to talk with your father sometime this week," he said.

He took one last kiss at the door before he disappeared into the darkness. Misty closed her front door and dimmed all the lamps but one, before she went to her room.

Drake had not been gone long before Misty heard her father arrive home.

* * *

The next week when Rachel sent Oscar to the woods to cut a basket of evergreens and gather pine cones to decorate her fireplace, she gave him an extra wicker basket to get some for Mr. Dalton's house, too. In the evenings she made garlands and wreaths to hang on their doors. The next day, she told Ellen,'' Why don't you drape it, Miss Ellen? Here's some pine cones. We can place candles on the mantel and tables.''

"Show me, Rachel. I've never done this before," Ellen confessed. Servants had always attended to such things at the manor house, but once she followed Rachel's instructions she was most pleased with her handiwork.

Drake could see that his sister was caught up in the excitement of Christmas approaching. "Drake, I've some gifts to buy so could you take me into one of the towns we went to the other day?"

"Of course I'll take you, Ellen. Shall we go tomorrow?"

"I'd love to."

Being the meticulous person she was, Ellen had gone to her room that night and as soon as she'd laid out the gown and cape she planned to wear, she sat and decided what she wanted to get for Oscar, Rachel, Misty, and Drake.

She thought about what each of them might appreciate. For Oscar she jotted down a wool cap to replace that old brown wool one that looked as if it should have been thrown away a long time ago. She put nothing down for Misty—she felt she would spot something in the emporium that would be perfect. So many things came to mind for her. For Drake, she would go to the tobacco shop to get him some of his cheroots, hoping they would have them.

For Rachel, she wanted to choose something she'd never think to buy for herself. Rachel was such a practical soul. She thought about a box of sweet-scented soaps and a bottle of nice toilet water.

The next day when she and Drake arrived in town, she politely dismissed him. "I want to shop on my own, Drake. I can hardly get lost on one main street. I know where the buggy is and I'll meet you in an hour."

Ellen's first purchase was Rachel's scented soaps and carnation toilet water. Remembering Oscar's cold-looking hands, she bought him the wool cap and wool gloves. She was now ready to shop for Misty. She remembered the lovely green of Misty's eyes, so when she saw the soft angora scarves with matching gloves she decided that this was the gift for Misty. She chose them in a brilliant green.

Then she was ready to leave the emporium to go to the tobacco shop, which was three doors away. There was a most pungent aroma as she entered—it was a little overwhelming.

But she managed to endure the aroma long enough to purchase Drake a supply of cheroots, as well as a fine carved wooden chest to store them in.

Drake had not been idle while he was waiting—he'd visited the jewelry store. He saw a pair of lovely sapphire earrings that he felt Ellen would like. She had such intense blue eyes that he thought they'd be perfect.

He'd actually had no intention of choosing Misty's gift today. He planned to make that purchase later after he'd given it more thought. As he was walking out of the store, he saw an exquisite string of pearls in the display case. Lying on the black velvet was a matching pair of the daintiest pearl earrings. They seemed perfect for Misty, so he asked the clerk to see the set.

"Lovely, aren't they? Perfectly matched pearls," the clerk remarked.

Drake examined them carefully. Then, without asking the price, he told the clerk he wished to purchase them. The clerk trembled with excitement—with this purchase he had sold more than he had in weeks.

Drake sat in the buggy until Ellen arrived with her packages. Then he leaped down to assist her into the seat beside him.

They traveled back to Dalton's Lair feeling very pleased with themselves.

Chapter 32

As Christmas drew closer and closer, Misty pondered what she could possibly give to Drake. Every free moment she'd had since before Thanksgiving, she'd sat in the afternoons and evenings knitting. She'd knitted enough socks for Jeff to keep his feet warm all winter. For Lavinia, she'd knitted a bright red sweater. Her pa didn't own a nice vest, so she was working on a woolen one for him.

But there was still Drake. And she would have liked to have a gift for Colleen and something for Ellen, since she would be with Drake during the holiday season.

As had happened several times in the last few months, she had Colleen Carver to thank for planting ideas in Mike's head. Colleen had remarked about the holiday gown she was making for herself, so Mike realized that Misty and Lavinia would like something pretty to wear, too. He'd come in that Saturday afternoon and told Misty to get dressed—he was taking her to town to buy dresses for her and Lavinia. "Buy Jeff a new shirt, too, Misty," he said.

When they arrived in Lepanto, Misty dismissed him—

she was sure he'd enjoy having some time to visit Colleen in her shop.

She planned to stretch the money he'd given her to get some extra gifts. She did buy Jeff a nice white shirt and Lavinia a bright red taffeta dress. But before she got anything for herself, she bought Ellen a bottle of scented bath oil and Colleen a delicate lace collar.

She counted her money to see what she had left. Then she looked around the stores, but she could not afford anything she would have liked to buy for Drake. So she bought yarn to knit a vest for him—she still had time to get it finished if she worked steadily.

She didn't buy a dress for herself. Instead, she saw a green velvet skirt and decided that with her white, long-sleeved blouse, it would do nicely for her holiday gown.

She had very little left after she paid for the velvet skirt—she thought it was lovely and knew she would feel very festive wearing it. She was in a happy mood now that she had gifts for everyone and enough yarn to knit a vest for Drake. Knowing him, he might just appreciate that more than anything she could have bought for him. She had chosen black yarn and gold buttons.

From then on, she spent every spare moment knitting Drake's vest. In the evenings after supper she went to her room to knit instead of being distracted by Jeff or Lavinia. She kept measuring the back carefully to be sure it wasn't too snug. The front seemed to go quicker than the back, and soon she was finished. She surveyed her work and was quite pleased by the time she had sewn the four gold buttons on the front.

Mike and Jeff had gone out on Sunday afternoon to cut a six-foot Christmas tree. Misty explained to Lavinia that it was too early to string the cranberry and popcorn garlands for the tree. Lavinia was just satisfied to see the tree in the corner of the front room. Like Rachel, Misty had layered the mantel with evergreen and cones. She had also mixed clusters of holly berries amid the branches.

Drake rode over that Friday afternoon and invited Misty to come over to his place on Sunday. "I have something to show you, Misty."

"What is it, Drake?" she quizzed him.

"No, no—you curious little cat! I won't give you one hint. You'll have to wait until Sunday afternoon," he said as he gave her a hasty kiss before taking his leave.

So Misty was left on the front porch wondering about his big surprise.

Drake and Oscar had gone out the first of the week to cut a fir tree. Oscar had nailed a wooden base to the bottom before they took it into the house. Ellen was very impressed by the beauty of the tree—she knew Drake had none of the heirloom ornaments they'd had back in England, but as she sat that evening staring at the tree she had a marvelous idea for decorating it.

She recalled that when she was in the mercantile they had large spools of silk and satin cord. She thought the tree would look beautiful draped with the red and gold satin cord.

The next day she urged Drake to take her to town so she could buy yards and yards of the cord. When they returned, Ellen immediately began to work.

Drake left her to do her handiwork while he went to the barn. Rachel was busy in the kitchen, but an hour later she strolled into the front room to see the splendor Ellen had created.

The red and gold satin cords were perfectly draped on the tall tree. Ellen stood on a stool placing a star she'd made out of cardboard and covered with the gold cord.

"Lord Almighty, Miss Ellen—never seen a tree prettier than this one!" Rachel declared. At the base, Ellen had draped a huge piece of white flannel she'd bought at the mercantile.

Ellen laughed. "Well, Rachel—I can't cook but tutoring children demanded that I be creative."

"Well, that you certainly are. It's a thing of beauty! Can't wait for Mr. Dalton to see what you've done," Rachel said as she walked closer.

Ellen got off the stool and sighed—she found herself suddenly exhausted. Sinking down into the chair, she told Rachel, "I'm not through with it yet, but the rest will have to wait until tomorrow."

"You just sit yourself there and rest—I'm going to brew you a pot of tea," Rachel said.

"Oh, Rachel, you are a dear! That sounds wonderful!"

Ellen had not realized just how hard she'd worked until she sat down. The tea Rachel brought was like a tonic and refreshed her.

Drake was as astonished at what she'd created. He was so overcome by all the effort she'd put into making their tree so beautiful that he reached down to plant a brotherly kiss on her cheek. "Thank you, Ellen. Thank you very much," he told her.

"Well, it's going to be my Christmas tree this year, too. Last Christmas was not a very happy one for me—I was alone at Dalton Manor."

Drake had a compassionate expression—he knew exactly how she must have felt. So he assured her, "This year will be better, Ellen. I know it is for me."

"Drake, you have every reason to be a happy man. You have Dalton's Lair, which you obviously love. Your life's going so well. You have Misty. I'm not blind, Drake. She adores you and I think the feeling is mutual," she said and grinned with a glint in her blue eyes.

"Yes, Ellen I do adore Misty—and I won't deny it."

"I was thinking, Drake, that if she was dressed in a fancy

gown, she'd outshine any young lady in London. Can you imagine her that way?"

"I've envisoned that, Ellen. But Misty's beauty goes beyond her lovely face and figure. She has beauty of heart and soul," Drake said in a serious tone.

"Yes, Drake, she does. I only had to be around her a short time to know that. Marry her, Drake! Don't let some other young man come around and take her away from you," Ellen urged.

"No one will take Misty away from me, Ellen," he vowed.

He was already thinking about asking Misty to marry him. But if he did, what would Jeff and Lavinia do without her?

He had to admit that Ellen's comments had taken him by surprise. The truth was, he'd never thought about marrying any woman until Misty came into his life. But then everything had changed.

He'd had very definite reasons for inviting Misty over for Sunday dinner instead of going over there on Saturday night. Now he just had to pray that the weather cooperated. He had plotted a way they might finally have a few moments completely away from everyone.

He couldn't figure how anything could go wrong. He had gone over every little detail. Surely fate would not be so cruel as to deny them a little time together.

On Saturday, Rachel came over as she always did and he dismissed her early. "I want you and Oscar to have a little free time," Drake told her.

"Well, that's mighty nice of you, Mr. Dalton. I'd like to go into Crowley this afternoon and if Oscar doesn't have to feed for you, we could stay as long as we like."

"He won't have to do it for the next two nights. I'll do it," Drake told her.

"You're not going to see Miss Misty this Saturday night?" she asked.

"Misty is coming over for Sunday dinner with Ellen and me," Drake said. The puzzled look on Rachel's face changed to a pleased smile. "Well, I'll come over Sunday morning to fix a good dinner for the three of you. Now, you sure you don't want Oscar to come over to feed Sunday evening?"

"No, I'll feed. It will give Ellen and Misty some time together before I take Misty home."

"Well, all right, Mr. Dalton. Oscar will be over early Monday morning then."

"That's fine, Rachel."

Drake was the first to admit it seemed a little strange not to be anticipating going over to see Misty on Saturday evening. But he could give it up when he had tomorrow to look forward to.

Rachel had been gone for over two hours and Ellen was completely engrossed in making the little ornaments to hang on the tree. She'd told him she was going to spend the rest of the afternoon getting the tree decorated before Misty came tomorrow.

Drake left the house to go out to the barn for over a half hour and when he returned to the house, all his plans were completed.

He came back feeling very smug that he had finally found a bower for him and Misty that would be cozy and warm. Ellen had been too occupied to notice the blanket he'd taken with him.

The two of them ate the dinner Rachel had prepared and Drake helped Ellen clean up the kitchen. The lamps were dimmed and Ellen put the last of her small ornaments on the tree.

Ellen bent down to kiss her brother's forehead when they had retired to the front room. "I'm going to retire to my room now, Drake. I'll get comfortable in my nightgown and read of a Christmas past. I have come to the part in Mother's journals where I was born and how she should never have had me, according to what the doctor had said. I think to myself, she had to have Susanne and Valeria also. Dear God, Drake—what a woman she was to have endured it all so long."

"She fought so hard, Ellen, to be with us—you and me," Drake said sadly.

"And we were too young to understand or know, Drake."

"Before she died, I knew and I'm glad I did," he said.

His pretty sister looked down at her brother and admitted she'd never had a beau. "I don't know, Drake. I really don't know that I ever wish to marry," she declared firmly.

Drake reached out to take her hands. "Don't feel that way, Ellen. Don't cheat yourself of what could be a wonderful life. All men are not like Father."

"I know you're not, Drake."

"But I'm not the only one, Ellen. Believe me!"

She smiled and said good night.

Drake lingered in his front room another hour before he dimmed the lamps and went to bed, too.

The next morning was bright and sunshiny. He was up and had the coffee brewing before Rachel arrived.

After he ate his breakfast, Drake left Rachel to go about her puttering in the kitchen. He went out to the barn to tend the stock. He knew Oscar must be enjoying his freedom from chores all day.

When Drake returned to the house, wonderful smells were permeating the kitchen. Rachel was preparing apple pies to put in the oven.

By the time he was ready to pick Misty up, he could also smell the aroma of cabbage cooking on Rachel's stove.

He asked her, "So what am I having for dinner tonight, Rachel? Do I smell cabbage?"

"Cabbage and a big pork roast. Roasted potatoes and green beans, Mr. Dalton. Think that will fill your stomach?"

"I think so, Rachel."

He went out the back door to hitch up his buggy. He'd

put a lap blanket on the seat beside him—it was a chilly afternoon.

Misty was ready when he arrived—she knew that the nice wool shawl Mrs. Walters had given her would not be enough to keep her warm, so she'd taken the worn coat she'd salvaged from her mother's things to wear over to Drake's. She wasn't too pleased about wearing it. It showed its age, but it was warm.

The bright wool scarf around her neck and the matching gloves might improve the look of the coat. Mrs. Walters had given her the scarf and gloves for Christmas last year.

Misty confessed to Drake that she was most curious about his big surprise. He told her she would find out very soon, but he added, "I have more than one surprise for you, love."

"Oh, Drake, I think you're enjoying teasing me!" she declared, her green eyes piercing him.

"It's only fair, Misty my love. You tantalize me every time I'm around you," he said and grinned deviously.

She smiled impishly. "I hope so, Drake Dalton!"

"Be assured you do, Misty Bennett," he told her. But what he said next was enough to fill Misty with overwhelming happiness. "One day, I'll tell my son or daughter what a tempting little flirt their mother was."

Misty sat there very quietly, absorbing what Drake had said.

Chapter 33

She turned to look at Drake, whose eyes were looking straight ahead down the dirt road. Did he realize what he had just said to her? It had been a spontaneous remark, but to her it was a marriage proposal. But she had to admit it was not the traditional way a man proposed to a woman.

However, Drake Dalton was not like any other man she'd ever met. So she said nothing and just sat with a pleased smile on her face. That he intended for her to be the mother of his children had to mean that she would also be his wife.

The truth be told, Drake had made an impulsive remark and was not aware of the impact his words had had on Misty. He had just given vent to his thoughts at the moment.

He helped her down and waited to take the buggy to the barn—he wanted to see her reaction when she entered the front room and saw the magnificent tree.

When he ushered her through the door, Misty gasped as her eyes went wide with wonder at the splendor in the corner. All she could manage to say was, "Oh, Drake!"

"Ellen created all that beauty, Misty. I couldn't wait for you to see it."

Ellen came into the room at that moment and received Misty's praises about the tree. "It did turn out rather well, I have to say. Please, come and sit down, Misty. It's so nice to see you again."

"I've been anxious to see you again, too," Misty said as she took a seat. Drake excused himself to get the buggy to the barn and allowed the two of them to have some girl talk. But he didn't have any intention of sharing his lady with his sister from now until dinner time. He had other plans for the two of them.

After he returned to the house to join Misty and Ellen, he sat there for the next hour trying to curb his desire to whisk Misty out of there.

When the clock struck four, his impatient nature won out. He rose from the chair and announced to Ellen, "If you'll excuse us, Ellen, I want to take Misty to the barn to show her our new family member before it gets dark. Come, Misty, let me help you on with your cape."

"Oh, we have a mother cat who sought refuge in Drake's barn to have her four kittens," Ellen said.

Drake draped Misty's wrap around her shoulders and took her hand to lead her toward the door. The bright sun put a dent in the chilly December day—Drake was just glad it wasn't raining.

They walked close together, Misty's arm entwined with his as they neared the barn. She asked him, "When did you find the kitty there, Drake?"

"Last Tuesday. She arrived sometime in the night and staked out the empty stall to give birth to her kittens. She was completely snow white, Misty."

"Oh, really?"

"Two kittens are white like her and there's a solid black one and a little striped monkey."

Soon she saw the little family cozy in the warm corner

of the empty stall. Misty bent down to gently pat each of the kittens and stroke the mother cat, who seemed oblivious to their intrusion.

It was only when she sat to pet the kittens that she noticed that the entire floor of the stall was covered with blankets. Her green eyes looked up at Drake, who was hovering behind her. There was a thick layer of hay spread over the length and width of the narrow stall and over it had been draped soft woolen blankets.

"You did this for the cat family, Drake?"

"No, love—I did it for us. It's to be our haven where we can be completely alone. Damn it, I'm weary of never having time with you," he declared.

"Oh, Drake," she said and smiled up at him, seeing his determined expression.

He grinned. "I'll keep you warm, Misty. I promise." He removed her coat and flung it over the stall's railing. With that, his firm-muscled arms went around her waist to draw her closer. His hungry lips met hers and a liquid fire began to flow through Misty. When he finally released her, he urged her down on the blanket with him.

In a lazy, unhurried manner he removed her gown and undergarments. There was no time to get chilled for Drake's naked body was quickly searing her flesh.

As his lips caressed her breasts, she began to undulate against him. Soon both of them were raging with a mounting fever. Drake knew he was out of control—he had waited so long for this moment. He gasped as Misty suddenly swayed against him urgently. She moaned with pleasure as the fire consumed her utterly and completely.

Finally, like smoldering embers, they lay together on the blankets and hay. But Drake knew they could not stay as long in their little bower as they would have liked.

"Love, I don't want to leave but Ellen could take a notion to come out here to join us and the kittens." He smiled down at her as she lay with her long hair fanned out on the blanket.

Misty had a very serious look on her face as she declared, "Drake you have to be my mirror. Lord, I don't want to go back to the house with my hair tousled. Your sister would immediately suspect what we've been up to."

He had already gotten up and slipped into his pants and was buttoning his shirt. "I'll be your mirror, love."

By the time she had put on her undergarments, Drake already had his shirt buttoned and sat yanking on his boots. He took a comb from the pocket of his coat. "You see, love, I even remembered that you'd need this to put your lovely hair in place."

He ran the comb through his own thick hair before handing it to her. By now she had slipped into her gown and Drake had turned her so he could fasten the back. He could not resist leaning over to kiss her. "You didn't get chilled, did you, Misty?"

"Chilled? Mercy no, Drake! I still feel flushed," she said and grinned.

When she had run the comb through her hair, Drake assured her she looked exactly as she had when they'd left the house. He told her he was going to stay awhile to remove all the little telltale signs of their tryst. "Don't want Oscar spying these blankets in the morning—I made all this possible by relieving him from the feeding tonight. I'll join you as soon as I get this done."

Misty returned to the house alone. Ellen was beginning to wonder why they were gone so long.

Misty explained that Drake was taking over Oscar's feeding chores tonight. "I came ahead to the house so we could start warming up dinner. I'm sure Oscar is probably enjoying his evening off," Misty casually commented as she began to remove her coat.

Ellen seemed to accept the explanation. Misty went back to the kitchen and put some kindling in the cookstove, remarking about what a darling little cat family it was. She was just glad that mother cat and kittens couldn't tell tales.

Drake folded the blankets and decided he would take them back to the house under cover of darkness when he put the buggy away later.

Smoke curled from his fireplace chimney and cookstove. He had to admit he was ready to sit down to a hearty dinner.

He did eat like a hungry wolf, causing his younger sister to tease him. Once the meal was over and Misty and Ellen had cleaned up the kitchen and returned to the front room, Misty realized that she couldn't stay too long. Tomorrow was a workday for her pa, so it would be an early morning rising for her.

At nine, Misty announced that she should be getting home. "Pa has to be at the mills at seven, so that means getting up early."

Drake went to the barn to get the buggy and also took the opportunity to toss the blankets in the back. A few minutes later he and Misty were rolling down the dirt road that ran along the riverbank toward the Bennetts' place.

Just before they arrived, Drake said in a sincere tone, "Misty, I wasn't talking frivolously about telling my sons and daughters about their mother. You are to be my wife and the mother of my children. I—I just don't want to bring my bride into my house with my sister living there. I hope you understand my feelings about this. Can you give me time to work all this out?"

"Drake, you know I can. It wasn't your fault that all this happened. To know that you love me is all I need. And I do believe you love me."

His arm pulled her closer. "Always know that, love! Never doubt it. But should you find yourself carrying my baby, come straight to me. I'd want to know, Misty. You promise me?"

"I promise you, Drake. I would tell you," she vowed.

They said their good nights at Misty's front door and

Drake returned to his buggy. Going back home, he noticed that the night skies were no longer clear. Clouds blotted out the stars and moon. They seemed to be moving up from the southwest. Oscar had told him that this usually meant rain because the moisture moved in from the Texas coast and traveled up into Arkansas. In the spring, summer, and autumn, it could mean rain but when it was winter like it was now, it could mean sleet or snow, depending on the temperature.

Ellen had dimmed the front room lamps as soon as Misty and Drake had left. The little pup remained at Lucky's side and didn't follow her into her room.

She was so engrossed in her mother's journals that she did not hear Drake enter the house about an hour later. He saw her lamp still glowing and figured she was propped up in her bed reading the journals. Every few days they had a conversation about what she'd read. Each time they talked, Drake sensed Ellen's fury building more and more.

By the time she'd finished reading the journal this wintry night, she knew she and Susanne had been conceived because their father had raped their mother. Some would say it was a husband's right to have his wife whenever he wished but Ellen's independent nature rebelled against that. She vowed no man would ever take her against her will. She'd fight to her death before she'd allow that to happen!

She had planned to put the journals aside and read no more until after Christmas Day because she wished to be in gay spirits for the holiday.

When she woke up in the morning, she heard something pelting her window panes. She got out of bed to look outside, and saw it was ice pellets.

When she went into the kitchen, Rachel said, "Ain't fit for man or beast out there today, miss. You keep yourself inside so you won't fall like Mr. Dalton did."

"You don't have to worry about that, Rachel. I'm not sticking my head out the door. Ice scares me to death."

Rachel told her she was starting her stew early so she could get back home. "Mr. Dalton done told me he wants me to get home before it gets much worse. Oscar has stored up plenty of kindling and firewood so Mr. Dalton won't have to go out to the shed."

Ellen could see how treacherous it was outside when she watched the two of them go the hundred feet to their house. Oscar jammed his pitchfork down into the ice-covered ground to get a steady footing. He had also brought another pitchfork so Rachel could do the same thing.

The sleet was still falling at one that afternoon with no signs of letting up. Ellen stayed on the roofed back porch until she saw them go through their front door.

By the time the afternoon was over, Ellen was feeling very pleased with herself. She'd kept the fire going in the cookstove and the stew was simmering nicely. Little by little, she was learning how to do things she'd never had to do before. She couldn't exactly explain why she was getting so much gratification out of such simple tasks.

But one's thinking changed, living here in Arkansas, and Ellen was realizing it more and more. Those around her—Rachel, Oscar, and Drake—had become aware of her completely different attitude.

They all liked this Ellen better!

Chapter 34

There had been only a few times when Mike Bennett had not been able to get to the mills on winter days, and this morning was going to be one of them. He saw how treacherous it would be to travel once he tried to lead the team out into the barnyard, so he jumped down from the wagon and led the team right back into the barn.

He couldn't afford to have one of his team break a leg. If it was this bad where he lived, he knew a lot of the other mill workers would not be showing up either. He went back into the house and announced to Misty, "Can't make it. The horses and the wagon wheels were slipping. It's slick as the devil out there."

"Isn't this early, Pa, for this kind of weather?

"Yeah, it is. Hate to think what January and February could bring. Me and that old wagon could have made it fine in a three-inch snow," he declared as he removed his wool cap and jacket and hung them on a peg.

He wasn't at all happy about losing a day of wages. He

needed every penny with the holiday coming on. He had gifts to buy for his children and Colleen.

At least he knew what he was going to get for Lavinia—Colleen was going to purchase that for him. She had offered to do so the last time they were together. She'd told him about the loveliest dolls she'd seen at Rector's Mercantile. She remembered how helpless her husband had been buying things for their Maureen, so she'd asked Mike if he wanted her to pick something out for Lavinia. "They're gorgeous dolls, Mike," she'd said. He'd eagerly accepted her offer. But there was still Misty and Jeff.

But Colleen's gift was the one that bothered him the most—it had to be just right. He thought that he might ask Misty what she thought would make a nice gift.

Mike knew what he'd like to buy for her, but that had to wait. He'd like to buy her a gold wedding band.

It was a slow-moving, quiet day around the Bennett house. Jeff put the last touches to his wooden horse while Lavinia contented herself by playing with her doll or sitting in Mike's lap.

Misty spent the afternoon wrapping gifts and stringing garlands of cranberries. She wished she had all the lovely ribbon that Ellen had used to drape their tree. But her mantel looked very festive and smelled of pine and evergreen.

Mike was glad to see the sun burst through the clouds by mid-afternoon. He told Jeff and Misty to remain inside, as there was still a thick glaze on the grounds around the house. He took charge of feeding the chickens, slopping the hogs, and feeding the horses.

Misty moved around the kitchen to finish cooking supper and thought about how much her pa had changed. This time a year ago he wouldn't have been so concerned about his children's welfare. What had turned her pa so bitter toward them back then? Now she knew that he could be caring and kind. She had to credit Mrs. Carver for bringing out the best in him.

Perhaps, it was thinking about this and trying to measure the past with the present that sent her to her room after supper to take out her mother's journals.

Lavinia was already tucked into bed and Jeff and her pa were still in the front room. Neither of them would intrude, so she got into her nightgown and began to read the journal which her mother had begun to keep about the time she'd married Mike Bennett.

Misty read for over an hour before she stopped to just sit and think. It was obvious, knowing how she felt about Drake, that her mother had not loved her pa when she married him. She had been in love with another young man who'd left Crowley.

She'd obviously given up hope that he was going to return. Beth's only reason for encouraging Mike Bennett was that she feared she was expecting, so theirs was a fast and furious courtship. Mike Bennett had fallen hopelessly in love with the lovely, fair-haired Beth.

Three days after she married Mike, she discovered that her panic hadn't been for naught. She *was* expecting!

When Misty opened up the journal again, she read for another hour. As Ellen had been disillusioned about what she'd read on the pages of her mother's journal, Misty was also disillusioned and the pain hurt just as much.

The very private musings her mother wrote disturbed Misty, for she'd always looked upon her mother as such a saint. Beth looked down her nose at Mike Bennett and what she considered were his crude ways. It seemed that Beth was always comparing Mike to her "lost love."

She wrote that she wished she was still living with her parents and had waited for this man to return to Crowley instead of rushing into marriage.

Finding herself with child devastated her, but Mike was overjoyed. Misty read that her arrival gave her mother no joy. Mike had been a doting father in the beginning, or tried to be, but Beth was determined to cool his ardor as she wanted no more children.

The journal Misty was reading was quite different from Ellen's. Her mother wrote almost daily as an outlet to preserve her sanity, but Beth made entries every few weeks or months. Beth was not being abused by her husband. In some ways her coldness to Mike was a punishment to him.

After Misty's birth, Mike found he had a woman who kept his house clean and cooked his meals but he always felt her body stiffen when he touched her. So being the red-blooded man he was, he sought his pleasure other places for the next six years.

Beth knew and she really didn't care as long as he didn't try to make love to her. There was an entry which particularly caught Misty's interest. Her mother had written that the man she had always loved returned, but he returned with a bride. She was devastated. It seemed that he and his bride had settled not too far from the Bennetts' place, so Misty wondered who it was.

The hour was getting late and Misty knew she had to rise early in the morning, but she couldn't close the journal. She hoped that her mother would reveal who the man was.

The next pages were about Jeff and how his birth came about. Jeff was conceived because Mike came home drunk and forced himself on his wife out of utter frustration.

Beth was a crueler woman than Misty would ever have imagined, for she wrote that when she found herself pregnant with Jeff, she set out to make her husband pay for having his way with her.

Misty had been six when Jeff was born. She had no inkling of what was going on between her parents. Beth seemed the perfect mother and Mike went off to work daily. But now she could understand why there was no talking between them at the dinner table. There were no smiles, either. They were stiff and cool with one another. Misty could understand the desperation they both felt now that she knew what it was like to love a man as she did Drake.

By ten, Misty was wiser and observed things that she hadn't noticed at six. She'd seen her pa reach out to touch her ma's hand or shoulder and she always jerked away from him.

Reading her journal tonight, she knew why. The next pages told Misty why her mother became more and more depressed as the years went on.

She wrote that each time she saw the man she loved go down the road with the bride he'd brought back from Tennessee, it was like a thorn in her side.

They owned a farm and lived in a fine house. Beth saw how nicely his wife was dressed as she sat in the buggy with him. Beth wrote that if she hadn't been so foolish, she could have been riding in the buggy with him and been married to a landowner instead of a mill worker.

Midnight came, but Misty was too entranced by now to put down the journal, so she kept reading. Four years passed after Jeff was born before Lavinia was conceived—once again Mike had forced himself on Beth.

Beth had written that Mike was a sentimental fool who would not be denied, so she found herself carrying his third child.

In late September Lavinia was born and after that Beth had made few entries. They were nothing but one woman's bitterness and hatred for two men: the man she was married to and the man who'd caused her pain and disillusionment most of her life.

Misty wondered if she would learn the name of the man her mother truly loved—she only had a few pages to read, but her eyes were becoming so heavy. She knew she would pay in the morning, but nothing could have made her stop reading now.

Those last three pages left Misty feeling very sad about the mother she'd always adored, and she'd already decided that in the morning this journal would be tossed in the cookstove. She never wanted Jeff or Lavinia to read it.

Beth's last entry was two months before her death and reflected the hate that had gnawed away at her life and destroyed her.

On the last page of her journal she had written a message to the two men in her life. She wrote that she hated Ed Walters for leaving her in Crowley when she was eighteen and wondering if he was coming back after he'd robbed her of her virginity. She wrote that she hated Mike, had never loved him, and had always found him a clumsy oaf.

Misty didn't believe that her pa had ever read the journal and she was determined that he never would, but she was convinced that her mother had wanted him to. Like it or not, Misty had to accept the truth. Her mother was a vindictive woman and certainly not the paragon she'd envisioned all those years.

Misty was glad she'd read this journal even though it made her feel very sad about her mother. She now knew the truth and understood many things that she never would have had she not read the journal.

Now that her father was finally a happy man he could give of himself as he'd wanted to do for years. But Beth had created within her and Jeff this mistrust of him. This was her revenge—to keep his children from admiring and respecting him, and it had worked quite effectively for a long time.

The truth be told, Mike Bennett was a man starved for love and affection and Misty now understood his brief episode with Georgia Gordon.

Colleen Carver had not found him a clumsy oaf and her love and understanding had been exactly what Mike had needed. It had brought out the best in him and Misty would forever be grateful to her.

Chapter 35

Reluctantly Misty crawled out of her bed in the morning. There was still ice outside, but there was a bright sun overhead. Misty fired up the cook-stove as Mike entered the kitchen. She told him, "There's still a lot of ice out there, Pa. You may still have a hard time making it to the mills."

"I got to get in this morning, Misty. I can't miss two days. Just brew me some strong coffee."

Her green eyes looked at him in a different light than they had before. The despicable journal was already burning in her cook-stove. The coffee pot was heating as she busily moved around the kitchen to cut some ham and get the eggs out to cook his breakfast.

While she was doing that, Mike banked up the fireplace with two large logs—he cautioned Misty not to allow Jeff to go out of the house today unless the sun did wonders.

A half-hour later, Mike left. Misty watched how cautiously he guided his team down the drive to the dirt road. She could only hope he made it to the mills safely.

He got onto the main road just fine so she finally turned

away from the window. While Jeff and Lavinia slept for another two hours, Misty went to the front room and sank down in one of the overstuffed chairs.

Amazingly, the bright sun did rid the countryside of its icy glaze by noon. Rivulets of water were all that remained of the sleet which had covered the ground.

Mike had no trouble getting home. He left the mills shortly after five, but the daylight faded so much earlier that dusk was already shrouding the countryside when he pulled up to the barn.

When he walked into the kitchen he said, "Do I smell what I think I smell? You baked your pa a cherry pie today?"

Misty smiled impishly. "You're right, Pa."

He put his big arm around her and gave her a fatherly hug. "You're a dear, sweet daughter, Misty. Sorry I've not told you that as often as I should have."

Her green eyes looked up at him warmly. "We all have our regrets, Pa." In a more lighthearted manner, she said, "I think I have a pretty nice pa."

She turned to check her pots and Mike's eyes lingered on his daughter for a brief moment.

Obviously, the last few months had made Misty's memory fade about what a miserable father he'd been for so long.

But Misty had her own musings as she went about setting the table. She had so harshly misjudged her pa.

She wanted to make up to him for that time when there was no love in her heart for him.

Chapter 36

Having loved a man and been loved by him, Misty had more understanding about her parents' relationship. It was an ill-fated marriage from the beginning, she realized after reading the journal. It had also made her understand why her pa had become such an embittered, constantly angry and short-tempered man.

She and Jeff just happened to be the innocent victims of the fury he felt due to his frustration. Lavinia had been spared, which was the reason her little sister warmed to their pa as she and Jeff couldn't.

Mike Bennett would have been astonished at her mature comprehension after she'd read her mother's journal. He had known Beth kept a journal but after she'd died he never had any desire to read it. He'd lived through all those years of misery!

By the time she died, he had no feelings toward her one way or the other. He felt no love—that had been killed slowly but surely. He didn't feel hate, either. He just looked at her and felt a kind of pity.

Such a pretty girl she'd been when he'd married her. Then he saw a woman turn ugly—there was no beauty in her heart and soul.

Trusting soul that he had been, he had no inkling that his wife loved another man. He had thought her reluctance to come to him was just shyness. Coming to Crowley a short time before they were married, he knew he had a reputation as a happy-go-lucky dude who could be a hellraiser from time to time, so he'd figured Beth had heard those tales.

But after they were married he was a faithful husband until after Misty was born. For another two years he tried, figuring it was just that she was afraid of getting pregnant.

Mike remembered the first time he strayed. Misty was three and Mike had begun to feel like his home was only providing a place to have his meals and sleep. His bed was cold and lonely, so he sought solace in Crowley with a pretty young widow who was more than willing.

He knew he would soon have a reputation as a philander. He saw the looks on people's faces—all of them were feeling sympathy for Beth.

So Mike became a loner—the only friends he had were his buddies at the mill. The so-called respectable neighbors like the Walters, Perkins, and Boyingtons didn't come around when he was home, but he knew they came to call on Beth.

It was just before Jeff was conceived that Mike began to wonder if Beth had ever loved him. He and his buddy, Jeb, had been out drinking one Saturday night and Jeb suddenly announced he was going home to his wife. He'd told Mike, "Why don't you go home to yours, Mike, old boy? You got a mighty sweet little daughter and a real pretty wife, if I remember right."

Mike was just drunk enough to have a loose tongue. He told Jeb, "A lot of good it would do me, Jeb. No, I'm going where I know I'll have someone welcoming me."

SWEET SEDUCTION

Jeb had asked, "You telling me what I think you're telling me?" Jeb found that hard to believe, as Mike Bennett was a rugged, virile man who most women found very appealing.

"That's what I'm telling you." Mike had replied.

"Well, I'll be damned! Known Beth all her life and just figured as fast as the two of you got married she must have fallen head over heels. Everyone in Crowley thought she was really sweet on Ed Walters but he left for Tennessee. Then you came to Crowley and swept her off her feet. At least, that's the way I had it figured."

Jeb left to go home, but Mike stayed to have another drink. He was drunk when he left. If it was Ed Walters haunting her, he decided he'd blot him from her thoughts.

So he didn't accept her refusal when he crawled into bed beside her. Jeff was conceived that night.

But there had been no gratification for Mike and frustration only festered in both of them for the next nine months. But Jeff's birth lightened Mike's spirits, for he had himself a fine little son. The next several months he didn't pay visits to the pretty lady in Crowley.

Nothing he did impressed Beth—he found their house a cold, loveless place. What really pained Mike was the looks he got from his little green-eyed daughter. He knew the influence Beth was having on her and that bothered him.

There was only one more time that Mike tried to make his wife wipe out the memory of her lost love and that was the night Lavinia was conceived. After that, he never attempted to touch Beth again. He let her live in her little world and he lived in his.

He had satisfied himself that it had been Ed Walters Beth had harbored love for all those years instead of him. It had happened after Beth found herself pregnant with Lavinia. She had been terribly cruel that night, wanting to punish him as she felt he was punishing her.

She had put him through sheer misery from the moment

he'd gotten in from the mill late that afternoon. Mike was tired and weary. Misty and Jeff had already left the room. He was almost four and she was already playing the little mother to her younger brother.

Never had Mike accused Beth of anything, but that night he let her know that he knew why she'd always been so cold to him. He no longer tried to please her.

"Beth, we're a sad lot, you know? I'm sorry I'm not Ed Walters. I'm much sorrier that we ever married," he said as he left the kitchen, leaving Beth to ponder how he could possibly have found out about Ed Walters.

The remaining time they shared together was hellish for both of them. Mike found that he dreaded coming home in the evenings. He was restrained in the front room after supper—Beth dominated the time with Misty and Jeff.

There was no question about it—Mike was ready and willing for the promiscuous Georgia Gordon a few months after Beth's death. She was like a breath of fresh air and good at building up his male ego.

But now, Mike regretted the neglect his children had suffered. God knows, he had tried to make up to them for the way he'd failed them during those four months Georgia had dominated his life.

Misty had made him think that perhaps he had done that.

That was why he wanted to give her a very special Christmas gift this year—she had been the one who had kept this family running so smoothly when he had not been there.

There was only one more Saturday before Christmas. Mike had to make that afternoon count. Jeff was going with him so he could buy some gifts with the money he'd saved.

When they got to Crowley, Jeff took off in one direction and Mike went to the mercantile. He wished he had Colleen with him to pick out a winter coat for Misty. Colleen had suggested it after she'd seen how worn Misty's coat was. She'd even suggested a color which she thought would be attractive.

So when a clerk offered to help him, he told her he wanted to see a winter coat in a rich green shade of wool. He had to describe his daughter as he hadn't thought to ask Colleen about the size.

The lady smiled as she told him, "I think I've got just what you're asking for." She showed him a lovely wool coat with a soft matching velvet collar and cuffs.

It proved to be the most expensive garment he'd ever bought for his daughter. He went to shop for Jeff next—he felt the best thing he could get for him was a warm winter jacket and wool cap.

He owed so much to Colleen. She had taught him how to love again. He had never been as happy as he was now. It was her he had to thank for bringing out the best in him.

Misty had suggested a nice piece of jewelry for Colleen. "Something dainty, Pa!"

Buying for Misty and Jeff had been no problem, but he roamed around the jewelry store looking at various things. The pieces he picked out and priced were beyond what his pocketbook could afford.

The clerk made a suggestion and pulled out what Mike thought was a very pretty etched gold locket. "It's a nice-looking locket, I'll grant you, but it isn't exactly what I had in mind," Mike told him.

"Oh, but it isn't a locket, sir. Look," the clerk said as his fingertips flipped the gold dome to reveal a watch. A slow smile came to Mike's face as he mumbled, "Well, I'll be dang! Come to think of it, it does look like a tiny man's pocket watch."

"Yes, sir—it's a new thing and they say the ladies are really taking to them. Just got my first ones in a week ago and I've already sold two. Rather nice-looking gold chain on them, long enough for the lady to flip it open to see the time."

Mike remembered what Misty had told him about something dainty. This little locket watch was only about an inch wide—that was surely dainty enough.

The price was affordable, so Mike eagerly purchased it and walked out of the jewelry shop proud as a peacock.

He hoped Jeff was winding up his gift buying—once he loaded up the buggy with his purchases, Mike would have to stay there and wait for him.

But when he was walking down the street he saw Jeff sitting in the buggy. As he came closer, he saw a big smile on Jeff's face, so Mike knew his son was as pleased as he'd been about his shopping.

"Got mine all done, Pa. How about you?" Jeff asked.

"Got mine done, too, son," Mike said as he loaded his packages in the buggy and leaped up. Jeff told him, "Pa, I'd liked to have got Mrs. Carver something. She's so nice. But after I bought Lavinia's gift I didn't have another cent left."

Mike reached over to pat Jeff's hand warmly. "Colleen would be happy to know that you wanted to buy her a gift, so don't worry about that at all, Jeff."

Mike Bennett had no idea what it meant to his son to have an affectionate touch. All of his pa's gestures of affection, like tousling his hair playfully or giving him a fatherly hug, were something Jeff had starved for during the early years of his young life. Just the look of warmth in Mike's dark eyes when he'd looked at him was so different from the pa he'd known in the past.

Like Misty, he knew that part of the credit belonged to Mrs. Carver—she was such a warm, outgoing lady, so different from that haughty old Georgia Gordon.

For Misty, seeing the two of them march jauntily up the front steps was a wonderful sight. She was sure this was going to be their best Christmas ever!

She teased the two of them as they came through the front door. "Well, you two must have bought out the town."

They laughed, declaring that they had surely added some

cash to the tills of some of the merchants. Jeff confessed that he'd spent all of his money, and Mike said that after buying groceries he had little left.

"But Christmas comes only once a year so what the heck!" Mike said, smiling.

Jeff didn't stay in the front room but dashed back to his room. Just as quickly, he came rushing back and tugged at his pa's arm to bend down—he had something to whisper in his ear.

Mike bent down to hear what his son had to say. Jeff told him that he couldn't bring the little wooden wagon he'd bought for Lavinia into the house. Jeff had thought Lavinia would love pulling the wagon around the house and yard with her doll in it.

But Mike quickly had a solution. "I'll store it in the barn, Jeff, when I take the buggy there."

"Yeah, Pa. She ain't going to find it out there."

Mike left the house to take the buggy to the barn and as he was walking back to the house he spied the high-stepping stallion of Dalton's beating a path up his drive. Mike had to admire the fine beast. He was thinking what a fortune that animal must have cost Drake.

He waited for Drake to ride up and leap off the stallion. "Afternoon, Mr. Bennett. I hoped I'd catch you before you left for Lepanto. I've something I need to talk with you about."

"So let's talk, Drake," Mike said, finding himself curious.

"Well, sir—it's about Jeff. I'd like to give him something for Christmas but I would want your permission first so I thought I'd best ride over here this afternoon to talk to you. I want to give Jeff that little roan mare of mine he loves so much."

Mike was staggered. "Dear God, Drake, that's quite a gift!"

Drake smiled. "I know. I don't need her but I couldn't

pass up the good buy she was. Oscar bought so much feed that I could furnish plenty for the winter."

"Dalton, I don't know what to say. You're a most amazing man. Guess I'd be a fool to deny Jeff such a gift. I find it overwhelming!"

"I know, Mr. Bennett. But your son, as well as your daughters, were warm and friendly faces in this strange new place I landed in. They all mean very much to me."

Mike could not help being impressed by the straightforward manner of this young Englishman.

"Wealth doesn't buy you happiness and contentment, Mr. Bennett. A lot of people fool themselves about that. I was born into wealth. I don't say that to boast, but it didn't bring me the happiness I found right here in Arkansas."

"You go ahead and give Jeff Beauty then, Drake."

"Thank you, sir,"

The two of them walked to the house together—Misty was completely taken by surprise to see Drake. He was not due to come over until the next day to take her over to his house for dinner.

She gasped, "Drake, I hadn't expected to see you this evening."

He laughed. "I didn't get mixed up on the days, love. I just had a need to speak with your pa about something. Remember what I mentioned to you?"

Her green eyes darted from Drake to her pa. Mike grinned and assured Misty that he'd given his approval. A pleased smile brightened Misty's face—she knew how thrilled Jeff would be.

Mike left the two young people in the kitchen and he thought that the next thing Drake Dalton would want to talk to him about was his pretty daughter. If he was any judge of a man, Dalton was smitten.

Well, he'd also give his approval for that, because on his proposal he knew Misty was in love with Dalton. He'd known that since the night she and Drake had joined him and Colleen at the square dance. He knew the look of love on a man or woman's face. It was on both of their faces that night.

Right then, Mike turned his attention to getting himself ready to go over to Lepanto to see his ladylove.

Chapter 37

Drake had not intended to stay long in Misty's kitchen but he did manage to steal one kiss before Lavinia rushed in. He teased her, "I like all those little curls around your forehead, Misty."

"Oh, Drake—I look a mess and you know it!" she giggled.

"Most beautiful mess I've ever seen," he called as he took his leave.

Misty went to the window to watch him leap up on Duke and ride away before she turned her attention back to her pots on the stove.

Little Lavinia stayed in the kitchen with her. "You don't look a mess to me, Misty." Misty was aware that those keen little ears didn't miss a thing.

"Thank you, honey," Misty said and smiled down at her.

Supper was ready for the three of them shortly after Mike left to go to Colleen's for dinner. Once they had eaten and her kitchen was put in order and the dishes dried, Misty spent a quiet, lazy winter night with her little brother and sister. But she also had a lot of time to sit by the hearth to just think. She had to ponder how she would feel the next time she faced Ed Walters, knowing what she now knew.

What she really questioned was the sudden absence of Geneva and Ed Walters.

Misty analyzed everything. The Walters' attitude had been different ever since the time Geneva had heard about her and Drake being in the jewelry store. She realized that Geneva had come over that morning to admonish her in a motherly way about that. But Misty had quickly let her know that there was nothing to be admonished about. She had openly admitted to the fact that Drake had bought her the earrings. But she had also let Geneva know that some busybody was real eager to create some gossip.

What Misty could not know was that Sabrina had planted a few seeds of doubt in Geneva's mind. She had done it in a most subdued way. She'd told Geneva the gossip about Misty and in the same breath she'd said how much she admired her and Ed for the things they'd done for the Bennett children.

Sabrina had said, "Well, a lot of women would have been jealous. Everyone around Crowley knew that before Ed went to Tennessee and met you, he was sweet on Beth Bennett."

All this was news to Geneva. Ed had never spoken that much about his early life and she'd never questioned him. The fact that he had courted Misty's mother gnawed at her constantly for the next few weeks. All kinds of crazy questions paraded through her mind. Was that why he enjoyed having Beth's son over here? Was it why he never minded what she bought for the children? As the weeks went on, Martha even wondered if Misty might be Ed's daughter.

But then she chided herself for the thoughts she'd been harboring about her husband and Misty. She should have known better and paid no attention to a busybody like Sabrina. Everyone knew her as the town gossip.

That night she'd told Ed, "I must get over to see Misty.

It's been weeks since we've stopped by there. Maybe we ought to go over next Saturday, Ed."

"Fine, dear."

But when they had stopped by the Bennetts' place on Saturday afternoon they found no one home. Jeff had gone to town with his father and Misty and Lavinia were strolling in the grove to pick up some more pinecones.

Later that day, it was Geneva's misfortune to be cornered in the mercantile by Sabrina. She suspected she would be forced to hear a juicy tidbit of gossip before she could get away.

"Bet you aren't seeing your little friend Misty much anymore. Hear that Englishman is beating a path to her door," Sabrina was delighted to tell her.

Geneva tried to defend Misty this time, so she told Sabrina, "Well, Misty is old enough to have a beau, Sabrina. I haven't heard anyone faulting the young man. We've heard very nice things about him. It's said he's completely transformed the old Benoit place."

"Yes—yes I've heard about that," Sabrina quickly remarked. She sensed that Geneva wasn't interested in gossip, but she decided to toss one more little morsel about Misty's father squiring a woman over in Lepanto.

"Yes, I know about that, too, Sabrina," Geneva told her.

"Well, Geneva—seems you know as much as I do so guess I'll will be moving on."

Geneva couldn't have been happier.

Mike and Colleen made their plans for the holiday that Saturday night when Mike went over there for dinner. She told him her daughter and her fiancé were coming for Christmas Day—they were spending Christmas Eve with his parents and family.

"Can you spend Christmas Eve with me and my family?" he asked.

She smiled. "Well, I would have been heartbroken if you hadn't asked me." Her eyes twinkled brightly and Mike was reminded of an impish young girl—he'd seen that look in Misty's eyes many times.

He reached over to give her a big hug. "You knew I wanted you with me Christmas Eve unless it interfered with plans you and Maureen had."

Similar plans were being made by Drake and Misty. She told Ellen and Drake, "You two must come to our house on Christmas Eve. Besides, Ellen, you could meet my family."

"I'd love to meet your family, Misty," Ellen said.

"We'll be there, Misty. I'm going to bring Beauty over the day before—Oscar will follow me in the wagon with the feed. I can hardly wait 'til Christmas Eve. I'll bring the little pup for Lavinia, too" Drake told Misty.

"Oh, I can't wait to see her face, Drake," Misty said.

"I'll have to give her her Christmas gift the minute we get there because that little monkey will be scrambling to get out of the basket." Drake said and laughed.

There were no private moments for Drake and Misty as there had been on her last visit, except for the ride over to his house and the ride home. But that provided enough time for many long, lingering kisses.

Drake told her of the nice invitation he and Ellen had had from Rachel. "She wants us to have Christmas dinner with them. They're like Ellen and me—they have no family around here either."

"That'll be nice, Drake. They're both good friends."

"I've been lucky to have them, Misty. They seem like family to me in a way."

Misty smiled. "And I think the two of them feel lucky to be living at Dalton's Lair."

"Hope so—I want to keep them a long, long time," he declared.

With so many plans for the holiday whirling around in her head, Misty also had to remember her dear old friends like the Walters. She was beginning to wonder if one of them might be ill as it had been so long since she'd seen them.

But it was a little too far to walk, so she wondered if her pa would object to her using his buggy after he returned from the mill.

She knew he had no time to take her over there during the week and certainly not on Saturday afternoon.

That Monday evening after dinner, she told him of her concern about the Walters. "They haven't come by in so long and they've been so good to me, Jeff, and Lavinia. I'd like to bake a cake to take over there, Pa. Would you let me use your buggy after you get in from work? It would mean supper would have to be about an hour late, but it could stay warm on the back of the stove."

Mike saw her expression of genuine concern about the Walters and he remembered the little dresses Geneva had made for Lavinia and Misty.

"You can take the buggy, Misty, but you'll be after dark getting back so I want Jeff to go with you," Mike insisted.

"Oh, thank you, Pa! I'll take Jeff with me," she exclaimed, thrilled that he had agreed.

A cake was all she could think of to give them as some kind of Christmas gift so the next morning she baked an applesauce cake. Jeff was very excited about their jaunt over to see the Walters.

She had a nice beef roast simmering with potatoes and onions. There was fresh-baked bread on her cupboard counter so their dinner would be ready to serve once they returned. Around four, she told Jeff, "Go and get yourself cleaned up so we can go as soon as pa gets home."

At five, she had changed into one of her better dresses and brushed her hair so she, too, was ready.

Mike did not stay to talk with any of his buddies after work as he often did. He got in his wagon to head for home and arrived there shortly after five. For such a large man, Mike was agile so he had the buggy ready for Misty hastily.

Just as hastily, Misty and Jeff boarded the buggy, Jeff holding the cake on his lap.

It was a most delightful surprise for Geneva and Ed to see Misty and Jeff. The four of them sat in the parlor catching up on the news. It meant so much to the Walters that Misty was concerned about them.

Misty told them about her pa's new lady and how much she liked Colleen. She also sang Drake Dalton's praises and Jeff chimed in.

When Misty heard the clock chime six she leapt up to say she and Jeff had to be going. "I've supper to get on the table, but I feared I wouldn't see you two before Christmas if I didn't get over here this week."

After fond farewells and warm embraces, Ed and Geneva stood on the front porch watching the buggy disappear into the darkness.

"Oh, Ed—I couldn't be more pleased. Misty and Jeff seem so happy!"

When they went into the house and Martha began to putter around her kitchen, Ed went in with her. He had something to say that would forever remove doubts about him where Misty's mother was concerned.

"Misty could have been my daughter had I not left to go to Tennessee when I did. I courted Beth for a little while but I never got serious, if you know what I mean, Geneva?"

"So it was a short courtship, Ed?"

"Lord, yes. Beth was a pretty thing and Misty looks so much like her, but her ways are nothing like her mother's. Misty is so natural and honest. Beth was never that way. She put on airs that I found perplexing the few times I was with her. No, I can honestly say that had I not come to Tennessee and met you, I would not have continued to court Beth."

"Well, you did come to Tennessee, Ed Walters, and I'm glad you did," she said with a loving smile.

"Not half as glad as *I've* been all these years, dear," he assured her.

For Misty, it had not been an easy encounter with Ed Walters, after what she had read in her mother's journals. But by the time she left the Walters, she was convinced that Beth Bennett had lived in a fantasy world. Her mother seemed to suffer from a young girl's crush on an older man who had never felt the same way.

She was going back home feeling much better now, knowing Ed and Geneva were both fine. Her pa was right—it was dark before they got home.

Jeff tended to the horse and buggy when they arrived and Misty rushed into the house. Mike laughed. "Hey, honey—slow down. You're not all that late. See—me and Lavinia have the table set and the food's nice and hot."

She lifted the roast out of the pot and sliced it. By the time Jeff got to the house, Misty had the huge platter sitting in the middle of the table. She ladled some of the rich brown juice over the roast and potatoes.

"Lord, that looks good Misty—I'm starved," Jeff declared as he flung off his jacket.

Perhaps it was the late hour, but all of the Bennetts were as hungry as wolves. Misty was amazed at how her huge roast had diminished. They seemed ready to get to their beds a short time after dinner.

Chapter 38

On the Sunday afternoon before Christmas Eve, Drake and Oscar left Dalton's Lair, Drake atop Duke and leading Beauty. Oscar followed in the flat-bedded wagon loaded with feed.

Expecting Drake sometime Sunday, Mike had cleaned out a stall in the barn for the new horse. Both he and Colleen had agreed that they wouldn't be together this weekend—he'd be coming over to get her Monday evening.

Mike didn't want to be away when Drake arrived with that feisty little roan mare to tell Jeff that the horse was his. Misty was just as excited as her pa. Lavinia didn't know what was to take place—they didn't dare tell her for fear she would give it away.

As far as Misty was concerned, her house was clean and her baking done for the holidays. She was ready for the holiday.

As it would happen when Drake and Duke came trotting up, Mike and Jeff were walking from the barnyard to the house. Jeff excitedly exclaimed, "It's Mr. Dalton, Pa."

"I see that, Jeff," Mike said with an amused smile.

Jeff rushed ahead of his father to greet Drake. "You—you going to let me go for a ride on Beauty, Mr. Dalton? Are you and me going riding, this afternoon?" Jeff asked anxiously.

By the time Drake leapt off Duke, Mike had come up to join them. Drake's eyes darted from Jeff to his father, who was standing slightly behind his son.

"No, Jeff, I can't go for a ride this afternoon. It's up to you and your father when you go for a ride on Beauty. Jeff, this is my Christmas present to you. Beauty is yours!"

Jeff just stood there frozen, unable to speak for a minute before he looked back at his pa. "Pa—Pa, he says Beauty is mine," Jeff stammered.

Mike patted his shoulder and smiled. "I heard what he said, Jeff." Never would he forget the look on his son's face. It was a very special moment.

Jeff rushed to Drake, throwing his arms around him. Drake patted his head and said, "You just take good care of her, Jeff. That's all I ask."

"Oh, I promise, Mr. Dalton. I promise Beauty will get the best of care," Jeff assured him.

Oscar sat in the wagon thinking it was a miracle of a Christmas Mr. Dalton had given that young man. Just to see the young lad leave Drake's side and walk to the mare to rub her was enough to tell Oscar that Dalton didn't have to worry about Beauty getting the best of care.

"Can I take her for a short ride, Mr. Dalton?"

"Ask your father, Jeff."

Mike gave his permission and then Oscar guided the wagon toward the barn where three of them unloaded the feed sacks.

When all the sacks were in the barn, Mike invited the two of them into the house for a cup of coffee. They told Misty about what had just happened.

She laughed softly. "Jeff will probably want to sleep in Beauty's stall, Drake."

"Now, I wouldn't want him doing that and catching himself a good cold," Drake said and smiled.

"Well, if I ever find him missing from his bed, I'll know where to find him," Misty declared.

Jeff had not returned by the time Drake and Oscar were leaving.

When they arrived back at Dalton's Lair, Oscar said, "You sure gave that young man a Christmas he'll remember for a long time to come. Never saw such an excited little fellow. Animals are interesting creatures. I could tell that Beauty likes that young man, too."

"They got along from the first. That's why I wanted Jeff to have her," Drake said as he removed the saddle from Duke.

"Yes, sir, the two of them will have a lot of pleasure together," Oscar said as he unhitched the team and led them into the stalls.

"You know, Mr. Dalton, if we humans were as smart as animals we probably wouldn't make so many mistakes. They let their instincts guide them. We ought to take a cue from them."

"I agree with you about that, Oscar," Drake said as the two of them parted.

Ellen had been a little crestfallen that no holiday festivities were going to take place at Drake's. They were having Christmas dinner at Oscar's and tomorrow evening she was going over to Misty's with Drake. But after all, she reminded herself, she was the intruder here. It was only natural that Drake would spend the holiday with his friends.

Except for Misty, Ellen realized she had no friends here. She considered Rachel and Oscar friends, but she had a need for young friends. Dear God, she thought, springtime was so far away!

She yearned so for the bustling streets of London. Driving

in a carriage through the dense fog during the winter months would have been a most welcome experience. Dining with one of her sisters in one of the many quaint little inns would have been such a delight. Drake seemed to have put all his English customs behind him, adapting himself to this new country's ways.

She wondered if Valeria and Susanne and their husbands had gathered at Dalton Manor to spend the holiday with their father and his new bride, Lady Margaret Henthorne. It seemed to take forever to get any news from England. She'd written both of them the moment she'd arrived, but had yet to receive a letter.

Back in England many things had happened that Drake and Ellen wouldn't learn about until long after the holiday. Devin Dalton was no longer the lord and master of Dalton Manor. He was the master of nothing—and never would be again—for he had been rendered completely helpless when he'd been thrown from his thoroughbred early in November.

As Oscar had said to Drake, animals are ruled by instinct, and apparently this fine thoroughbred that had been abused by Devin sought his revenge. So Devin was thrown and tromped on by the horse whose spirit Devin could never break.

Lady Margaret was told by a crew of doctors that there was nothing to be done for Devin. The damage to his brain was permanent. So he had no use of his legs, nor could he speak.

In her own way the arrogant Lady Margaret was as overbearing and selfish as Devin had always been, so she quickly decided to move back to her own estate. Dalton Manor had never impressed her. The truth was, once she'd married Devin she'd found him to be nothing like the man who had so ardently courted her. He had immediately tried to break her will, which didn't work with Lady Margaret. She was as strong-willed as he.

There was nothing naive or innocent about Lady Margaret. She never allowed her estate, Meadowbrook, to be sold. Devin had never learned of her other holdings even when they were in the throes of passion.

Lady Margaret was a shrewd and clever woman who could parry with the likes of Devin Dalton—he came to know that shortly before his death.

He also found out something else about her. She wouldn't tolerate his having an affair if he wanted a little diversion. Lady Margaret would have sought a young lover, which Devin knew she could do. She wasn't what Devin would have called a real beauty but there was a certain air about her that attracted gentlemen. He had seen this when they'd attended social affairs.

Lady Margaret never let Devin forget this after they were married, so Devin was a faithful husband. What he'd never suspected before his accident was that his bride of only a few weeks was finding him a bore.

So that was why, after his accident, Lady Margaret moved back over to Meadowbrook and hired nurses to tend to her helpless husband so she could resume the active lifestyle she'd enjoyed before she'd married. So Dalton Manor was closed and the servants dismissed. The truth be told, Lady Margaret could not have cared less about what happened to Devin's estate.

But Susanne cared—she and her husband consulted with Lady Margaret to see what they could work out with her in order to make the estate their home. For Susanne, it was very important, as her mother was buried on the grounds.

They found Lady Margaret most agreeable to their terms, so Dalton Manor was returned to the Dalton family. Susanne's husband sold their property and they moved into the fine old mansion. They planned to celebrate their first

Christmas there with their firstborn, who had arrived in early spring.

Misty had decided she would serve baked ham for Christmas Eve and turkey for their Christmas Day feast. She had also decided that with their small house filled with guests, she could not possibly have a sit-down dinner. Her small kitchen table would not accommodate that many, so she'd decided it had to be a buffet. Her baked ham was studded with cloves and the crocks of baked beans were seasoned with molasses and brown sugar. There were relishes and boiled eggs—her kitchen table was covered with food. Jeff had caught enough fish for her to make a pot of fish chowder, so she'd put bowls out on the table.

By the time Drake and Ellen arrived, Misty was dressed in her green velvet skirt with a frosty-white, long-sleeved blouse. Mike and Colleen had arrived shortly ahead of them and were placing her gifts under the tree.

The room was aglow with flickering candles on the mantel and tables, as the aromas of holiday time greeted Ellen and Drake.

Ellen carried some of the gifts as Drake had his hands full toting the wicker basket containing the pup. The lid kept popping up—she didn't like being confined.

Drake didn't hesitate, telling Lavinia, "Honey—here's your Christmas present. Hope you like it."

Lavinia giggled and rushed to sit on the floor beside the basket. At that same moment, the lid rose and the pup's curly black head peeped out.

Lavinia shrieked when she and the pup had their first encounter. It was instant love as Lavinia cuddled her while she jumped about and reached up to lick her cheek.

"It's really mine, Mr. Dalton?"

"She's yours. You'll have to think about a name for

her—I left that for you," Drake said as he turned to go back to his buggy to get the other gifts.

Everyone in the room knew that Lavinia's Christmas had been made if she hadn't gotten another gift. Misty told her, "That's Lucky's pup, Lavinia."

Lavinia turned a quizzical eye up at her sister. "Couldn't be, Misty, 'cause Lucky's a boy."

Everyone was roaring with laughter when Drake came back in to hear Misty explaining to Lavinia, "No, honey, I meant that Lucky is the pup's father."

"Oh, good! I'm glad Lucky's the father," Lavinia remarked, her attention already back on the pup.

Misty could feel proud about her scrumptious buffet. Ellen told her, "Mercy, you amaze me, Misty. To think that you cooked all this delicious food yourself just dazzles me! I can't imagine doing something like this."

"Just a little practice at the stove," Misty declared.

But Colleen had walked up and overheard them. "Oh, no, honey—some women stand over a cookstove for years and never cook such delicious food. You have a real talent."

By the time Drake had complimented her, too, she was feeling very pleased and in very festive spirits as they gathered around the Christmas tree.

Colleen suggested they sing some Christmas carols before they exchanged gifts. She proceeded to lead them in singing some of her favorites. Mike was amazed to discover what a lovely soprano voice she had.

By the time all the gifts were passed out, Ellen was feeling so consumed by warmth and sentiment she felt close to tears. She'd never known such people. She could understand why Drake felt as he did about this place.

Drake and Mike pranced around the room, displaying their new knitted vests like proud peacocks. Colleen was overwhelmed by the unusual gift Mike had given her and insisted that Mike fasten it around her neck immediately.

Misty was mesmerized by Drake's gift. Like Colleen, she

had Drake fasten the pearls around her neck. She took off the other earrings he'd given her to wear the pearl earrings.

She looked so exquisite wearing the pearls with her snowy white blouse, Drake thought as he looked down at her. Her warm green eyes looked up to tell him how lovely she thought the pearls were.

"No gem could ever be as exquisite as you, love. Never!" Drake told her, aching to reach down and kiss her.

When they finally had a brief private moment, he told her how he'd always cherish the vest. He didn't restrain himself from taking her two small hands in his to bring them to his lips and murmur softly, "Those dainty hands worked many hours to make this for me and that's why I will always treasure it, Misty, my love."

Maybe it was the sentimental tone of the evening that made Misty softly whisper, "I love you, Drake Dalton."

"And I love you, Misty Bennett!" he told her just as candidly.

It was late when the two buggies left the Bennetts' house. They traveled in different directions, Mike taking Colleen back to Lepanto and Drake heading for home.

Colleen confessed to Mike, "I should have had you taking me home an hour ago but I was having such a good time I didn't want to leave."

"I'm glad you enjoyed yourself so much. It was the nicest Christmas Eve I can ever remember," he said.

The occupants in the other buggy were having a similar conversation. Ellen was the chatter-box, not Drake. He didn't have to ask if she'd had a good time. He knew she had!

"And Drake, I've some exciting news. You know that lovely Mrs. Carver? Well, she and I sat over in the corner and talked for quite a while."

"Colleen Carver is a very gracious lady and a very successful business woman in Lepanto."

"I know about her bakery, Drake. Remember—you took me in there a short time ago."

Ellen sensed that her older brother was preoccupied by his own thoughts and had been since they'd left.

"Well, she told me about a lady in Lepanto who needs a companion. She's an elderly, wealthy woman. Mrs. Carver says that she lives in a fine house and has a cook and a housekeeper in her home but needs a companion to take her out in her gig and certain things like that. I could do that, Drake."

She kept chattering on about what Colleen had told her about Agatha Fortis.

"You know her, Drake?"

"No, honey, I don't. I haven't had a chance to get to know too many people around the area yet, Ellen," Drake confessed.

"Well, I was just overwhelmed by Mrs. Carver's generous offer that she come to your house and take me over to meet this Mrs. Fortis after Christmas. Isn't that nice of her? She said she'd arrange the meeting for a Sunday afternoon," Ellen told him excitedly.

"Well, I think that's just wonderful, Ellen," he said. But then this entire evening had been glorious for Drake Dalton.

What Ellen had just told him couldn't have made him happier, for when he'd left the Bennetts' a few minutes earlier, he had made a decision.

When those green eyes of Misty's had looked up at him and she'd told him she loved him with such sincerity, Drake knew that he was going to ask Misty to marry him.

She was the only woman he'd ever want to wear that cherished ring he'd taken from his mother's jewelry case back in England. It would be Misty's wedding ring.

Drake was sure Adrienne Benoit Dalton would have approved of his bride. Misty was everything he had envisioned his mother to have been when she was Misty's age. He imagined her as a breathtaking beauty with her sweet, virginal innocence when Devin Dalton came into her life, breaking her spirit and robbing her of her dignity.

Drake wanted only to give all his love to Misty and never break her high spirit. He wanted her to be the mother of his children but never would he force himself on her. Theirs would be children of their love for one another.

Tonight he knew that he wanted Misty sharing the rest of his life with him!

Chapter 39

When all the Christmas Eve farewells were over, Misty got a very sleepy little sister to bed and made her new pup a cozy spot right beside her. The little pup seemed as weary as Lavinia as it cuddled on the blanket and fell asleep.

The pup had its name—it was to be called Sweetie. Once Lavinia and her pup were taken care of, Misty turned her attention to the kitchen, but she'd already decided that the cleaning up could wait until morning as she was completely exhausted.

She more than welcomed Jeff's assistance in getting all the food stored away. He observed that there wasn't that much left. Jeff also noticed that his sister looked exhausted. When they dimmed the lamps in the kitchen, he told her, "Why don't you go to bed, Misty? You look tuckered out."

"I think I will, Jeff."

"I'll take care of all the candles and lamps in the front room. You just go to bed."

She was so sleepy that she forgot to remove the pearls from her neck and ears when she took off her clothing to get into her nightgown. So exhausted that she didn't know when her pa returned from Lepanto or when he, Lavinia, and Jeff woke up in the morning. She slept past the breakfast hour, so Mike fixed their breakfast on Christmas Day.

Misty could not believe how late she'd slept when she did finally rouse from her bed. When she ambled into the kitchen to get a cup of coffee, she found two bowls in the kitchen—Sweetie's food and water.

The kitchen was ghostly quiet. Two cups of coffee made her more alert—when she was ready to get dressed, she had to admit she was glad there'd be only the four of them here for supper. She saw her pa and Lavinia out in the back yard with the new pup. If she was to guess what Jeff was doing, she would suspect he was taking his little mare out for a ride.

It was a quiet day and evening around the Bennett house, and Misty welcomed that. Mike instructed his young son how much feed he should put out in the morning for Beauty. He had also laid down very firm rules for Lavinia about keeping her pup's water bowl filled and feeding her. He impressed on her that Sweetie was her responsibility.

Lavinia assured him, "I'll take good care of Sweetie, Pa. Misty won't have to do anything, I promise you."

"All right, sugar," Mike said and smiled for he had no doubt that Lavinia would tend to Sweetie.

The lovely doll Colleen had bought for her was neglected because Lavinia was so occupied with Sweetie. Misty stood at the kitchen window observing her trying to get Sweetie to stay in the wagon Jeff had bought so she could take her for a ride. But Sweetie always jumped out, which frustrated Lavinia. Misty watched the expression on her sister's face when she couldn't get the pup to do what she wanted her to do.

* * *

SWEET SEDUCTION 349

Both Ellen and Drake welcomed the fact that they could sleep late on Christmas Day—Drake had told Rachel not to come over that morning. He assured her he could prepare breakfast for the two of them.

Rachel appreciated his offer because it gave her more time to devote to the dinner she was preparing for the four of them.

Ellen had stuffed herself so much the night before at Misty's that she didn't want anything to eat the next morning, so she had a couple of cups of coffee. She would never have believed it, but she had aquired a taste for this coffee that Drake drank all the time.

As she sat there at Drake's kitchen table, sipping her strong black coffee, she thought about this strange place she'd arrived in and found herself so disillusioned. Truth was, she hadn't had such a grand time for as long as she could remember as she'd had in the humble little Bennett cottage.

Christmas Eve in the elegant parlor of Dalton's Manor had never been that stimulating. Never had she felt herself so surrounded by warmth and love. Her mother, Ellen mused sadly, was capable of being very loving when Devin wasn't around. Then she became reserved and stiff.

What tales she was going to have to tell Valeria and Susanne when she returned to London! But Ellen knew that her thinking was changed forever after this venture. That first week, she would never have thought she would feel as she did now.

She was glad now that she'd come to this new country and spent time with Drake.

The evening at Oscar and Rachel's was not the spirited occasion of the previous night, but Ellen enjoyed it nevertheless. She thought it was very sweet of them to invite her and Drake to dinner.

Rachel had knitted Ellen a lovely scarf and gloves in a

berry color. She said to Ellen, "Don't know about England, Miss Ellen, but winters can get mighty cold."

Rachel had also knitted Drake a warm wool scarf. They both greatly appreciated the gifts.

It was much earlier when Drake and Ellen walked back home than it had been when they came back from Misty's.

"Well, another Christmas has come and gone, Drake. I hope Valeria and Susanne had as nice a holiday as I've had here with you."

"Ah, honey, I'm glad. I can't remember a nicer one. I'm ready to face the new year with high hopes for Dalton's Lair," he said.

Ellen wondered if his plans included taking a bride. She couldn't imagine that he wouldn't be asking Misty to marry him soon—it was obvious to her that he was head over heels in love.

But she said nothing of this as they approached the house. Instead she told him, "Well, seeing what you've accomplished in less than a year, Drake, I'm sure next year will be grand for you."

When they got inside the door, Ellen didn't stay long in the parlor. She told Drake she was going to her room and write Susanne and Valeria a long letter about the glorious holiday. But she hesitated for a moment. "You know, I must say I miss that adorable pup, Drake."

"Just goes to show how things grow on you. I think old Lucky misses the pup, too," Drake said and grinned.

Drake spent the rest of the evening alone in his parlor, mulling over something Oscar had told him he might want to look into for the next three winter months. There were many acres of dense woods on his property and Oscar told him, "Logs float up and down the St. Francis and Little River all winter long, Mr. Dalton. The lumber mills around Crowley and Lepanto do a thriving business during the cold weather."

Drake had to admit he could well afford to enrich his

coffer—he had spent a tremendous sum of money over the last seven months. So far, everything Oscar had suggested had been the right moves for him to make.

Misty wasn't the only one weary by the time the Christmas holiday was over. Colleen felt the effects of the late night hours, too. All the excitement of Christmas Eve left her a little tired the next day when she had Christmas dinner with Maureen and her fiancé.

Maureen displayed the lovely diamond on her finger and announced that they were getting married in May. "Will you bake my wedding cake, Momma?"

Colleen hugged her and assured her she would have a very special wedding cake. Maureen teased her mother, asking, "Will there be two weddings in the Carver family this year?"

"You'll be the first to know, my darling Maureen," Colleen said and smiled.

She took her usual order to Agatha Fortis on Friday and told her about a young girl she felt might fill the position as her companion.

"An English lady, you say? Well, now, that might be very interesting."

Colleen said, "Yes, Mrs. Fortis. She came here to live with her brother, Drake Dalton, who inherited the old Benoit estate. I'm sure you know of that land. He's been here several months now. A charming gentleman, I must tell you. I met his sister during the holidays and she, too, is most gracious but terribly afraid she won't find tutoring work here."

"Not stiff as a poker then as I've heard a lot of English people are?" Agatha Fortis quizzed Colleen.

"Not at all, Mrs. Fortis, but then you'd just have to form your own opinion. She's a very mature young lady, certainly not a giggling little scatterbrain like a lot of young girls. But then Ellen is around twenty-one or -two, I think."

"Could you bring her here to talk to me, Colleen? I know how busy you are and I hesitate even to ask this," Agatha said.

"I have Sundays off, Mrs. Fortis, so I'd be most happy to bring Ellen over on a Sunday afternoon if that would be all right with you."

"This Sunday? The sooner the better, as far as I'm concerned, Colleen, dear. I've been isolated in this house for over a month now. Can she handle a gig?"

"I asked her that and she had her own gig in London. She's the daughter of Lord Devin Dalton."

"Well, Mercy lord—wonder why she ever left?" Agatha asked, sitting up in her chair.

"She wasn't happy after her mother died, she told me. I gather that Ellen is a very independent miss who didn't want just to be the daughter of an English lord. That's obvious, or she wouldn't have been tutoring for over two years."

"I think I might like this young lady very much. I might be the answer to her dilemma and she could certainly be the answer to mine," Agatha Fortis declared. So she asked Colleen to bring her the next Sunday at three. She also told Colleen that her own mother was English and she always observed her traditional teatime at four in the afternoon.

"I'll bring her at three, Mrs. Fortis, so the two of you can have tea at four if you wish."

The next morning Colleen got in her buggy to go out to Dalton's Lair to see Ellen. She had Maureen open up the bakery while she was gone.

Ellen was elated and told Colleen, "I'll be delighted to have tea with her. You make her sound so interesting. She obviously isn't ready to be confined just because she's impaired and elderly."

So it was arranged that Colleen would pick her up Sunday afternoon around two to take her to Lepanto. Ellen had very exciting news for Drake when he and Oscar returned to the house after their ride through the woods to survey the trees on his land.

Drake said he'd be delighted if Ellen found a position that would please her. To himself, he remembered that at Dalton Manor, a person could easily have privacy, but not here in his little home. He and Misty had had nowhere to go to be alone except to the barn.

But going to the barn was not going to happen again, Drake had already decided. There was a long winter ahead and he didn't intend to wait until spring to make Misty his bride. He wanted her here in his home, sharing the cozy warmth of his hearth together.

Colleen left Dalton's Lair to return to her bakery to find Maureen a nervous wreck because she'd been so busy. Maureen declared, "God, Momma—I don't see how you do this every day. I'm worn out."

Colleen saw all the empty trays and asked her daughter if she could possibly handle the front of the shop one more hour so she could get another four dozen cookies in her oven. A few minutes later, she came back to the front and told Maureen in a breathless voice that she was going to be forced to hire someone to deliver her orders and help her in the kitchen. "It's becoming too much for me to handle, but I've been making more than I ever have. So how can I complain? I thought it would be a slow week but it hasn't been. I'm glad Mike isn't coming over until tomorrow."

Maureen looked at her, surveying this petite woman and admiring her so much. She had not really helped her that much in her shop. Not until today had she realized how hard she must have worked to build this bakery into such a prosperous business.

Maureen stayed on until Colleen took the cookies from her oven and refilled her trays. Colleen had everything ready for her afternoon shoppers when they came in. When she closed, she had four deliveries to make so if she was lucky she'd get home by six or six-thirty. If she had a delivery man, it would be so much easier, she realized.

Maureen finally prepared to go home. As she was going out the door, she made a flippant remark that Colleen pondered later that evening. Maureen said, "You ought to marry Mike and have him help you run the bakery. He could do your deliveries, for one thing. His wages at the mill have to be meager. From what Eric tells me, he could work there another ten years and not make any more."

Her pretty daughter breezed out of the bakery to head for home and get ready for her date with her fiancé. Colleen had a quiet moment to reflect about how easy she'd made life for her one and only daughter. She didn't regret a moment of it, but she *had* pampered and spoiled her. When she compared what Misty had had to do at her age, she knew Maureen would not have been able to cope.

In fact, by the time she closed her door and loaded the four orders into her buggy, her head was whirling with the suggestion her daughter had made. By the time the orders were delivered and she pulled the buggy into her drive, she was thinking that Maureen's suggestion made very good sense.

If she and Mike were married and he was in the shop to help her, it was a way to solve their dilemma: his earnings at the mill could never support the two of them. She would never give up her thriving business; as crazy as it might seem, the wages she would have to pay for a young man to come in to help her would probably be about what Mike made at the mill.

She was so weary when she entered her front door that she sank down into one of the overstuffed chairs and kicked off her slippers.

She relaxed there for a half-hour before she pulled herself up and began to move around the house. While she put together a light dinner and brewed a fresh pot of coffee, she

SWEET SEDUCTION

was thinking how much she was going to enjoy sleeping late in the morning.

After dinner, she took a warm bath and got into her nightgown. By the time the clock struck nine, Colleen was tucked into bed. She reminded herself that she had to go out to Dalton's Lair tomorrow by two.

She was glad Mike was not due over tomorrow until seven—he knew nothing about her plans to take Ellen over to Mrs. Fortis's.

Her sleep was sweet and swift—her head had barely hit her pillow. She slept for twelve hours before awaking refreshed and ready to meet the day.

As she'd promised Agatha Fortis, she had Ellen Dalton in the woman's elegant parlor at three. She told them she would return at five to pick Ellen up to give them a chance to get acquainted.

Somehow, Colleen knew that they would get along magnificently. They certainly did. They had tea at four, Agatha finding that Ellen had the gracious manners she wished her companion to have. She also had a vivacious way about her that Agatha liked. She summoned her housekeeper to take Ellen upstairs so she could pick out her bedroom. There were four that Ellen could choose from.

It was a huge mansion, far grander than any home Ellen had been in since she'd arrived in Arkansas. The entire house was elegantly furnished. She chose the one across the hall from Mrs. Fortis's suite.

Mrs. Fortis had already told her she had permission to ride any of her thoroughbreds anytime she wished. She assured Ellen she would have a lot of time to do whatever she wished. "I'm not a demanding old harridan. I want a companion to help me do the things I used to do so I can stay as active as possible."

"I understand, Mrs. Fortis. You already have a housekeeper and a cook."

"That's right. I used to take myself anywhere I wanted

to go in my gig. Well, I haven't been able to do that. You like to play cards, Ellen?"

"Oh, yes," Ellen said.

"Know how to play poker?"

"No, I don't."

"Doesn't matter. I'll teach you, and in no time you'll be beating the socks off me," Agatha said and laughed.

Agatha was a lady who came straight to the point. She told Ellen what her salary would be, plus her room and board. It would be pleasant for Agatha to have someone to share her evening meal. "So shall we give it a go, Ellen? Are you interested?"

"I'm willing if you are, Mrs. Fortis."

They had only one other thing to discuss before Colleen picked Ellen up—the day she'd arrive.

Agatha suggested, "Enjoy New Year's Day with your brother and come over here the next day. Would that work out for you?"

"That would be fine. I'll plan to get here Wednesday morning," Ellen replied.

"I'll look forward to seeing you, Ellen. I have a feeling that you and I are going to get along just fine, my dear," she said with a bright twinkle in her eyes.

Chapter 40

Colleen could tell Ellen was very excited as they drove back to Drake's place. "I really like her, Mrs. Carver, and I'm very grateful to you," Ellen declared.

"Well, when I met you I thought the two of you might just be a perfect match. She wanted someone gracious like you for her companion."

"I'll be moving over there the day after New Year's," Ellen informed her.

Colleen laughed. "My goodness, Agatha *is* anxious to have you over there."

After getting Ellen back to Dalton's Lair, Colleen was very contented as she traveled toward home. Now she had her own evening to plan since Mike was coming over for dinner.

It was going to be a simple meal—she was sure Mike would understand when he learned about her busy weekend. Mike was not persnickety about food. He seemed to like everything.

She actually had an hour to spare before she began to

putter in her kitchen. When her table was set and her food was simmering, Colleen went into her little parlor and sat by the hearth. She poured herself a glass of sherry to sip as she waited for Mike's arrival.

Mike had never been late when she'd asked him to dinner. Colleen had always admired him for being prompt. She had no patience with people who didn't keep their promises.

That afternoon when Colleen arrived home she had found Maureen's note telling her where she was and would be for the evening. That was another thing Colleen insisted upon.

Dinner was quiet and relaxed—Mike seemed ready for a low-key Sunday evening. She told him about her hectic day.

"And then after all that, you had me hitting your door. Colleen, you work too hard," Mike declared as they sat in the parlor by the hearth.

"Well, I'm going to hire someone to help me, Mike. I must. I'm going to hire a young man so he can make my deliveries."

"Why a young man, Colleen?" Mike asked straightening up on the settee.

"Real simple. A lot of young women can't handle a buggy and their parents would not want them delivering orders after dark. I can understand that."

"You mean that would be all he'd be doing?"

"Hardly. I'll hire someone for a full day, six days a week," she said. She explained how long it took her to mix all the doughs, starting at five in the morning. She also told him what had happened just during the short time she'd had to be away from the shop while Maureen was running it.

"Why couldn't she have made up some more cookies when the trays were empty?" asked Mike.

Colleen smiled sheepishly. "My pretty daughter never helped me in the back of the bakery. She's only been in the front. I've pampered Maureen, Mike. I realize that now, but it's too late. She and Eric are to be married in May."

"I wondered if you hadn't overindulged your daughter by carrying all the load," Mike confessed.

"I have, Mike. But she didn't have a father like other girls her age so I tried to make up for that."

"I understand, Colleen. I really do."

"Thank you, Mike. I don't regret anything, but I'm glad you understand. It means a lot just to have you to sit here and talk with me about it."

"Now what will you have to pay a young man to work for you six days a week?" he asked.

"Well, I don't know. It will take a special young man to put in such long hours—from early morning until after five in the afternoon—so I must offer a wage to make it worth his while," she said, becoming very serious and businesslike.

When she told him the salary she was going to pay her new employee, she was hardly prepared for his response. He had such a sober look on his face she knew he wasn't teasing.

"Would you consider hiring an older man who would work his guts out to help you? If you would, then I'm applying for the job."

Her hand caressed his cheek. "You're serious, aren't you, Mike? But I couldn't ask you to make that sacrifice."

"What sacrifice, honey? Hell, I've never kidded myself about my job at the mill. I'm going nowhere there. I'm just a laborer and that's all it will ever be until my back gives out or I get hurt on the job. And I'm no young dude anymore."

Colleen nodded, knowing he'd spoken the truth. She smiled slowly as she told him, "You're hired, Mike Bennett. But you've got to mix that dough exactly as I instruct you," she teased.

"Yes, ma'am—you're the boss lady. Now, if I prove to be good can I expect a raise in six months?" he asked playfully.

"You may, and if you don't work out I might just have to let you go and hire another man," she taunted.

"You won't have to do that, Colleen. You'll see. I want to help you—that would give me so much pleasure. I don't mind hard work and long hours. I've known nothing else since I was fifteen."

"Oh, Mike, I'm so excited. The thought of you there with me making the shop work more effectively and taking so much of the load off me is all I could ask for. I can't believe how busy I've been since autumn. Sales have grown constantly."

By the time they said their farewells, they had decided that Mike would come to work for her on the ninth of January.

"I don't owe them more notice than that, Colleen. If they laid me off, as they have some men, they would tell me one day and I'd be gone the next. I've worked at that same mill for over eighteen years and I'm not making much more than when I started. But what could I do? I had a wife and a family to support."

"Oh, Mike—you haven't had a very easy life, have you?"

"No, I haven't, but then I've never gone hungry nor has my family. I'm sure I was always a big disappointment to Beth. But she knew she was marrying a mill worker, not a landowner."

Colleen listened to him talk, realizing it was one of those rare times that he'd ever mentioned his wife. She sensed that theirs had not been a happy marriage. At least, she had had a happy marriage until her husband had his ill-fated accident.

"Mike, it's going to be a wonderful year for both of us. I just know it! I'm really looking forward to the two of us working at the bakery together."

He was holding her in his arms and he admitted, "You know something, Colleen? I'm as excited as hell about it!"

After he had left, Colleen realized that it was a big gamble—it could be the solution for both of them or it could break up a relationship she'd enjoyed very much.

Time would tell, she told herself as she prepared to go to bed to meet that early morning hour when she'd have to get up and go to the bakery.

Since Ellen was going over to Mrs. Fortis's with Colleen on Sunday, Drake rode over to Misty's while she was gone. He wanted her to come over to spend New Year's Day with them. "Regardless of what Jeff said, I'm eating some of those black-eyed peas. I want good luck this next year," he said and laughed.

Misty giggled. "I'll cook them for you, Drake, but you're going to feel just like Jeff."

She also advised him to pick her up early—it took several hours to simmer the peas. On New Year's Eve, she had cooked a pot of black-eyed peas for her pa, Lavinia, and Jeff and made up a big pan of cornbread. She had also cooked a huge cast iron pot of white beans, which she knew Jeff liked, so he wouldn't go hungry. There was more than enough to take a huge crock to Drake's the next day.

The first thing she noticed when she arrived was a group of valises lined up in the parlor.

Ellen was bubbling when she greeted Misty. "I'm going to be a companion to Mrs. Fortis, Misty, and I have Mrs. Carver to thank for finding me the position. I'm going over there tomorrow."

"Oh, Ellen—I'm so happy for you. I don't know Mrs. Fortis but I've heard about her. The family has lived over in Lepanto for as long as I can remember."

"Well, I may not see you for a while, Misty, but I'll be thinking about you. She told me I can use her buggy to visit Drake so I'll come to see you, too."

"You must, Ellen."

Drake had to admit that Jeff was right. He took one taste of the black-eyed peas and grimaced. Misty broke into a giggle, but she had the other pot of beans and ham ready to serve to him and Ellen.

"You must remember, Drake, when people in the South had been ravaged by Yankee troops and there was nothing left in their pantries, anything would have tasted good. They had nothing in their barnyards—no chickens left to fry or roast. Their vegetables had been carried away. A pot of black-eyed peas and some cornbread became a feast—they would not allow their spirits to be broken by the intruders. Southerners were a proud breed. Ravaged and raped, they still looked down their noses at the crude Yankees who invaded their beautiful countryside."

For all that had been done to them, nothing would force them to give up, Misty said. Drake and Ellen listened intensely to her tales of the war.

"The North had no victory, really. The South rose quickly again and the freed slaves didn't find the road to glory all that wonderful once they got up North," Misty declared.

In a lighter vein, Drake suggested he take Lucky outside and see if he might like some of the black-eyed peas, and Misty agreed.

As it would happen, when Drake returned and Misty and Ellen had dimmed the lamps, he announced that Lucky had turned his nose up.

"You've got a pampered dog, Drake."

"Guess you're right, Misty. You know what else? Snowflakes are falling."

"Then maybe you should get me home, Drake," Misty said.

It was a lovely wintry night when Drake took her home as the light snowflakes pelted their face. It wasn't sticking on the dirt road at all. Misty snuggled close to him, her wool scarf draped around her hair. As Drake pulled his buggy up to the Bennetts' gate and before he leaped down, he paused. He didn't want to delay asking her to marry him any longer.

"Misty, it's the New Year and I want to spend the rest of my life with you. Marry me, love," he declared as the two of them sat in the buggy.

Could he have possibly realized how much she yearned to hear him say what he'd just said. She'd dreamed of it so many times. But now that he'd finally uttered the words, she found herself completely breathless.

Finally her arms encircled his neck as she murmured softly, "Oh, Drake—I'll marry you whenever you say. My heart has been yours since the first afternoon I met you on that country road."

"If we could, I'd say let's get married tomorrow. But I'll try to be patient until I can get Ellen settled in at the Fortis place. Let's start planning our wedding, love."

"Why not sweethearts' day, Drake?"

"Sweethearts' day?"

"Yes, I'm speaking of Valentine's Day, Drake."

"That's so far away, Misty. Six weeks would drive me crazy," he declared.

"Oh, Drake," she said and laughed. "You choose the date, then."

"I'm a greedy man where you're concerned. What about two weeks from tonight?"

"That sounds wonderful to me, Drake. I'm just as impatient as you are. Now I believe that dreams really do come true."

"I knew that when I first met you, love," he said as he took her in his arms for one last kiss.

Chapter 41

Ellen did not have Drake load all her valises in his buggy on Wednesday morning when they prepared to depart for Mrs. Fortis's place. "I'll get them later, Drake. After all, what if it doesn't work out?"

That remark was enough to dampen Drake's mood after the plans he and Misty had talked about. "There's always a little adjusting to do, Ellen. Look how it was when you first came here," he pointed out.

"Oh, I know, but Mrs. Fortis has already told me I can use her gig to come over to see you whenever I wish."

"Well, it sounds to me like you've found a very nice lady to work for, Ellen. I can't imagine that the two of you won't get along."

Ellen was ready to leave after she'd gone to the kitchen to tell Rachel goodbye. "Come and see us over here, Miss Ellen," Rachel told her as Ellen was turning to leave.

The snow was only about an inch deep, but it created a beautiful winter scene as they started down the road. It was a short trip from Dalton's Lair to the Fortis estate. Drake had only to meet Agatha Fortis to feel his younger sister would be working for a very gracious lady.

She had great dignity about her. Although she walked with the aid of a cane, her white head was always held high.

He also found her to be a lady who didn't hesitate to say what was on her mind. She told Drake, "I heard about your arrival here in Poinsett County, young man. You stirred up a little gossip in our little community."

"Well, I wasn't aware of that, Mrs. Fortis," Drake said and smiled.

"Oh, a handsome young Englishman arriving here was enough to set a lot of tongues wagging. All these pretty little Arkansas girls will be vying for your brother's attention, Ellen," Agatha said.

Ellen laughed. "I think Drake has already found himself the prettiest girl in Arkansas, Mrs. Fortis."

A twinkle came to Agatha's sharp eyes as she smiled at him. "You don't waste time, do you, young man?"

"Not if I can help it," he said and grinned.

Agatha insisted that Drake stay for a light lunch with her and Ellen and he could hardly refuse. He wasn't hungry but the lunch was delicious. Obviously, there was a very good cook in the Fortis kitchen.

As they ate, Agatha confessed that she wasn't one to like a hearty breakfast as her husband did. By the time they'd finished, Drake had learned that Agatha Fortis was an entertaining and witty woman.

"Jefferson always called himself a lark because he got up at the crack of dawn. I slept late, so he called me an owl—I liked to stay up. You know, when I think about it, I guess it was a miracle that we stayed married all those years," she said and laughed.

Drake left feeling very happy that his sister had found the perfect job. He had no doubt at all about Ellen's welfare—he sensed that Mrs. Fortis liked his sister, so he decided that it was up to Ellen to adjust to Mrs. Fortis's ways.

* * *

Agatha was certainly not a demanding woman who expected Ellen to be at her beck and call. In fact, the minute Drake left, Agatha dismissed her to get settled in her room, saying she would see her at dinner.

They had a nice, relaxed evening. After dinner they played card games—Agatha didn't attempt to teach Ellen to play poker that first night.

By the time the next two days and nights had passed, Ellen was feeling comfortable in her new surroundings. She had taken morning rides on one of the thoroughbreds. Agatha observed her from the window and saw that she sat well in the saddle. There was no question that Ellen was not a novice—she was an expert equestrienne.

Agatha was ready to test Ellen's skill guiding her gig. She was more than ready to make a long-anticipated jaunt into Lepanto.

So the next afternoon, the two of them boarded the gig. Agatha was such a tiny lady that the tall, willowy Ellen had no problem giving her the extra hoist she needed to get to the gig's seat. Ellen found her a most admirable enjoyable friend.

Oh, how Agatha Fortis disliked her helplessness! Ellen would always smile when she heard her fuss and cuss that "no-good leg" of hers, as she called it.

One of the first stops they made was at Colleen's bakery. Colleen could tell that they were getting along fabulously. When they prepared to leave the shop with their purchases, Agatha told Colleen, "Now that I've got Ellen, you won't have to run out to my house to deliver my orders, Colleen dear."

Colleen smiled, "I don't mind, Mrs. Fortis but, it's so good to see you getting out again."

"It's absolutely glorious to me, Colleen. I thank you again for bringing Ellen and me together."

Colleen watched them get back into the gig and head up the main street.

Agatha's next stop was at the emporium to purchase a large supply of thread so she could work on her needlepoint during the winter months ahead. She'd been out of thread for weeks.

"You need to shop for anything, dear?" she asked Ellen.

"Not a thing this trip, Mrs. Fortis. I got so many nice gifts for Christmas—scented soaps, scarves, and gloves—that I find myself needing nothing."

"Well, I guess we'll head for home then," Agatha said as they exited the emporium.

Ellen realized when she helped her into the gig that Agatha's stamina was spent after the two stops they'd made. And Agatha realized by the time they approached her home that Ellen could handle a gig with the same expertise she had with the thoroughbred yesterday. She had a jewel and she knew it!

By the time the weekend came, Ellen was convinced that everything would be fine between her and Mrs. Fortis. Agatha was happy to hear that she'd like to take the gig to go over to her brother's to gather up the rest of her things.

"Of course, honey, and have a nice visit with your brother. I want you to have plenty of free time for yourself," Agatha told her. But Ellen had already found that out. The time she shared with Mrs. Fortis was so pleasant. She enjoyed the evening meals with her. Some evenings she liked playing cards but there were other nights when she enjoyed going into her husband's study to read for hours. She had revealed to Ellen, "I was this poor little country girl and Jefferson Fortis was a wealthy gentleman who took a shine to me for God knows what reason. He married me and then educated me. I couldn't read, Ellen."

"And he taught you?"

"Yes, dear. He taught me so much. He opened up so many worlds to me."

"That's a wonderful story, Mrs. Fortis," Ellen said.

"It was amazing—I couldn't believe how smart I became after being married to Jefferson for five years. I not only learned how to read but how to add and subtract. When I asked him how he became so wealthy he always told me that he knew how to add and subtract," Agatha said and laughed.

"So he didn't have a wealthy father?"

"Hardly, Ellen. He came from a poor farming family like mine. He was thirty-five when we married and I was only fifteen."

"Mrs. Fortis, you're fantastic! I know I'll learn so much from you," Ellen said.

"I'd like to think that, Ellen. I never was blessed with a son or daughter to pass all this *wisdom,* as you call it, on to. So I hope I can do it for you," Agatha declared as she rose from her chair. She was ready to go to her bedroom. The trip had tired her.

When Ellen came rolling up his drive in Mrs. Fortis's gig, Drake was just finishing his second cup of coffee and preparing to ride over to the Fortis estate.

Oscar had gone into Crowley and picked up the mail. There had been a letter addressed to Drake and Ellen from Susanne. It told about what had happened to their father two months earlier as well as her plan to take over Dalton Manor.

Drake had read the letter—it was obvious that Lady Margaret wanted to rid herself of the responsibility of Dalton Manor. The truth be told, Susanne wrote, she also wished to be rid of Devin Dalton, but she could not think of a way do that.

Drake had read the letter twice. He wanted to feel compassion but he didn't. All he could think of was that Devin now found himself in the helpless position that Drake's dear mother had been in for over twenty years. No, he felt no compassion!

At least, now he could return to England and go to Dalton Manor to visit his mother's grave as Susanne and her husband would be living there.

He gave Ellen the letter when she arrived. She sat at his kitchen table reading it, sipping a cup of coffee Rachel had served her. Drake knew that reading their mother's journal had brought out Ellen's obviously cold response. She gave Drake the letter. "What is it about poetic justice, Drake? Father has surely received his."

Drake knew exactly what she meant—a man like Devin Dalton could have no more tormenting damnation than to be rendered helpless and at Lady Margaret's mercy.

As he helped Ellen carry out the remaining valises, he asked her, "Guess this means that you're happy over there?"

"Oh, yes, Drake. She is such a charming lady—I've thoroughly enjoyed myself this week. I've ridden her thoroughbred and we've gone into Lepanto. I think she's enjoyed our time together, too. Yes, Drake—I'm very happy over there," she said and smiled up at him.

"Well, then I'm happy, too!" He decided he would tell her about his and Misty's plans to be married in two weeks. He had not told Rachel or Oscar.

Ellen gave him an exuberant hug, declaring, "Oh, Drake I couldn't be happier. I liked Misty the first night I met her. Oh, I'm so excited!"

"I'm glad you approve of my bride-to-be, Ellen."

She got up in the gig and looked down at him, smiling. "Everything has worked out perfectly, hasn't it, Drake? I have my position now, so I won't be underfoot when you bring your bride here. That's the way it should be."

Drake agreed but he didn't say so. Instead, he said, "Seems it's going to be a good year for both of us, Ellen."

She put the gig in motion and gave him a nod.

The next morning Drake did tell both Rachel and Oscar about his plans and they were as delighted as Ellen had been. Rachel said to Drake, "You got to let me know the number of people I'll be cooking for, Mr. Dalton."

"Oh, I will, Rachel. Misty and I have plans to make before I can give you the number. It won't be a huge guest list—I know few people here."

"Well, Mr. Dalton, you're going to have the prettiest bride in the country," she declared.

But Drake already knew that!

That evening when he had had his dinner and he and Lucky were all alone in his small parlor, he read Susanne's letter over again. It was apparent that Ellen's reading of the journals had hardened her heart toward their father.

Drake was thinking about a day in the future when he and Misty would sail for England. He would show her London and the fine old country estate where he was born and raised. What meant so much to Drake was that he could finally visit the grave of his beloved mother.

He would also take her to Paris to meet Bayard. He even knew the time of the year when he'd want to sail.

Nothing was more beautiful than Paris in the springtime. He wanted to visit there again with Misty. They'd ride in a carriage down the boulevards lined with cherry trees in full bloom. He could see her green eyes sparkling with life and excitement at the beauty of it.

Drake was a man full of dreams of the future. For the first time in many months he went to his bedroom to take out the velvet case and look at his mother's exquisite emerald and diamond ring which would be Misty's the day they were married. There was also the delicate emerald bracelet, which would be his wedding gift to her. Never had he regretted stealing into his mother's room that night to take these cherished possessions.

Lady Margaret certainly didn't deserve them. From what he gathered from Susanne's letter, Devin had met his match in this woman.

Drake only hoped that Susanne and her husband would

not settle into Dalton Manor and have this woman play some dirty little trick on them. Susanne's husband was a shrewd lawyer who came from an influential family in London. Before he had allowed Susanne and himself to move over to Dalton Manor and put his property up for sale, he had tied up all the loose ends legally. He had not trusted Lady Margaret at all.

Kendall Spencer, Susanne's husband, had no great love for Devin. So he had no compassion for what life had dealt him. But he loved Susanne dearly.

Drake would have liked him had he known him.

Just as everyone at Dalton's Lair happily greeted the news of the wedding, everyone at the Bennetts' house was jubilant. But Mike was filled with mixed emotions—Misty would be sorely missed when she moved over to Dalton's Lair. He realized what a tremendous load Misty had carried for him. She had been the housekeeper, cook, and nanny. In two weeks all of those responsibilities would fall on him and Jeff—Lavinia was still too young. God, he was going to miss her!

He also knew that things were going to be very hectic for him after the wedding. Two weeks was a short time to try to adjust to this new arrangement. Now that he'd agreed to leave his job to go to work for Colleen, he would be away from home longer. So he was happy about Misty's upcoming marriage, but he was also facing a dilemma.

At least, he was truly happy for Misty. He knew that Drake Dalton loved his daughter.

Chapter 42

Colleen was delighted to hear Mike's news about Misty and Drake. But she was also perceptive enough to understand Mike's apprehensions. "It'll be fine, Mike. It'll take more of your time but Misty deserves to have her happiness." She seemed to have a solution for everything. She pointed out that Jeff could take charge of Lavinia and the house when he was away during the day. If they couldn't have their usual Saturday nights together, then so be it.

"Mike, Misty carried a heavy load for you since your wife died. She was so very young. I hate to tell you, but my Maureen would not have been able to do it."

Mike could not argue with her—it also made him realize how much he hadn't appreciated all that Misty had done since Beth died.

Once again, he realized what a wise woman Colleen Carver was. She was like no other woman he'd ever known. He had loved Beth with all his heart and soul until slowly and insidiously that love had cooled, but he'd never admired her as he did Colleen.

Had Beth been faced with the challenges Colleen had, he doubted that she could have met them.

He went home that evening feeling much better about everything than he had when he'd arrived at Colleen's. But then that was always the way she affected him.

Misty and Drake had enjoyed a glorious Saturday evening at his house. She had set the table and served up Rachel's fine dinner. Together, they'd cleaned up the dishes and dimmed the lamps in the kitchen to go into his parlor.

Drake had told her the latest news about Ellen and about the letter from Susanne. He said it was time that they turn their thoughts to themselves and their wedding. Like Drake, she had few people to invite except her family.

His adoring eyes danced over her face. "I've always wanted to see you in a fancy gown, Misty. I've found a seamstress I wish to take you to on Monday. She can make your gown. You'll never have but one wedding day and that will be your wedding day with me."

"No, Drake—I'll only have one wedding day and that will be with you," she declared.

It was a wonderful night for the two of them since they had Drake's home completely to themselves. It had been so long since they hadn't shared an evening either with Ellen or Misty's brother and sister. Their courtship had been a rather frustrating one.

They both had a laugh about that. In the bedroom that she would soon be sharing as his wife, she and Drake made most passionate love before he took her home.

As they were boarding his buggy, Drake declared, "God, I'm glad we'll be married before winter really sets in here in January. You'll be here with me and I won't have to worry about getting over to your father's place to see you. We'll be here, all cozy by my fire."

"Drake, you're such a romantic—most people wouldn't think this about you," she told him.

"Guess I got that from my French mother—I sure didn't inherit it from my father."

Misty's eyes looked deep into his. "You detest your father, don't you, Drake?"

"Yes, love, he can go to bloody hell and I wouldn't care." The look on his face was so intense that Misty knew it was a hatred which went so deep that Drake would feel this way the rest of his life.

On Monday, Drake arrived at the Bennett house to get Misty and take her to the seamstress. As it would happen, it was the same seamstress who had made Georgia Gordon's wedding gown.

Molly Bergan was immediately impressed by the aristocratic Drake Dalton when he and his lady entered her shop. He told her exactly what he wanted her to create for his bride-to-be.

Molly listened to him describe the details of the gown and smiled as she began to make a sketch on paper. "Does that look like the gown, Mr. Dalton?"

Drake scrutinized the drawing and grinned. "Well, it bloody well does! You're an artist as well as a seamstress, ma'am.

"That was my heart's desire when I was younger but things didn't work out that way. Fortunately, I have a nice supply of white satin and lace so even though it's short notice, I'll be able to get the gown made for you. This is a slow time—all the ladies have bought their dresses for the holidays."

She then turned her attention to Misty, who had been sitting there very quietly. Molly urged her to come with her so she could take some measurements. Misty rose to follow Molly to the back of the shop. Molly showed her to a small room so she could slip out of her gown. For Misty, it was a new experience—she'd never been measured for a gown made by a seamstress. Molly suspected this when she came cut of the small dressing room clad only in her undergarments.

Molly told her, "This will only take a few minutes. My, you're such a tiny little thing."

Molly measured her bust, waist, and hips. Then she took the measurement from Misty's waistline to her ankles and also the measurement from her waistline to her shoulders. "One more and we're through," she said and smiled. She whipped out her tape again to measure the length of Misty's arm to her wrist.

"Ah, Misty—you're going to have a lovely wedding gown," Molly declared. "You may get dressed now and we'll join your young man."

A short time later, Misty and Drake were leaving the shop. Molly promised to have the gown ready the day before the wedding, but she asked Misty to come to her shop in a week for a fitting.

Misty was a little awestruck seeing the white satin and lace that her gown was to be made of. When she and Drake were in the buggy, she told him, "Oh, Drake, I've never seen such lovely material. I've never had such a fancy gown. I think I'll be afraid to wear it."

He laughed, "Well, it's time you did have a fancy gown, love." Privately, he was thinking that Misty was going to have more fancy gowns now that she was to be his wife. He'd noticed how she'd carefully surveyed Ellen's gowns—Ellen dressed modestly but Misty appreciated the fine fabrics. His other sisters dressed more flamboyantly than Ellen.

Drake did not stay long at the Bennetts' when he took Misty home—there were things needing his attention at his place. Oscar had not been feeling well this morning so he wanted to get back to help him with the late afternoon chores. Rachel had told him that morning that she feared Oscar was getting a chest cold.

When he got home and changed his clothes, Drake went to the barn. He only had to look at Oscar to know he wasn't feeling well. He told him, "Get on home, Oscar. I'll finish these chores. Have Rachel doctor you up—stay in bed in the morning and I'll take over."

"Oh, Mister Dalton—I can do it," Oscar protested.

"I'm the boss around here," Drake admonished him gently.

Reluctantly, Oscar did as his boss ordered him to do. Drake finished up the feeding of his livestock and returned to the house to see what was waiting for him in the pots on his stove.

The next morning, Rachel told Drake how grateful she was that he sent Oscar home early. "Bless you, Mr. Dalton, for being such a considerate man. Oscar really needed to stay in bed this morning. He coughed all night long but wasn't coughing as much this morning."

"Well, you stay only a short time here today, Rachel. The house doesn't need cleaning. Fix me a big old pot of that good vegetable soup or beef stew—I can keep it simmering on the cookstove. Then go on home to tend to Oscar and make him behave."

Rachel did as he suggested and started a pot of stew. Before she left, Drake told her he was also going to do the feeding this evening. The entire day and evening in bed, plus Rachel's rich broths—and ointments rubbed on his chest—did wonders for Oscar. He was feeling much better by Friday morning. He was up and dressed by the time Rachel was getting ready to go over to Drake's.

Shortly before he would have left the house, there was a knock on the door—it was Drake. He made his conversation with Rachel short and sweet. "Tell Oscar to stay inside. There a chilly mist starting to fall. I'll feed this morning, Rachel."

Rachel didn't have a chance to make any reply—Drake was already going down the steps. So she went to the kitchen and informed Oscar, "Well, in case you didn't hear what your bossman said, he said for you to stay in. There's a chilly mist outside."

Oscar sat at the table, shaking his head. "Never knew a man like that one and sure never worked for anyone who gave a dang about me like he does. Well, Rachel, you give him a full day's work since I can't. I can putter around the house here and get things done for you then."

Rachel got her coat on and tied the wool scarf around her hair to head for Drake's house. When he returned from the barn, she had a fine breakfast ready—Drake ate it with relish.

She went over each room in the house, dusting and cleaning. She filled all the lamps with oil. Expecting Miss Misty would be coming over tomorrow evening, she baked a couple of pies for their dinner.

She was tired when she returned to her own home late that afternoon, but Oscar had their dinner ready. Rachel was grateful—she was ready to sit in her chair and prop her feet up on the footstool.

Oscar announced, "Tomorrow, I'll be able to do my job."

Saturday morning was a glorious contrast to the miserable chill of Friday morning. Ellen took one of Mrs. Fortis's thoroughbreds out for a brisk ride. When she returned to the house an hour later, she had a flush to her cheeks. She hadn't put her hair up in a coil as she usually did when she went for a ride. With her hair flowing around her shoulders, Ellen looked much younger.

She rushed into the parlor, where she knew she would find Mrs. Fortis at this time of the morning, to tell her what a delightful time she'd had.

As she breezed through the parlor door, she stopped suddenly when she saw that Mrs. Fortis was not alone. Dexter Harlton knew immediately who she was but Ellen had no inkling who he was. She did know he was very nice looking and she guessed him to be about Drake's age.

Agatha realized Ellen was feeling slightly embarrassed about rushing into the parlor, so she beckoned Ellen to join them. "This is my nephew, Dexter Harlton, Ellen. Dexter, this is the young lady I've been telling you about, Ellen Dalton."

Dexter rose to greet her. "Aunt Agatha has been talking about nothing but you, Ellen. It's a pleasure to know you and to know she has someone like you living here with her."

"Nice to meet you, Mr. Harlton," she replied.

She took a seat on the settee beside Agatha, who told her that Dexter lived some fifty miles away in Memphis, Tennessee, but he'd come here to check out some land he'd heard was up for sale. "Dexter will be staying here this evening and tomorrow."

"How very nice," Ellen remarked.

Dexter watched her graceful hands remove her gloves. Everything about her intrigued him from the minute he saw her enter the parlor. Her tall, willowy figure was clad in a tailored riding ensemble of brilliant blue twill. The moment she spoke, he heard the distinct English accent. She looked so radiant and her blue eyes were sparkling so brilliantly as she'd rushed into the room. With her long hair flowing around her shoulders, she looked even younger than she actually was.

Ellen lingered a few minutes longer before she excused herself to go upstairs to change. She looked over at Dexter to tell him once again how nice it was to meet him.

"Please, Ellen, just call me Dexter. I'm going to feel ancient if you call me Mr. Harlton," he said and smiled.

"Oh, now I wouldn't want that," she said, returning his smile.

When Ellen had left, Dexter told his aunt, "She's most charming, Aunt Agatha!"

Agatha had been observing her nephew and already knew that he was very impressed by her new companion. "She certainly is. I expect I might have you visiting me more often."

Dexter grinned. "If I make this deal, then I can assure you I'll be darkening your door often. In fact, I'll be moving here from Memphis, so I guess I'd better get on over to the place and see if it is what I was told it was. I'll be back here before the dinner hour, Aunt Agatha. I remember that's promptly at seven."

"Hope it works out for you, Dexter. It would be nice to have you so close by."

"Did you know the Gordon family, Aunt Agatha?" Dexter asked as he got up, preparing to leave.

"Knew him but I never met his wife. So she's selling her husband's land, eh?" Agatha asked.

"Yes, she remarried, I was told."

The prattle in Crowley and Lepanto that Agatha had heard a few years earlier had indicated that she and Georgia Gordon would have nothing in common, so she never sought to know her.

What she did not know, until her nephew told her, was that Georgia and old Cyrus Heller had gotten married. She'd known Cyrus for years. She could not imagine him and this Gordon woman being compatible.

"Shows you what can happen when you're isolated, as I've been until Ellen came here. I hadn't heard about the marriage," Agatha said as he started for the front door.

A planter from the area had been in Memphis and told Dexter about the land being put up for sale. He'd remarked about it quite casually because he knew that Dexter's aunt lived nearby. It surprised Turley Underwood that Dexter didn't know about it already since he knew Miss Agatha, as he called her. She usually knew everything going on in Crowley and Lepanto.

Cyrus had urged Georgia to put her vast acreage up for

sale after they'd been married a week. He'd told her she didn't need to fret about running that land when he could provide her with anything she could possibly want. Georgia had to admit she didn't want to be bothered with it, either. She was living in an elegant house with servants who catered to her every whim. Cyrus was a doting husband who demanded little of her. He'd even presented her with the silver chest containing all his former wife's exquisite jewelry and told her to choose what she wanted. Georgia wanted it all.

So she was willing to put the land up for sale—Cyrus had told her she could take the money and do whatever she wanted with it. He certainly had no need of it.

So Georgia put a low price on the land and the house as she was just eager to be rid of it. Dexter was a sharp businessman and he had only to spend three hours over at the Gordon property to know it was a steal so he immediately decided to buy it.

By the time he left the office of the gentleman handling Georgia Gordon's land, it was past five. As he guided his gig back toward his aunt's home, he realized he was going to be her neighbor.

Dexter was delighted with the house on the property. He had a few changes in mind, but it was spacious. Being a bachelor, he was already thinking about changing one of the bedrooms into a study. He had no qualms about giving up his law practice in Memphis—people in Crowley and Lepanto would also need the services of a lawyer. Dexter had lived very frugally the last few years in Memphis, never touching his inheritance from his father's estate. He'd never bought any property in Memphis as some of his lawyer friends had urged him to do. He rented an apartment—he and his cocker spaniel, Rusty, lived very comfortably there.

He was thinking of Rusty as he rolled down the country road toward his aunt's house and how happy he would be to have that big yard to roam around in.

He figured that by the first of March he could be settled here in Poinsett County. It was obvious that when this Mrs. Gordon had left her house, she'd taken nothing with her. The price included all the furnishings, so he was in the highest spirits by the time he arrived at his Aunt Agatha's home.

His exciting news had to wait until the dinner hour—the parlor was deserted, so he knew his aunt must be upstairs having a rest. Ellen would probably also be in her room.

He'd put in a busy day since he'd gotten up before dawn to leave Memphis. He was ready for a warm bath and a change of clothes.

He also saw that he was in need of a shave, so Ellen and his aunt were already in the parlor when he finally joined them. Ellen was as impressed by his handsome features as he was with her when he saw her in her gown of a soft mauve.

Agatha teased him, "You were almost late."

"But I made it," he said and laughed. "With all that traveling, I felt a bath was in order as well as a clean shirt, Aunt Agatha." He bent down to kiss her cheek.

"Well, sit down and tell me all about it. You know how curious I am, Dexter," Agatha prodded.

"The Gordon land is mine. At least it will be when all the paperwork is done. I got myself a heck of a deal, auntie. This lady, Mrs. Gordon, left a completely furnished house which I can move right into. Couldn't believe she'd have left all that nice furniture there."

"I can, Dexter. She had no need of it, marrying the wealthiest man around these parts. She went to an even finer home than hers."

Ellen didn't know who they were speaking about but it was apparent that Dexter had purchased some property nearby. She could tell from the expression on Mrs. Fortis's face that she was delighted.

Agatha looked over at Ellen and realized she was being

ignored and remarked, "Forgive us, dear, but I was just so anxious to know how Dexter's land deal was going to come out this afternoon. It's grand news."

Dexter chimed in, "Yes, Ellen—I'm going to be living close by so I can pester my dear aunt. She's obviously happy about that."

"That *will* be nice, Mr.—uh, Dexter," she said and smiled.

Agatha laughed. "Well, I have to admit you're not the pest you were when you were little. You know what this young man did when he was small and his mother had brought him over here?"

With a twinkle in her eye and looking from Mrs. Fortis over at Dexter, Ellen asked, "What did he do, Mrs. Fortis?"

"Well, his mother, Cecile, and I were in the kitchen having ourselves a nice little chat and thinking what a very good little boy Dexter was being back in the sitting room. Well, what was keeping him so occupied was he was sitting on the floor by the basket where I kept my crochet work, slowly unraveling the shawl I was making for myself."

Ellen broke into laughter, "Oh, no."

"Oh, yes. I was livid. I didn't wait for his mother to paddle his bottom. I did it!" Agatha declared.

"Believe me, Ellen—I never touched anything in that basket again."

The rest of the evening was filled with laughter. Mrs. Fortis had many tales to tell, most of them humorous. Only once did a look of sadness cross her face and that was when she spoke of her sister's death when she was only forty. "Dexter was Cecile's only child and I never had any children, so we have a small family, Ellen."

"That's why it will be so nice that you and Dexter will be living close together, Mrs. Fortis," Ellen said.

After dinner, Ellen felt she should excuse herself. She felt it only proper that she leave the two of them alone for the rest of the evening.

Dexter wanted to ask her to stay but he didn't. He felt she wasn't intruding at all. Quite the contrary—she had made the evening even more enjoyable.

Dexter knew one thing by the time he escorted his aunt upstairs to her room: he wanted to get to know Ellen Dalton better.

He found her the most interesting young lady he'd met in a long time!

Chapter 43

Dexter knew he should have started for Memphis earlier than he did but he also knew his aunt's habit of having Sunday brunch since she liked to sleep late in the morning. So he stayed to enjoy the brunch with her and Ellen.

When he said his goodbyes, he gave his aunt a kiss and then his blue eyes darted over in Ellen's direction. "I'll be seeing you two in a couple of months. Maybe a little sooner, if I can manage it."

Agatha and Ellen watched as he guided his gig out of the drive. Then the older woman took Ellen's arm, her other hand gripping her cane, to go back into the house.

Ellen smiled as she listened to Mrs. Fortis grumbling as she led her back to the parlor. "Damned old leg! Acting up on me today."

"Maybe tomorrow will be a better day, Mrs. Fortis," Ellen said. She took her over to her chair by the hearth and got her comfortable. Picking up the soft wool afghan, she covered Agatha's legs. "Let's get those legs warm while you work on your needlepoint. Maybe it'll make that mean old leg feel better."

Ellen had such a gentle way about her that Agatha found her very understanding about someone ailing as she was. When Agatha mentioned this to her, Ellen explained that her mother had been ill often. "I—I guess that's why, Mrs. Fortis. Now I wish I'd done even more for her," she declared, remembering her mother's journals.

"Thank you, dear. I'm just fine! Now you go do whatever you'd like. I'm just going to sit here and work on my needlepoint." When Ellen had left, Agatha was thinking that just when she had found herself the perfect companion, that good-looking nephew of hers was going to come back here in a couple of months to take her away. She'd seen how Dexter was ogling her. Oh, she'd feel like scalping him if he did that!

For Misty and Drake, it was wonderful to have little paradise back on Saturday evenings now that Ellen was no longer there. This Saturday night they were making plans for their wedding. Their only concern was the harsh January weather.

Drake said, "Now I know why there are so many June weddings."

"We'll just have to hope we'll be lucky, Drake,"

What Misty did not know was that Drake had remembered several details for his bride-to-be—he'd ordered an array of lacy undergarments and some white silk slippers from Molly. He'd also gotten a cluster of silk orange blossoms for Misty's hair.

When Mike had called on Colleen that Saturday night, she had given him a box to take home for Misty. "Just tell her this is something I thought her mother might have chosen for her wedding night, Mike." Mike found out the next day that Colleen had bought Misty a lovely gown and robe trimmed with ecru lace.

By the time Drake took her home that evening they had chosen fourteen people to gather at Drake's for the wedding ceremony. Misty reminded him that Rachel had no need to bake a wedding cake—Colleen had insisted that she make the cake and a variety of other pastries.

Drake had located only one minister in Crowley. His name was Jeremiah Hadley a Methodist minister who had just recently come to town. He agreed to come to Drake's home the following Saturday afternoon at six. He was a bachelor and very nice-looking, so the young ladies had been flocking to his church on Sundays.

When Drake told Misty good night, he said, "This is the last Saturday night I'll be saying good night, love. Next Saturday night you'll be my wife."

Misty's head was already whirling—was it possible that all this was really happening to her?

The next week was somewhat bittersweet, even though she was thrilled about becoming Drake's wife. When she was packing her possessions, Jeff and Lavinia would roam into her room to see her emptying her drawers and lament how they were going to miss her.

"But I won't be that far away, Lavinia. Jeff can always ride over on Beauty to get me if you need me," Misty had said, trying to soothe her little sister.

She had told Jeff the same thing. She'd also instructed him about many other things he'd have to tend to at the house while their father was away.

On Friday, late in the afternoon, Drake arrived in his buggy and came to the door with his arms laden with packages. He'd brought Misty her wedding gown and a multitude of other things he'd bought for her. His surprise for Lavinia was a frilly pink taffeta dress and a big pink velvet bow to wear in her hair.

He gave Misty no more that a peck for a kiss—he had a

million things on his mind to make sure tomorrow night was absolutely perfect for his bride.

Colleen had already asked Mike to pick her up early so she could help Misty get dressed. "Maureen and Eric can come in his gig. I want to arrive earlier than that, Mike. This is such a special night for her."

Mike understood what she meant and loved her all the more for trying to be a mother to Misty.

"I'll pick you up early, Colleen. I know Misty will appreciate you being there to help her," Mike said.

Misty was feeling like Cinderella when she looked at her exquisite gown—she'd never seen anything so gorgeous. When she opened the other packages and found her white silk slippers, they could have been the crystal slipper that Cinderella wore to the ball. All the lacy undergarments made her realize what a doting husband Drake Dalton was going to be.

She wondered how she'd been so lucky to capture the eyes and heart of such a man. Her life had seemed so hopeless before she met Drake and after that everything started to change. Surely the two of them were meant to meet that summer day.

Before Drake had ridden off late that Friday afternoon, he'd told her, "It's going to be a glorious day tomorrow, Misty. The sun's going to shine on my bride."

He had been right, for the sun was indeed shining brightly when Misty rose the next morning. It was her wedding day but she still had to pinch herself to believe she wasn't dreaming. At six this evening she was going to stand in front of Drake's hearth and become his bride.

Her family was very sweet to her all day, insisting that she take it easy. So she was not allowed into the kitchen to do anything.

Mike Bennett told his daughter, "We might as well get started shifting for ourselves now that you're not going to be in charge, Misty. Truth is, we should have all been doing more all along. I know that now."

His words meant a great deal to Misty as she listened to him and sipped her morning coffee. He told her how he'd been having talks with Jeff and Lavinia for the last few days.

"Lavinia is going to have to be responsible for that pup of hers, feeding and watering it. She can set up a table and dry dishes. You were doing that for your ma, as I remember. Jeff's a good dish washer. 'Course, I don't have to give him any orders about caring for Beauty. He'll do that," Mike said and smiled.

Misty had no doubts about that. But there was so much else to running the house that she knew Jeff couldn't handle. There was the evening meal to be cooked—and the baking.

But Mike shrugged those concerns aside. "My dear Colleen has assured me that our house won't go lacking for breads or pies. We'll just be sharing more Saturday nights over here rather than at her house. I don't have to tell you what an understanding woman she is."

"No, you don't, Pa. I love Colleen," Misty confessed.

"We'll be fine, Misty. You'll see. I'll cook the evening meal after I get in from work and Jeff can handle getting the wood in. He can also feed the chickens and hogs. I'll tend to my horses."

"Sounds like you've got everything well planned, Pa. I'm glad to hear it for I have worried about what would happen after I married Drake," Misty confessed.

"Well, don't fret your pretty head about that. You just put your thoughts to being a happy bride. I think you're getting yourself one hell of a man. That's all I want for you. There's no greater blessing in the world than to love and be loved by someone, Misty."

Misty's green eyes looked deep into his. "Pa, I believe that, too."

Perhaps Bennett was feeling emotional because his oldest

was getting married today but he reached down to embrace her. His voice cracked as he told her, "I love you, Misty, even though there was a time when you didn't think so."

Misty was also feeling very emotional. "But now I know. I understand things I could not have understood when I was twelve or thirteen. Remember, Pa, I took Ma's journals and I read them. I don't have to tell you how I always worshipped her but she was a woman I didn't understand after I read the journals. She was so bitter!"

A sad expression etched Mike's face and he gave her a nod. "One day we'll speak of this but not today. Today is your wedding day, my little Misty."

Misty agreed that nothing sad should mar her glorious day, so the subject was dropped. She left the kitchen to see about packing the things she would be taking over to Drake's tonight. Her pa was going to take them over there this afternoon, since his buggy would be filled with passengers this evening.

Misty had had her bath and had put on the fancy lace undergarments. She sat on the bed, an amused smile on her face, for he seemed to have known her measurements exactly. She was pulling up her stockings and getting ready to slip into the white silk slippers when Colleen knocked on her door.

"I thought maybe I could help you with your gown, Misty, so I had your father bring me over early," she said as she came in. "Besides, I wanted to be sure you had all the things that they say a bride must have. I knew you had something new, but you must have something blue, something borrowed, and something old. I think I have it all for you."

She opened a small bag and took out a blue garter, a lace-edged handkerchief of hers, and a tiny leather prayer book which Colleen said had belonged to her mother. "I carried it when I was married. I did have a very happy marriage, Misty. I certainly wish that for you and Drake."

"Oh, Colleen, you're so thoughtful. Thank you very much," Misty said. She slipped the blue garter on her leg and laid the prayer book and handkerchief on the bed.

Colleen helped her into her wedding gown and fastened the many little white satin-covered buttons at the back. Misty put the pearls Drake had given her around her neck and on her ears.

With the cluster of silk flowers pinned to the side of her head and toilet water dabbed at her throat and behind her ears, she turned to face Colleen.

With her fair hair and the flowing white satin gown, Misty looked ethereally beautiful. Colleen gasped, "Oh, Misty dear, the angels in Heaven could not be lovelier than you!"

Colleen was sure that when Mike saw his daughter as she emerged from the bedroom, she saw a mist of tears in his dark eyes. Jeff and Lavinia gasped at how pretty their sister looked.

Misty was so happy that the weather was perfect as they traveled from their house to Drake's.

Certain traditions, like the groom not seeing his bride until she came down the church aisle to join him, could not be observed for Drake and Misty. He was there to greet them when they arrived as he had been to greet the minister.

But when they did arrive, Colleen insisted that she and Misty go to Drake's bedroom until Maureen and Eric arrived. Ellen and Mrs. Fortis had not yet arrived. Colleen said, "Your father is very excited about walking you down the aisle to Drake and the minister, Misty."

Drake had insisted that Rachel leave the kitchen and sit in the parlor with Oscar when he and Misty said their vows.

Once Ellen and Mrs. Fortis arrived about the same time Maureen and Eric did, Mike came in to the bedroom. "It's time to take you to your groom, Misty." As Mike led Misty out of the bedroom, Colleen followed them out and took a seat by Jeff and Lavinia.

For Misty, it seemed strange for the minister to address

her as Melanie as she exchanged her vows with Drake. The ring he slipped on her finger took her breath away—she'd never seen anything so magnificent.

The look on Drake's face as he put the ring on her finger was serious and intense. His eyes looked into hers with great depth. A few feet away, Ellen was aware of it, but she didn't find out until later that it was her mother's emerald and diamond ring Drake was giving to Misty.

Some might have called it a simple wedding but to Misty it was absolutely wonderful. The minute the service was over, Rachel and Oscar made a hasty exit from the parlor to the kitchen to serve the champagne.

The moment the service was over and Drake had given his bride a passionate kiss, Agatha Fortis turned to Ellen. "You were right when you told me that your brother had already chosen the loveliest girl around here. She is gorgeous! But then, Drake is the best-looking man I've seen in years!"

"Misty is not only beautiful, she's so genuine. You'll like her, Mrs. Fortis," Ellen said.

Drake or Misty drank very little champagne as they visited with the Walters, Mrs. Fortis, and their other guests.

Maureen was so impressed by the wedding that she told her mother, "It makes me want a wedding at home instead of at church, Mother."

Colleen said, "Forget it, darling, with the list you have. My little home would never accommodate them."

The guests sat at Drake's dining table to enjoy the feast Rachel had prepared. Later that night, Misty sat in the parlor to open wedding gifts. One of the most cherished gifts she and Drake received was the quilt Geneva Walters had made for them in the Wedding Ring pattern.

The first of the guests to leave was Ellen and Mrs. Fortis—Ellen thought they should be getting back home, even though Agatha was still enjoying herself very much. Agatha Fortis was a very earthy lady and after she had had a chance to speak with Misty, she'd come to a conclusion. "Your brother will never get bored with her, Ellen. She's a little charmer."

"I told you that you'd like Misty," Ellen said.

"I liked her very much. There's nothing fake about that young lady. I liked the way those green eyes look straight at you when she's talking to you and that warm embrace she gave me because she felt like doing it. That's a good measure of a person, Ellen. I don't like people who can't look me straight in the eye—I never was taken in by smooth talkers."

Maureen and Eric made their exit next, followed by Mike, Colleen, Lavinia, and Jeff. Rachel was still laboring in the kitchen washing up dishes with Oscar drying them.

As soon as their last guests had left, Drake grinned as he said he was going to release Lucky from his prison in the spare bedroom. "Get yourself comfortable, love, while I take him out for a stretch."

The first thing Misty did was rid herself of the slippers. She always found that slippers cramped her feet—she'd spent too many years going barefoot or wearing sandals.

While Drake was tending to Lucky's needs, she sauntered into the kitchen to say good night to Oscar and Rachel. She took charge as mistress of the house by telling them to put the food away and not worry about all the dishes.

"You've had a busy day and night, Rachel. Those dishes can wait until morning," she said.

"If you say so, Miss Misty."

"I say so, Rachel." Misty smiled and walked over to embrace her and thank her for the dinner.

"You made it a very special night for me. Your dinner and Mrs. Carver's wedding cake were enough to delight any bride. You and Oscar just get on home to bed. You must be worn out."

Rachel couldn't argue with her. She was bone tired and Oscar had still not regained his strength from his chest cold.

When Drake came back with Lucky, the kitchen lamps were dimmed and Oscar and Rachel had gone home.

Drake found his bride sitting in front of the fireplace in her stocking feet, looking very comfortable and relaxed. She had amazed him tonight. He would have expected her to be nervous and uncertain but she had not been at all.

Lucky seemed very content to curl up by the hearth. Drake announced, "Snow's falling, but it doesn't matter now because you're here with me. I don't care if we get snowed in."

"I just hope that Ellen and Mrs. Fortis get home all right," Misty said.

"They'll be fine. It won't be that deep before they get home. Ellen runs a fine gig. She had her own in England, Misty. We had harsh winters, too."

As long as everyone had time to get home safely Misty didn't care if it snowed all night. She was home—home with her husband!

Chapter 44

The snow did continue to fall and the logs in the fireplace crackled and sparked. Lucky slept peacefully next to the hearth while Drake and his bride sat feeling so cozy as they sipped a glass of champagne.

Before he'd gotten the champagne for them, he'd asked if she wanted to get into something more comfortable. If so, he'd offered to unbutton all the little buttons down her back. But Misty said, "Not just yet, Drake. I'll never wear a wedding gown again and this one is so beautiful I want to wear it a little longer."

He grinned. "Then wear it, love. I'll go get our champagne." He went into the kitchen and chanced to glance out the window. Snow was falling so furiously that he couldn't see Oscar's house. The grounds were starting to get covered.

He came back to the parlor and proposed a toast to the two of them. This was the moment he had decided to give Misty the emerald bracelet—he wanted it to be very private. When she had taken the first sip, he set his glass down and reached into his shirt pocket. "Hold out your hand and close your eyes, Misty love."

"Oh, Drake!" she sighed happily, wondering what he was up to now. So she set her glass down and did as he asked. She felt the weight of something being placed on her wrist. When she opened her eyes she saw the emerald bracelet and she gasped at how lovely it was.

"You're spoiling me outrageously, Drake Dalton! The beautiful ring and now this bracelet—oh, Drake, you didn't have to do all this. My grandest gift is having you as my husband."

He bent over to kiss her. "Both of your gifts, the ring and this bracelet, were not bought by me, Misty. They belonged to my mother. They were her two favorite pieces of jewelry so that was why I took them before I left England."

"You took them, Drake?"

"I took them without asking my father's permission shortly after I was told of my mother's death, Misty. It's a long story and I'll tell you about everything on the long winter nights when we're sitting around our fireplace. But knowing what a curious little miss you are, I'll tell you this much tonight. My mother was very unhappy. She was not loved by my father. She and I were very close and I detested him. I knew she'd want me to have this ring and bracelet so I went immediately to her room and took them. You see, I'd made up my mind the minute she died that I was leaving Dalton Manor."

"Knowing this, I shall cherish them all the more, Drake," she declared.

"Somehow, I feel that wherever she is right now she'd be very happy about the beautiful girl I took as my bride."

"I'd like to think that and I want to know about her, Drake."

"You will."

"What was her name?"

"Adrienne."

In that candid way of hers which had impressed Drake from the moment they'd met, she said, "Drake, we will name our first daughter Adrienne to honor your mother."

He grabbed her and embraced her. "Ah, Misty—there is no other woman in the whole world like you. Anyone could see why I lost my heart to you the first afternoon we met."

She giggled, "Now Drake Dalton, you probably didn't lose your heart *that* quickly." There was a glint in her green eyes.

"I probably did but I didn't realize it until a little later. But it didn't take long for me to know that I felt differently about you than I had ever felt about any other woman, Misty."

She found herself suddenly enclosed in his arms. Drake kissed and wooed her as though it was their first time making love. His lips and his hands moved with a slow, gentle touch as if he was sweetly, sensuously seducing her.

As she had the first time they'd made love, she surrendered to his searing touch. As their bodies fused and clung together in flaming rapture, Misty gloried in the ecstasy of being loved by Drake.

She didn't realize until the next morning that she hadn't removed her pearl necklace or the emerald bracelet. She stretched lazily and smiled when she realized how quickly everything had happened last night once Drake began to kiss her. He had obviously gotten up ahead of her.

Propping herself up on the pillow, she pulled the coverlet up around her breasts. Such nimble fingers her husband had—she could hardly recall getting out of her wedding dress. It was apparent she'd never changed into the lovely gown Colleen had bought for her!

She finally urged herself out of bed and gathered up her undergarments. Drake had hung her wedding gown up this morning when he got up.

Wearing her robe, she left the bedroom in search of her

husband. But he was not in the house so she poured herself a cup of coffee. Rachel wasn't in the kitchen, either.

Misty looked out the window and saw the imprints of Drake's boots. He'd apparently made his way to Oscar's house earlier. There had been quite a snowstorm during the night. Suddenly he entered the kitchen with a red nose and flushed face.

"Well, good morning, love! We're snowed in."

Misty got up to pour a cup of coffee for him. "You look like you could use something hot. I saw how deep it was from the imprint of your boot."

He took off his wool jacket and cap and joined his bride at the table. "Didn't want Rachel trying to come over here. I rather doubt that she even owns a pair of boots," he remarked. "By the way, do you have any boots, love?"

"No, Drake, I don't."

He leaned over to kiss her. "Then we're going to town soon and buy you a pair."

She prepared her husband a hearty breakfast of ham, eggs, and biscuits, which was no problem for Misty since she'd done it all the time for her family.

As the two of them were eating breakfast, Misty said, "I can handle breakfast in the mornings, Drake. Rachel could have more time to herself. I'm not used to being so pampered."

"Well, maybe it's time you had a little pampering, Misty, but I'll tell Rachel she doesn't have to come over until noon. She can still have some chores to see to over here or she'll be hurt and think her services are no longer needed. She and Oscar are very proud people. They like to feel like they're earning their keep."

"Oh, Drake—I'd never want to hurt Rachel's feelings. But she'd still enjoy having her morning hours free—she's not a young woman anymore."

Misty always amazed Drake. He watched her clear away the table after they'd eaten their breakfast. She prepared the dishes for washing, then crumbled the two biscuits remaining in the pan and called out to Lucky. He got one and she took the other one toward the back door.

"Where are you going with that, Misty?" Drake asked.

"I'm putting this out for the birds, Drake. They need food on a cold winter's day."

Drake sat at the kitchen table, thinking to himself that he could have looked the world over and never found someone like her.

It was midday before Misty finally got dressed in one of her little sprigged muslin gowns. She told her husband that since she was going to cook tonight she'd better see what was left from Rachel's grand feast.

A few minutes later, Misty announced that she had little to do to provide a nice dinner. "There's turkey and baked ham as well as two loaves of bread and two pies, Drake."

The sun came out around two and the snow began to melt. Drake let Lucky out to romp while he gathered logs for the fireplace and kindling for the cookstove. After they ate dinner, they cleaned up the kitchen together.

When they were settled in the parlor, Drake lit up one of his cheroots. "I'm glad you're not one of those little violets who can't stand the aroma. I'd have to go outside to enjoy my smoke."

"I love the smell of it, Drake. May I take a puff?"

"Are you serious, Misty? You really want a puff?"

"Drake, you ought to know that I don't say something I don't mean."

He passed his cheroot over to her. He had expected her to gasp and choke but she didn't. She took not one but two puffs before handing it back. "I like it, Drake."

"Well, I bloody well would not have believed it! What tales I'm going to tell our children about you, Misty Dalton!"

She laughed. "Well, I'm going to have some tales to tell them about their father, too. He must have been an expert at removing ladies' gowns. You did it so quickly. I'm sure you had a lot of practice, Drake Dalton, before you met me."

"Ah, Misty—the only lady's gown I'll ever remove is yours. I wouldn't lie to you and tell you I hadn't known my fair share of ladies by the time I came to Arkansas. But you were the first and the last since I arrived here.

Ellen and Mrs. Fortis had made it home safely but the snow had fallen heavily during the last mile of their trip. By the time Ellen had Agatha into the house and took the gig to the barn, she knew if this kept up it was going to be a real snowstorm.

By the time Mike and Colleen got to his house and a sleepyheaded Lavinia was in bed, Colleen felt no concern about Mike getting her home. Her concern was whether he could then get back here to his two children if the snow kept falling.

An exhausted Jeff gave her a warm embrace, saying, "I'm going to bed, too, Mrs. Carver."

She kissed him on the forehead and told him good night. As she waited for Mike to return to the front room she looked out his front windows. The dirt road was already covered with snow. She was glad Maureen and Eric had left a half-hour ahead of them. They were home by now.

When he joined her back in the front room, he asked, "You ready to head for Lepanto, Colleen?"

"I'm ready, Mike. What I'm concerned about is whether you could get back home to your kids. You could always stay at my house if it got too rough."

"Then you stay here tonight and I'll take you home tomorrow. It's coming down like cats and dogs out there."

Colleen took a look out the window. "I'll stay here, Mike. I don't want you to get me home and then not be able to get back."

While Misty and Drake were having their wedding night

champagne, Mike and Colleen were enjoying a cup of coffee. He tried to soothe Colleen. "Maureen will surely understand that I couldn't get you back home since we were still at Drake's."

Colleen laughed liltingly. "Thank God, Maureen's going to be married in the spring."

Mike grinned deviously. "Think about it, Colleen. Both of us could be grandparents this time next year."

"You could, Mike, but I better not be or Eric's going to know what a fierce temper I have."

"You, Colleen? I can't recall ever seeing you in a fit of temper."

"You've just been lucky," she replied lightheartedly, beginning to feel more relaxed about having to remain for the night.

Mike went to the kitchen to fill up their coffee cups. When he had served her, he asked her to excuse him for a moment. "I'm going to get some things out of my bedroom. I'll sleep with Jeff tonight. I wouldn't dare subject you to sleeping with Lavinia. She's a little kicker," he said, laughing.

"Oh, I would have survived, Mike. Maureen did the same thing when she was Lavinia's age."

Mike gathered up his work clothes and folded the bed back neatly. While he was not gone that long, it was enough time for Colleen to sit by the warm hearth in the quietness of the room and begin to drowse off. It had been a long, exciting day—she'd put in a busy morning and afternoon by the time Mike picked her up at five.

Mike saw her sitting there nodding her lovely head, so he walked up quietly to sit down beside her and gently put his arm around her until her head was resting on his shoulder. "Honey, I think it's time for you to get to bed," he murmured softly in her ear.

Colleen looked up at him with a lazy look in her dark eyes. "I guess I was falling asleep."

She flung her arms around his neck to kiss him good

night. Mike gave her a tender kiss. Something about the gentle way he held her and the soft tenderness of his kiss made Colleen flame with wild desires that she'd restrained for months.

Mike sensed it—she clung to him like she had never done before. He had certainly not planned to seduce her tonight just because she was staying under his roof, but dear God, he was a red-blooded man. So his own passion fired as he held her close.

But he still was in control enough to whisper in her ear, "Oh, Colleen—tell me—tell me to stop right now if you don't want me making love to you. Otherwise, I'm going to do what I've wanted to do for months."

"Oh, Mike—I'm tired of fighting it," she moaned softly.

He lifted her off the settee and carried her to his bedroom. Closing the door, he dimmed the lamp and Colleen discovered what an ardent lover Mike Bennett could be. She also realized how hungry she was for a man's intimate touch.

He could have stayed there in her arms all night but there were the two children to think about. He reluctantly rose from the bed. "I'm going on into Jeff's room, darling. But tell me before I leave that you don't regret it."

"No, Mike—I don't regret it. One more kiss before you go," she said, smiling up at him.

He eagerly obliged her!

Chapter 45

Before Mike crawled into bed with his son, he looked out the window and saw that the snow was still falling heavily. He could not even see his barn to the west of his house. He might have misled Colleen; he might not be able to get her home tomorrow.

He was the first one to wake up the next morning. When he got dressed and had a fire blazing in his cookstove, there were still flurries whirling around. However, by the time his morning coffee was ready, the flurries had ceased.

But when he walked out to his barn he saw how deep the snow was as his boots sank into it. When his chores were done, there was sun shining through the clouds.

Almost everyone was still asleep inside his house—the smell of his ham and bacon cooking roused Lavinia. She came into the kitchen in her long flannel nightgown, announcing that she and Beauty were hungry.

Mike looked down at her and smiled. "Well, you and Beauty are just going to have to be patient. Pour yourself a glass of milk."

Jeff was the next one to saunter into the kitchen. Mike hoped to sit down to his own breakfast and feed his two children before Colleen emerged from his bedroom. Getting herself dressed in the same fancy dress she'd worn to the wedding, she finally came into the kitchen. Mike sat at the kitchen table and had another cup of coffee as she ate the ham and eggs he'd prepared for her.

"We had ourselves a hell of a snowstorm overnight, Colleen. There's a good five inches out there," he said.

"Oh, God, Mike!" she sighed.

"Well, the sun's bright now so we'll give it some time to do some work for us," he told her.

After the previous night, everything had changed for Colleen and Mike. After breakfast, they spent time talking about their future. Neither of them had any doubts now that they wanted to be together for the rest of their lives. Jeff was busy with a new whittling project and Lavinia was occupied with her doll, so they had a lot of privacy.

Mike confessed, "Oh, Colleen only two things stopped me from asking you to marry me many weeks ago. I don't have a fine home to offer you and I have Jeff and Lavinia."

She gave him a taunting look. "You mean after last night you're not going to make an honest woman of me?"

"Oh, honey—I'm ready to marry you anytime but you wouldn't want to come over here to live with your shop in Lepanto."

"What about a May wedding?"

"Are you serious, Colleen? Nothing could make me happier!" Mike exclaimed.

"You're already at the bakery with me, working by my side, Mike. When Maureen marries, my house would accommodate your family. Lavinia and Jeff could have their own bedrooms. Of course, I'd expect to share my bedroom with my husband. Would you be willing to sell your place?"

"Nothing holding me in Crowley—I'm ready to start planning a May wedding, Colleen."

By noon, he went out to measure the depth of the snow to see how much it had melted. When he came back in, he told her that they'd best give it another couple of hours.

Colleen realized this man she loved was very handy in the kitchen as he started puttering around to get a pot of vegetable soup started for their supper tonight. In her fancy gown with Misty's old apron around her middle, she sat at the kitchen table helping him prepare the vegetables as the soup bone simmered.

"I'm learning all kind of things about you, Mike Bennett," she said. There was nothing lazy about him. He'd been up well ahead of her, tending to his livestock and feeding his children their breakfast. She'd sat in the kitchen, watching him carry logs in for his fireplace. He had had Jeff go to the shed to gather up a couple of loads of kindling for the cookstove. Now, he stood in the kitchen peeling potatoes to put in his soup.

He had suddenly stopped peeling his potatoes to exclaim, "Damn, Colleen, I just thought about something. What would I do about Beauty? It would break Jeff's heart to have to give up that horse."

She threw her head back and laughed. "Oh, Mike—I always forget what a serious man you are. We've got over four months to expand my little carriage house where my bay's quartered with my buggy. A stall for Beauty would not take that much more room."

"I could work on that myself."

"You see, Mike? We'll work everything out," she assured him.

It was three in the afternoon when Mike and Colleen started toward Lepanto. He had no trouble getting her there or returning home.

That evening, he was as elated about his own future as he was about his daughter's. He'd never expected to feel this way again.

Colleen had had no reason to fret—Maureen was not at

all concerned about her. She told her mother, "I knew Mr. Bennett wouldn't be able to get you home and get back to his youngsters. In fact, I pushed Eric out the door so he wouldn't be stuck here all night. That would have set tongues to wagging, wouldn't it?"

They both had a laugh about that.

On Misty and Drake's first trip into Crowley after their marriage, they went to the emporium and he purchased a fine pair of leather boots for her. He also took her back to Molly's dress shop to be measured for three light woolen gowns, which he felt she should have for the winter months ahead.

Molly was delighted. In the last month, he had enriched her coffers tremendously. There was no doubt he was indulging his young bride. Few gents around these parts did that. Her other client who bought lavishly was Georgia Gordon Heller.

Most of the local ladies made their own gowns. There was a time when she'd stitched many lovely gowns for Mrs. Agatha Fortis but she understood why she hadn't been in recently. She was elderly now and no longer entertained as she used to.

On the gowns she prepared for Misty Dalton, she allowed wide easements so seams could be let out a few inches. The very perceptive Molly felt sure that Misty would be expecting a child before winter was over. Drake Dalton was such a virile, handsome devil!

Like Molly, Drake kept thinking that Misty was going to announce that she was expecting their child but she didn't. Misty had no inkling that her handsome husband was anxiously anticipating this. Life for her at Dalton's Lair was so much simpler than it had been at her former home.

She always got up with Drake and fixed their breakfast. Rachel came over around midday to tidy up and do chores.

But Rachel found herself with more free time on her hands; once she put a chicken or a roast in the oven, Misty would tell her that she would tend to it so Rachel could go home. She and Misty never had any conflicts in the kitchen. Like Drake, Rachel was also waiting for her to announce that she was expecting.

The rest of January went by, and February came and went. By then, Misty had no doubt that she was indeed carrying Drake's baby. She had wondered if she might be a few weeks before they were married—she remembered what Drake had told her if she might find herself pregnant.

This baby had not been conceived on their wedding night—it had been that Sunday afternoon in the horse stall. But she was one of those women who didn't show pregnancy early. When they had married, her tiny figure had not changed at all. Now that they'd been married a month, it still had not changed.

Drake certainly had no inkling that his bride was about ten weeks pregnant. Rachel was the first to suspect it when Misty complained that she felt sick to her stomach. When it happened the next day about the same time, she was having her morning coffee. "Lord, Rachel—I haven't had anything to eat since last night's supper," she told the housekeeper.

"Feel like you're going to throw up, Miss Misty?"

"Yes, but I didn't yesterday and don't think I'm going to this morning, either."

"You had any other things happening to you like feeling lightheaded, Miss Misty?"

"No, Rachel. Wha—what do you think I might be coming down with?" Misty's green eyes were looking up at her, questioning.

"Well, Miss Misty—hope you won't think I'm being too nosy but have you missed a monthly period lately? If you have, I'm thinking you could be pregnant."

"So feeling queasy like I have the last two mornings is a sure sign?"

"Sure is." Rachel remembered that Misty had no mother to talk to about such things.

A slow smile spread over Misty's face. "No, I haven't had my period, Rachel. So maybe I *am* pregnant with Drake's baby. You think he'll be happy?"

Rachel laughed. "Oh, miss—I think he'll be fit to be tied! Time he became a pa just like it was time he got himself a pretty bride. I was so happy when he told me the two of you were to be married."

"What else should I expect, Rachel? Guess I'm pretty naive about such things. Mama never got a chance to talk about them with me," Misty confessed.

"Well, that queasy feeling will pass in a short time. You'll find your waistline will put on an inch and then two inches and your breasts will become fuller."

"I haven't noticed my clothes feeling tighter yet."

Rachel smiled. "Well, honey, you're not far enough along yet. Give it a few more weeks."

Like an enthusiastic child, Misty jumped up from the table. "I'm going to measure my waist, Rachel."

Rachel watched her dash out of the kitchen and stood there with an amused smile on her face for a moment before she turned her attention back to her stove.

The last time Misty's waist had been measured was when Molly was fitting her wedding gown and that had been a month ago. She took her waist measurement a second time, then sank down on the bed, her long lashes fluttering nervously. After what Rachel had just told her, Misty was now convinced beyond any doubt that she was pregnant.

She pranced around the bedroom, a smug smile on her face. She could hardly wait to tell Drake that he was going to be a father before next winter came. If she was calculating right, her baby would arrive late in August.

She sat in their bedroom for a while, just thinking. She

felt exactly as she had the night she and Drake had been married. She felt she should pinch herself to know for sure she wasn't dreaming.

Becoming a mother didn't frighten her at all. After all, she'd been like a mother to Lavinia and Jeff. She laughed softly thinking of Jeff being an uncle and little Lavinia becoming an aunt.

What about her father? How would he react when he found out he was going to be a grandfather?

When Misty returned to the kitchen, her face was glowing. "I'm surely expecting, Rachel! I surely am! I've put another inch on my waist and I didn't even know it."

Now Rachel was caught up in Misty's excitement. Wiping her hands on her apron, she walked over and gave her a warm hug. "Well, well, well—Dalton's Lair is going to have its first heir! What a grand event that will be! Can't wait to tell Oscar."

It was late afternoon when Oscar and Drake returned from Crowley with a wagonload of supplies. The Christmas holiday and the wedding had left a lot of the pantry shelves bare. Drake was a man who liked to plan ahead, so he purchased enough staples to have them covered if foul weather moved in during the next four or five weeks.

Oscar took charge of getting the feeding done while Drake unloaded the wagon.

When Drake had carried the last load into the pantry, Misty said, "I'll have a hot cup of coffee ready when you get back from taking the wagon to the barn, Drake."

"Ah, love—that sounds good to me." He gave her a quick smile before he dashed out the door.

When Drake came back to the kitchen, he took Misty in his arms and told her, "It's such a welcoming sight to see you here when I come in as I did this evening. God, Misty, I'm the happiest man in the world."

She was bubbling so with her exciting news that she was finding it hard to keep from telling him right then. But she found herself being kissed by her husband.

When he released her, he gave her a devious grin. "Better stop right now or I'll have you burning my dinner and I'm hungry as a wolf," he declared as he began to rid himself of his wool jacket.

Misty smiled and turned her attention to the stove to stir up the beef stew Rachel had been simmering all afternoon. Their table was already set—she had only to take the pan of cornbread out of the oven and ladle up the stew.

As they sit there eating, Drake was filled with dreams about what he was going to do when spring came. "Before spring comes, Misty, I'm going to look around for a fine little mare for you to ride like the one I gave Jeff. That way, we can take rides together. You'd like that, wouldn't you?"

"Oh, I'd love it, Drake."

"Can't believe how quickly the winter is passing. I thought it would be endless but here it is February already. Oscar tells me the worst of winter will be over in another month. I didn't know what to expect since I wasn't here at this time last year."

Drake was famished—he had two generous bowls of stew and Misty was surprised to see that the entire pan of cornbread was almost gone. She'd had only had one piece.

"Tell me, love, what color would you like your little mare to be? Shall it be black like Duke or a roan like Beauty? I'm going to start looking around next week."

"No, Drake," she replied.

With a startled look, he asked her why. "I thought you told me you'd love to go riding with me when spring came," he muttered, still crunching on the last morsel of cornbread.

She smiled slyly as she told him,. "And I would love to ride with you, Drake darling, but when spring arrives I should not be riding a horse. I'm sure I'm pregnant, Drake."

She heard a slight choking sound as he swallowed that

last bite. In a stammering voice he asked her, "You think so, Misty?"

"I'm almost certain, Drake. I've got all the little signs, so Rachel tells me. Are you happy about it?" she asked because he had such a strange look on his face.

When he finally found his voice, he said as his hand reached across the table to take hers, "I'm so happy that I'm speechless, love. It bloody well scares me to be as happy as I am, and I mean that!"

"Oh, Drake, I couldn't be happier and I just wanted you to be, too."

He laughed nervously. "Bear with me a few minutes—I'm so bedazzled, knowing I'm to be a father. You see, I'm still floating up there in the heavens because you're my wife. Now you're to give me a child! I—I just thank God I came to this place called Arkansas and found you."

"It was my blessing, Drake Dalton, that you came here."

Part IV

The Promise of Spring

Chapter 46

Misty enjoyed thinking about the conversation they'd had at their kitchen table the night she told him about her pregnancy. Had Drake not entered her life last summer, she knew that her life as well as Jeff's and Lavinia's, would never have been so happy. Misty could never forget what he'd done for her and his generous gestures to her little sister and brother.

In the kitchen of Oscar's house, Rachel was also bubbling with the news by the time they sat down at their dinner table.

"Well, I'll be damned! Mr. Dalton will be busting his buttons!" Oscar said and laughed.

"Well, thank goodness it'll be a summer babe and we won't have to fret a snow or sleet storm," Rachel declared.

"Oh, God—yes, thank goodness for that! You ever delivered a babe, Rachel?"

"No, Oscar, and I don't want to," she told him.

Misty noticed a change of attitude in both Rachel and Drake during the next two weeks. They both watched her like a hawk. She actually felt herself getting vexed but then she knew just how much both of them cared for her. But she felt fine and had no intention of sitting around twiddling her thumbs.

She finally told Rachel, "I wish you and Drake would relax, Rachel dear. I'm fine. I'm just carrying a baby—women do it all the time."

"Can't help it, Miss Misty. This is a special babe," Rachel said.

A few weeks after her wedding, Misty had a chance to tell her pa about her news. Colleen's bakery did a thriving business in the winter, so both Mike and Colleen went home in the evenings feeling exhausted. Since Misty's wedding—and the night Colleen had surrendered to Mike—their time together on Saturday nights and Sundays had also changed. It was more than just a courtship now. It was two middle-aged people planning their future together as husband and wife.

So every Sunday during February, Mike went over to Colleen's to work on the extension of her carriage house and on Saturday nights he stayed home with Lavinia and Jeff. By the end of March, he had built the extension which would house Beauty, so he was ready to cut through the existing wall of the carriage house.

Colleen surveyed his carpentry and praised him. "Well, I not only have myself a fine baker but a carpenter, too."

It was the first weekend of March before Misty finally saw her family. Drake had ridden over to invite them to dinner at Dalton's Lair. For Mike, it was a perfect time to accept the invitation—he hadn't planned to go over to Colleen's until the next evening. Lavinia and Jeff were eager to see Misty. They hadn't seen her now for over six weeks.

Had Jeff not appreciated his sister before, he certainly

did now. He realized just how much she'd done for him and Lavinia now that he was shouldering more of the load.

It was a lovely Saturday evening with Misty and Drake. Mike had never seen his daughter look so radiant. She wore the new bottle green light wool gown Molly had just made for her with the little emerald earrings Drake had given her before they'd married. On her finger was the most exquisite ring—and Mike also noticed her emerald bracelet.

When they had finished their dessert and before they left the dining table, Misty announced to her father, "Pa, are you ready to be a grandfather?"

A slow grin came to Bennett's face. "I'm ready, honey! Are you telling me I am?"

"I'm telling you you're going to be."

Mike gave her a warm, fatherly embrace. "My little daughter's going to be a mother. Can't wait to tell Colleen the happy news."

Jeff suddenly had a broad grin on his face, too, as he asked, "So that's going to make me an uncle, ain't it, Misty?"

"It sure does and Lavinia will be an aunt," Misty said and smiled at both of them.

"Hope it's a boy," Jeff declared. But Lavinia quickly retorted that she hoped it was a girl. Mike, Drake, and Misty began to laugh at the two of them.

Drake spoke up. "Now one of you two may just have to be disappointed, I fear. Just hope it's a fine, healthy little baby—that's how your sister and I feel."

"Guess you're right, Mr. Dalton," Jeff replied, for he considered that Drake was right about everything. He had swelled with pride when he saw that his carved horse was displayed on the fireplace mantel.

They left for their home around nine. Later, Drake thought to himself as he watched Misty move around the house that he could detect a slight difference in her waistline.

Four weeks later there was no question about her

expanding waistline—she finally admitted that she'd let out the seams in two of her gowns as far as they would go.

"Lord, Drake—you're going to see me in my nightgown and robe all day if I wish to breathe," she laughed.

"Oh, Misty love, why haven't you told me how uncomfortable your gowns have been? We'll get you over to Molly's to get some new things."

"I just didn't think it would all happen so fast," she said.

"Love, it's the end of March," he reminded her.

"But it hardly seems possible, Drake. Winter will be over soon. Guess I have a right to be getting a little bigger, don't I?"

"You certainly do, Misty. Now, Monday morning we're going to Molly's—I want you to be comfortable."

Seeing them enter her shop came as no surprise to Molly. The minute Misty took off her cape, she could see how her gown was miserably tight around her waist.

Anticipating that Mr. Dalton might be bringing his bride into her shop soon, she had stitched up a sample gown designed to accommodate a lady who's expecting. She showed the sample frock to Misty.

"Oh, Molly—that looks divine! Look, Drake," Misty exclaimed as she saw the full-flowing material of the dress.

Without any hesitation, Drake told Molly, "Make my lady five such gowns in whatever materials and colors she chooses."

When they were preparing to leave, Molly told them, "Take this one home with you today, dear. I have a pattern already cut. If you would like, I'll deliver the first two as soon as I finish them so you'll have some changes before I can get all five of them sewn."

"Oh, Molly, that would be wonderful!" Misty exclaimed. She could understand why it would take more than a week for Molly to get five such beautiful gowns finished.

Molly was more than happy to provide this service for the Daltons—March was a very slow month around her shop. January and February had not been that good, either. She could not hope for an increase in business until Easter was approaching.

Now that winter was almost over and spring was only a few weeks away, Ellen wasn't so sure she wanted to sail back to England. Many things had tempted her to stay right here in Poinsett County. Needless to say, she was elated over Drake's news that he was to become a father and she was going to be an aunt. But something else had happened to Ellen. She had fallen in love with Dexter. He declared his love for her and wanted the two of them to be married.

But there was one thing that troubled Ellen. If she should marry him as she wished to do, what would happen to dear Agatha? Someone would have to be hired to fill in for Ellen during the winter months. Ellen had become more than fond of the elderly lady and she knew that few companions would give Mrs. Fortis the care she'd given her.

When she and Dexter had gone out for rides in his gig or ridden their horses around the countryside, they'd talked endlessly about how they could solve that problem.

Dexter had told her, "Oh, I know there's one easy solution to our dilemma, Ellen. We could marry and move into Aunt Agatha's. But I have my own place now. I'm enthusiastic about it—I want us to have our own place. I don't want to live under Aunt Agatha's roof as much as I adore her."

"Oh, I know, Dexter. Truly I do, for I, too, wish to be the mistress of my own house."

"That's what I want, Ellen, for the two of us. Darling Aunt Agatha will be the mistress of that house of hers until the day she dies. It wouldn't be our home," Dexter said.

"Then we must find someone we both trust to take care of her before we get married."

"I know, Ellen, and we will. I love her, too. But I plan to tell her about my plans to marry you, Ellen darling, because she has to get used to the idea that someone else will be living with her. But we'll be close by and can drop in on her often."

The old saying about March coming in like a lion and going out like a lamb was certainly true. The last week of March and the first week of April gave way to much milder weather.

Misty could not have been happier to see spring. She was tired of being sequestered in the house so much. Just to be able to walk around the yard with Lucky trailing along with her was delightful.

She swore if she'd been able to get outside more she would not have put on so much weight, but Rachel kept telling her, "Honey, you're not that big to be as far along as you are. I think it's going to be a little girl."

When Ellen came over to see them the first week in April in Mrs. Fortis's gig, Misty was overjoyed. She was even more elated to hear that she wasn't going to return to England as she'd planned.

"You can tell my big brother that I'm staying right here and marrying Dexter as soon as we can find someone to tend to Mrs. Fortis."

"Oh, Ellen! I'm so happy for you! I'm glad you're going to be so close to us," Misty said.

She and Misty had a nice two-hour visit before Ellen had to leave without getting to see her brother—he'd been in town working out a deal with the lumber company.

Misty and Ellen did not see one another again until May at the wedding of Colleen's daughter. During the reception Colleen found a private moment with Misty. She felt it a proper time to tell Misty something she'd been anxious to tell her for weeks. "Now that I have Maureen's wedding behind me, I'm ready to plan my own. I hope you'll approve. I love your father dearly."

Misty's green eyes flashed excitedly. "Oh, I couldn't be happier, Mrs. Carver. You certainly do have my approval!"

A month later, Misty and Drake attended another wedding and reception, and by now Misty was becoming very heavy with her baby. What made Misty happiest was that Jeff and Lavinia seemed very content about having a new stepmother.

The old Bennett property went up for sale since Mike and his children were now living in Lepanto. Lavinia's pup, Sweetie, and Jeff's roan mare, Beauty, were also housed there.

Mike and his children had adjusted to Colleen's lifestyle easily—he'd sold his team of horses and old wagon to his friend, Jeb. He had nothing to rush back over to Crowley to see about once he closed the doors to his house. His life was here in Lepanto with Colleen.

They worked daily in her bakery shop and business was flourishing. Then they came home in the late afternoons to a warm family circle.

Jeff and Lavinia found out immediately that Colleen laid down very strict rules for them—but then she lavished such love on them that they wanted to please her.

Mike was delighted about the way Jeff and Lavinia had adjusted to their new surroundings. Colleen had made a very special effort to make both their bedrooms comfortable.

Colleen's energy never ceased to amaze Mike. She was like a whirlwind, constantly in motion. Like Drake Dalton, Mike Bennett had never been happier!

Chapter 47

Spring had come to the Arkansas countryside and the signs of it were everywhere. Wildflowers bloomed profusely in the pastures and by the sides of the dirt roads. Trees and shrubs were budded out, and the birds were chirping their sweet songs of spring.

Maureen and Eric were married, as were Mike and Colleen. Ellen was now able to marry Dexter for she'd found a very good, dependable lady to come to live with Mrs. Fortis. She and Dexter were to be married in July. Love and romance were in the air, Misty enjoyed thinking.

Her nursery was ready and waiting for its occupant to arrive. The chest was filled with a lavish layette—Drake had bought enough things for two babies, but Misty didn't dampen his enthusiasm.

Being married to Drake had made her love grow deeper and deeper. She could not have had a more doting husband. The larger she'd become the more protective he and Rachel were. Every time she took a stroll, she knew someone was at the window checking on her. Drake was extremely watchful during the evening hours when the two of them were alone.

When July came, he was apprehensive about taking Misty to Ellen's wedding. "Oh, love—I fear that's going to be too much for you."

"Drake, I'm going to Ellen's wedding. I'll be fine. The baby isn't due until the end of August, Dr. Sloan said."

But he had insisted that she allow him to go to town to shop for their wedding gift so she wouldn't have to do it.

The day he was preparing to go to town, she said, "Buy a blue garter, Drake."

"A blue garter? Why a blue garter, Misty?"

"I want to give it to Ellen for good luck as Colleen did for me."

"A blue garter you shall have, my love," he said and grinned as he went on out the door.

The next week they rode in Drake's buggy to the Fortis estate. It was an absolutely beautiful day. Agatha Fortis's home was a profusion of colorful flowers. It was a small gathering, since Dexter and Ellen knew very few people.

After the wedding and dinner at Agatha's, Ellen and Dexter planned to spend their honeymoon at their own home a few miles away.

There was one sentimental moment for Drake when he saw his sister in her white wedding gown, wearing her mother's pearl and diamond earrings. Pinned just below her high lace collar was the matching brooch. Adrienne Dalton would have been pleased.

His father must have given those exquisite pieces to Ellen after his mother's death. Drake was sure he had also given certain pieces to Susanne and Valeria. He wondered what Lady Margaret had received after she'd married Lord Dalton. Drake couldn't help feeling resentment if she touched anything that had belonged to his mother.

But he didn't dwell on those bitter thoughts long—this

was a joyous occasion. However, he did insist that they leave shortly after dinner.

Misty seemed fine but he didn't want to press their luck. "We're leaving now, love. I think you've had enough excitement for one night. Come, let's say our farewells," he urged.

Misty was not about to admit it, but she was feeling very weary so she gave Drake no fuss as he led her by the arm to say goodnight to everyone.

He knew he had made a wise decision—she was falling asleep before they were halfway home.

When they got home and he'd helped Misty get undressed so she could get right into bed, he went back into the parlor to have a nightcap and smoke a cheroot.

It was so quiet in the parlor without Misty. He took Lucky for his late-night roam before he dimmed the lamps to go to bed.

High up in one of the pines, he heard the hooting of an owl. Long after he had returned to the house, he could still hear the screech. When he got into bed beside his sleeping wife, he could still hear that damn thing hooting.

The next morning he and Rachel were in the kitchen—Misty was still sleeping, so he knew how tired she must have been from going to the wedding.

"You hear that old hoot owl last night, Mr. Dalton?" she asked as she set his plate of bacon and eggs in front of him.

"Sure did, Rachel. Thought he'd never stop all that racket."

"Don't like those owls around a house like that. It's—it's a bad omen," she declared.

Drake had learned over the months that Rachel knew a lot of old wives' tales. "So what does that mean, Rachel?"

"Means death, Mr. Dalton. Means a death or death message. That's why I've never liked them."

Usually, Drake would have shrugged her comments aside but somehow, he couldn't during the entire day. All he could think about was that something would happen to Misty or the baby. She was so tiny and she'd grown so large. He'd heard of women dying when they delivered a child.

Misty was unaware of the torment her husband went through during the next few weeks. July passed and the month of August arrived. Misty didn't care what Doctor Sloan said about the baby's arrival—she was counting from that day they'd made love in the the barn. She was never going to go until the end of August.

Rachel agreed—she could swear the baby had dropped during the last week. That evening when she returned home, she told Oscar, "You or Mr. Dalton will be riding for Dr. Sloan any time, I'm thinking."

"Really, Rachel? But it ain't the end of the month," Oscar reminded her.

"Well, just remember what I said, Oscar," Rachel declared smugly.

Late Sunday afternoon, Oscar did remember what Rachel had said for Drake rushed over to get Rachel and dispatch Oscar to get the doctor. Misty was in labor.

She'd said nothing when the first pains began about midday but she could not conceal the ones she was experiencing now.

The truth was, Drake felt utterly helpless and awkward. Rachel could hardly tend to Misty and calm him, too, so she sent him to the kitchen to put on a kettle of water and brew up a fresh pot of coffee. Knowing how slow first babies could be, she figured Mr. Dalton might need plenty of coffee before this was over.

During one of those periods when Misty was free of pain, she told Rachel, "Drake's going to be a nervous wreck before I have this baby."

"He'll survive. Fathers always do," Rachel said and patted her hand. "Oscar is already on his way to get the doctor, dear."

But what Rachel didn't dare mention was whether he'd

locate the doctor—it was Sunday and he wouldn't be in his office.

Oscar had not found him at home when he arrived in Crowley but luckily his next door neighbor was able to tell Oscar where he was. He and his family were out on Otter Pond having a family reunion picnic.

Doctor Sloan was just getting ready to take his first bite of watermelon when Oscar came rushing up. So he left his wife and children with the rest of the family to follow Oscar to Dalton's Lair.

The sight of his arrival greatly relieved both Rachel and Drake. The thought that they might be forced to deliver Misty's baby scared them to death.

Once the doctor arrived, he took full charge. Rachel and Drake sat in the kitchen sipping their coffee, but Drake couldn't sit still. He paced around the kitchen.

When Oscar had finished the evening feeding, he came in the back door to ask if anything had happened yet. Rachel told him he might as well go on over to the house—there was nothing he could do. "Me and Mr. Dalton will just have to wait it out, Oscar. Go on home and warm some supper up," she urged.

Drake suggested that she go on home, too, but Rachel quickly told him, "Oh, Mr. Dalton—I can't do that. Right now, I couldn't eat a bite. No, sir—I'm staying right here!"

Drake reached the point where he couldn't stay in the kitchen any longer. He had to know what was happening in that bedroom. He announced to Rachel, "I'm going in there!"

But what he saw when he entered the room was his wife at the height of her agony. He became very vexed at Sloan, who sat there calmly.

"Can't you bloody well do something to help her, doctor?" Drake barked.

"I will, Drake, when the time comes. Misty and your baby are both working very hard—I must wait it out and so must you. Birthing a baby doesn't happen in a couple of hours. It's nothing for a woman to be in labor over twelve hours. If it calms you, I can tell you Misty is going to have a quick delivery."

"Quick delivery? She's already been in pain for three hours," Drake declared.

By now, Dr. Sloan was becoming indignant. He told Drake if he wished to help, he should give her his hand to squeeze on when the next round of pain struck. Drake did as the doctor ordered.

For such a tiny hand, Drake felt a powerful grip as she began to undulate with the next round of pains. At least, it gave him the feeling he was helping just a little.

This went on for another seemingly endless hour. Drake stood there by the bed thinking he'd never hated his father as much as he did now. To think that his mother went through this agony to produce children she never wanted but were forced on her. Now that he was witnessing what his own wife was going through to bring this child of their love into the world it made an indelible impression on Drake.

Drake had no idea why the doctor suggested, "How about getting Rachel to come in here and you go have a little rest and a cup of coffee? By the way keep the coffee pot hot for me," Sloan added.

The doctor had a very definite reason for wanting Rachel there instead of Drake. This baby was a wee one but a real little firebrand. It was ready to be born.

When Rachel entered, she asked him what she might do and Doctor Sloan wasted no time in telling her.

He smiled, "Wish all my first deliveries were as fast and furious as this. Got ourselves a tiny little girl here just like her mama."

Misty heard his remarks but before she could say anything, another mighty assault struck and the doctor told her to bear down with all her might.

From the sound of Rachel's and Doctor Sloan's voices, Misty knew her little angel had finally arrived.

Rachel was there to take the little being from the doctor. It was a short baby but certainly not a skinny one. It looked like a little doll lying there in the blanket. She was a petite little thing like her mother.

Dr. Sloan told Misty, "You're the mother of a little daughter, Misty. Short little thing, just like you. I doubt she'll measure nineteen inches and if I were to guess, I'd say she weighs just a little over five pounds—but she's absolutely perfect."

In a weary voice, Misty assured him that that was all that was important. Rachel cleaned the baby so she could wrap it in a clean blanket and put it beside Misty.

"There she is, Miss Misty. Isn't she a doll?"

Misty had only to look at her to know that every pain had been worth it. Every little feature was perfect. Misty took each little hand to look at it. Her little cluster of hair was as black as Drake's, which delighted Misty.

Doctor Sloan had already left to tell Drake the good news. Rachel left the room as soon as Drake came dashing in.

Rachel and the doctor were both ready to have a cup of coffee, so they let Misty and Drake have this private moment alone.

In a weak voice, Misty said, "Adrienne has arrived and she's beautiful, Drake." When he saw his daughter for the first time, he was so overcome with emotion that all he could do was mumble, "Oh, God, love!" He just stood there for a few seconds staring down at the baby and Misty saw tears begin to stream down his cheeks. They dampened her face as he bent down to kiss her.

When he stood up, he asked, "Can I hold her?"

"Of course, Drake. You're her father."

Misty wasn't aware when Drake put the baby back beside her—she'd fallen into a deep sleep as he roamed around the room cradling the baby in his arms.

Dr. Sloan left shortly before ten—Rachel told Drake she was warming up some beef stew for the two of them. "Miss Misty is going to sleep for a while—she's exhausted, so we have to keep up our strength to do what's got to be done around here."

From that minute on, Rachel took charge. She knew her services were needed tonight.

"Mr. Dalton, you get yourself a breath of fresh air. Walk over to our house to tell Oscar I'm going to spend the night over here to tend to Miss Misty. When you get back, we'll have some stew."

Rachel had been right—Drake was hungry for the stew and some coffee. Old Lucky was whining for some food as well. She'd also been right about Misty—she and little Adrienne were still sleeping soundly at the midnight hour.

Rachel slept on the small daybed in the nursery. Drake dimmed all the lamps, and by the time his head hit the pillow he knew he would never know a day as special as this one!

Chapter 48

Oscar was sent to Lepanto to take the great news to Mike, Colleen, and Ellen. She wrote Dexter a note telling him where she'd gone and went immediately to the barn to have one of the young hands prepare the gig.

As impatient as they were, Mike and Colleen were forced to wait until the weekend to see the new baby. It was too late to make a jaunt out there by the time they'd prepared dinner for their own family. Rising at five in the morning meant that all lamps were dimmed at Colleen's house no later than ten every night.

Rachel had been expecting to spend more time over at Drake's, but he took charge of his baby as he did everything else. Actually, she was doing her usual routine over there and getting home at the regular time.

For young parents, Drake and Misty were amazing. The many things Rachel had expected to have to do were handled capably by Drake. He might have been a nervous expectant father, but now that his daughter had arrived he was calm and assured when he bathed her and changed her diapers.

Misty made a hasty recovery. She was not one to pamper herself and stay in bed longer than necessary. Five days after the baby was born, she was already moving around the house in her gown and robe.

Rachel went home feeling very confident that Mr. Dalton could handle the rest of the evening. He served the dinner which she'd cooked for them and washed and dried the dishes after dinner. Misty left him in the kitchen to attend to those chores while she went back to their bedroom to attend to little Adrienne. Once she had fed the baby and had her cozily snuggled in the wicker bassinet by the side of her bed, she joined Drake in the parlor.

It would be many weeks before she would finally put Adrienne in the crib in the next room. Drake adored her for being such a loving mother.

Ellen was overcome with emotion when she had rushed to Dalton's Lair the day after the baby was born and Drake and Misty had told her what they'd named their daughter.

In a sobbing voice she said, "Oh, Drake—how very happy that would have made her."

"Yes, Ellen. It would have," he replied.

When she got back in her gig to return home that August day, Ellen was deep in her own private musings. Should she ever be blessed with a daughter as Misty had been, she was going to tell Dexter that she'd like to name her Melanie to honor Misty. One day, she told herself, she must tell Misty how she'd changed everything around for her when she'd first arrived at her brother's house. Misty had no idea how that first encounter had influenced Ellen to think differently about so many things.

Once she and Misty had talked that night Ellen realized she'd slowly begun to change. Her stiff English attitude loosened about Drake's primitive new home and his bossy housekeeper, Rachel. She had Misty to thank for that!

By the time a golden autumn arrived over Poinsett County, Misty was fully recovered and by the end of November, she was riding with her husband over the countryside on the fine thoroughbred mare he had purchased for her. She was as black as Duke—Misty named her Midnight.

Thanksgiving Day was spent with Ellen and Dexter. Drake and Dexter had gone out to shoot a wild turkey for Ellen's dinner table. With the baby snuggled in a warm wool bunting, Drake and Misty had traveled over to Ellen's. Agatha Fortis was joining them and swore to the Daltons she'd never seen a more beautiful baby.

Colleen had extended an invitation to everyone for Christmas Day to be celebrated with her and Mike. Drake had firmly announced that Christmas Eve would always be at his and Misty's home now that Adrienne had arrived.

So it was, and a most glorious holiday season it was! During the winter months Drake watched many changes take place in his daughter. The long months of winter gave him time to think. One thing gnawed at him constantly during those long, cold nights. The day he'd gotten the letter from Susanne that his father had died, Drake found that he was finally rid of the bitterness he'd harbored for so long.

He was now ready to return to England and take his wife to the place where he was born and raised. He wanted her to meet Valeria and Susanne. And most of all, he wanted to take baskets of flowers to his mother's grave.

He said nothing to Misty as he began to make plans for the late spring. By that time, Adrienne would be almost a year old. He knew if they wished to leave her here under the care of Rachel and her doting Aunt Ellen, it would be fine. But the final decision would be Misty's.

When he was finally ready to tell her of his plans, Misty was very excited but he quickly found out she had no intention of leaving her daughter. "Adrienne will go with us or I won't go," she declared firmly. Drake could not have been happier—even the thought of being away from Adrienne that long devastated him.

He immediately made plans for his absence from Dalton's

Lair. Molly was given the largest order she'd ever had—Drake wanted his wife to be gowned in the lovely silks and satins he knew the ladies in England and France wore in the spring.

Molly worked day and night to fill his order. Misty was unaware of all of Drake's elaborate plans—she was too preoccupied with her daughter.

It was mid-April when they left Poinsett County, sailing for England on the first of May. Everything about the venture was exciting to Misty, who had never been out of the little county in Arkansas. She survived the ocean voyage with no ill effects. Drake learned that his daughter was very much like her mother—she was obviously a very spirited little miss, too.

When they were approaching the shores of England, Drake confessed, "I'm glad we didn't leave Adrienne back home. I would have been constantly wondering if everything was all right."

Misty reached over to kiss him. "I couldn't have left her, Drake. I would have been miserable."

It was a lovely day in May as the two of them took a hired carriage out to Dalton Manor once they'd disembarked from the ship.

Drake's arrival with his wife and baby daughter, took both of his sisters by utter surprise. They had a glorious reunion for the next five days. Valeria was expecting her first child and Susanne was expecting her second, so Drake met his little nephew at Dalton Manor. How pleased Drake was that the ghosts of the past were no longer there. Dalton Manor was a happy place now that Susanne and her family were living there.

Drake, Misty, and Adrienne visited the grave of his mother with four baskets of colorful flowers. As she stood there holding her baby's hand, she heard Drake's deep voice murmuring, "Mother, I finally got to come back."

Misty strolled quietly away so Drake could have some

time there by himself. He didn't linger much longer after he'd placed the flowers on the grave. He'd heard his daughter whimpering so he got Misty and Adrienne back to the house so Misty could put her down for a nap.

Drake was able to persuade Misty to leave Adrienne at the manor house so he could take her on a grand tour of London. It was quite an experience—Misty actually saw a palace where a king and queen lived. Drake enjoyed just watching her lovely face and flashing green eyes as he pointed all this out.

"Things like this only existed in the fairy tales that my mother read to me as a small child. Now here I am, seeing all these wonderful sights. I wonder how you could have wanted to leave all this to come to our strange new world," she exclaimed.

"Because I'd lived here all my life and seen all this time and time again. Besides, I have my own palace now that suits me just fine—and I have my own beautiful queen and a little princess," he said and smiled at her as they rode along in the carriage.

"How sweet you are, Drake Dalton!" she said as she reached over to plant a kiss on his cheek.

Before they returned to the manor house, Drake took her to a quaint little inn by the side of a pond. It was such a serene setting, with two graceful swans swimming nearby. Swan's Nest Inn was a favorite place of Drake's, and he introduced Misty to Dover sole which she'd never eaten before.

When they returned to the manor house, Misty was a little chatterbox as she told Susanne about seeing Buckingham Palace and Westminster Abbey.

Susanne found Drake's wife utterly enchanting. She was so sure of herself as she attended to Adrienne. There was no doubt about her being a doting mother. But this afternoon when Drake brought her back from their jaunt around London, Susanne saw a vivacious, sparkling-eyed young lady with a childlike quality about her.

Misty excused herself to go upstairs to check on Adrienne while Drake remained in the parlor with his sister. His sister admitted she'd never met anyone quite like Misty before. "Ellen has written long letters with vivid descriptions of Misty—she obviously warmed to her the first time they met. I don't think words can describe your Misty—one just has to meet her," she said and laughed.

"She's my whole world, Susanne. I never expected to be this happy."

"I know you are, Drake. It shows," Susanne said gently.

Drake and Misty stayed ten days in England before they left for Paris. He'd planned a week there before they returned to England to spend the last seven days before they sailed for home.

When they arrived at Bayard's apartment, Drake found that his uncle's life had changed as drastically as his own. Bayard was also a husband. He and Gigi had been married about a year now. Being a long-time bachelor, one might have expected him to marry a much younger woman but Gigi was about Bayard's age and as independent in her thinking as he. They'd met when she had rented the apartment next to Bayard's, but she had insisted on keeping her two-bedroom apartment after they were married.

She gave Drake and Misty a very simple, practical explanation. "I am an artist and I need time alone. I had a perfect studio set up in one of my two bedrooms so why should I give it up?"

She laughed lightheartedly. "Besides, where would my darling Bayard have made me a studio here in his apartment? It is a perfect arrangement, is it not, Bayard?"

"Perfect, chérie," he agreed.

As it happened, it was also perfect for Drake and Misty.

They had Gigi's apartment all to themselves as Gigi didn't work in her studio during their visit. She graciously entertained them during the day while Bayard was at his office.

Evenings were spent pleasantly in the apartment with Bayard's fine cuisine and vintage wines. The time went by swiftly as Drake and Bayard had so much talking to do.

But Misty was never bored as Gigi was most engaging. Misty would not have called her pretty, but there was something most attractive about her. She had a long mane of dark hair that she allowed to flow loosely down her back at times or pulled up in a huge coil at the top of her head. She was tall and trim, with a sensuous air about her.

She told Misty, "Oh, ma petite—I wish you two were going to be here longer. How I would love to capture your beauty on canvas! May I ask if I might sketch you, Misty?"

"Of course, Gigi."

While Drake and Bayard talked for the next hour, Gigi busily stroked at a pad. Misty was very impressed when she saw the finished sketch. It was almost eerie to look at the pad and see herself looking back.

Before it was time to leave, Bayard presented Drake with a gift he would treasure forever—It was a miniature portrait of his mother. Her parents had had it done when Adrienne was only ten because she was already such a little beauty.

"I'll be anxious to know how your little Adrienne looks at this age, Drake," Bayard said.

"Long before Adrienne is ten, Misty and I will expect you two to come to see us in Arkansas," Drake replied.

The seven days in Paris went by quickly and they traveled back to England. By the end of the last seven days there, Drake, was anxious to sail for home.

It was not until they were out on the Atlantic Ocean sailing homeward that they both confessed to one another that they were ready to go home to Dalton's Lair.

"Oh, Drake—I loved seeing all the glorious sights of

London and Paris, as well as meeting your sisters and uncle, but right now I'm so hungry for the sight of our little house."

Drake grinned. "So am I, love."

"Drake, make me a promise," she said impishly.

"What's that, love?"

"Let's never have a house as big as the ones Susanne and Valeria live in. They exhaust me!"

"Never, my Misty. I might not be able to find you when I wanted to. No, love—I don't yearn for such a place," he assured her.

It was mid-July by the time Drake and his wife and daughter were traveling down the dirt road toward their home. He swore that the air smelled fresher and sweeter. All he had to do was look in Misty's direction to see how her eyes were sparkling to know how happy she was.

She was thinking about the changes Rachel would see in Adrienne since May. Her little daughter was about ready to walk. Very soon there would be no baby in the house—they were going to have a toddler roaming around.

Misty had bought gifts for everyone while she was in London and Paris. Drake had purchased some fine French brandies and a fine briar pipe to give to Oscar.

The sight of Misty and Drake arriving back home was glorious to Rachel—it had been lonely with them gone. Time had hung heavily with no chores to do over at Drake's house.

Rachel and Oscar had a jubilant reunion with Drake and Misty that afternoon. Rachel left no doubts about how she felt. "I hope you don't make that trip too often—it was too lonely around here. Old Lucky's as skinny as a rail—he wouldn't eat for me."

Drake grinned. "We'll fatten him up, Rachel."

For Misty and Drake, it was wonderful to sit at their own

kitchen table and dine on Rachel's delicious dinner. Lucky also ate heartily.

Adrienne seemed delighted to be back in her crib. Drake and Misty were convinced that no bed they'd slept on while they were away was as cozy as theirs.

Drake realized just how exhausting the long journey had been for Misty. She was still sleeping soundly when he got up the next morning.

He went out to the barn to check on Duke and speak with Oscar. Rachel had tended to little Adrienne's needs—she no longer had to rely on mother's milk.

Rachel saw the changes in her—her crib was no longer able to confine her. Little Adrienne was ready to stretch her wings and fly.

It took days for Misty to tell Rachel about all the things she'd seen in London and Paris. Rachel was thrilled with the yards of delicate lace and the bottle of French perfume Misty had brought her from France. Misty had also bought some for Colleen and Ellen. Drake had insisted she buy several bottles for herself.

Drake found it amazing that when he took her in the European shops, her purchases were for everyone but herself.

But Drake didn't forget about her. He bought her a fur muff, fur neck scarf, and a bright green velvet chapeau.

The whole family gathered at Dalton's Lair to celebrate Adrienne's first birthday. As Misty had expected, she was already taking her first steps but she was also taking a fair share of falls. Rachel and Misty would often expect her to burst into tears but it rarely happened. Rachel exclaimed, "She's a tough little nut, Miss Misty."

"She is, isn't she? Well, I'm glad of that."

Their lawn party began at three. Colleen closed her shop early, insisting she be allowed to bake her little granddaughter's first birthday cake. Rachel also made some other desserts for the occasion.

It had been Ellen's first chance to see Drake and Misty

since they'd gotten back. She was most anxious to hear about her sisters as well as Misty's impression of England.

She also told them her wonderful news: she and Dexter would be having their own baby in February. But Ellen was not the only one to make such an announcement. Maureen was also expecting her first baby.

"What a family we're going to have," Misty exclaimed.

Of all the gifts Adrienne received, the one she enjoyed the most was Jeff and Lavinia's gift of a bright red ball. Jeff would roll it across the grass and Adrienne would toddle to retrieve it. Giggling, she would roll it back to him.

By five it was obvious that little Adrienne was ready to have her nap so Drake picked her up to carry her in the house. Her frilly pink organza dress was spotted with the icing from her birthday cake. Drake grinned as he announced to his guests, "Think Adrienne has had all the celebrating she can handle for this birthday."

It seemed to Misty that summer suddenly disappeared shortly after Adrienne's first birthday. It was golden autumn all over the Arkansas countryside. Drake and Misty took long, leisurely rides through the woods over his land. Often when Drake was busy around the place, Misty would take the gig and go into Lepanto to see Jeff and Lavinia or go over to visit Ellen. Once winter arrived, she would not be able to venture out alone some days.

But the golden days did not last—it was a short autumn. By the time the Thanksgiving holiday arrived, cold days arrived with it, prompting Oscar to tell Drake he felt they should store up more wood. So Drake went along with him to cut the wood and load it into the wagon.

Misty left Adrienne with Rachel so she could go into Crowley to do some shopping. During the afternoon when Oscar and Drake arrived with a wagon load and Misty had not returned, Oscar could tell Drake was getting concerned.

When she had not returned by four-thirty, there was no question about it—Drake was at the point of riding into town.

When he and Oscar had piled the last logs on the stack, Oscar alerted him, "There she comes, Mr. Dalton. See there, she's just fine!"

Drake heaved a deep sigh of relief but for once he was annoyed that she'd caused him so much concern. He left Oscar to finish up the unloading to go meet her.

By the time he approached the gig, he saw it was piled high with packages. His black eyes glared up at her as he inquired, "What did you do, Misty—buy out all of Crowley?

"No, Drake darling—I just got all my Christmas shopping done early," she said with a soft gale of laughter.

He broke into a smile as he went around to hoist her out of the gig. "Love, there's more than four weeks before Christmas," he reminded her.

"But I don't want to go to town in snow and sleet. Remember what happened to you last winter?" she asked. Her green eyes were flashing as she reminded him, "This is our Adrienne's first Christmas."

He didn't release her for a few moments but held her close as he planted a kiss on her soft lips. "Oh, Misty— Misty, love, how could I ever tell you how much I love you?"

Her hands went up to his face and her emerald eyes looked deep into his. "Just keep loving me, Drake. That's all you have to do."

Chapter 49

The next week Drake went into town to pick up their mail and do a little shopping. He was hoping he might have some letters from England or France by now.

Misty had done enough shopping for everyone, so he didn't have to buy anything for Oscar, Rachel, or Adrienne, but he had one special gift to buy. He was rather at a loss for what to get Misty.

Her armoire was full and, as Misty had told him, she had no need for a lot of fancy gowns. So he ambled up and down the streets to try to get an idea. He was just about to leave Crowley to head for Lepanto when he went by the one jewelry store in town.

Suddenly, his gaze fell on a lovely necklace with sparkling diamonds forming the shape of a heart which hung on a delicate gold chain. It was the kind of sentimental gift he wanted for his wife, so he purchased the diamond heart-shaped necklace and a beautiful, jewelry chest with mother-of-pearl inlay.

He was finally ready to head for the post office, pick up

his mail, and go homeward. The postal clerk handed him three letters, saying, "Just a minute, Mr. Dalton, there's also a big package for you." A few minutes later he emerged with a large, thin package about two feet by three feet.

Drake could not imagine what Bayard could have been shipping to him. His curiosity was whetted so much that he urged the little bay swiftly toward Dalton's Lair. When he arrived home and carried the huge package into the house, Misty became as curious as he was.

With fumbling fingers he tore away the wrappings and gazed at Gigi's artwork. She had done a portrait of Misty in oils from the little sketch she'd made that July night. She'd captured all of Misty's breathtaking loveliness in soft pastels. Misty's golden hair flowed over her shoulders, which were draped in a soft green silk that exposed just a hint of her cleavage. But it was the face and Misty's green eyes with her thick lashes that Gigi had managed to capture so completely.

Misty was so overcome with emotion that tears flowed freely and she could not speak. It was a very emotional moment for both of them.

It took Drake a few moments before he gained control of his emotion so he could call Rachel into the parlor to see the portrait.

Rachel was as awestruck and speechless as the two of them. She didn't hesitate a minute to suggest that it should hang over the mantel.

"You're exactly right, Rachel, and it shall be done tomorrow," Drake assured her.

After Rachel went back to her kitchen, Drake and Misty decided it was a night to share a glass of wine before dinner as they read their letters from England and Paris.

Bayard wrote a letter to both of them and Gigi wrote a letter to Misty, saying that she hoped she'd like her Christmas gift. She was so pleased with the portrait that she did a second one and a Paris gallery had placed it on display.

She delightedly told Misty she had never received so much as she had for that canvas. The vivacious Gigi wrote that the gentleman who'd paid such a high price quizzed her endlessly about the ravishing beauty's identity. She'd told him, "Ah, monsieur—that I will never reveal."

Misty had laughed, "Oh, that Gigi—she's fantastic!"

Drake had to agree with her, adding, "I'll wring that neck of hers should she ever tell who that lovely lady is."

Misty had to laugh—she realized that Drake could be a very jealous man. It thrilled her, but she quickly soothed him. "Gigi would never give that away, Drake."

During the Christmas holiday, Gigi's portrait gathered praises from everyone. It was a glorious Christmas Eve when everyone came to Misty and Drake's home for the evening.

The hour was very late when everyone had started for home and Misty had finally gotten a very excited little daughter to bed. Christmas Day was to be spent with their own little family, but Misty had insisted that Rachel and Oscar come for Christmas dinner.

Dexter and Ellen shared Christmas Day with Agatha Fortis and Colleen and Mike had Maureen and Eric over.

While Misty got Adrienne undressed and into her nightgown, Drake took Lucky out for his last roam of the evening.

By the time he returned, Misty was in the parlor looking very comfortable in her nightgown and robe. The log in the fireplace was crackling and Misty wondered if it was true that it meant that snow was on its way.

She heard Drake and Lucky coming in the back door. Just opening the back door told her how cold it was outside—the draft of chilly air permeated to the parlor.

Drake entered shortly to announce, "It's snowing like crazy outside, love. I hope everyone has arrived home by now."

"If they're not home, they're close to it," she told him.

Drake went over to the liquor chest to get a glass of the cognac he'd brought back from France and he invited Misty to have one with him. But she graciously refused, reminding him of how she'd tried to drink cognac when they were at Bayard's.

"I'll have a glass of wine, Drake."

So as he sipped his cognac, she sipped her wine. Knowing this man she loved so dearly, she knew she was about to give him the grandest Christmas gift of all. She allowed him to almost finish his cognac before she impishly said, "Drake, I've another gift to give you tonight."

Knowing by now that his Misty was a most unpredictable miss, he asked, "And what or where is it?"

"You're going to be a father again, Drake. I'm pregnant," she announced.

"Now tell me, love, how long have you known this time without telling me?" His dark eyes pierced her as he remembered how long she'd kept her pregnancy to herself.

"Only two months," she confessed.

"So it didn't happen in Paris—but back here?"

"Of course, Drake. Right here in Dalton's Lair, not Paris or England. This is home, Drake," she said as his arms went around her.

"Oh, Misty love, I hope I'll know more about how to help you this time than I did with Adrienne," he vowed.

There was so much determination in her voice that he never doubted her for a moment when she said that this time he would have a son.

It didn't matter to Drake Dalton whether it was a son or daughter, just as long as he had Misty's love. This tiny little Arkansas girl had changed his whole world.

His home was certainly no palace but it was his castle. Here he was the king and Misty was his beautiful queen. When he lifted her from the settee to carry her to their bed, he grinned as he looked down at her. "Well, after what you've just told me, I guess I know what my project is going to be during these winter months."

"What, Drake?"

"I have to get another room built onto this house, love."

Once they entered their bedroom, Drake sweetly seduced her as he had when she'd first surrendered to him. She'd never regretted that moment.

Drake Dalton had been the man she'd dreamed about all her life and she'd just been lucky enough to find him!

DON'T MISS THESE ROMANCES FROM BEST-SELLING AUTHOR KATHERINE DEAUXVILLE!

THE CRYSTAL HEART (0-8217-4928-5, $5.99)

Emmeline gave herself to a sensual stranger in a night aglow with candlelight and mystery. Then she sent him away. Wed by arrangement, Emmeline desperately needed to provide her aged husband with an heir. But her lover awakened a passion she kept secret in her heart . . . until he returned and rocked her world with his demands and his desire.

THE AMETHYST CROWN (0-8217-4555-7, $5.99)

She is Constance, England's richest heiress. A radiant, silver-eyed beauty, she is a player in the ruthless power games of King Henry I. Now, a desperate gambit takes her back to Wales where she falls prey to a ragged prisoner who escapes his chains, enters her bedchamber . . . and enslaves her with his touch. He is a bronzed, blond Adonis whose dangerous past has forced him to wander Britain in disguise. He will escape an enemy's shackles—only to discover a woman whose kisses fire his tormented soul. His birthright is a secret, but his wild, burning love is his destiny . . .

Available wherever paperbacks are sold, or order direct from the Publisher. Send cover price plus 50¢ per copy for mailing and handling to Penguin USA, P.O. Box 999, c/o Dept. 17109, Bergenfield, NJ 07621. Residents of New York and Tennessee must include sales tax. DO NOT SEND CASH.